THE
SILENT
CULLING

JEANINE MOLLOFF

TABLE OF CONTENTS

This book is dedicated to the 11 million who were brutally murdered by the Nazis. Of the 11 million persons murdered, 6 million were Jews. This mass murder took place while the world remained silent. This was—the silent culling.

Of that 6 million, I discovered after my copyright was established, a distant cousin who perished in the death camps. His name, by an odd twist of fate—was Max.

Never again.

I

SELECTIONS

Tʜᴇ sᴍᴏᴋᴇ ᴀᴅᴠᴀɴᴄᴇᴅ in the sky, a demon perched ready to crush its prey—eternally hungering. The time was nearing for 'selections'. Max cursed each day, knowing someone would live (if you could call this Hell-living), and someone would die. It was a sunny day, blue skies forming the backdrop for the foul black smoke, mocking the naked reality of this daily terror—adding insult to injury.

Such days made it more difficult to wish for the peace death brings, yet Max was hoping for death today. The Nazi machine had sucked dry all life, much like a vampire consuming marrow, leaving nothing but an empty barren husk. Death was lingering in between the silences, waiting for unseen release. Max was shriveled, drained and old, all thirteen years of him.

This was the legacy of the Nazi 'Final Solution', a thorough extermination of an entire people—much like spraying for roaches. Max wondered if roaches had it better; they had no foreknowledge of impending death—or worse, torture. After all, it wasn't until they stopped breathing, or felt the shell on their back break from the pressure of a human foot—that they sensed any pain.

Yes, the Nazis were cold blooded exterminators, and to them, the Jewish people were roaches. He closed his eyes and pictured the giant jackboot of the Nazi beast. It approached at full goose step then slowed, much as a snake closing in on a kill; the jack boot hovering above, less than a hair's width from its prey—teasing. Crumbs of delectable food mixed with dead flesh, clung to the sole of the shiny black boot, forming a moldy, blood soaked, crusty membrane.

The roaches then felt pressure being applied in measurable increments; enough to know pain—enough to feel their shells and heads cracking in half—slowly. Then, at the point of near death; the pressure eased. These half-dead roaches looked up at the blue sky, loving the blueness, the life of it all, hoping... then blackness hit. The boot, once again pinned them down—wringing any life out of their broken shells. Pressure dominated any other sensations; except for the actual spiritual sense of their souls leaving this hell. The boot then proceeded to another target while ghastly white elasticized hands attached to a voice coldly listed the dimensions of each crushed shell and it's 'torque.' The bored white plastic hands casually tossed each empty shell onto a garbage heap with a million other empty shells.

What the indifferent, plastic white hands and the dirty jackboots couldn't see would confound them, for above the mountain of dead empty shells—are free souls—in paradise. Max then knew that retribution and justice—by a higher power—would punish the guilty. The souls of the dead are free—in direct defiance of the Nazi beast. Max actually laughed.

A Nazi guard sneered at him, pointing his machine gun straight between the eyes. Max dropped his eyes in a move of contradictory self-preservation, but remained defiant on the inside, where the guard could not censure or monitor.

He understood the joke. His people were little more than roaches to the Nazis, and yet—their souls remained free. He remembered an old Hebrew song many Jews sang even in the death camps, which the Nazis mocked. The song, roughly translated was a message of eternal defiance—and faith. It simply stated, that..."though you have tortured, maimed and destroyed my body—you can never touch my immortal soul—for that is with the Lord."

Yes, it was a good day to die.

Suddenly the alarms went off; wailing banshees come to claim their prey. A young guard, maybe fifteen, kicked the old man sitting next to Max. This boy of a guard was blond, blue eyed and definitely well fed, for he had the scant remnants of an extra chin. The chubby guard kicked the old man again, this time with more ferocity. The old man refused to move, sitting stoically defiant, while his sallow skin clung to his bones like dried tissue paper. His Yamaka, or skull cap, which shows respect and obedience to YHWH, balanced precariously on his head.

This time he hit the old man in the face. Blood flowed through the crevices of his time worn expression beginning as a trickle and increasing to rivulets spilling onto the earth.

"Get up you old useless parasite," screamed the guard.

"I'll kick you until you rise or die; it doesn't matter to me." The black booted youth kept kicking with unending venom. It was as if the hatred and evil of an entire world were concentrated in one solitary boot. A mixture of spittle and blood flowed from the old man drenching this youth's polished black boot.

"Now look at what you've made me do; I'll have to take an entire hour cleaning and polishing this boot, just to pass inspection."

"You Jews leave a mess wherever you go. The least you can do is supply me with a wiping cloth for these boots." With that remark; the youth ripped the old man's rags from his emaciated body and laughed. "This is what you Jews call manhood!"

He then, unceremoniously lifted the 40 pound body of the old man by the beard, and threw him to the ground. Max heard a decisive crack. The old man's neck snapped like a toothpick. His yamalka remained, lovingly in place. Max knew; selections had begun early this morning.

"MAX, MAX, PAY attention! You have to choose. Piano or violin." Max's mother was determined to have a musician in the family. Max, on the other hand was equally determined to escape music lessons from Dr. Rosenkamp.

The truth was that his hatred for both instruments was only surpassed by his negative feelings for Dr. Rosenkamp. Not only were the lessons as enjoyable as having a tooth pulled without anesthesia, but Dr. Rosenkamp always sprayed when he spoke. Max thought that anyone educated enough to be called 'Doctor', could learn to control their saliva. Why couldn't his mother understand that soccer was just as enthralling as the piano or violin? It never ceased to astound him.

In the meanwhile, Dr. Rosenkamp was in the process of inhaling his sixth piece of Mama's fancy chocolates. Maybe it was his ninth. Max supposed that the accounting was purely academic since he suspected that Dr. Rosenkamp's main preoccupation was the pursuit of large quantities of edibles in as timely a fashion as possible. Max watched a dribble of chocolate sauce flow down the old man's craggy face, only to rest on his bearded chin.

"Maxie, listen to your mother—select." Dr. Rosenkamp sprayed again; this time a mixture of red cherry juice and chocolate sauce. Pellets of dark red and brown rained down on Mrs. Hirsch's mahogany coffee table. A pair of neatly manicured hands, with wiping cloth in hand efficiently mopped up the drippings.

"Maxie, select!" Drops of red brown sauce established caked scabs in Dr. Rosenkamp's gray beard. "You don't have to be Franz Lizdt or Beethoven—just proficient enough to have your fine arts requirement for entrance to the University. We're not talking about world domination, just a fine arts credit—select!" The veins in Dr. Rosenkamp's face were in a state of fine protuberance, practically geometrically parallel on each side, like legions of Romans.

Max was temporarily reprieved by the sound of glass hitting the floor.

"Sasha, you naughty cat, look at what you've done!" Broken, devastated crystal mingled with the hard wood floor, catching the light in angry tones of red, orange and yellow. Mrs. Hirsch's best crystal vase had been sent tumbling down to the floor by the upstairs neighbor's cat—Sasha. Sasha ran for cover.

Max never really liked that cat—until now, when he actually admired this singular act of defiance. Up till this moment; he viewed Sasha as a finicky, self-involved interloper, vying for his mother's attention. In fact, there were many afternoons when Max was enduring a punishment for some sundry infraction of the rules; when he found himself concocting all methods of torture aimed at this sniveling, fur-covered coward, whose very existence was an irritation. Sasha had indeed transformed species—from feline—to scapegoat.

Max visualized Sasha as a cat-goat hydra, poised and plotting a petty vendetta, carefully aiming certain goat anatomy 'parts', Dr. Rosenkamp's direction, timed specifically for the interlude—when he was bending over to engulf another dozen petit fours. Max began to laugh uncontrollably.

"Max Hirsch, I fail to see the comedy in this situation," shrieked his mother, hands on hips, daring Max to offer a rebuttal. "This is the crystal I inherited from Tante Sophie."

At this point Max knew his mother would begin her autobiographical diatribe about Aunt Sophie's side of the family not really being German—but French. Max knew this was a crucial point for his mother; it was her closest link to a sense of national identity, as she had only moved to Germany when she married his father.

Another crash was heard. This time it came from the direction of Goldman's Kosher Meat Market, two doors down. The noise was followed by a shrill operetta of insults, screams and 'friendly' machine-gun fire. All color drained from Dr. Rosenkamp's face. He knew these sounds and smells both historically and intimately. It had started—'Kristallnicht'—the 'night of broken souls.' The propaganda ministers would later explain it away as a crime prevention technique; but Rosenkamp knew better. This marked the beginning. Rosenkamp was deep in thought—traveling back to the secret hiding place of his youth, of his soul—back to Vladivostok and the Pogroms.

Flashes of blood caked memories passed in front of his eyes—memories which stained his soul and robbed him of any sense of even fleeting security. More flashes. This time, a split second picture of his infant sister, Chava; resting on a soldier's bayonet. Her tiny body pierced through cleanly; blood caked on the metallic surface, forming a crusty dark brown ring of equal proportions— marking the point of entry and exit. Chava's body was then ripped from the blade; her blood remaining to form a precise signature on the bayonet.

The Pogrom then threw her small broken body into the spittoon, laughing. An ugly voice from the soldier bellowed; "That's one less Jewish bitch we have to poke!" Laughter erupted from the small brigade.

At that point, seeing Chava's body discarded like trash; Rosenkamp lurched at the uniformed vampire, ripping flesh from his pasty white face. Bits of leathery skin and blood dug under his nails, while his body catapulted backwards into a spray of gun fire.

The Pogroms were breaking all the glass items and ripping up the furniture. Pieces of virginal white upholstery drifted onto Chava's corpse, like new fallen snow.

Rosenkamp felt a warm trickle down his stomach. He looked down and watched the blood drain out of his body and onto his dead infant sister. He would have gladly given his life's blood to Chava, if it would have saved her. Rosenkamp cried for his sister.

Max saw a tear travel down Dr. Rosenkamp's weathered face. For a minute Rosenkamp seemed a million miles away.

Rosenkamp woke from the remembrance, collected his faculties, and turned his attention to Max. "Max, get away from that window now! The police are dealing with the situation. Back to work."

Mama chimed in as well—"decide Maxie, piano or violin."

Max noticed the steely expression on her face, almost devoid of any emotion.

Another chorus of gun fire pierced the air; already thick with an ever present, consuming gray smoke, as bullets rained down on the glass and pavement. Mama could not break his need to witness. Max turned to face the scene unfolding down the street, neatly framed through the tenement's window. There was Mrs. Goldman running out of the building and down the street to this river of blood, where the militiamen were planted.

She lunged at one machine-gun armed youth, in a desperate attempt to stop the vandalism, missed her mark, and fell in the street. Coldly, in robotic motions, the teen age soldier turned, took aim, and shot Mrs. Goldman through the head, at point blank range. The bullet went clean through. It was if the soldier was 'shooting fish in a barrel.' Max would never forget the vision before him—the expression on Mrs. Goldman's lifeless face. It was the face of utter disbelief and horror. It was the face of paradise lost; the child's realization that fairy tales were never real, and all the fairy godmothers and kind handsome princes were—the big lie. A single tear remained isolated, frozen en route, from the corner of her eye to a still flushed cheek. It was the face of incomprehensible betrayal. Max would witness more faces frozen in terror—but none as haunting as the living death mask of Sara Goldman.

Two militiamen hoisted Mrs. Goldman's body onto a garbage truck; but only after rummaging through her pockets for loose change, jewelry, anything they could use in the name of the 'cause.' Suddenly a gangly swastika drenched hoodlum noticed Sara Goldman's engagement and wedding rings. He started to yank at her rings, but couldn't budge them. Wedging his black boot against her still tear stained cheek; he attempted to remove the rings, but to no avail. With impatience in his eyes, he took a dagger and in a sawing motion—cut the finger off. He then removed the rings and discarded the offending part—but not before parading his perverted fresh meat version of a 'red badge of courage', through the street with a gruesomely clownish celebratory dance. He was like a young child with a new toy.

A stray dog wandered past the spectacle. The teen aged soldier threw the ill begotten 'trophy' at the hungry mongrel laughing—"Here doggy—eat this." At this point, the entire militia brigade roared in unison with blackened laughter, while soldier-boy cleaned his hands on Sara's skirt.

The laughter was broken by a single scream, as Joseph Goldman ran into the street. "No! No! My Sara—you pigs—why have you done this?! Why?!" Joseph Goldman lay in the blood stained street, cradling his wife's face in his arms. (His pain was the pain of a thousand years. His sobs matched those of a million souls).

While in shock, he began to chant the Kaddish or prayer for the dead, for his Sara. One of the militiamen turned toward this act of love—this religious ritual—his face one of blind stupid hatred, and stepped toward Joseph Goldman. With one firm blow to the jaw; he sent the old man reeling across the street. Sara's head hit the pavement; her eyes heavenward. Somehow Joseph found within himself the strength of a much younger man, as he rose and walked back to his wife with a resolute and defiant eye.

The militiaman barked out a command to halt. Joseph heard nothing. The militiaman issued a warning this time to halt—or die. Joseph glared at the pig-child in the uniform sporting the deformity of the swastika.

In a fit of panic the militiaman-child aimed his gun, again shouting a high pitched warning. Joseph saw nothing but his beloved Sara lying in the street. He knew his duty—to Sara, to his love, to his G-d—to chant the Kaddish. It was his labor of love—to Sara and to G-d. Joseph saw the toy soldier lift his toy gun and take aim, while he kept walking towards his wife. A final warning was issued by the pig-child. He responded, once again, by lovingly chanting the Kaddish. Joseph never actually felt the bullet pierce his chest—only a warm, light sensation as he dropped to the ground.

JOSEPH GOLDMAN FIRST met Sara Rosen at a Bar Mitzvah party for his cousin Murray. She was the oldest daughter of Saul Rosen; the new cobbler who moved in two doors down. Sara Rosen had auburn hair which caught the sunlight even on the dreariest, most overcast days. Joseph first knew he loved her, when she laughed at his awful jokes. No one else did; except Sara.

She had the tiniest figure—a size 6. She claimed to weigh 115 pounds; but Joseph swore that 15 pounds of it had to be that gorgeous thick hair. If she ever had her hair cut; she would suddenly be underweight!

His Sara was also quite brilliant. She could wade through an unbelievable amount of disorganized information and design a logical plan, where there was once nothing but chaos. Most men weren't comfortable with the thought of a brainy woman; but Joseph cherished this quality. It never ceased to amaze him the hidden talents which this woman could draw upon with seemingly little effort. The only question which plagued Joseph was, what did this angel see in him? It did not matter, for he had decided at that party—Sara was the girl he would marry. There was no one else. She would be his lover, best friend, business partner and soul. It was just a matter of convincing Sara. Luckily for Joseph; Sara felt the same way.

Joseph and Sara were married five years later. Their courtship was very traditional. Joseph would 'call' on Sara every Sabbath. He would worship with her family every Friday night. They would sneak glances at each other from across the Shul. They had to be very careful for these were the days of ultimate propriety. In an orthodox synagogue; the men and women sat in separate areas of the sanctuary. There could no question as to his intentions, or Sara's father would not give his permission, much less his blessing. So they stole loving glances at each other, when every other pair of eyes was supposedly secured on the Union Prayer Book, p. 647. Joseph could feel the love, desire of Sara every waking moment of every day. She was his life. Unbeknownst to Joseph; the entire congregation spent many evenings—watching Joseph—watch Sara.

They were married on the 25th of September, just before the High Holy Days. Sara wore her grandmother's gown, which had been lovingly stored by her mother. The gown had pale organza lace over pure white satin. Sara wore a single pink and ivory cameo in the center of the high ruffled neckline. Her hair was up in a simple knot, small curls at each side of her sweet face. A silk veil covered her head until the end of the ceremony.

Joseph didn't remember what Sara wore that day—he only remembered how much he loved her. She looked like an angel sent from G-d. When the sunlight hit her hair, you could almost see a halo of sorts. Frankly, Joseph didn't remember much of the ceremony itself. He barely recognized any language at all. All he saw, or thought of, was Sara.

Everything seemed to move in slow motion that day, and if he could, he would have kept it that way forever. He wanted this moment to last a lifetime. And so it would; for in his eyes, she would always look this way her entire life.

H IS MIND SKIPPED ahead to the day he and Sara first opened their kosher meat market. She must have swept the floor a thousand times—no speck of dust had a chance. The counter was scoured and scrubbed to the point it glistened. Everything had to be perfect; in preparation for the Rabbi's inspection. Without the Rabbi's blessing; they could not open for business. They had to have his blessing, as well as his oversight on specific procedures for each cut of meat. This is what it meant to be a kosher meat market. Joseph recalled the time he tried to explain the idea of 'kosher' to his neighbor, Mr. Steigetz. It had to be the funniest recollection of his life...

"I understand, Goldman—your meat market has to be clean—as mine. What's the big deal?" Steigetz was shaking his head in confusion so vigorously that his threadbare toupee began to slide.

Joseph bit his cheek to refrain from laughing at his friend's near mishap, and said, "It's not just clean, but it must have the Rabbi's blessing in order to be sanctified and pure. It's as much a religious act, as a dietary one. Kosher is not just a difference in food preparation, but a way of showing our respect to G-d and his commandments." Joseph was aware that Rabbinate tradition forbade sharing information about Judaism with outsiders, but he chose to break this doctrine regularly.

He understood the rationale behind this intellectual and theological segregation; that it was regarded as thinly veiled proselytizing, or conversion of non-Jews;—but argued against the validity of that theory. Joseph often wondered if this type of self-imposed interfaith exile—contributed to already existing levels of bigotry and Anti-Semitism from the outside community. After all, how can a man or a race defend themselves against lies when they refuse to speak up in their own behalf? Most people view the person who fails to speak up in their own defense—to be guilty as charged, solely by their silence.

In other words, silence is seen as an admission of guilt. Joseph often argued to his Rabbi that this self-imposed silence contributed to the growing credibility of the xenophobic Nazi party. In response, his Rabbi started to pray for Joseph's misguided soul; and chided Sara to help rid her husband of this craziness. Sara would in turn, raise her voice to new levels of 'excitement' as she explained how they needed the Rabbi's blessing to remain in business. Jewish customers would not patronize a meat market which was not 'kosher', and their business could not remain 'kosher' without the Rabbi's blessing. (Forget 'goyim' or non-Jewish customers—they would never lower themselves to help a Jew—in business or otherwise.)

In Sara's mind, it was nothing more than a practical business matter. To Joseph, it was a matter of logic and principle. It made no sense to continue a practice of segregation.

He could not see any virtue in hiding. Perhaps outsiders feared that the Jews had something to hide—because of their life in the shadows. Sure, there were some influential individuals involved in the outer periphery of politics as it related to business; but the average Jew was too busy trying to survive. Most Jews honestly thought that politics would ignore them if they only obeyed the laws, no matter how archaic—and remained silent about any unusual occurrences.

Joseph would never know how prophetic his words and thoughts would be some day—as he now began to equate silence with death—(as he danced with death lying there in the middle of the street, bleeding out).

In spite of these constant altercations with religious leaders; Joseph was regarded as a pious man holding peculiar ideas. Many times, he was warned by the religious leaders to keep his dangerous new ideas to himself. Joseph reasoned that the religious establishment feared social and political repercussions from any radical notions, such as integration.

His mind wandered past to another time—a time of heated discussion with the Rabbinic and Council of Elders. The future of his business was actually in jeopardy. The meeting was held in the Rabbi's study, a room he thought was held together at the rafters by musty books and equally musty notions. He looked up at the clock. It had stopped at the stroke of one minute past twelve. It would be rewound before the meeting. One of the committee members entered to prepare the timepiece. Joseph mused that this clock befitted the room and its daily occupant—both had ceased to move forward—trapped in a cold, pseudo-intellectual twilight zone.

"Joseph, we are ready to begin. The Elders are waiting." The face of his dear friend Myron Katzman suddenly looked drawn and worried. Even though they differed in opinion often; Myron remained his closest friend.

"It's good that the Elders are kept waiting; that way they can practice their scowls. We wouldn't want the old women of the congregation to think that these Elders aren't doing their duty. I'm ready for my verbal spanking." Joseph followed his old friend into the sanctuary where a committee of ten, (in addition to the Rabbi), were seated in naked, rickety wooden chairs. Each and every one of the ten had long beards and longer sour looking faces.

Joseph leaned towards Myron and whispered; "Is a minion really necessary?"

Myron hushed his old friend; "They aren't joking Joseph—you may very well lose your business standing in the community."

Joseph wondered how many outsiders would have understood the meaning of his minion joke. He figured that his Reformed American cousins would have no knowledge of the minion, or communal prayer for the dead. This committee had collected ten men to 'bury' his business and reputation.

What this committee could not understand, was that his ideas, new ideas, new questions—could not be buried, at least not forever. The truth changes for no man.

Words came from the center of the ancient oak table. "Joseph Goldman, you stand before this committee for the sole purpose of responding to concerns expressed by the community regarding your questionable activities with outsiders." The voice belonged to Saul Lutzkenstein—a cynical old rip in Joseph's eyes, always laboring to vindicate cruelty through 'ecclesiastical superiority.'

Joseph once claimed that Saul was trying to collect 'brownie points from G-d.' In truth, Saul was the ultimate modern-day Dathan—a slum landlord squeezing every ounce of economic lifeblood from his own kind; while forwarding reports on 'suspicious' behavior to the authorities, albeit as a conscientious citizen. He often paraded around the neighborhood adorned with the entire collection of religious artifacts—the Talis or prayer shawl, yamaka, requisite copy of Torah commentary and Torah pointer. In another life; he could have been his own circus sideshow. A low chuckle came from down in Joseph's soul. His old friend Myron shot him a stern look of warning. Joseph had never seen Myron look so worried, or tired.

Saul began his verbal assault; "You have been observed collaborating with non-Jews and reportedly discussing theological concerns in great detail. It has been brought to the attention of the Elders, that you have been critical of the Rabbinate. To some this could be construed as blasphemy; a spiritual turning on your own. It is wondered how you can accept the Rabbi's blessing for your business if you have such questionable thoughts. How do you answer these concerns?"

Joseph thought long and hard, (for an entire two minutes), and replied; "You say that I have been speaking to non-Jews, outsiders. This is true. You also say that I have issued opinions critical of the Rabbinate. This is also true. I cannot argue with these 'observations', nor do I feel any remorse or shame. As for my questionable thoughts, I have a question of my own."

Saul glared daggers at Joseph, but responded; "What would be your question Joseph?"

"How can you or any other mortal presuppose such 'abilities' as to know my thoughts before I have come to such knowledge? Are you as G-d? Do you occupy the same moral plane, and if so, where is your proof of such a dubious achievement?"

Saul's face morphed into an ugly study of angry colors—from gray, to red and finally purple, in the time it took the clock's secondhand to complete a single rotation. "You dare mock this inquiry?! Do you realize your business—your livelihood is in peril?!"

"Yes Saul, I know—that's why I am here. Believe me, I have other things I'd rather be doing, like having a tooth pulled."

The minion recoiled back into a snail-like formation from this pseudo-farcical barrage. Never had they witnessed such arrogance.

Lutzkenstein issued a venomous reply; "Joseph Goldman, you have mocked this inquiry, the Rabbinate, our traditions and authority. You have had contact with goyim, and have provided no acceptable explanation or apology. We cannot have outsiders mixing in—they might bring dangerous ideas to our young."

Before Saul had a chance to finish his diatribe, Joseph interjected; "That's true Saul, they might actually have to think and question. If that were to occur—where would we be?" Joseph's eyes were glistening with the excitement a glimpse of the truth inspires. He went on to add; "Whether you believe me or not is of no importance. I did not intend to mock this proceeding, much less our faith. I love my faith, my G-d. I do not, however, love some of the outdated traditions that fail to make any logical sense in a changing world. I do not believe that the Lord's will was for us to separate ourselves from the world around us. If that were the case, we would not have the thirst for knowledge which abounds in our culture. Weren't we deigned to be a 'light to the world?' So, why are we cringing in the shadow of the Nazi beast?"

The minion was largely unmoved, stony in their terrified choral silence. Joseph continued, "Is there anyone here who would doubt the debt we owe to Moses, or Joseph?"

The minion uttered a collective hushed gasp. The silence had a choke hold in the room, making the air stale and old. A previously uninterested member of the inquiry board suddenly looked up and challenged Goldman. "Are you comparing yourself to the likes of Moses or Joseph?" His name was Abraham Cohen, an Elder that even Lutzkenstein approached with caution, at least in calmer times.

Joseph chuckled, shaking his head as if he had just shared an 'inside joke', as his American cousins would say. "No, I would never presume such a thing."

Abraham Cohen pointed a long, bony finger at Joseph, challenging him; "Then what is it that you DO presume? I am confused by your monologue and would like to understand."

At this point Lutzkenstein interrupted; "What is it you that you need to understand? Joseph has blasphemed against our traditions, and now mocks this inquiry board. How clear a picture do you require old man?" Lutzkenstein knew his misstep, even as he uttered the challenge.

Abraham Cohen looked up at Lutzkenstein with a newfound fierceness in his soul, to the point that his eyes glowed like two meteors exploding. "It is said that I am old—this is true. It is also said that I move very slowly—also true. And though observation of past behaviors is vital to study; it would not be prudent to confuse my slowness of movement—with slowness of thought. I want to hear his reasoning."

The room exploded with silence. Seconds stretched into many minutes as the full force of his statement fell on the consortium. This was the lamb subduing the lion. The hour hand on the ancient grandfather clock changed position and resumed a deadly frozen stance. The sound of time ticking away to eternity pounded away at the walls. Never was there such a morbidly noisy, deafening silence.

Abraham broke the palpable silence. "Explain your reasons for this statement regarding Moses and Joseph. I need an explanation."

Joseph noted that the old man never looked more alive as he responded; "None of us gathered here would question the heroic status of Moses or Joseph."

The minion all shook their heads in an affirmative chorus; resembling discrete parts of a single, well-oiled machine—all but Abraham Cohen, who was listening motionless but thoughtful.

"What we all fail to recall, is that in their time—Moses and Joseph were regarded as dangerous, warped and yes—even somewhat blasphemous. Recall, that as a youth, Joseph was sold into slavery by his covetous brothers, later to become second only to Pharaoh. He lived as an Egyptian, among idol worshipers, and saved both Egyptians and Israelites."

"Go on." The voice was Abraham Cohen's—his eyes aglow.

Joseph continued. "Moses was to be the deliverer, and yet—even then— we had Dathan—the traitor, in our midst. The people, at one point were ready to desert the new teachings Moses received from the Lord—and go back to Pharaoh. With Dathan's urging—they forged an idol of gold, and sinned in the eyes of the Almighty. It was at that time, the Ten Commandments were seen as alien—and suspect."

"But, did not Dathan's presence serve a purpose," queried Abraham. "Perhaps his evil ways served as a foil, to separate out the 'wheat from the chafe' among the people. In this way, the Lord could see which of his people were truly virtuous, and which were merely fearful and self-seeking." Abraham Cohen's expression suddenly glowed with new enlightenment. "I am beginning to see your point. Perhaps the true evil was not in Dathan, or in the obviously open sinners, but in the silent majority willing to be ruled by fear—shunning compassion, reason and truth."

Joseph smiled, and Abraham returned the same self-effacing smirk. It was a smile which betrayed the owner in an episode of prideful humility.

Lutzkenstein's face grew dark with hatred and fear. His plan had failed— for the moment.

Footsteps wound down the hall, as a pair of time worn hands replaced an equally old stethoscope. The hands were calloused and wrinkled, as though they had been through many battles. Doctor Katzman looked exhausted. "His prognosis is poor. He has lost much blood, and unfortunately I do not have hospital privileges open to me, so I cannot operate safely." He rubbed his eyes until they could have fallen out of the sockets.

"There are no hospitals open?" The question came from Rosenkamp his face possessing the look of a weary time traveler stranded in another era. Rosenkamp already knew the answer, but still asked—as if the act of voicing the question could somehow change the pre-ordained outcome.

"The Nazis have not only rationed food and gas, but access to medical facilities. Jews are not permitted on hospital grounds. In essence, we have been cut off from medical care." Dr. Katzman then shot Rosenkamp a look which was the very embodiment of sheer, naked horror, adding; "Those few souls, who are accepted into hospital—are never seen again. Even worse—their bodies are never viewed by family. The rumored atrocities are unspeakable." Katzman had the dead eyes of a man who had lost all hope.

"So, it has begun," Rosenkamp stared straight at Katzman with an ancient buried anger that penetrated through Katzman's fear, like blood festering pus seeping out of a gangrenous wound.

"Yes. The roadblocks have begun. I have heard stories of 'protective' walls being erected around the Warsaw ghetto, as well as similar ghettos in Germany and France. No one is allowed entry or exit without a specified official pass." Katzman definitely had the look of the walking dead, as he made this admission.

Rosenkamp removed his bifocals, inspected the lenses at a distance and placed them in his pocket. "Last time—they tried to destroy us with the cavalry—this time they plan to entomb us in the ghetto."

Katzman placed his tired hand on Rosenkamp's shoulder and continued; "There is more. Certain individuals are missing." His look was somber. "We have been instructed to never speak of this, to anyone. Such discussion will result in one's own 'disappearance' or death."

The terseness of the dialogue only served to betray the tension hovering in the room. There was a 'Maginot line' drawn above these earthly characters, taunting fate and events, to perform as a tightrope walker—minus a net—with only concrete, mortar or grace to greet it's eventual gravity bound body. History had taken on a persona all its own, with life events colliding to Earth like a dead fallen star. Rosenkamp wondered how much longer he had. He knew his 'luck' had been exhausted, as he looked back at Goldman's battered and bloodied shell of a body. These barbarians had not only shot the poor man; but they felt the necessity to break most of the bones in his old frame. He reminded Rosenkamp of a marionette—with all his strings severed—everything suddenly went limp.

Katzman also glanced back at his dying patient, wondering why the seemingly most ardent religious cynic of this ward, would suddenly risk his life to chant an age old prayer, for which he never professed any ascribed belief. "Why did he antagonize them? What did he possibly hope to gain by this spectacle, which cost him his life? Did he think this would bring Sara back to him?" Katzman's eyes were, once again, wet with fear. He reminded Rosenkamp of a hunted doe staring down the barrel of an old shotgun. "What will this sudden religious fervor bring down on the rest of this neighborhood? Couldn't he have kept this quiet?" Beads of perspiration formed in small clusters on Katzman's wrinkled brow.

Rosenkamp looked once again at Goldman's broken body, and challenged Katzman. "What would you have him do; divorce himself of any genuine feeling when he's faced with his wife's mutilated and still body? No. He did the right thing; he refused them satisfaction." Rosenkamp went on to say; "Perhaps if more men would stand their ground against these cowardly butchers—Joseph and Sara Goldman wouldn't have had to die. We have the moral right to self-defense against those who would commit acts of genocide." His face had the firm resolve of a much younger man. His jaw was granite and his hands were steady.

"You do not truly advocate disobeying the local authorities?!" Katzman was beginning to replace his surgical instruments into his wrinkled and weathered black bag; back turned away from Rosenkamp.

"I fail to see where we have any other alternative. This gangsterism is escalating while our people have become far too passive and obedient." Rosenkamp was looking far into an unknown distance.

"But that would mean—civil war. So many more would die, and for what—your pride?" Katzman was white as a living corpse.

Stolid in his convictions, Rosenkamp went on to say;"You ask, for what purpose would such an insurrection serve—

"Sara"—a faint, ghostly voice came from the direction of Joseph's torn body. He could barely breathe, yet his mind was racing—back again to the inquisition board.

Lutzkenstein was drilling away at Joseph, pounding his fist on the Rabbi's study table; "You have been consorting with goyim, gentiles—giving no thought to our traditions, our ways. Joseph Goldman, it seems that you are Hebrew in name only—particularly when it benefits your business. If it were not for your wife; it is doubtful that you would have responded to this board of inquiry!" Lutzkenstein's eyes were two blood filled sockets aglow. In Joseph's mind—Saul Lutzkenstein was Satan, reincarnated.

"My wife may have convinced me of the questionable value, much less the importance of this inquisition, but..."

"You mean 'board of inquiry.'" Saul quipped at Joseph.

"No, I 'mean' inquisition."

Saul Lutzkenstein's fists were concentrated so strongly on the Rabbi's table that the skin covering the knuckles had transformed to an almost colorless, deathly manila yellow. He continued with his barrage, "You must realize the gravity of such a position. Our community finds itself in a rather tenuous situation—we cannot afford to antagonize those in power by mixing outside of our own people."

"Why is that Saul? By what circumstances do our people find themselves in that tenuous position which you desperately want maintained?"

"Is that an accusation?" Lutzkenstein's face was filled with desire, much like a sexual afterglow.

"No not an accusation—rather a mere statement of fact." Joseph saw; Lutzkenstein take the bait.

"Based on what foundation? Need you be reminded of the penalty for bearing false witness against thy neighbor, Joseph?" Lutzkenstein was ready for the kill. (Cat toying with prey.)

"No Saul. I am very aware of such a penalty, and I am not so eager to forfeit my life, much less my family name." (The volley continues. Mouse teasing Cat.)

"Are you so reckless, that self-destruction comes naturally?" (Cat losing grip.)

"No, but though honesty and loyalty do come with strife; they are necessary parts of my soul." The room was swallowed whole by a thick warm blanket of silent fear. None of the committee members wanted to face the real enemy, for it might taint their own names. The community leadership had failed to lead. Denial and retreat were the policy of the day in a dangerously changing Europe. (Everyone had heard 'stories' whispered in dark corners, never to see the light of day). The predominant attitude was that of complicity, based on blind compliance with the violent demands of the silent majority. It was simpler to allow a chosen few to interpret confusingly insane ordinances, rather than risk antagonizing governmental powers. The room was suffocating in warm, toasty fear. So thick was the stench of indecision; it could have been a leech draining blood from a lifeless body. Such was the body politic in the Rabbinate according to Joseph Goldman.

"How long has it been since any of us have freely expressed our thoughts concerning this town, this Germany, or for that matter—this world? Why should we lie down and die—and then say 'thank-you' for the dubious privilege? I for one, will not. We have been issued dictates which limit our freedom of movement, freedom to work, or to worship without fear of retribution." Joseph Goldman continued his speech with a defiant step and an adamant voice.

"How many of our people have simply disappeared? One day they are loving members of our families, our community—then they are gone. All we do is whisper in the shadows, and chant in the synagogues to salve our collective conscience. Yet we take no direct action. We even fail to publicly speak the names of those taken from our midst—rather we ostracize their surviving family members. Why do we quarantine their loved ones? Why do we allow a self-imposed body of elders to dictate the community or personal response to such political criminality—all in the name of keeping this false peace, which is actually a surrender—an act of communal suicide—without the courage of Masada?"

Joseph walked around the dank room, looked at the inquisitors, and lowered his head. All around him, he saw what he savagely resented—hypocrisy borne from fear. These men had not lost their faith; they had taken such rich, ripe fruit and strangled it to little more than a dried husk, containing no life. Why did he bother? He knew why. There were individuals, families outside the ruling elite of the Jewish community, questioning and demanding investigation and reform. There were people who wanted to integrate, mingle with outsiders, if for no other reason but curiosity.

Joseph had a self-awareness that many successful Jews had long since lost to a false sense of security, purchased by their own affluence. He knew that the seeds of bigotry were ignorance, segregation and fear, with hard economic times serving as fertile soil for economic and social marginalization.

The self-imposed segregation of Jews only aided and abetted the bigots. When we allow outside 'others' to define and present 'who' and 'what' we are; the imminent violence which bigotry harbors—is invited 'to the party.' This problem was complicated further by the simple fact that a silent majority of affluent European Jews were apolitical. They espoused no beliefs, and saw no reason to venture beyond the professional borders of their own small world.

Unfortunately less affluent Jews namely the poor—paid the political price, for the arrogant, child-like beliefs of wealthy Jews. Poor Jews knew about rising xenophobia and anti-Semitism—they had no choice. Poor Jews knew all too well the political role of churches pushing the violence of anti-Semitism. The rich could escape the Pogroms; hide their wealth, and come to America—the poor had no such escape clause. Joseph had an American cousin who lived in a lovely house in the USA. He complained bitterly about being denied access to the 'country club' of their choice. This was their myopic view of anti-Semitism.

Eventually this cousin, Myron Goldenhersh, changed his name to Richard Gold. Problem solved. Myron didn't look 'ethnic', (dark blond thinning hair)—he looked like Goyim. Since Myron was 'passing' for white and Christian; he kept his mouth shut about religion. (Be discrete—it's nobody's business.) Myron's faith was kept in a plain brown paper wrapper, like a dirty book—only read when hiding in the shadows. Joseph viewed this type of affluent Jew, as an enslaved coward who embraced his shackles.

Some saw Joseph's attitude as unfairly targeting the successful—it wasn't. Remaining silent about injustices dished out to minorities, is merely a more subtle form of evil. It is that very role of cowardly silence which supports and nourishes the bigot. This type of moral coward espouses no beliefs, and sees no reason to explore beyond the borders of their own self-imposed spiritual prison.

These cowardly collaborators could not bring themselves to witness what the political evidence of the day so clearly spelled out, nor could they face their own history of silence. It wasn't that the Spanish Inquisition, Pogroms or the murderous proclamations of Hitler's buddy—the Grand Mufti—had been forgotten; they were merely filed in their collective memory, in an intellectual 'dead letter' department.

Joseph realized that these perceptions flooding his mind were wasted on a collection of rabbits. If change were to occur; it would have to come from the people, and not the imposed elite.

Much as he desired; further debate only served those like Lutzkenstein— hired tools tasked with thwarting any seeds of freedom. Joseph saw Lutzkenstein clearly for the first time—as a dirty weed strangling any growth. Lutzkenstein was there to maintain the 'selective blindness' and silence of the Jewish community, regarding their homegrown political and psychological enslavement. Lutzkenstcin was the local 'overseer.'

Just as Joseph was ready to walk away from these cowards; he noticed a curious division in the minion' emerge. Rather than remain seated in one united body; certain members were forming two or possibly three disparate discussion groups. Lutzkenstein looked panicked. His stranglehold was loosening. Joseph looked up at the clock again, and could feel each second ticking off its short, premature life, only to be followed by more seconds, dying at the hands of this cold, indifferent, lifeless instrument. How each dying second was like our people, he thought; sacrificed to the beast. The clock seemed to stare back at Joseph in icy blackness; ticking away strands of his life. He knew then; indifference was the executioner.

Joseph looked up once again, and issued a warning later recognized as prophetic; "One day this board will awaken only to discover our people slaughtered on the altar of political cowardice. Our own silent refusal to call out centuries of historic slander merely emboldens slavers desperate to use us as the ultimate political scapegoat. We will never have peace or freedom unless we expose this slander as nothing more than evil lies, which serve as a convenient public distraction from the very real crimes of political dictators."

"Since this is an alleged religious body; I will speak to the Torah on the right and moral obligation to self-defense. Torah clearly states a right to self-defense; which is described as a duty to our families and to future generations. I fear that by the time we rediscover our full heritage, my life will be a memory. Be warned; it is impossible to placate slavers—they must be eradicated—otherwise we are guilty collaborators by our own silence—our own collective 'sin of omission.'"

Lutzkenstein saw his opening. He could paint Joseph as a crazy zealot, and still emerge as the voice of reason. He could almost offer thanks for this gift—if he actually believed in G-d. "It is quite obvious to this board that you have some very strong convictions concerning Torah, and our entire body of law. We can only commend you on such scholarly intent, though the execution of such study is questionable."

"Questionable in what way?" Joseph returned Lutzkenstein's steady glare.

"The execution," vollied Lutzkenstein. The smirk on his face was evil incarnate.

"So my intent is commendable, and my execution condemnable? That is certainly an interesting paradox."

Lutzkenstein raised one bony finger and added, "More prophetic than you will ever live to know."

An icy wind bellowed outside begging to be fed raw flesh and bones. It howled with the fury of a banshee. Joseph found himself lulled into an almost hypnotic trance watching the clock—watching life drain away. He surveyed the gray, colorless room one last time, realized the enormity of the situation, and said; "Well, I won't tire this honorable body any longer. My wife and I will be waiting for your decision."

The minion was stunned by Joseph's sudden retreat. It had no rhyme or reason—this capitulation. Finally, the Rabbi straightened up his bent frame and posed his question—his only question. "Why do you recant previous testimony through this retreat? You spoke to the sin of silence, in the face of overt sin—yet now you entertain your own 'sin of silence'?" The outside storm subsided for a few seconds, followed by a furious wind slamming the door open. Rain pelted the tile lined doorpost; the ferocity reduced to a constant droning din.

"Rabbi, it is clear that Joseph has realized his error and is throwing himself on the mercy of the committee. If you ask me, he should have considered his business and his wife's sensibilities at an earlier juncture." The voice belonged to Lutzkenstein, accompanied by an eerie glow in the sole light bulb poised directly above his head. He had the look of a demon, preying on an innocent lamb.

The Rabbi directed a stern look which carried a warning to Lutzkenstein, so fierce that the entire enclave had to lower their heads. "I believe that this question was directed towards Joseph, and am confident in his ability to provide a rational explanation." The Rabbi continued, "Perhaps this inquiry has lost its way in terms of its mission. We are not here to stone you. We are only trying to gather information and study your side of these accusations."

Joseph fixed his gaze on the rain falling outside and asked; "Isn't this a theological stoning?" A pall fell on the minion, as if they collectively stopped breathing.

The Rabbi, hurt by the testimony, yet still trying to find the truth asked, "Joseph why are you so hostile? We are your people. It is very difficult and frightening—this fixation with outsiders and their ways. Though it is not specifically forbidden by the Torah; our traditions frown upon this direction you have been taking. Have you not placed any value on our time honored traditions?"

"Rabbi, have you ever considered that our traditions are not nearly as important as Torah itself?" Another deadly hush fell over the room.

"Joseph, at the times of our history when we had nothing—no country, no freedom to worship, no protection, no food—we had our traditions which gave us a sense of identity. Without such traditions, we would have surely lost our way, as our people did in the desert, for forty years during the Exodus from Egypt."

"Rabbi, it is curious that you mention the exodus. It seems that the role of tradition has taken precedence over the Ten Commandments and the covenant sent by G-d through Moses his messenger. Our people lived in Egypt for some generations, and adopted Egyptian 'traditions.' It was through the slavish attention to tradition; that Dathan was able to introduce corruption to our people."

The Rabbi saw an opening and seized the opportunity. "But Joseph, those were Egyptian traditions, not Hebrew—as you have so rightly stated. They were not borne of our own."

"Rabbi, have you forgotten that many of those traditions were adopted by another messenger of G-d; Joseph. He not only saved both peoples from starvation, but assimilated into an alien culture, while maintaining his Hebrew faith." Joseph looked at his neighbors and continued, "Why do we find this idea of integrating into a larger society, so frightening? Is our faith so fragile that we must segregate ourselves from differing ideas in order to"...

"Maintain our ways? Yes, it is necessary. We cannot allow outside ways to contaminate our community." The voice and words came from the unseen depths of raw hatred—Lutzkenstein. The light in the room gave off a pasty yellow aura. The clock had stopped.

Joseph glared at Lutzkenstein, noting the dead clock adjacent to his skull like features, and responded; "One of these days we may find ourselves the victims of that same dogma." Joseph would never live to realize the full ramification of his prophetic statement.

The committee sat with bowed heads intense with the decision before them. Joseph knew; the discussion was over—this was the time of judgment.

"He's dead." Rosenkamp's soul was drowning in a flood of renewed self-loathing as he reported this cold, clinical fact. It was as if bureaucrats in pristine little white coats entered the room with the power to arbitrarily decide who will live and who will die. No emotion; just a cold, action-reaction sequence delivered in sinc with the midnight hour.

Katzman noted the exact time of death. "Joseph Goldman, deceased at midnight, November 9, 1938."

Rosenkamp turned towards the ghoulish antique gargoyle clock. It had six pentagrams engraved in its face. These wooden tattoos were reminders of time past, when evil, fear and superstition ruled the domain of man. He thought of the previous owner, a 'scrubby Dutch' social democrat, who sold this usually defective device at an outrageously high price, all the while bitterly complaining, about having to 'sell to a Jew.' How curious that suddenly this timepiece became accurate, to the exact second.

INHABITANTS BEGAN TO pick up violated, devastated shards of glass—which had established primacy as the newly twisted window on their reality. It was morning. Sunny skies dominated, setting off a symphony of broken reflected colors, like a malformed degenerate rainbow, imposing its dominance onto the bloodied street. Clean up continued; old women were hunched over newly paved streets, (complements of the German Worker Corps); their calloused hands serving as unnatural appendages—glued to the blackened surface. The washer women were beating time worn rugs into submission.

Cleanliness must be maintained, there is no tolerance for unsightly dirt at any level. These women took pride in their work—for that is what they were taught—a tradition of order that cannot be questioned. After all, who would question the unquestionable? Such a thing would be akin to questioning the entire order of things. These philosophical issues were left for the Rabbis and Town Elders.

As the washerwomen continued to dutifully club all life out of their 'charges' (for carpets are incapable of screaming in the dark, or witnessing acts of genocide); clouds of dust flooded the hollow street pathways. All you could breathe, taste or smell, was the moldy dust—it clung to the pores.

This is all that remains—dust and memories. Rosenkamp was deep in thought once again. His thoughts were invaded by a piercing sliver of glass penetrating the warm, fleshy part of his hand. A spot of blood appeared and dried in the exact timing of a heartbeat. The old man bent over to taste his own blood. It had no true flavor, just a weary saltiness seeming to belie an emulsification of a soul which can no longer feel pain. But Rosenkamp knew; this was a fraud—a cheat. Pain still remained with many in the collective memory. There were such things as ghosts, apparitions—they haunted the inner recesses of the mind when presented with the appropriate stimulus. Until then; such ghosts remained cocooned in the subconscious, daring fate to disturb them, just like Pandora and her deadly box of sins.

These ghosts were as dust. That was to be the legacy of Wiemar—dust. No great paintings, literature, medical miracles or deep philosophical insights—only dust. Like the starved remnants of some noble beast after having been ravaged by vultures; even the skeletal carcass will disintegrate into—dust.

His hand returned to the shattered splinters of some family item—an heirloom perhaps, and continued his search. Somewhere he would find Sara Goldman's Star of David. This could not replace the theft of her wedding bands, but the family needed some shred of religious and sentimental dignity. Something, anything, for the memorial service. Very few possessions from the Jewish sector remained after Kristallnacht, as the Nazis encouraged ransacking. They didn't even wait for the corpses to go cold. "Even jackals wait that long', muttered Rosenkamp in a barely audible voice. A shadow fell over his searching extended hand.

"Such mutterings are best left for the silent criticisms within the mind. The voices of dissent are far too soon, the voices of the dead." Rosenkamp was face to face with Lutzkenstein. The eyes of conscience met those of amoral self-interest.

"Lutzkenstein, such altruistic statements from one so esteemed are such a gift." Rosenkamp could feel the bile rise and flood his mouth. It was worth it, to aggravate the enemy.

"All the better to lead you to correct thinking, my dear Rosenkamp. His face aglow with the thrill of the chase.

"Why don't we dismiss the formalities and discuss the ground rules of this 'hunt'—assuming foolishly that you play by any." Rosenkamp felt ice cold electricity surge through his soul. Yes, he thought—Joseph Goldman was right. Silence is death. We can no longer fail to see the Dathans in our midst. Like those at Masada—never again.

Lutzkenstein was prepared for the next volley. "There will be a new world order—those who are incapable of assimilating, face definite...censure." His face never looked more grotesque.

"Definite censure—that sounds more like a cartoon than an ultimatum. You can improve upon that feeble attempt Lutzkenstein."

"Heed my words Rosenkamp; those who fail to bow rebellious heads before the new world order—are in danger of extermination." Shadows cast on Lutzkenstein's craggy face were a tainted, stale yellow. His eyes were sockets of inky black, reflecting no light. Outside of the Council's chambers, camouflaged by the murky glow of faulty electrical wiring and dim bulbs—he was truly a ghastly looking creature.

"Extermination by what authority?" As Rosenkamp issued the challenge; he already knew the answer. Treasonous collaborators often have a look of self-imposed importance and position. Before he had an opportunity to continue his search; Lutzkenstein interrupted, slamming his solid oak cane against Rosenkamp's skull—sending him careening to the ground. Lutzkenstein surveyed his work, visually inspected his victim, grinned and walked away.

Rosenkamp's head reeled in a counterclockwise direction. Sights were replaced with sounds of screeching rubber meeting pavement. Sirens wafted in mid-air, alternately switching pitch between two deviant qualities of shrill. The air was saturated with a peculiar odor. It sliced through the early morning fog like marauding battalions. All this penetrated through Rosenkamp's painful stupor. As the pain began to subside; he looked up and whispered to the wind..."et tu Brute?" A mournful laugh escaped from his inner depths, something he knew Lutzkenstein would never comprehend.

He imagined a caricature of ..."those crazy Americans," standing in full uniform applauding his verbal attack on Lutzkenstein. Perhaps the Americans were not so crazy. Perhaps the blind obedience demanded by the Reich is the real insanity.

Rosenkamp's mind traveled further along this 'stream of consciousness' line of thought—while absorbing the emotional and physical pain inflicted on his weary body. Through his head trauma, he realized that this journey may have been worth the initial difficulties.

Beginning to hallucinate. He could actually smell the pain. Multiple shades of gray began to flood his line of vision, swirling into a cartoon like gas, forming a series of generic looking boxes. Within a few moments of this head trauma induced stupor, the newer boxes grew progressively darker and larger than the earlier incarnations. They then started to form a processional, accompanied by a noxious odor, so deceptively sweet that it burned at the moment of contact. Soon this odor, rather presence, began to consume all the empty boxes in the processional, enveloping them into invisibility.

Then a curious thing happened. As the gas subsided, Rosenkamp saw the emergent boxes sprout arms, then legs. Like unsteady toddlers, these faceless boxes, clumsily began to march. Soon they were marching in unison to a demented looking goosestep, during which they started to grow facial features. The features morphed into absurdly exaggerated ugly caricatures. Rosenkamp could feel the cold shiver of wicked cowardly indifference; the kind that comes with the blind conformity of people abandoning their own humanity. His body had gone cold as a corpse. These boxes had the faces of his gentile neighbors.

KRISTALLNACHT WAS MERELY the beginning. Security patrols were thereafter dispatched to 'protect' Jewish property; while Jews were rounded up, beaten, forced to perform slave labor at the local 'patriotic' work camps—and 'disappeared' or murdered. Adding insult to injury; heavy taxes were imposed on Jews to pay for this additional protection, as aliens in the very country many called home.

Max saw firsthand this 'big lie'—for what it was—cowardly thievery. He witnessed nineteen year old thugs with IQ's equivalent to their shoe size; remove all his family's possessions for the 'protection of the Aryan volk'. Any possessions not made of useable materials, such as metals, precious stones or expensive art; were shoveled into large, rat infested manure heaps. Max and his family were then evicted from their home and corralled into the newly created Jewish ghetto.

The Hirsch's occupied the room next door to the Steinmachers. The Steinmachers were an elderly couple raising their twelve year old niece, Ruth. Max had decided in the eternal span of five minutes, that Ruth was the girl of his dreams. She had long black hair and big dark eyes that could swallow you up in their unbridled innocence. Max first attempted some conversation with Ruth the Friday his mother invited the Steinmachers over for Shabbos dinner. His younger brother, Henry, knew it was 'true love' when he counted the thirteen times Max tripped on his own already overgrown feet. It was all Henry could do to keep from laughing uproariously. (It was all Max could do to keep from dropping baby brother out the sixth floor window). Max shot Henry a three second warning glance, which Mama interrupted before things escalated. She must have built-in radar, Max thought. But, John (the eldest of the three brothers)—knew better. Mama was a bit of a silly scold; but underneath the veneer, she had an acute ability to judge intuitively a person's temperament and worth.

John wished that our religious leaders had Mama's practical knowledge of real life, but he instinctively knew this 'movement' to the ghetto was the first step, of a one-way trip—to oblivion. Though only fourteen; he read many foreign (and thus illegal), newspapers. Billed as treasonous propaganda, these newspapers were dangerous to obtain, but a small underground resistance movement managed to sneak such valuable information into the Jewish ghetto. John had friends he kept secret from his family and the 'official' Judenrat community. He considered the Judenrat to be a group of cowardly old men who sold their own people into slavery—for the temporary 'safety' of political alliances.

John hated these hypocritical old weasels; adorned with Hassidic curls and other symbols of outwardly imposed martyrdom. Thank G-d his mother did not believe with the Hassid! He regarded them as a people defined by their oppressors. They never moved beyond the time of the Spanish Inquisition. Rather than studying Torah—they reacted to historic genocide, and altered Torah interpretation to fit their experience. Nothing ever changed from tradition. They were such a predictable target—easily identified, totally segregated, while congregating en mass. To the Nazis it was as easy as shooting fish in a barrel.

The Diaspora had been a blessing; leading Jews to many countries, but especially to America. Conversely, these people led by the Judenrat were inviting genocide to their front door. Lambs blood on the doorpost was unnecessary; conformity dictated by enemies served as the signpost for mass murder. His contemplation was abruptly interrupted by laughter—at Max's expense.

Poor hapless Max felt a warm trickle on his lap, before he realized where his tea had been deposited. The room suddenly drowned in laughter, as the skin on his face convulsed from embarrassment at his plight. Unknown to all, this laughter had an expiration date—soon.

"You see how attentive my sons are to the pretty little girl. Well no harm done, at least the floor got some tea." Mrs. Hirsch felt some level of sympathy for Max—he was growing up so fast. She looked over at Ruth—noticing the worn expression of worry on her far too thin, young face. Would these children ever see a spring dance? Would they ever know the joy of a piano recital? She instinctively knew the answer.

Mrs. Hirsch found an old rag and mopped up the spilled liquid. Ruth crouched to help Max's mother, but was ushered back to her chair. "You are a guest in this home, sit, visit." Max saw his mother smile with genuine approval. He could not remember when his mother last smiled at anything he did—in his entire 11 years on this earth.

Mr. Steinmacher repositioned himself in the chair—trying in a vain attempt to ease the pain. "Can I get you a pillow for your back?" Sophie Hirsch was very worried about the frail old man.

"You are too kind, but I am afraid this condition is what the doctor calls 'degenerative,' nothing helps." The old man gave Sophie the look of someone who knew he was dying. Sophie understood. She realized then that Mr. Steinmacher was one of the fortunate ones. When the pogroms really come; he would already be at peace. His eyes would never witness a loved one dying or worse, being mutilated, tortured and violated in all sorts of hellish manners. Yes, Sophie knew what was coming, and had to face the terror of being powerless to stop any of it. The propagandists would say that she would not be able to 'arrest new developments'. She mused how propagandists love to camouflage evil acts with neutered language, and all covered up with a dollop of sweet vanilla coating.

This second sight of Sophie's weighed on her soul as psychic quicksand, blurring the vision of millions of suffering faces. She could feel the thickness of her fear; smelling it like the burning of human hair and flesh. Sophie hated these visions and sensations, but couldn't ignore them. Nor could she share these thoughts with the Rabbi, (much less now with the Judenrat eavesdropping on the community)—in the name of 'friendly relations.' After all, when do 'friendly relations' jail your family in a rat infested ghetto?

Beads of sweat broke loose on her brow, forming a boundary between her eyes. Max noticed the sudden look of age in his mother's face, for the very first time. His attention did not drift for very long from Ruth, as she was once again, in the line of his gaze. His mother was just tired, after all she had lost her house, furniture, clothes, money, and was now forced to live in one dirty, grime encrusted room. You could hear the mice and rats 'sing' at night. What an odd way to think of rodents, that they 'sing.' Sometimes the chirping could almost muffle the gunshots outside.

Max shook his head and saw Ruth again. He had forgotten all prior thoughts. His dreams during the night and otherwise were monopolized by the vision of Ruth.

II

Barbed Wire and Shattered Dreams

MONDAY MORNINGS WERE always the most difficult. A new dictum or ordinance was posted on the kiosks outside the ghetto walls. Residents of the Jewish ghetto were held responsible for observing these ordinances, even though only selected individuals were provided restrictive passes to venture beyond those same ghetto walls.

Needless to say; such passes were rarer than a virgin in a whorehouse. Max wondered if his mother would be shocked that he knew of such things. That he knew what a whorehouse or a brothel was, much less the extent of their services. The streets provided an education all their own. Neither the state nor the Judenrat could totally control the street. Amidst all the oppression; there was some freedom in the street. No police state could maintain real control over all things, all the time. There were too many thoughts, sights, sounds, smells. The smell of life and death spread over the land, in spite of the Third Reich's insane attempts at such elusive control. The street would always escape the Nazis. Little did Max know how important this information would be in the future, for his very survival.

This Monday the kiosk contained detailed instructions, in print small enough to practically require a microscope. Sasha Berkowitz, the resident counterfeiter, was able to reproduce the appropriate packet of papers required to obtain access to the nearly disappearing information. Luckily the SS guards weren't overly literate, or there would have been questions.

"Papers Juden!" The voice emanated from a pimply faced youth; his brain, clearly in neutral, and testosterone in overdrive. This child in an emerging man's body felt empowered, and thus superior to the multitude of Jewish doctors, businessmen, scientists, professors, etc.—and all due to his Aryan genetic code. This was his entitlement, his inheritance, his birthright, without having to earn any of this newly granted authority. Sasha rolled his eyes upwards in his head, reached in to a trousers pocket and offered up a crumpled paper with a series of ignominious stamps emblazoned on the surface. The youth looked disappointed as he sighed; "All is in order, you may proceed. But remember Juden; curfew is prompt and the penalties for violators are severe." The youth suddenly looked wizened and evil beyond his years.

Sasha did not look back . He was going to complete his assignment. As the kiosk grew closer, so too did the realization of impending gnawing danger. Sasha had to obtain official information on the latest dictums, but also leave a coded message for the underground resistance. Sasha was a Zionist to the bone. He despised the Nazis and the collaborators that called themselves the Judenrat; the old men that preached passive acceptance of this genocide, thinly disguised as 'national defense.'

He was to meet a red-headed girl at this kiosk, wait for the appropriate password, and give the coded response. He had to communicate to the operative the anticipated timeline for sabotage jobs. The final coded message was expected soon, but then code guidelines changed suddenly. Apparently the word was out; both names and physical descriptions of suspected resistance fighters had been supplied to the SS by the Judenrat 'government'. In return, the Judenrat leaders were rewarded with new positions of authority and additional food, gas and money rations. The clock was ticking—boxcars lying in wait—death camps ready.

Storm clouds began to accumulate in the distance. The configuration of clouds formed a prison wall against the narrow horizon. A purple haze emerged, giving the sky a ghoulish glow. Massive red curls approached with an air of determination; the courier, a small girl with a large stride. She carefully examined the kiosk announcements as she dutifully ignored Sasha's presence. The rules of the kiosk were specific—no conversation for fear of censure by the guards. Sasha played along, positioning his body by the notices posted two weeks ago. The girl stood by this week's notices and began to speak in careful tones while staring ahead at the everlasting kiosk.

"Shabbos is approaching; dusk will soon fall."

It was now Sasha's turn to reply; "the preparations for Shabbos are not complete—the Rabbi will be upset."

"But Mama is busy preparing the meat and cheese pie." The red headed girl had a deadly serious look as the corners of her mouth developed small beads of perspiration.

Sasha had to maintain composure at this remark, as any slight tremor of the hand, or small remnant of a gesture could arouse suspicion. This was quite difficult, considering the girl's statement was such obvious nonsense to anyone with a basic knowledge of the Hebrew community. Meat and cheese are never combined in a dish. It is forbidden to mix cheese or milich, milk products, with meat. That combination has always been against the laws governing kosher food. Pork products are also forbidden, but this example is more widely known and the Nazis might detect the ruse. Still it was difficult not to laugh at such an utterly stupid mental picture.

Sasha envisioned his mother setting the table with her very best china—the place settings she inherited from her great grandmother—white bone with delicate blue flowers along the edge. The four crystal wine glasses are placed on the lace covered table with love—one for Papa, Mama, himself and the widower Rabbi. He can see in his mind's eye each prayer being recited to perfection for Shabbos, with the wine, challah and the candles all set with meticulous care, when Mama finally enters with a greasy meat and cheese pie—the kind the British love. But, this is not all, for after Mama presents the main dish—a final touch is introduced. She proceeds to top this dish of grease, this floating pool of slimy sludge—with an enormous dollop of fresh whipped cream. Consequently, the Rabbi proceeds to experience a peculiar change in his pallor—from light pink to rancid green. At this exchange; the Rabbi runs from the room, through the front door—his portly body creating a new breezeway where the doorbell had been. Mama then pleasantly serves the main course—reminding everyone that seconds are available.

What a thing to contemplate at this time of woe and atrocity—meat and cheese pie with greasy whipped cream. Sasha realized that this image was probably as sane as anything else in this evil, insane age.

The red-headed girl continued; "we must conclude our business quickly; Mama will be very angry if we are late for Shabbos."

Sasha redirected his attention to the situation at hand. "You are right sister. Mama sent her list of provisions. They must all have the Rabbi's blessing." Sasha handed the girl a pocket worn list which was rapidly intercepted by a cold, white hand.

"Juden, passing propaganda is a treasonous act; one punishable by death." Sasha and his red haired compatriot froze—both hearts combined into one slow, steady beat. Time itself had frozen and transformed into a dead, gray, moldy cocoon.

The voice continued in confused disbelief... "this is merely a grocery list." The blond head whipped back in sneering derision, as his laughter filled the area of the kiosk. "No wonder you Juden are so easily vanquished; when you should be arming yourselves—you plan recipes for meat and cheese pie." The guard's mocking laughter was welcome relief. (Definitely preferable over an execution). The blond mocking voice then inquired; "what do you do with this chicken schmaltze? Do you use it for your men's virility?! Maybe you will grow a beard instead of curls?" A wicked laugh emanated from this vile coarse youth, much like an incantation. "Here, take your little shopping list. You will find actual food to be scarcer—than your manhood."

The guard's hair had the cast of dirty dishwater, as opposed to the Aryan golden blond sheen. It lacked luster and failed to catch the sun's last remaining rays before dusk. Sasha and his companion began to leave as the guard suddenly barked the command to halt. The two children stopped dead in their tracks; hearts barely registering life. "Juden, I forgot to give you something. Look in my face—remember this face—for some day I will be someone of importance."

With that last remark the guard summoned bile from the depths of his poison filled organs and spit in Sasha's face. "Never forget your tormenter. This is our duty—to torment and exterminate. It is your duty to serve—and be exterminated. Be glad of your role in this destiny—without the hunted; the hunter would not be needed." The guard laughed once again as the two children walked home in the cold darkness of night. Sasha could feel the sting of this vermin phlegm against his young face, and remembered; "I won't forget. I'll hunt you down until the end of my days, or until both of us die in the attempt."

The entrance to the ghetto was lined with barbed wire, broken glass and shattered dreams. Crumbling, rat infested brick walls surrounded what had previously been thriving, middle class neighborhoods. Sasha had parted company with the red haired messenger and prepared for reentry to the Judenrat governed prison. The few hours of freedom he had bought by risking his life, left the bitter taste of pending betrayal in his mouth, as he played the role of victim once again.

Only a handful of people knew of his double life. There was desperate need for the information he obtained. Movement from the ghetto was expected very soon. Underground leaders had relayed information from official British, German and American sources. Sasha crept through an opening in the barbed wire, and headed for the alley. The sound of footsteps nipped at his heels, as he felt his legs slide out from underneath him; head hitting pavement.

"HE'S AWAKE." THE voice sounded cold and mechanical. "Perhaps now we will obtain some useful information—rather than the ravings of an unconscious stupor."

"I never claimed immediate results;" the second voice whined.

The first voice went on to say; "You did mention results which would be useable, not nonsensical drivel about meat and cheese pie, the Rabbi, and his mother not approving. May I remind you—we are running out of time—the second phase is already under way. The information we obtain from members of the Underground is vital to our cause; lest the Fuhrer be embarrassed by any failure."

"We will not fail. These are merely Jews. They can't even send adults; they have children fight for them." The subordinate voice clearly insulted by mention of failure, due to lowly Jews. This voice belonged to Dr. Klinkelshaun; a Nazi butcher claiming to be an expert in hypnosis and analysis. His only training—the dubious treatment he received at the Berlin…Sanitarium…as a patient. Klinkelshaun was a paranoid schizophrenic with delusional tendencies accompanied by acute bouts of psychosis—according to the official diagnostic report. After the mass 'liberation' of what was termed political prisoners from the prisons and sanitariums; Dr. Klinkelshaun found himself with suddenly acquired 'medical' credentials—bogus credentials—but acceptable to the Third Reich.

Now, he faced this eleven year old child, who supposedly possessed vital information, concerning the coordination of ghetto activities by some alleged underground movement planning to liberate Jews, Poles, homosexuals, gypsies, Catholics and other 'mud races.'

The commandant's voice boomed; "A failure due to a Jew bastard is intolerable insult. The Fuhrer would lose valuable political ground with the Italians and the Occupied French Vichy governments. They have no moral imperatives concerning mud races, providing their precious art, and traditions are not disturbed by anything as untidy as war. In any case; this diatribe is distasteful, and I have a dinner engagement at five." The Commandant closely examined the manicure he maintained with a phobic interest. He monitored his nails frequently; not a speck of dirt was evident. They were white as snow, as he bleached them nightly. He discovered long ago that soaking them for exactly an hour produced the desired result. He could not tolerate a single microscopic amount of dirt; it was too dangerous a possible contaminant.

One manicurist was promptly executed because she had left one nail with a slightly ragged edge. The bullet lodged exactly between her eyes with an equidistant space from point of entry—to point of exit. This had been determined by post-mortem measurements relating to cranium size.

Again, Klinkelshaun had been minimally useful, but his constant excuses were growing tiresome. Commandant Eiselhauf reexamined his nails and asked; "How much longer will this take?"

Klinkeshaun responded as he readjusted the IV on the boy; "I will require an additional hour in order for the boy to be lucid."

"That is not acceptable;" Eiselhauf detecting an imperfect edge on a nail. "I don't care if the drugs impair his memory or not; I require information. Strap the boy to this chair and I will demonstrate how the Third Reich makes informants out of miscreants."

Klinkelshaun perched Sasha up against the back of a rickety wooden chair, laced the leather strap through the wooden slats, and secured the boy tightly. The drugs were beginning to subside and Sasha was becoming far too aware of his surroundings and his predicament. Sasha felt a loss of oxygen, paired with a restraint so severe that it began to cut into his flesh.

"That is secure. Now my foolish young friend; you will learn compliance, before you die. But don't worry your death will be at the hands of our premier scientist Dr. Klinkelshaun, director of psychosocial anomalies. I promise it will be unique. You'll be the subject of papers submitted to the medical and scientific community. Of course no one will recognize the body or remember the name, but that is the price of academia."

Commandant Eiselhauf flashed a broad grin which immediately transformed to a deranged ugly scowl.

The commandant signaled Klinkelshaun to begin the official interrogation. Klinkelshaun began by producing several surgical instruments on a cold rusty metal tray. The commandant continued; "As you can see, Dr. Klinkelshaun possesses many talents—including self-taught surgical skills. I understand that he has honed these abilities on some of our inmates here at camp."

Sasha glared up at the commandant. "You mean he butchered innocent people, because he is a lunatic the Nazis released from the crazy house."

"You are quite perceptive, but that knowledge won't aid you now. Perhaps you would like to know what we have planned."

Sasha refused to respond. He knew any response would increase the Commandant's perverted enjoyment. The Commandant continued; "We have prepared your castration. You do not need to worry about any future disfigurement however."

Sasha glared at his tormentor, felt the hatred of a hunted animal and asked; "Why is that, you sick pervert? You like playing with young boys after they are dead?"

Sasha never saw the blow. He only felt the impact of a solid iron poker against his skull and neck. He heard a loud pop, followed by total silence and immobility. Sasha was deaf and paralyzed on the right side of his body. Fear had now been replaced with insane laughter. He realized that this Nazi Commandant would be cheated out of his cheap thrill. Whatever happened next; Sasha was determined to protect the underground freedom fighters. He now knew that his life was the price of this battle.

The Commandant bashed Sasha's head once again, using his riding crop as a weapon. The crop instantly dug into the child's flesh, but Sasha made no outcry. Eiselhauf had become more enraged by this insolent child's silence, and he struck again. Sasha felt nothing, though the child could see his own blood cascading down his shirt. Eiselhauf's rage became so animalistic that even Klinkelshaun was fearful. Eiselhauf paced the outer perimeter of the room then suddenly bent over as if in a chilling pain. He clutched his head and Sasha watched as Eiselhauf's eyes rolled to the back of his head. He more resembled a rabid dog in the final throes of the disease—than a man.

"I cannot bear this pain. You have taunted me for the last time," screamed Eiselhauf at some imaginary foe. Sasha noticed that Eiselhauf was not directing his gaze at him but at some blank point in space.

Eiselhauf continued his argument with these 'inner voices,' for nearly an hour. Finally, his own inner demon surfaced as he derided his invisible tormenter. "He will promote me. I am not incompetent. Don't call me that—you are the crazy one. I could never have cannibalized the entire body. You were there too."

Eiselhauf's screams had reached a new fevered crescendo as he continued with his perverted litany of complaints. "It was your idea to dissect and cannibalize him while he was still alive." Eiselhauf then released a blood curdling noise which sounded less than human, as he proceeded to grip his head as if in unbearable pain. Newly trimmed fingernails dug into his own flesh and drew blood as he went on with this erstwhile dialogue. "No, no I am not a coward. I can proceed I tell you; I have no problems taking care of the boy."

Eiselhauf's eyes grew even larger, like bloody robotic members in a pair of empty flesh sockets, devoid of life. "It is of no accord that he resembles my son—he is an enemy of the Reich—a member of a mud race."

Eiselhauf's body followed the non-existent voice as he rambled; "You want proof, fine I can do it. I will demonstrate." In what seemed to be a millisecond; Eiselhauf lurched out at the boy—his face more resembling a steel vice as opposed to anything close to human, ripped off Sasha's ear—with his bare teeth—the organ fixed in his canine incisors. Screams then flooded the area allowing no oxygen to circulate. It was inconceivable that a human being could utter such sounds, but Eiselhauf was beneath humanity. Sasha remained silent and could only see the trail of blood from his shoulder snake down to the floor, ending at Eiselhauf. Blood caked in concrete-like formations, between the Nazi fangs and the offending part. Eiselhauf stood there, making no movement—then as if directed by an unknown force—pushed the appendage into his mouth, chewed—and finally swallowed.

MORNING HAD ARRIVED and Sasha was greeted with a congested sensation on one side of his body. Darkness engulfed his mind, shrouded his thought, vision, hearing, like a dense blanket. He became more intensely aware of a dank odor, much like newly planted soil. It had that coolness, that ripe closed-off scent which choked off all awareness of anything else. He was able to move one finger and could feel the moist clay compacted tightly around his hand. The rest of his body was rigidly pinned. Particles of soil crumbled and fell into his eyes. It had a stinging, burning effect. Sasha could taste the soil in his mouth as he screamed for help. None would be forthcoming.

THE REMAINS OF a young boy had been unearthed a thousand yards from the ghetto walls. Misha Berg and David Gernstein had been assigned to a rubbish evacuation detail by the local S.S. Movement had already begun from the ghetto to the 'work camps.' Such camps were established to 'provide employment for the Juden burden which the noble Aryan race has supported.' So it was written and presented to the League of Nations when Hitler began his expansion into Czechoslovakia. This was the propagandized introduction of the concentration camps to the 'civilized' world. World diplomats nodded in blind agreement, including the United States representative. There were no protests of record, no pesky, inconvenient questions.

It was a cold grey morning that found Misha and David picking out rubble with bare bleeding, frostbitten hands. Misha was busy working to free a large stone, when he called over to David. "There's something under here. It might be a land mine. I need help." David released his burden and made his way over to Misha. "You think it might be live?"

Misha replied; "I don't know, but we better clear it out. The soldiers are watching and if we appear idle, one of us may not be here to complete any additional tasks for our own protection."

David responded; "You mean this protective custody the Nazis have so generously supplied from the kindness of their stony little hearts?!" Both men chuckled at this often heard piece of verbal excrement known to intelligent beings as dog shit. (Some politicians call it public relations).

Misha countered; "How could we have survived a mere two thousand years without such help and blessings?" With hand held to crotch, Misha continued; "And to think the Judenrat were so very cooperative—the transfer to protective custody was completed so efficiently."

David kept picking stones from the earth while muttering something about... "a Dathan by any other name."

A soldier from the top of the hill fired off a few stray bullets that grazed the ground near the two old men. The trajectory halted two meters from the intended target. Misha and David continued digging; this time in relative silence until stumbling upon a gory discovery. It forced Misha to bend over and lose his morning food ration. Another bullet whizzed past as a result of such inactivity. David helped Misha up and they proceeded to unearth the remains of a human hand. It was badly decomposed, but appeared to belong to a child. Remnants of skin hung on the skeleton, maggots busily feeding. The nails on one hand had grown into the local limestone deposits. David began to dig more furiously; his hands pummeling the red-brown soil resulting in cracks and breaks, bleeding earth rich.

The sight was ghastly in terms of its purely evil nature. This child's eyes were open, fixed in an upward bound direction. Large clumps of softly yellowing young skin loosely draped the skeleton; while half of this child's facial bones were nakedly exposed. The child had been buried without his clothes and there was evidence of castration and emasculation. David turned the body over to discover further incidence of trauma—the child had been raped. To add to this; an ear had been ripped off.

David felt a surge of hatred course through his veins. How could any human commit such atrocities? He suspected this was merely the beginning, this unnatural butchery; this assault on humanity. Sodom and Gemorrah was thriving in the world, the very same place that permitted such things to happen, while remaining blind and silent to these crimes.

He ventured deeper into his mind, and realized the full power of—the sin of silence. When victims of evil are 'invisible' to the world—the very same world becomes Satan's garden. Yes, that's it; the temptation of the garden wasn't about knowledge, but the choice between sight and invisibility. It's simpler to invoke selective blindness, rather than see what is difficult or hideous. Such 'invisibility' or 'visual silence' has received a more modern moniker—appeasement. In other words, give the blood sucking beasts what they want, and they will cease to be hungry.

Apparently, the Judenrat never understood the nature of gluttony; more 'feeding' produces more appetite. David sensed the horror that this beast feeding, namely the Third Reich, would never get its fill. The 'feeding' would continue—the beast never satisfied. When one source of prey was exterminated; the beast would pursue other sources of prey. Like a multi-headed hydra; new heads emerge as the old are attacked and decapitated. The horror never ceases.

David disregarded the S.S. guard shrieking, harpy-like in his face; he only saw the cold, vapid blue eyes which lacked any warmth. He could count the blue veins emanating from beneath this creature's thin pasty skin. They seemed to pulsate with intensity independent of the creature. David realized this young guard was frightened. The little bastard's life was dependent upon work completion. David knew by the look in this teenager's face—he had control. Refusal to complete the task would hurt this cowardly parasite. David also realized that this tactic would probably cost him his life, but each moment stalling, might cost the Nazis in the long run. Besides, what time had this young child, buried alive—bought the cause of freedom? It seemed only right to avenge this affront to humanity. The boy understood this—and now David did. It was a matter of mere seconds before David found himself lovingly hunched over this child's body—a bullet in his back.

THE LIGHT OF first dawn bled through the sky, rendering the darkness impotent. The return of day brought new opportunity; Frau Schmidt had acquired a luxury settee at bargain prices. Never during her married life did she ever consider the possibility of owning such a treasure. It was beyond her wildest dreams. Who could guess this new Fuhrer would so improve the economy? He had found the traitors and leeches that were depriving the rest of us, while they lived in the lap of luxury. So why need be concerned with their protective imprisonment at this time?

Her nephew, Ralphie also had a new position as a direct result of the Reich's efforts. The baker two doors down had fresh goods in his shop—and at reasonable prices. And the butcher actually had healthy cuts of meat for sale in the neighborhood, and not merely pushed aside for the military. It was amazing how much these Jews consumed. The stories from the propaganda ministry must not only be true, but understated. These were the only conclusions Mary Schmidt could appreciate.

Fresh meat, available baked goods; these were the seeds of civilization. The settee made it approach 'paradise' in the ghetto. Mary Schmidt had higher hopes; that this ghetto could actually thrive. Under this new leader and his legions; this was possible. The enslavement of the 'Jewish problem'; brought hope for Mary Schmidt—to become middle class.

The kiosk down the street was wallpapered with such a multitude of notices, warnings and dictums that the papering grew into a second skin. This kiosk was exactly three doors down from Mary Schmidt's rent controlled apartment, and adjacent to her favorite shop—the bakery. Mary lived for the heavenly strudel only Baker Herr Dobin could create. The man had such talent, vigor, such sensitive hands—and strudel. Mary stopped by his door sometimes just to absorb the pleasant odors, like a more sophisticated woman would sample expensive perfume. Besides, Herr Dobin was a widower and Mary a widow. A marriage between the two would merge her two greatest loves, baked goods and Herr Dobin's secure income.

The object of Mary Schmidt's desire was a simple man, quite content caring for his business, helping his friends and observing the Shabbos. This was his second month of acquaintance with Sophie Hirsh. He was very greatly impressed with this brave strong woman, who seemed to possess endless pride. Such qualities were rare in men, much less a small woman. And to think, this evening he was to spend in her most charming company. Herr Dobin began to contemplate each grey hair in his beard; how they were uniformly spaced and planted in his fleshy cheeks! Even graveyards lacked such geographic precision. He then thought of his wife's grave. The Jewish cemetery had been desecrated a year ago, and her memorial stone had been 'appropriated' for the Nazi war effort.

Enough of such grim thoughts. There was nothing that could change the past. He was about to spend a few hours in the company of a delightful woman; a widow herself. Herr Dobin glanced at his pocket watch, noting that once again, this monster chose to halt its ministrations. He hit the face of the timepiece with his fleshy index finger, and shrugged both shoulders in resigned disgust. Sophie was waiting.

Sophie Hirsh was busy preparing for the Shabbos. Herr Dobin was expected shortly. He had always been a good family friend. Her husband had valued Herr Dobin's sense of duty and compassion. When Albert Hirsch could not gain an apprenticeship; Herr Dobin stepped in and shamed the elders into providing one. This had been some five years before their marriage. Her dead husband had been a watchmaker. He was able to take any dilapidated timepiece, no matter how abused, and bring it back to life. Even the antique colossus of a clock in the town square had been resurrected by her Albert. He had been a good husband and father; teaching their three sons the very same craft.

Oh, how the boys complained! They were young children who would rather have played ball, or fight some imaginary army of monsters, than learn such a common trade. But Albert was firm; the boys must have a trade, as good Samaritans like Herr Dobin would not always be around. In fact, Sophie must have thought Albert was almost paranoid about this insistence, but she loved her husband and supported his decisions. So the boys learned the trade of watch-making. At least they would be able to feed themselves.

"Mama. Mama, Herr Dobin has arrived. It's time to begin Shabbos." Sophie looked up to find her oldest son, John, impatiently tapping his fingers on his already outgrown shirtsleeve.

"Herr Dobin, forgive me. I don't know what I could have been thinking." Sophie's face was flushed like a young girl receiving a suitor for the very first time.

"Frau Hirsh, forgive me for I have arrived too early." Herr Dobin's face was genuine with concern for his lovely hostess. She worked too hard, he thought. "I believe the boys and I can finish preparations while you rest." Herr Dobin signaled to Sophie's three sons to assist him in the Shabbos activities. The boys responded like three interlinking cogs in a precision Swiss timepiece. Herr Dobin merely set the mechanism in motion.

With the dexterity of an orchestral conductor Herr Dobin sent hand signals to each son, which met with a uniform and swift response. Finally with a great sense of harmony, all four men were seated at the clap of Herr Dobin's hands.

Sophie was astounded. She had never seen her sons so cooperative. Herr Dobin began Shabbos prayers. Afterwards, meager plates of food rations were juggled between those seated at the table, with the skill of circus performers.

Sophie began the conversation. "Herr Dobin, we cannot begin to express how much your visits mean to our family. Good friends in these times are as rare as gold." Herr Dobin shrugged in modesty. Sophie continued. "You take a great risk bringing us extra baked goods and sugar rations. If you were to be caught… " Her voice grew lifeless with more somber tones. She had to maintain control; emotional attachment could not betray everyone's confidence in her calm faith. Such was the role for Sophie.

Herr Dobin interrupted his hostess; "My dear Frau Hirsh, the Nazis will not notice that their baked goods are less sweet or their waistlines less plump." Herr Dobin reviewed this brave family, and realized how fortunate he was, to be in a position to befriend them. "Besides, if that repulsive Frau Schmidt drools over my pastries once more; I may forget what the Torah has instructed about tolerance!" The entire family groaned with laughter, to the point that it was difficult to discern between tears of hilarity and those of grief. Such were the times. (Joy was found in small islands intertwined with unbearable sorrow. The journey to discover the difference was just beginning).

Max was passing the challah to his mother when a deafening explosion struck the frail door like lightning. Bullets punctuated the holiday bread known as challah, disintegrating it in seconds. Sophie was automatically murdered, half a clip of machine gun spray pumped into her body. The sight was typical; one of her soft brown eyes had been shot out of her skull, a blood filled socket remained in its stead. Ten uniformed bodies occupied the one room apartment in a space of less than ten seconds. Nine of the 'soldiers' surveyed the room, and then proceeded to beat John, Henry and Herr Dobin senseless.

A tenth soldier ducked under the makeshift table, only to find two horrifying discoveries—his own excrement—and Max. Here this 'patriot' soldier of the Third Reich had to face the ultimate atrocity—his own victim, eye to eye. There were no slogans or heroic images to hide behind; just the hunter and the hunted. Somehow in the space of a second; the Reich's promises rang hollow, newly festered with the rank odor of evil. It wasn't supposed to be like this— this new world order. The toy soldier's senses failed him; no sight, sound, touch or smell could escape from the reality of the situation. His mind went numb; the only reality being the sensation of his mouth greeting the open barrel of his gun.

The explosion blew Max across the room. Remaining soldiers stripped the Reich uniformed body of any ammunition or valuables. The helmet was deemed unsalvageable due to blood, bone and brain tissue—baked on from the force of such direct fire.

Max lay there with the open space of death choking off his air. He did not feel the beating, (supplied via courtesy of the storm-troopers), nor did he become aware of his surroundings until the lull of the cattle car came to a screeching halt at their final destination. Selections had begun.

MAX WOULD LEARN later in life that this young soldier, who committed suicide in front of his very eyes, was a transplanted American of German ancestry, named William Bakker. The contact would come from Bakker's own family in Sioux City, Iowa. It seems that Bakker was an early sympathizer with the National Social Democrats of the Midwest United States. William Bakker, alias 'Billy'—was one of some sixty-six teens forming the membership of the local German-American Bund's Youth Aryan Corps, in his hometown of Sioux City.

Billy's father had been an active elder in the local Methodist Church, and long favored the 'science' of eugenics. In truth, Billy had never seen a Jew before this. Of course if one ever came to Sioux City; they better not expect service at the local diner or IGA! Like other groups, they would just know that the appropriate boundaries were to be respected as time honored traditions. Billy's father would often say; "Us White Christians forgave the unbeliever, the pagan, and even the lowly 'Jew." His father would begin each diatribe with a history of the world and the genetic ordering of things. "The white Christian will eventually control all business, schools, and churches. The colored races will be protected from their own innate 'weaknesses."

Jeddediah Bakker, otherwise known as 'Jed' truly believed what he preached, and he taught this to his only son, Billy. Billy's mother had died in childbirth when he was five years old, and Jed attributed this tragedy to 'weak genes.' Jed also passed this explanation on to Billy, inferring that her death was some sort of punishment for a hidden sin. Billy never told his father, or anyone else this, but he hated his mother for deserting him. It was the only explanation. Why else would no one discuss the facts of his mother's death, other than it was a 'female' problem? Billy felt a searing humiliation on holidays, when other church women heralded in their families, (like chickadees behind the proud mama hen).

He received charity gifts on Christmas from these same women, usually discards other children would mock. Billy's very existence seemed to carry an unspoken scarlet letter of shame, just for having the gall to be alive. When he asked his father for details of his mother's death; his father issued a severe scolding, shaming him for questioning God's will. This was usually followed by a beating or 'whooping.' (Apparently, God's will was only shared with his father and other 'worthy' Aryan warriors. Children were not admitted to the show).

Billy grew into a young man of nineteen years, when he met proud card carrying members of an Iowa chapter of the 'German-American Bund' or the 'Young Aryans.' He was instantly swept up by the new found adoration he experienced for the first time in his life. He wasn't sure if he believed what they had to say at first, or that it was just something convenient to believe. The reason was irrelevant, because he belonged to a greater cause and that was important. It was as if he had been starving his entire nineteen years, and suddenly found psychological sustenance.

Soon his new friendships grew into something more; a growing loyalty and belief in a cause. At that point; it was only a few short steps to blind obedience and 'true' belief in the 'principles' these angry young men espoused. Billy had sworn his life and allegiance to the Nazi cause. The Jew had become his special enemy.

Once again, Billy had never met a Jew before his encounter with Max that evening, (both cowering under the bullet riddled table). It didn't really matter; he knew as well as his friends in the Young Aryan group knew—that the Jew was the bane of the world. For all their crimes against White humanity; these Jews had to be punished. His duty was clear; the automatic, pre-ordained sentencing made it easier. Billy didn't even have to wait for FDR's declaration of war; he was long gone. It must have been a full eighteen months before the official Declaration of War for WWII, which found his passport and other necessary papers ready to go, and officially enlisted on Germany's side.

His first encounter with the German army was rather grandiose. The full complement of brigades and troops were set to march in Berlin on a special parade route, banners ablaze, people lining the streets—an event replete with pomp and circumstance. It was calculated to have the emotional power of what some may call a 'religious experience.' Not only was it colorful and dramatic; it was effective propaganda. Billy truly felt a part of something larger than himself, larger than life. In his mind, he was part of some great plan to rebuild the world. Billy had graduated to a higher purpose. It was a far cry from the corn fields of Sioux City, Iowa.

As they goose-stepped down the winding streets towards the town square; it seemed as if the entire regiment was one giant, well-oiled machine, devoid of any humanity. Hundreds of average men completed their hypnosis induced journey, by marching around the courtyard in unison as if it was part of a choreographed ballet. A sea of legs flooded this demented dance. The entire courtyard was drowning in legs.

Billy's soul seared with pride, enough to overwhelm his previous 'bumper crop' of shame from Iowa, (which normally grew like mangy weeds). (Yes, his shame was as hardy as Iowa corn, easily transplanted, firmly rooted and able to flourish in even the most barren soil). He had arrived.

Orders to move were issued that same hour. 'B' company was commanded to locate and eradicate the Jewish scourge infesting the local ghetto. Billy's company was feted, liquored up and transported to the site. An entire block of buildings was targeted for 'ethnic' cleansing.

The soldiers entered the buildings and initiated the local genocide. Only relatively strong, able-bodied males were to be spared. Women, children under age twelve, and the elderly were expendable 'collateral damage', or as Berlin called them—'useless eaters'. Billy was fevered for the assault; Italian wine numbing his senses. Even his inebriated state could not prepare him for this naked carnage. Nothing could.

The 'battle' began in confusion; bullets seemingly taking on a life of their own, spasmodically jerking during their ricocheted journey. It didn't matter who or what was hit; it was the trip there that counted. Such is the life of bigots and bullets; neither one is able to demonstrate any conscience—the kill is the thing.

Billy wasn't quite prepared for either role; he was simply there. The rest of the story was related to Max's family forty years later, in a letter from the Bakkers. Apparently, the Bakker's developed a sense of repressed guilt, and felt the need to be forgiven.

Max remembered the young soldier and felt remorse. Billy Bakker signed up to kill Jews; yet when faced with the insanity of genocide—he blew off his own head. It wasn't reparation or justice, but it was a sort of demented apology. It was a beginning.

MORNING HAD ARRIVED. The cattle cars were ripe with cow manure and human fear. The fear grew, generating a stench unlike any others— it had a life all its own. That's the first thing Max remembered—the smell. It lingered on all things and grew with an intensity befitting raw energy. Bodies tumbled out, all looking tired and worn. Some had already been beaten; others were fresh from the cities wondering what this protective custody would mean for them.

It was the dawning of cold dead winter. The visible effects of arctic temperatures were evident as piles of manure released live steam from its captivity. Max watched this with a sense of twisted fascination, wondering about any human release. In terms of fantasies meant to cloud the conscious mind with subconscious nonsense, (a natural anesthetic); this wasn't very appealing, this steam escaping from the dung heap, but it was there, with no other solution in sight. It was real.

Rolling clouds of smoke dominated the heavens in the rear confines of the camp. Max could see the short squat buildings marked SHOWERS, in ugly German letters. They were like overgrown beasts from a previous age, ready and eager to feed on all living things in their path. A line formed to one side of each building; old men, women, small children, all standing deathly silent in the raw wind. Max never saw any of those faces again, at least not in a humanly recognizable form. Not what some would call human. People walked into these buildings- - but—they never walked out. Max wondered what happened to the bodies. Theories abounded among the other prisoners, spoken in whispers, in the shadows. Max became old as death itself, the day he discovered what happened to the bodies.

The beatings began in the morning. Whoever survived with some strength was assigned to the work detail. Those remaining too weak to work were sent to the 'showers.' Once again, the first 'shower selections' consisted of women, small children, tired old men and any cripples. They were separated out earlier in the day, perhaps to contemplate their fate; that is those who understood. The panic escalated as the day drew closer to its inevitable end. Families were physically torn apart and ordered to publicly strip. They were told hot showers awaited them. When anyone asked about their loved ones; they were told that their entire family would also receive this treatment. Their absence was merely a glitch in scheduling times.

Max knew somehow that those 'showers' had to be a disguised slaughterhouse; he just wasn't sure how they disposed of the bodies. Why would the Nazis waste a precious resource such as water, on showers for enslaved Jews? Max soon found the answer. During his work detail he pretended to find new garbage. When the guards weren't looking he hid underneath a jeep parked by the showers.

From this bowel of German machinery he noticed an open door. The building was like a large barn, but there were no showers. Instead Max saw industrial size hoses resembling the kind that release car exhaust. Max knew; the plan was to gas these people to death. There were no air vents or windows. He had to find a way to warn his people; to stall the Germans. Surely if we were to be murdered; we should go down fighting.

It was all so antiseptic; a silent killing factory—only using mass production techniques. The concentration camp genocide was conducted cleanly, under the camouflaged guise of providing 'showers' to prisoners—while administering poison gas. Cleanliness was a secondary issue; how to dispose of the bodies posed a particularly distressing nuisance. The Nazi High Command needed its Pontius Pilate moment.

Max wandered to the back of the building marked 'SHOWERS'. He was going to find the truth. Hearing some footsteps coming closer, he hid under a parked jeep. After the soldiers passed, Max snuck into the building. The 'shower' room was larger than the other rooms. Behind the 'showers' was another room, fully accessorized with multiple ovens. Max realized—it was a crematorium.

The force required to cause a severe concussion could be achieved by the application of a baton to the back of the human head, as Max then discovered. A heavy hand, armed with a metal baton struck Max so severely; it took a day for him to regain consciousness. He awoke to a stern, ugly, pocked marked German face, that of a Lieutenant, who obviously enjoyed his newly found importance over a captive audience. Max felt a new crack on his head from this sycophant. He merely turned his head the other way. The Lieutenant was issuing orders, and demanding answers.

Unfortunately for him, the beating Max endured rendered him now unable to respond to any questions. He heard an oily, adolescent voice boom away; "So Jew boy, you want to find out how our showers work? We can arrange for you to join your friends."

The Lieutenant then motioned for the military police, with one wave of his soft, pink hand. "Take him to the shower area. I'd say have an enjoyable life, but we both know that won't happen."

Max was promptly carted off to another section of the camp.

III

PEDOPHILES AND
GENERALS

MAX HAD BEEN summarily deposited into a long line of women, young children and the very old. Everyone was stripped naked. As instructed, they were waiting for the 'showers'—while a tone deaf amateur band from the local secondary school attempted to play Wagner. Band members were young women dressed in crisp white shirts and navy blue skirts, (the kind often worn to Sunday school). Some of the girls wore dainty pink ribbons in their hair, smiling as they played this—(off-key)—funeral dirge.

Max's mind raced to a time and place some distance from the here and now. He was getting ready for his high school entrance exams, and having to choose between piano and violin. Why didn't anyone ever listen to the propaganda and just analyze the meaning, the implications? For that matter, why couldn't he just play soccer or rugby? His mind raced as he realized the way they were scooped up and massacred. The Nazis weren't hunters; they were cowards doing little more than 'shooting fish in a barrel.' None of the adults believed this could happen. We had been told for so long to 'forget' past injustices. We were heading into a new era where we could purchase our 'right' to exist, through appeasement. It was all so very civilized, at least externally, but the inner workings of such policies were vile to the core.

Max thought further; it's too much like that 'big lie' theory, Hitler gushes about. He had read it in Mein Kampf; a forbidden book for a Jew. The idea was simple. Tell a big lie over and over again and look like you really believe it. When confronted with facts contradicting your lies—just keep lying. If the liar maintains this pattern; eventually a sizeable majority of sheep come to believe this 'big lie'; and it becomes their gospel. After a while this 'big lie gospel', takes on a life of its own, growing to such monstrous proportions that it devours any truth blocking its path. At least this is what it seemed. Why would people rather believe a lie than the truth? Was it just easier? These same German Aryans wouldn't believe a fast talking 'snake oil salesman,' so why do they believe lies that are equally absurd? And then the ugliest truth of all dawned on Max; they wanted to believe these lies. The Nazis embraced the 'big lie' as the perfect excuse for slavery and mass murder. They were nothing more than a bunch of thieving, murderous cowards.

Max felt the bile from his gut surface to his mouth. He could not resist the release, and vomited on the guard leading him to the 'murdering place.' It felt good. The guard screamed, "You filthy retarded Jew bastard!" The guard then threw the child to the ground, concentrating his efforts on his soiled trousers and boots.

All the guard could do is look at his boots in abject horror. He hated such filth. It struck a chord in his fanatic, (almost phobic), German upbringing. "Clean it up, you sniveling little coward!"

Max lay there unable to move. The guard lifted one jackbooted foot and placed it precisely on the boy's windpipe. Max couldn't scream; he couldn't breathe.

"Too bad Jew boy; you won't even make it to the showers. You will die right here. The only tragedy is my disappointment. I was looking forward to seeing you die slowly. Oh well, life can be cruel. Don't you think so?"

The guard's laughter was echoing through Max's mind when the sound of a bullet piercing helmet and skull, interrupted the 'joke.' Max's remaining breath was suffocating under the added pressure of a collapsing body striking him.

A tall Weimar Colonel had signaled the order for the Lieutenant's execution of convenience. With an additional slight wave of his hand, two more guards were carting away the body, while a third helped Max to his feet.

"Take him to my personal quarters. I will interrogate him there." The Colonel looked at the small boy hungrily. "I need absolute quiet and privacy during the interrogation. No one is to disturb us for any reason."

With that comment Max was escorted to the Colonel's private quarters. One of the young guards, a private, spoke to Max. "You shouldn't consider yourself too lucky; the Colonel likes little boys, especially ones that haven't any beard yet."

Max shot a vengeful look at the private, but remained silent.

The private continued; "don't worry, when he's through with you, he doesn't give you to the other officers. He isn't that crass; he merely sends you back to the showers."

Max felt his mind race. He had to find a way to escape. He considered lunging at this guard's weapon, of making them execute him now, of running wildly, of… "Here's your honeymoon suite. Have fun Jew girl." The laughter from both guards was raucous, as they threw the boy into the quarters of this known pedophile officer, of the Third Reich.

Max heard the door bolt from outside. He was trapped in this pedophile's lair. He raced to the window only to find it also securely locked. He searched the room for some object to break open the window. Nothing was available. Max then looked for some sort of weapon—anything—he'd rather go down fighting than be a willing participant in his own rape. He found a fashionable fireplace poker with a sharp golden tip. It probably couldn't kill, but it could gouge out an eye and give him the opportunity to escape.

He had to find a way to hide this peacock of a weapon. He had to find a secure hiding place secure that would not be easily discovered; yet still be able to access it suddenly. Could he find anything to incapacitate, or even poison this Colonel? He ran over to the latrine and opened the medicine cabinet. There were aspirins, suppositories, after-shave lotion, a halfway used syringe and a bottle labeled 'morphine.'

Max grabbed the syringe and inserted the tip into the bottle of morphine. He made sure that the syringe was full and the bottle was drained. Max remembered Dr. Rosenkamp's warning about air bubbles in a syringe being able to kill a person. You had to tap the syringe first, and check for any such air bubbles. Max carefully omitted these steps. He knew that this Colonel would only release him if—Max released the Colonel—from life.

Max then took the syringe and set it down on the milky white basin. He began to search for some sort of string or twine, and found an old piece of dental floss. Taking the dental floss, he tied the syringe to the tip of the golden poker. This could work—but there was still a problem. How would the plunger be pushed to release the drug? Max detached the syringe. He was going to have to administer the dose in a closer proximity. Would this be enough morphine for a lethal overdose? Max heard footsteps and a door close. This would have to do. Max hid the syringe under his vest.

When Max walked into the main room, he was shocked to find the Colonel standing in the doorway—totally nude. What was even more shocking was the fact that the doorway was open for all to see.

The light escaping from the door hit the Colonel's white hairless body in a way that made him look iridescent, much like the old vampire stories. Yet the Colonel was worse than a vampire; he sucked the life out of children by raping them. At least the vampire had the decency to kill his prey. Max looked around and realized that he was unarmed, having partially dissected his makeshift weapon.

The Colonel remained standing, presenting himself in full glory, looking hungrily at the young boy. He spoke, and it seemed as if the words came independent of their owner. "Come here—I'll not harm you—I love little boys." A flash of teeth, perfectly white, belied the blackness of this pedophile's evil soul. Max maintained his distance from this animal, with his blindingly white teeth.

The Colonel spoke again. "Very well, I shall have to come to you. But I warn you, if you persist in being uncooperative, then I shall have to play rough. You may find that outcome stimulating perhaps?"

The grin flashed again, only this time Max saw white hot rage replace what was previously amusement and sexual desire. The Colonel lurched at Max, falling on top of his feet. Max struggled to pull away, but the greater weight of the Colonel's body rendered him immobilized. The Colonel lay on top of the child and began to strip him from the waist down. He clutched greedily at the boy's trousers, scraping and clawing like a mad dog—nothing was enough.

Max twisted his body like a small alley cat, and bit down hard on the Colonel's hand, drawing droplets of blood—forcing his release. The Colonel stared in amazement at his injury—Max's red badge of courage. He screamed at the boy. "You little Jew bastard! I'll make it rough on you—then I'll see you shot, dismembered and fed to the dogs!"

His teeth flashed like venomous fangs as he pursued his prey with an unrelenting vigor. His body seemed to ooze and slide past any furniture barriers Max hurtled his direction. In an instant the Colonel lurched at Max and engulfed his juvenile body, much like a cobra swallowing the young of another animal. Max was pinned underneath the Colonel's body so securely this time he could barely breathe. His eyes looked heavenward as he prepared himself for the worst, when he saw an unlikely instrument of rescue—a rather ornate porcelain tea pot.

Max stretched a desperate hand towards this delicate weapon of desperation. The tea pot moved slightly, perhaps an inch. Max concentrated all his strength on the teapot. He needed a few more inches in order to grasp that small intricate handle. All that stood between Max and some temporary freedom was this perfectly formed virgin white porcelain handle. It had pink roses and white lilacs laced onto its unblemished form. Not a single rose bud or lilac bloom was missing, not a single detail was forgotten. No orphan flowers for this artifact.

Max stretched still further, to the point his fingertips skimmed the milky white porcelain, grazing its surface skin, but not quite engaging full contact. Max thought his arm would pop out of its socket but that was far more comforting than the Colonel's steaming hot breath down his neck. Max made one last starving reach, muscle spasms screaming from every joint in his arm and side. The Colonel was clawing once again at his now torn trousers, when Max gripped the thin handle.

Emancipated slivers of crafted porcelain flew across the room as the fine rosebuds and lilac blooms were sacrificed in one liberating smash. The Colonel's body went limp and heavy onto his intended victim. Max began to roll the Colonel's equally milky white body off of himself, when he saw a new shadow fall over the mantel clock facing him.

The voice attached to the shadow—was cold, robotic, and very German. In a powerful base it barked commands at the soldiers. Two SS soldiers lifted the Colonel's body off Max. All this was spoken in German. Max understood and spoke German, Hebrew and English—so he knew what had transpired.

Apparently a General was sending the Colonel away to be imprisoned somewhere, though the location was not revealed. Max was relieved, horrified and confused simultaneously. The Nazis had always looked the other way when officers or officials of high rank raped children, babies, dead bodies, animals, whatever their particular perversion. As long as it was one of the 'mud races'— it was practically state sanctioned by the high command.

This punishment of the Colonel, no matter how deserved, just didn't fit the pattern. The General read the expression of disbelief on Max's face, but maintained the icy cold stare which denied any emotion. He motioned with one finger to a third guard, and Max was escorted to a specified location which also remained unnamed, unspoken. The S.S. guard blindly obeyed—another robot without a conscience.

As Max was ushered out of this chamber of horrors, he noticed that a clock overwhelmed by the General's shadow—had stopped dead. Max desperately wondered how much would that elegant clock be worth to the General— in human lives. Could he become valuable enough to survive with his brothers and hopefully escape?

The guard threw Max towards the interrogation room like a limp rag doll. Max stumbled for a few steps, turned back and in a desperate voice said to the General;

"That mantel clock is broken. I can fix it for you Herr General."

All motion dropped dead with this bold utterance, as if time stood still, like a movie freeze frame.

The General looked back at Max, raised a single eyebrow, and with a grin equal to the Cheshire cat, answered; "So little man, you claim to be a watchmaker, do you? The grin flattened horizontally to form an ugly scowl. The General continued; "The best watchmakers in Germany have proven unable to repair this clock. Why do you think yourself more competent?"

Max looked the General straight in the eye, never blinking and said; "Because Herr General, I am fighting for my life, while their sole concern was mere reputation."

Everyone in the room stood frozen in fear, with the exception of Max and the General. The guards could not believe the utter gall of this young boy. This brave display by a young child, only added to the bile and moldy resentment festering in their cowardly bellies. Jews were not supposed to possess such raw courage.

The General chuckled; "Very well, I will test your knowledge. Perhaps the best watchmakers in Germany demand too high a price. How much do you think a Jew's life is worth these days?"

Max jumped on this chance; "Fixing your mantel clock, which is bound to be a priceless antique, is the issue of worth. By the looks of the piece, it must be over 150 years old."

The General tilted that same solitary eyebrow Max's direction and asked with that cold, robotic voice; "How did you surmise that information? You are a mere child, perhaps only ten years of age."

Max responded; "My father was an expert watchmaker and he taught me such things."

"So you are a watchmaker's son. Fine, I will give you the opportunity to prove yourself."

That was the last word Max heard from the General for a month. As the General motioned to a guard; Max found himself locked in another well-furnished room, waiting to discover his fate. He would receive an answer soon enough.

COLONEL HERMANN GOFF awoke, cold and chained to the wall of a dark, dank cell in the brig. Much like a child, unable to believe the reality of the situation; he pulled at the ball and chain in an exercise of futility. Both were nakedly solid. He looked around the cell, blinked several times as if the blinking could somehow alter the reality. Nothing worked. Pulling at the ball and chain again; he nearly dislocated his shoulder. After twenty minutes of straining, he released a scream which came from the depths of utter despair and fear.

SS guards heard the screaming throughout the complex. No one was interested. The compound was flooded with bland indifference. If fear could be given a distinct voice; this would be it. Nothing else could describe the sounds escaping past places where the mind and body moved past living—and transmogrified into a fear based hallucinogenic state. These desperate cries penetrated the night, piercing, guttural and feral. The Colonel ceased to sound human. The cries morphed into a homunculus of pain. Yes, this was the voice of abject terror. This was the voice of arrogance turned sideways. This was the voice of angry hypocrisy.

No one came to see the Colonel for a week. Food had been pushed through a slot in the prison door. None of the metal tins had been collected, but were left to accumulate by the door. Most of the food had been left to sit. Mold had begun to grow on the uneaten portions. The mold was the only sign of life as the Colonel sat in a dazed condition; his body mutated into a non-distinct curved shape.

The second week of his captivity the Colonel received a visitor; the General. As the door opened, the light nearly blinded him. In fact, the light was actually painful, and he covered his eyes for several minutes as the General spoke.

"Colonel Hermann Goff, you have been detained temporarily due to several improprieties."

The Colonel looked up but had to shield his eyes from the light once again, as soon as they made contact. "What do you mean my General? I have always done my duty as an officer." A sense of pleading invaded his voice, which sickened the General.

The General continued in a cold tone. "You have been seen with a juvenile male in rather intimate circumstances. Now while the Reich has unofficially sanctioned such alternative arrangements, that is, as long as the juvenile is of a mud race; new considerations have rendered previous judgments politically incorrect and dangerous."

The Colonel looked up once again and blinked incoherently. He more resembled a confused, trapped animal. As he spoke there was a sound of trepidation in his voice;

"What do you mean my General—politically incorrect?"

The General paced the width of the cell and proclaimed; "We are about to sign a treaty with the French and the Italians, and possibly the Americans. This treaty is of course a ruse to lull them into a false sense of security. This will give our friends, the Japanese, time to stockpile weapons and organize supply lines."

The Colonel was shocked by this revelation. He heard rumors of similar plans, but no officers officially admitted to such. The Colonel felt an insane surge of hope, as he immediately fantasized that the General had planned this imprisonment to serve as cover for a covert mission.

The General went on; "As we understand the situation in diplomatic terms; we require additional time to boost this stockpiling initiative."

The Colonel began to beam as he assumed that his role in this drama was about to unfold. The General noted the change in Goff's expression and realized he had correctly 'read' the Colonel. He took particular delight in the next announcement; "Your sexual liaison with this child has proven to be an embarrassment, and an unnecessary liability to the Reich."

The Colonel felt his heart race to the point it nearly ripped through his chest wall. The General added; "Though we can do a certain amount of public relations damage control; your situation is specifically problematic."

The General took a long, deep puff off his cigarette securely positioned in a pointed holder resembling a stiletto. "The Americans are rather squeamish about such arrangements as yours. Considering the backwards nature of American prudishness, your situation could distract and derail the entire plan."

The Colonel's heart beat even wilder than before; "But my General—how would the Americans know? There would be no such activity during an arranged visit." His voice was pathetically pleading.

The General thrived on such torture. "You have proven to be an unworthy risk."

"How my General?"

"Need you ask? Several SS officers disguised as guards and as prisoners, saw you prancing about naked, attempting some clumsy form of sexual gymnastics."

"SS officers were disguised as prisoners? How could this be?"

"I suppose there is no harm in sharing this information with you at this juncture. We have been planting SS officers specially trained in espionage, in camps as POW's. They can then infiltrate and discover underground agents, on both sides." The General released a slow steady smirk long enough that it seemed to eclipse the rest of his face.

The Colonel felt an icy dead pain explode through every point of his body. He was drowning in fear.

The General went on; "During this interim period, we have, if you will forgive the term—'exposed' numerous traitors, collaborators with the underground, tax evaders and other problems. In the process, we have also identified various embarrassments. You have proven to be such a problem. It's a pity. Your service record is impeccable. If you had been more discreet, the hands of time, or is it fate, would have been kinder."

The General looked away from the object of conversation. The Colonel had ceased to be a living creature, and was now a troublesome waste product— one to be summarily disposed of. "You are to be sent to Auschwitz."

The Colonel barely heard the words when he crumbled onto the cell floor, folding himself into a fetal position. He heard the echoes of the General's words like a cruel noise ringing incessantly in his ears.

"Consider yourself a part of history, though a very temporary fixture. You will personally experience the efficient implementation of the Final Solution."

The General's malignant words grew to deafening heights as Goff's head exploded into blinding white pain. Biting down on his own lip so firmly, he drew blood, ripe red juice. The General withdrew from the cell.

Colonel Goff never acknowledged the large yellow star newly pinned to his grey shirt. None of this seemed real. How could this be? He was an officer of the Third Reich, a member of the master race, always the poster boy for an Aryan advertisement. He closed his eyes and refused to envision anything except his own officer's quarters and his own bed. Soon this ghoulish nightmare will end. That's right—all this horror—in time—will soon pass.

G OFF SAT STARING at the series of numbers being carved into his flesh
with the tattoo needle. The needle itself was filthy, caked with dead blood,
and iced with rust. He noted the point of entry into his pasty skin, how the
needle pierced through at one dominant point, but never found an exit coordi-
nate. He could imagine the needle going deeper still, becoming lost in a sea of
flesh. It went far deeper, burying itself in dark hidden recesses, much like the
depths of a dirty secret.

He heard a voice bellow "Next", and he was efficiently shoved into another line. This was truly a line of the lost. His world was now one of never
ending lines, some of which crossed over, some which merged to a single point
and some which eventually became socially invisible—as if they never existed.
Intellectually he knew these lines would inevitably converge to a violent conclusion, but that thought was like a newly discovered scent—meant for the
pleasure of others—not for those purchasing the item.

He found comfort in these lines. They were dependable. Colonel Goff
spent many days and nights contemplating and respecting these lines. Then
one day he found himself in a rather different line.

THE SUN BARELY peeked over the horizon, when Goff found himself in the midst of two long, cold, perfectly parallel lines. They led to a matched pair of buildings that resembled makeshift barracks. People walked into one end of each building, but they never walked out. Goff could barely determine the length of the lines over the sea of bodies standing—waiting. A young SS guard barked the order demanding that all prisoners strip. Goff stood immovable, certain the order did not pertain to him. This demeaning order was directed at the Jews—not an officer of the Third Reich. He stood stony, solitary in a self-imposed isolation. He looked naked—fully clothed.

Everyone who had previously worn a yellow star was now stripped of all material possessions—all except Goff. An SS guard approached wearing a grin spanning from ear to ear. "Strip Jew!"

Goff ignored the remark as it obviously had nothing to do with him. The SS guard marched directly into Goff's face and reiterated, "Strip Jew!"

Goff looked up slowly, deliberately, as if mentally preparing to challenge the guard's sanity. He declared, "Since I am obviously not a Jew; you must be directing that command elsewhere, but I implore you to do so—some distance from my person." Goff turned his back and began to hum.

The young guard's disbelief was only equaled by his indignation. As he paced the 'presenting' line, his pallor went from Aryan white to raging purple in the amount of time it takes the second hand of a clock to complete a single revolution—the span of a solitary minute. This guard could not believe the insanity of this Jew prisoner. What else could he be, except a God forsaken Jew? Returning to the scene of an enraging conversation; the guard used long, strident steps as he made his way back to this curiosity of a prisoner. In a confident and large voice he barked the command; "Strip you crazy stupid Jew—or I'll have the SS assist you."

Goff looked up once more and barked back; "You are clearly the insane one or merely slow mentally. In either case; you are most definitely out of order. Stand down or I'll have you taking my place in this line—preparing for your execution."

Goff's eyes flamed with the excitement of such a prospect. He was filled with a sense of omnipotence. Goff could clearly feel a thrill as he berated this uniformed simpleton.

In fact as he stood and contemplated the various ways he could defile this toy soldier; a grin positioned itself on his pseudo-aristocratic face. He imagined caning this idiot, glorifying in each deliciously tortured scream. Goff could view the soft broken flesh of his rump; two delightfully shaped crescents—round and pink. The only thing lacking is youth. If this toy soldier were of a prime age, (say between 9 and 13), then paradise, even amidst this inferno of filth—would be his. He was in his own fantasy world. Yes, such a twist of fate would prove to be quite delightful, but this wrong fate, this time and place, would not allow for such delicious delights. The Fates knew this, but Goff failed to notice the obvious. He was a prisoner about to be executed in the most humiliating manner devised by man. He was to be gassed to death under the guise of being 'given' a shower.

Goff then heard a calm soothing voice whispering in his ear. "This is merely a ruse, something to confuse the allies. The road to glory lies before you. Merely open yourself to the word, the truth and the way. The Fuhrer is benevolent to the faithful and obedient; the truly worthy."

Goff's grin suddenly transformed to a look of pure religious mission. The guard stood there, totally flummoxed both during and after the tirade, as Goff demonstrated the most insane behavior he had seen to that day. Sure there had been Jews muttering what passed for prayers while waiting for their turn in line; waiting in line for the executioner—but it was a one way communication ritual; they didn't expect a direct answer. This lunatic was conducting a conversation with an invisible companion.

The guard watched, amazed as Goff went on; "Yes, I understand the concept my Fuhrer. This peon standing here—how do I gain access to the secret weapon with this…human barricade?" Goff's eyes adopted the look of the true believer. He was the newly commissioned emissary of the uncovered plot.

The guard continued to watch this obscure prisoner 'dialog' with his non-existent commander. As if receiving a top secret communique; Goff 'returned' a salute to his invisible Fuhrer, and suddenly ran back towards the one-way alley behind the barracks. The young guard returned chase, once again finding Goff muttering to this same unseen 'commander.' After completing his abrupt conference with his imaginary 'superiors' Goff 'saluted' once again, before he lunged at the guard, fangs fully extended.

They scuffled like two school boys, clumsily scratching and clawing for the machine gun that would grant one of them, sweet freedom. Neither one could fight worth a damn; so they rolled on the ground pulling, screaming and tearing at each other's hair and face, with oafish vigor. Goff seemed pinned down at one point, unable to move his arms or torso. At that instant he sent his knee flying into the guard's groin. Pain surged through the guard's body as he fought to maintain consciousness. The pain was too much; it exploded in his head.

The guard's pistol lay on the ground, inches from what Goff considered to be the young, 'empty' uniform. He managed to reach the pistol lying between him and the toy soldier, twisted his body to face his prey, and fired all five rounds. He lay on the ground; hunched over the uniformed munchkin and caught his breath. After this temporary rejuvenation, he hovered over the dead body and hissed; "So you were going to order about the official emissary of the Fuhrer. Little did you know; I was sent on a secret mission to discover any double agents or underground workers."

Goff then felt for a pulse on this unfortunate pile of human cannon fodder, but no pulse was evident. He lay there triumphantly with the toy soldier enjoying the sight, smell and feel of his appetizing prize, for (what seemed to him), an unknown period of time. Time was an irrelevant commodity in his reality.

He soon muttered in a low, guttural voice; "Dead bodies can also serve a purpose of pleasure." Quickly Goff stripped the toy soldier from the waist down. The body had not yet begun to stiffen. Goff looked around, saw nothing, but heard footsteps coming toward his prey. Like a small predatory animal defending his kill; he dragged the body, face down, into another gangway between the barracks. There he massaged the dead man's buttocks. They were round orbs with a delightful separation that would soon send him to paradise. He kissed the orbs, licking them with his tongue, tasting the dead flesh of his sex. Hungrily, he separated the orbs and sodomized the body. Goff lost himself in this release and repeated the sex act until he was spent. He then lay there licking the object of his sex, eating the flesh, kissing the hard dead penis.

He was gurgling gibberish when he heard footsteps. It was the General once again. Apparently he had received multiple reports regarding an insane Jew prisoner claiming to be the new emissary of the Fuhrer. The General was in the area assigned to other business concerns and wondered if it was that stupid reprobate, Goff. Somehow he was not surprised. The General motioned for Goff to be sent to his quarters.

Two SS guards lifted Goff off the dead body he had been molesting. Fresh saliva and drool hung from his mouth, attesting to his conquest. He smiled broadly, smugly, as he was carted to his next destination. The General viewed his prize from one end to the other. The game was cat and mouse, and that poor dumb bastard Goff had no idea—that he was the mouse.

The General did so enjoy his games; but this comedic twist was growing weary and it was time to move on to other more interesting toys. It seemed fair to the General; after all Goff enjoyed HIS toy soldier, which he killed, played with, and would have disposed of in good time. Goff had become a problem which then morphed into the General's toy of sorts, and was now a problem once again. There was just one final detail required to make the game more entertaining. Goff was about to discover the gruesome details.

IV

AND WAGNER
PLAYED ON

GOFF FOUND HIMSELF once again in the General's care. He surged with a newly found confidence, created by the thought of a secret mission for the Fatherland. He had suspected all along that this torture he was forced to endure was merely a ruse to establish a 'deep' cover, as it was termed in espionage circles. The order for this deep cover must have come from the inner circle of the Fuhrer, perhaps the Fuhrer himself. They required someone who could appreciate the earthier aspects of the street life, someone who could mingle with those of 'different' persuasions, who could gain the confidence of those same street elements. Goff felt vindicated in the eyes of the Supreme Command; all this suffering had been for a grander purpose.

He strutted around the General's quarters, assessing the cost of the private label cigars, and smelling the brandy housed in ancient crystal snifters. Yes, he was sent there to be briefed on an urgent secret mission. He sat back in a large overstuffed settee, taking in the atmosphere of importance, all the while failing to notice the simple fact that his trouser fly was wide open.

The General entered the room and Goff flew to attention. His salute was weak from imprisonment, but the form was exact and according to military protocol. The General returned the salute in a strict, formal military manner, and motioned Goff to fall at ease. (The ensuing conversation was the part of this 'cat and mouse' game, that the General relished most of all). He then motioned for Goff to—once again, sit on that same overstuffed settee (which practically swallowed the small office). Goff was reassured by this action on the General's part—this new familiarity. Yes, this had all been a necessary cover, so he could begin work as some sort of double spy.

Leaning over, the General politely offered Goff a cigarette, which he happily accepted. It had been a long time since his last cigarette. Such luxuries were non-existent for most prisoners, except for those with either 'special' talents—or double agents. Goff took a long, deep puff and began to listen as the General spoke.

"You have once again posed quite a curiosity in the camp. I kept hearing tales of a crazy lunatic Jew, who constantly insisted that he was actually an officer of the Third Reich."

The General carefully flicked an ash into a crystal ashtray as he continued; "Eventually the rumors spread from the local gossip, traced back to camp officers—including enlisted men—up the military food chain—until it surfaced in Berlin's top circles." The General inhaled long and hard on his cigarette, studying the evolution of intricate smoke curls as he went on; "It has become such wild gossip that foreign visitors have been relating the same stories."

The General inhaled again and began to chuckle amicably with Goff. Goff, further wishing to ingratiate himself with the General laughed in synchrony. He felt his stock had risen. The General bent over the coffee table, and crushed his cigarette in another ornate gold ashtray, shaped like a gargoyle sporting promising springing claws. "These stories finally surfaced at the American Consulate and visiting entourage, which resulted in very difficult discussions. Apparently, the gossip also included your previous indiscretions."

Goff's face froze, stony with fear and anticipation of what was to come next.

The General added; "The Americans broke off talks with the Reich, citing irreconcilable differences with aspects of our social order. Their politicians were unable to devise a ruse that would conceal your pedophilia."

In a cold antiseptic voice the General proclaimed; "As the official emissary of the Reich; I am here to personally supervise the resolution of this situation, and to facilitate a positive version of events, that will correct this idle gossip." He signaled for the SS Special Duty Guards to gather Goff. A knowing look between the SS and the General was exchanged. The fate of this parasite had been sealed.

"The Fuhrer's inner circle communicated quite clearly that an example must be set. The order was given that you are to be fully aware and conscious as your sentence is carried out."

Goff wilted in the arms of the SS like a soggy dish rag. The General's orders seemed to be given in slow motion as he proclaimed; "You are to observe the execution of various Jews that were selected as choice 'specimens', to be cremated—live. You will watch as the remains are picked through by hungry dogs, knowing full well that you will be the final fatality."

Goff was removed by the SS, his feet dragging in time to the guard's rhythmic strides. This was so unfair, so sub-human—so cruel. How could they do this to him? What evil had he committed to warrant this horrifying final punishment? The pain, the endless pain of his own flesh burning down to the bone—leaving death as the only respite from such agony. This was supposed to happen to Jews and other mud races, not him. How would his handsome face burn? Would his eyes explode, while the remainder of his dead flesh flicked away, or would he remain conscious—feeling the endless, constant flames scorching, consuming his body? He could not watch these Jews go to this hell. He would not watch this hideous exercise in cruelty. He closed his eyes tightly; so much so that all light had been cut off to his vision, and especially to his sick soul.

The guards led him outside to a separate viewing stand used for visiting dignitaries.

There, he was bound to a pole, hands secured tightly behind his back. He turned his head as the General gave the order for the Jews to be led to their execution. The General directed a signal to the guard to bind Goff's head to the pole also. "You will watch this down to every detail."

Goff closed his eyes defiantly, "I cannot!"

The General gave another signal and Goff's eyes were pried open by an SS guard with hands like a vice. He stood there maintaining the pressure. Goff looked more like an amphibian with his eyes overextended—than human.

"You will notice how the Jews strip down so easily, line up, and passively walk inside the crematorium building and to their slaughter. They suspect that 'the showers' await them, but after entering the building, they are strapped to the slab, waiting to be placed in the oven." The General leaned over and chuckled on the next remark; "It's the waiting 'in repose' on that slab—that drives them over the edge. You see, they are forced to view the inside of the crematorium oven, fully ablaze, as they watch the last seconds of their miserable lives drain away like runoff waste. It is quite a show." The General continued his diatribe; "As you can surmise, I have made a study of torture practices, and subsequent effects on any potential survivors. You might say that this war presents unusual study opportunities over multiple subjects. I intend to take full advantage of such a golden, or should I say a 'muddy' opportunity—after all they are a mud race."

Goff's face was blank and white. He was determined to maintain some dignity; the General would not get that level of satisfaction. Goff could guarantee this in his mind; or so he thought. He was soon proved wrong. It was merely a matter of seconds on the clock.

The General looked at his prey and began toying with it. "We have arranged a unique entertainment so your experience will be particularly enriched."

Goff's eyes raced toward the General; he was fully aware of this technique, he had used it himself frequently. This tantalizing of prisoners was an acquired skill, much like riding a bike. In fact Goff was as practiced at the art of torture as the General, equally skilled using both physical and emotional triggers.

He was determined not to take the bait, for he knew this game, and would play it by controlling the only factor left to his personal armory; subversive emotional repression. Or so he thought. He was proven wrong again. Nothing could have prepared him for this next sight. Before Goff's brain could register what his eyes were witnessing, his ears were bombarded by missile like projectiles of Wagnerian movements.

These musical projectiles pierced the skin of the ever present fog. The music permeated everything, adding a false dimension of civilization. Evil always preferred an elegant disguise; its true face being too grotesquely hideous to directly view, much less sell, to unsuspecting souls. Ironically, Goff then found himself strengthened by these proud powerful strains—this regal nocturne—until he viewed two unusual prisoners in the lines. They were unusual for a few reasons; the most obvious being, that this elderly couple was fully clothed—and the lesser known reason being that—there were Goff's parents.

His mind halted at that very second. He was paralyzed. Goff seemed to witness this drama unfold further as some sort of passive observer.

The elderly Goff's were really quite ordinary looking—bespectacled and mundane. Both were rather plump and rosy cheeked—presenting a stark contrast to the actual Jewish prisoners. Frau Goff still had a kitchen apron securely fastened around her midsection—as if subdividing two equally indistinguishable sections. The apron was a crisply starched white linen bib and skirt, encircled by an embroidered ruffled boundary.

Goff thought to himself; "Did his mother ever cook in that lovely apron, or was it merely a prop?" He reasoned that it must be a prop, for there was never even the slightest hint of a stain anywhere on the garment. Come to think of it; that apron was like his mother—no stains in sight—always the appearance of cleanliness. How he loved that apron!

Goff couldn't hear his parents desperate pleas—they were home tending to their small garden. It was time for the spring carrots.

Though he was positioned in plain sight of the beheadings; he never saw the event. He envisioned his mother's plump hands cradling an apple strudel in the skirt of that same apron, as opposed to her amputated head reeling on that virgin garment.

The General leaned forward to note the glossed over look on Goff's face. The exercise had failed. The subject was expected to be hysterically raving at this juncture. Instead, the same subject was smiling, reality being light years away.

Goff was released from his bonds, stripped, and sent to join the other prisoners at the end of the line. These prisoners were sent, at gunpoint, directly to the waiting slabs in the crematorium. Before he was sent to his reward; as a final irony or insult (depending on the interpretation), his naked body was clothed in his mother's blood soaked apron—embroidered ruffle intact.

Goff shed a single tear which traveled down his face and neck, and whispered, "Thank you".

He entered the crematorium last. The General left the spectacle broken; and Wagner played on.

WILLY BRANDT HAD a good job with the railroad. He was a lucky man. Since the Fuhrer took power—wages had steadily gone up and jobs were more plentiful. Every day his wife Greta would pack a lunch pail and send him off to work. He and his wife had three plump children ages five through fourteen. The oldest child Franz was proudly enrolled in the German Youth Corps. Here Franz learned the values of family and country loyalty. He participated in enriching activities, marches through the town square, informational pickets in the ghetto section and sometimes surprise 'patriotic' events after dark. Naturally his parents wholeheartedly approved of such politically correct meetings. Franz had become a serious boy; gone were the days of frivolity and wasted youth—he was becoming a good Nazi.

Willy Brandt served as a conductor on the local railway for an entire year to date; driving loads of surplus metal and other commodities. On occasion he hauled railway cars filled to the brim with furniture, jewelry, and expensive art which had been appropriated from the Jews, and returned to the state. He was amazed at how these Jews could hoard! They were traitors filled with avarice. A Jew's appetite for wealth knew no bounds. Willie was sure of this, as certain as there were stars in the sky. He really didn't have any problem with such acquisitions; after all these people were enemies of the state, greedy leeches feeding on the German people.

Realistically speaking Willy Brandt had never met a Jew. His part of town had always been segregated from 'those kind' partly due to economics—but mainly due to church tradition. Before the Third Reich, Jews were a topic of conversation often consisting of long vitriol citing them for all of the world's suffering.

Willie had seen books complete with official drawings of Jews. They were resplendent with elaborate masks painted to resemble good Aryan folk, but the hooks which secured their masks invariably slipped and the truly hideous face of the Jew—would peek out. Yes, the hooks, (much like fishing hooks), were one telltale sign. Another dead giveaway consisted of a set of small, sharp horns which could be viewed if a Jewish man forgot his skull cap, or a Jewish woman failed to coif that thick wild hair into the accepted bun or snaked braids neatly arranged on top of their head. It was also cited in these important books that Jewish women had a third breast. This third unnatural breast carried poisonous milk which was used to murder Aryan babies while they suckled. Yes Willy Brandt had heard the stories and seen the official books. The subject of Jews, (in the flesh), had been broached during an announcement, regarding some additional shipments of surplus materials sent for disposal, in sealed steerage and cattle cars. Willy had some concerns—after it was disclosed that the surplus materials to be hauled, were dangerous Jewish prisoners—murderers, rapists, child molesters, charlatans and the like. The cattle cars were sealed as a safety precaution. Rumor had it, that some of these Jews had been known to bite off a man's finger, ear or similar appendage. Willy Brandt knew his duty and was ready to do his part for Fuhrer and fatherland. He was prepared for the dangerous, grisly, Jewish prisoners. He was not prepared for the truth, or his eventual consequent reaction.

Nothing could absolve Willy of his eventual sin of omission; that is once he came to that understanding. His day of enlightenment would occur exactly one month to the day that he had been hauling human freight. For now, Willy joined his 'colleagues', (who numbered in the hundreds), in their morning sojourn to work; lunch pail in tow, driving unsuspecting victims to the death camps in those hermetically sealed cattle cars.

These railroad operators grew to know each other. They shared stories about their families, hobbies, hopes, aspirations, how they thought the economy was going, and what kind of job the Third Reich was doing. These train operators all formed a 'conversation collective'—almost like a hive mentality. They moved in chorus—walking to work, walking home, opening their nearly identical lunch pails in almost perfect harmony. There are those who might have cautioned a simple man like Willy; that talking openly could prove quite dangerous. At least in a more normal society, this type of council would be wise. But nothing was 'normal' in those days.

Ironically the hunt and eventual persecution of deviants resulted in a highly abnormal ghostly remnant of a society. Withholding conversation—no matter how mundane, would be cause for investigation. So the coerced camaraderie continued, some of which was transparent to mentally swifter individuals—but totally lost on Willy.

He had just driven his twelfth load of human contraband, when a new assistant conductor joined the line. His name was Rudy Berman. Rudy was a small weasel of a man, compactly built and sharp eyed. Several of the men, (operators and SS guards), knew to keep their distance. Rudy Berman was no ordinary worker; he was what was termed a 'traveler'. Such men and women disguise themselves to infiltrate or 'travel' the national public works—in this case the railroads, sniffing out 'undesirables'.

And where 'travelers' were concerned, Rudy Berman was the best. Past jobs, (or as Rudy like to put it performances), included posing as a butcher, a dentist, a shoe peddler, a member of the local Jewish Judenrat, and even a Catholic priest. The Catholic priest was the most difficult; considering the required forgeries of authentic church documents necessary to make the fraud look legitimate. Luckily, the Reich had sympathizers in the Church hierarchy, looking to 'transform' the present official church leadership. Obscure priests on the lowest rungs of the ladder were known to have 'disappeared'—but their identity papers conveniently resurfaced in the right places at the right times, ready to serve the needs of the Reich.

Hell, Rudy was so convincing—he even officiated over the marriage of ten couples, in the name of the Church. Somewhere in the middle of Yugoslavia, ten couples are unwittingly 'living in sin' and multiplying numerous little bastards. Rudy actually smiled. It was one of those rare occasions.

Now he was here at the Auschwitz railroad evaluating the entire process. Apparently several high ranking Reich officials were convinced that a problematic situation was emerging. Eager to squelch rumors of any impending embarrassments—a full investigation of all personnel—even the local brass, was authorized. So, Rudy became a new assistant conductor working under Willy Brandt. Willy had no clue regarding his future path. This was one case where ignorance was truly relative bliss.

A dark, gray morning began with the cattle cars pulling into Auschwitz. Already overused breaking systems were screaming against the iron tracks, flaming sparks escaping from the binding ties. Smoke rose from the sooty buildings and seemed to suffocate the pores of any living thing. Smoke was a dominant force. It was one of the few elements liberated on any basis in that geographic location—that set of coordinates on a map—that Hell—that Auschwitz.

Willy Brandt unloaded himself off the train and viewed his meal. His wife had packed an overstuffed limburger sandwich complete with a thick piece of onion and some homemade strudel. It was secured in his pail so tightly that the contents practically exploded out of the container. A few rays of sun peeked out onto Willy's lunch pail. The pail had been scrubbed till it had a luster, shining like gold. Yes, Willy must have done something very right he reasoned—for the gods had smiled upon him. He studied his distorted reflection on the pail's smooth, unblemished surface. His eyes were mismatched in the reflection—one being overly large, while the other small and beady—much like a dead, dry raisin. His nose was broad and flat with dirty enlarged pores.

Willy could not believe this—he was always so clean about himself. Every morning he would scrub his face using the same meticulous pattern—till the skin glistened like pure new fallen snow. Willie knew that he was no movie star in the looks department, but this reflection was truly ugly. He refused to look at it any longer. What does a reflection in a lunch pail really mean? It's not a true picture. It's not a mirror. Willy felt reasonably secure in his own mental reassurances; such doubts were not only unfounded—they did not really exist. He was merely having a moment; probably due to some stale meat. Life was definitely not too hard for him at this time. Willy was looking up at a few passing storm clouds, when he heard several large, resounding shots. Bullets struck metal, releasing a cloud of stale turbid air.

Willy looked up at this release of force only to see his first load of dangerous Jewish prisoners up close. He had never looked any of them straight in the eye. Hell, he had never met any of these people before. What he saw sickened him. Released from a cattle car the size of a small kitchen; tumbled out one hundred people, as they were being rounded up and assigned numbers. Of the hundred, some sixty people were already dead.

Willy marveled at how so many were literally stuffed into so small a space. He saw the dead bodies piling up, one on top of the other. The SS guards systematically bayonetted the bodies on the top of the heap; in order to finish the kill. Fatally injured slaves were again, 'useless eaters.' A permanent blood stained area was being created on the ground, from the displacement of these bodies.

Willy began to lose his lunch. As he vomited into his pail; he first noticed the stench. It permeated everything, sticking to his pores like a second skin. How could he have missed this? After Willy finished emptying the contents of his stomach into his lunch pail, he noticed how many of the dead—had been young children and babies.

One body was more painful to witness than the others; a young boy, about twelve—the same age that his Franz was when he joined the Hitler Youth Corps. This boy however had his eyes posed fixedly at the sky. No movement—no life—just his frozen dead eyes and an unspoken question. How could this Jew look so much like his Franz as a younger child? This was impossible, yet here Willy found himself staring into this dead child's face. He turned away violently; then realized his dangerous error. Beads of sweat collected on his forehead and upper lip—which became streams flooding the deep crevices of his dirty, worn face.

Life had not always been good to Willy; and blaming others for past injustices—real and imagined—had been convenient; perhaps the only convenience afforded him in this life. And now he felt a stabbing pain in his soul. This can't be. This was victory. He had a dependable job, plenty of food in the pantry, and what seemed like a secure future for his children—one of which resembled this dead boy.

It wasn't supposed to hurt like this. Yet it did. Willy looked all around him; feeling the consummate eyes of the Gestapo, the other railroad workers, and those Jews all centered on him. All the eyes of the world were on him. His vision became blurred, faces and bodies merged in new and perverse combinations. Jumbled legs were fused onto collar bones and decapitated heads were walking on raw, overworked knuckles. And then that dead child looked up, wide eyed at Willy, and spoke a single, solitary, word—"Why?" The 'why' echoed in his ears in deafening, resounding tones. He had no answer. The question pounded in his head, developing a life of its own; overgrown like a gnarled vine choking off another young plant. He could feel that rope like vine wrap gently around his neck—caressing his Adam's apple. This caress morphed into the warmth that only a tight choking grip brings to the death dance.

At that moment, Willy choked. The air being supplied to his lungs was halted and his head was swimming. A vice like grip had a chokehold on his emotions.

"Dumpkoff—move!" The voice was young, arrogant and loud. Willy felt piercing stony eyes laughing at his moment of weakness. He looked up and snapped to attention. "I'm moving sir, yes sir. Pardon my blunder sir."

"Just move!"

"Yes sir. In a split second. I'll be so rapid and quiet too; you won't even know I've been here."

"Move!"

Willy jumped out of his skin on this last command and was backing out of the way; when he saw the child's body being thrown onto a rat infested dung heap with the other bodies of the newly dead. Willy had never felt the burning of shame—until that moment. This feeling seared his eyes, burning holes in his conscience. This was not the way it was supposed to be. Something was very wrong.

At that instant, Willy felt a tug on his shoulder—his heart in his throat. Nothing to fear; no melodramatic hand of fate—just the new assistant conductor, Rudy Berman. "It's time to go. We are behind schedule. "

"Ya, you are right." Willy's face was pale and drawn, withered like a dead tree before the fall. He put his hand to his forehead and wiped some perspiration from his brow. He had been sweating heavily, so much so that his hair was matted like a badly groomed amateur pimp. The two men headed for the freshly fueled (and now empty)—train.

Willie realized; this train was a morgue on wheels. He was the conductor of a mobile tomb. The thoughts came faster and more jumbled. His mind was a flood of crosscurrents all going in opposite directions. He knew his duty, yet how could that boy look so much like his Franz? How is this even the slightest bit possible? Could the Fuhrer be mistaken? A thought even more black crossed his mind; could his Franz have been a part of this work detail, this 'special project'? What if that boy wasn't really a Jew? Surely a child so normal looking had to be a good German.

Rudy Berman could see that Willy was deep in thought, and obviously troubled. This might be the opening he was searching for. He began his subtle plot with simple commiseration. "What a day. Such a mess, why did we have to be detained for that nonsense?"

Willy muttered something inaudible.

Rudy continued; "Why can't the Gestapo clean up their own mess? Do we look like janitors; or worse yet—stable boys shoveling sub-human garbage?"

Willy shot Rudy a wild angry look; nostrils flaring like a dumb, wild bull that didn't have the sense to know when he was about to be made into steak.

M AX HAD A strange dream; he was resting on a luxurious settee in a stranger's apartment. The room was tastefully decorated, lots of over-stuffed cushions and red silk brocade on the draperies. The brocade really caught his eye; it was the deepest red he had ever seen, whether in a dreaming or wakeful state. It was a red that seemed to go on forever, like an endless stream of blood.

Max shut his eyes and dreamed some more. He was standing along a river bank watching the tentative eddy of current move lazily downstream like a movie running in slow motion. There were some freeze frames; at points where the sunlight reflecting on this river glistened as the light met the normally dull syrupy flow.

It was a halting, blinding effect. The current then began to change, and the wind became colder than the previous soft breeze. This blood river gathered speed and the current was foaming white froth like are rabid dog gone mad.

Max just stood and watched as a whirlpool formed in the red and white mixture. It grew in both size and force till it swallowed the entire blood river. As Max stood there in total fascination, the whirlpool continued its metamorphosis beyond known reality.

A vaguely human form emerged from the center of the whirlpool. It was composed of the blood river with all appendages intact, but lacking a face. Even though this river had become stone cold; the blood river beast forming before Max's eyes was boiling like an overcooked lava creature springing to life. The bloody lava emerged as a dominant force, overwhelming the shore. Max could see the outlined forms of those he knew to be dead, mired inside the beast. The old man Max befriended in the ghetto was there, but his face was trapped in a mask of pain. He had been executed by Nazi soldiers for refusing to participate in a sidewalk execution of an accused dissident. They impaled him through the heart and laughed as his frail body hung from the bayonet. His murder served as a grisly warning to those who refused to execute fellow Jews or righteous gentiles. Max stared in disbelief as he recognized old neighbors and friends that he knew—had been killed during youth raids in the ghetto. Max rubbed his eyes, blinked, and cried at his next vision, that of his mother drowning inside the beast.

All of these images emerged from this misshapen perverted form, one right after another, like malformed figurines—poor caricature imitations of their real life counterparts. The blood river beast then continued to grow, eventually to giant proportions; commensurate to the size of a house. It changed color from deep red to purple, and then to pure black.

The beast had become a living gelatinous substance flooding the banks of the river. Max stood by the riverbank, still as a tomb, as the black ooze climbed up his legs. For some reason, unknown to Max—he was unable to escape. Rather, his feet were cemented to the riverbank's edge.

The beast was coming closer and Max was positioned like an insect trapped on flypaper—waiting for the inevitable. The blood river was inching closer still, though now it was more of a black tar. Everything it touched became as one with this Black Death. Max was petrified with fear.

Then an odd thing happened; Max began to sink into a pool of this new black tar. In a matter of seconds—his feet had merged with the cold black earth. His ankles soon followed; then his knees, hips, waist and shoulders. By the time his head was buried; all sense of self was lost. A zone where time and space had no relative coordinates or meaning was spinning around his essence. It couldn't be called a soul; that's for the lord to determine—but it was a gathering of elements, of being, which transcended previous realities. He was one with the greater spirit.

As this realization dominated his mind, a sense of calm settled over him. He was in a place where no one, not even the Nazis could hurt him. At that point, his body began to feel incredibly light. Like a helium filled balloon; he emerged from the bottom back to the surface. He popped up like a piece of escaping burnt toast.

Max was covered from head to toe in the black ooze. If formed a hardened skin so thick that his features, even his limbs were barely perceivable.

That's when Max woke up. He saw the General's slimy stare and realized where he was. He popped up off the settee, much like the toaster effect in his dream.

The General took it all in when he said; "So, you are back with the living—at least temporarily."

Max took the luxury of rubbing the sleep from his eyes. The General continued; "How alert are you Jew boy? I have a job for you. You could call it a 'baptism by fire.'"

Max looked up and for a few seconds saw the General in triplicate. Additionally, all three of them were swirling in opposing directions. The General's voice came from a void distinctly separate from his body. Max listened as the General said, "I'm waiting for an answer, and I am not accustomed to waiting."

Max returned his volley with the same blank stare. Now there were only two Generals. The General walked right up to Max, used a cold blooded voice and said; "I have lost an efficient officer—in part—due to his indiscretion, but largely because of your worthless Jew carcass. You had better be one Hell of a watchmaker boy!"

Max's vision was beginning to come into focus. The General was an unwitting port in a storm. Max spoke; "My brothers."

The General shook Max vigorously, totally unaware of his future role. Max looked straight in the General's eyes and said; "I won't fix any watches or clocks unless my two brothers are here with me."

The General was so stunned by this outright insane defiance—he dropped the boy. "What did you say?"

A deafening silence followed for an immeasurable period of time. Neither character could continue—they were both too amazed. Time had stopped for them. Max quietly issued the ultimatum again; "I won't fix any watches or clocks unless my two brothers are here with me."

The silence clung to the air, saturating the room. Max realized something very valuable at that moment—this General who was attempting to intimidate, desperately needed him.

There was room for negotiations; and Max was willing to gamble anything to save his brothers. He didn't know why this evil old man needed him, but this was the wedge he had been looking for. He had to hold firm, no matter what the threat. It was his only chance for survival.

The General's mouth dropped open—he could not believe the raw courage of this boy, this Jew. Turning away from Max in an effort to disguise the shock and fear he felt; an altered strategy was emerging.

"Very well, I will see to it that your brothers are here with you. What are their names?" (General slithering towards his prey.)

It worked. Max could hardly believe his ears.

"John and Henry Hirsch."

Max realized he may have been in these chambers for a much longer time period than he previously thought. His brothers will not be easily located—that is if they survived the daily' selections'. Yet he could not appear overeager; that would ruin the negotiation.

The General arched an eyebrow and said; "There is no guarantee that your brothers are here, much less alive. I will send the SS guards to discover what they can."

The General then asked with a sardonic crooked grin; "What will you do if your brothers are dead?" He made his move; he had Max in check and expected checkmate. The General was not ready for Max's answer.

"Then I won't fix any watches or clocks for you, or anyone else."

The General's eyes flashed both anger and fear as he replied; "Then you will die in the crematoriums."

Max reiterated; "That may be, but you won't have that antique clock fixed."All the color in the General's face drained away in a matter of seconds. Max knew that he had leverage, but didn't fully realize the gravity of the General's situation.

The General turned his back and try to contain his own fear. How could he allow a mere child—a Jew—to intimidate him? It was incomprehensible. He had to think fast in order to maintain control. "Your brothers will be located within the day—dead or alive. If alive, you shall have your wish."His voice lingered on the air like a foul stench, as a wide eager grin spread from ear to ear. "If dead, then you shall repair the antique clock before you eventually share their fate, and all at my leisure."

Max returned a hateful glare and said; "If they are dead; I just might make sure that clock never works again—and I'll go to my fate laughing."

The General saw the boy's eyes glow with the thrill revenge brings. It was clear at that moment frozen in time that this boy was beyond fear. What Max did not know, but suspected, was that the General had his brothers spirited away in a separate barracks for 'special' political prisoners; well out of reach from the 'daily selection' process. Max's gamble was about to pay off. The General issued the command to summon the two children. They were standing beside Max within the stroke of an hour.

Max had to use every ounce of self-control to maintain this deal. If he displayed any emotion including joy, whatever psychological edge he had over the General would be diminished if not totally destroyed. So delicate was the timing of this deal; the slightest demonstration of emotion beyond bland inquiries about everyone's health, would result in three more bodies being added to the day's mass grave.

Max began the charade; "John, Henry, it is good to see you. I trust that you are in good health and feeling productive?"

Henry had a dazed look; his eyes swallowing up the rest of his face. Max redirected the salutation to his older brother, John. John understood instantly and ran with the opportunity; "Yes brother, we are both in very good health and feeling a need to be exceptionally productive." The brothers shook hands like two seasoned old men brokering the deal of the century. Henry stood there, again his big eyes devouring the moment.

The General was nonplused; but he could almost feel a slight respect for these children, these same Jewish children who displayed more courage and sanity than that reprobate Goff. In fact the General's feelings of the moment were quite mixed—a most dangerous position for him. Not to worry—this was a momentary phase or lapse, soon eradicated. Resolve and decorum resurfaced with this self-assurance. He was not to be done in by a mere child. The General soon interrupted the exchange of greetings. This entire strategy and counterstrategy, action and reaction completed in the time span of a heartbeat. The General interjected; "Enough of the family reunion—it is time to work."

The three children looked upward but heaven was nowhere in sight; just the cold dark emotionally empty eyes of the General. He continued the instructions directed mainly towards Max. "Your brother will be responsible for the implementation of this task, while the two of you wait in an adjoining room."

Max glared at the General, for he knew what was coming—a double cross. No wonder this man was a General for the Third Reich.

"I have a watch that is badly in need of repair. Your brother, Mr. Max Hirsch, 'master' watchmaker has precisely one hour to accomplish the task. If he succeeds while you wait; then all three of you will be fed and kept safe for one additional day. If he fails—one of you will be summarily tortured and executed."

John leaped up, rage coursing through his body and said; "That's insane, surely we can help our brother. All three of us were taught these skills."

The General motioned to the guard to restrain John. The General then signaled the guards to force open Henry's mouth. A rifle was summarily shoved into the child's mouth—the General grinning the whole time.

"As I was saying; your brother has one hour."

Max replied in a tight but controlled voice; "Nothing in our agreement ever indicated a time limit—much less one so unreasonably short. Surely you want quality."

The General, viewing Max from a still superior height sneered back; "Time is always a limiting factor. We are all entombed in time from the womb to the grave. But, since you require more time—I will grant your wish."

Max braced himself for what was to pass.

The General issued his proclamation; "You have precisely one hour and one minute. A single second over the time limit—"

Max interrupted. "We know all too well; however since this task must be a test..."

"Test? You are so mistaken; this is the real thing, my Max Hirsch." The General smiled. He was an insecure devil incarnate.

MAX WAS LED to a smaller room, barefaced alarm clock set to pronounce the verdict, one way or another—exactly one hour and one minute, from this time. Before him lay a variety of jewelers and watchmaker tools; most had been damaged or sabotaged to some degree, just barely workable. Max knew the trick; if he used any of these tools he would prove expendable to the General, proving any competent watchmaker would suffice. He had to design his own tools of necessity, from literally nothing.

Max first removed a bent piece of wire from his suspender hook. It was hidden there precariously designed to feign a necessary support, though far from its true purpose—on the surface to fix watches—and later—to pick locks. From the inside of his left shoe came a small broken partial toothbrush; the next tool in his makeshift arsenal. Its composition consisted of two bristles in the width exactly equidistant from the three bristles in the length, forming a makeshift cross. Some double thick thread was his final weapon. He began to work.

Thoughts of his brothers, family, and the horror of this reality were presently banished from his mind. He had to steel his emotions at least for sixty-one minutes. His small hands scurried in a flutter of manic activity; eyes never looking up to check the time. Time would be called soon enough; the race would not go to the swiftest, but to the most cunning. Like the Olympic runner in a relay—you never look back; it breaks your stride. Somehow, instinctively you just know when to pass off that baton. Max knew this as he continued work on his mechanical patient.

Max's fingers continued in a barrage of disciplined yet frenzied movement, though his reflexes seemed as if in slow motion, compared to the whirlpool of thoughts flooding his mind. Eye to hand coordination ran at breakneck speed as he manipulated that tiny wire. Max had not always paid attention to all of his father's lessons, but this time mastery counted. It had been raised past the level of a fine art—to blunt survival.

As the final minute approached, Max was fighting the clock. The door swung open and the General's shadow blanketed the room with his presence. The General spoke; "Well my little protégé, Judgment day has arrived." A smirk on his face emerged as he continued the verbal torture; "I am sure your brothers are eager to see the results of your labor."

At that moment an SS guard violently pushed Max into the outer reception room, almost inviting him to drop the timepiece; providing an excuse to maim or kill one of the remaining unnecessary brothers. Not that the General needed an excuse to commit those additional murders, but the burden of guilt his prey would feel would be so much greater. Such was the nature of these bigots; they derived strength from brutalizing others. They were psychic vampires. Max did not provide the General such an excuse; he balanced his load like an angel dancing on the head of a pin.

Much to the General's shock; Max somehow miraculously repaired the watch without using any of the bogus tools and materials. The General had the tools soaked in some sort of lubricating oil, and any handling would have penetrated the coating. Max knew this espionage ploy from the stories his father told him before the war. So many Germans were convinced the Jews were liars and cheats that lubricating a tool would prove that it had been used. Wiping off the oil would also prove use. Max's ingenuity would fascinate the General to his own eventual detriment. He would soon grow to place an unusual trust in this boy, and would later view Max's yet, unseen abilities, as prophetic.

The General produced a second time piece—this being an exquisite Swiss bob, accurate to the second. The General examined and reexamined both timepieces. The silence in the room swallowed all sound except for the ticking of the two functional watches. Each timepiece was accurate to the millisecond.

Over the next three weeks Max repaired some twenty watches, clocks and assorted timepieces much to the General's irritation and fascination.

By this point his two brothers had been secreted away in an additional room adjoining the General's suite—but still separated from Max. There were permitted to see each other only at mealtimes. Max earned temporary safety for his labors and additional protection for his brothers as payment for his services. Mealtimes were always an exercise in duplicity. The three brothers had their own special sign language that made its debut before each could read. It was a combination of signals and letters which formed invented spellings. The trick was obvious to the boys; even if the Nazis deciphered the letters, the invented spellings would seem like idiotic gibberish.

In actuality, every third letter formed was the corresponding letter two spaces prior. That was one component. The other component consisted of vowels. There were none. Rather than vowels, the numbers one through five substituted for a predetermined vowel. If the boys wanted to; they could reverse the order of vowels back and forth by signaling 'upside down', for reverse. The Nazis merely attributed these behaviors to the craziness of Jews. A final complication was the fact that the letters were composed from phonetic Hebrew—but purposely misspelled. Misspelling of several languages—Hebrew, German, Russian and Polish was common in the Jewish ghetto.

The Germans fed into the notion that Jews were mentally retarded or slower but the actual motive was concealment. What the Germans dismissed to stupidity would not be closely examined. This was critical for any chance of survival. Every Jew kid in the ghetto for any period of time—knew this. Those new to ghetto life, from more affluent backgrounds, were at a distinct disadvantage. Such 'street' survival skills had to be learned or acquired in very rapid succession. There was no room for error. Such 'street' skills served Max and his brothers well at this juncture.

THE EVENING MEAL eventually became commonly shared time for the General, Max, John and Henry. The General had taken a type of perverted interest in Max which confused all of them. His interest was beginning to reach an obsessive level. Even the General's top aides questioned this behavior amongst themselves, though never openly. It was during this time that Max became acutely aware of the General's constant nightmares.

Actually half the camp heard his night terrors, even against the backdrop of these all very real terrors. The General's fits as some called them, were a routine nightly occurrence. The first evening Max witnessed these subconscious ramblings; he was left exhausted and confused. The General was being hunted, apparently by something so vile, he was left shaking uncontrollably in his sleep. No one else in the camp dared to listen to his ravings—it would prove fatal. Max wandered to the doorway of his quarters and pressed an ear to the door. The General was in fine form this evening. "No—spare me—I see the omens! I will obey—spare me!"

An animalistic gurgling sound, along with a piercing scream penetrated the night wind. Both emanated from the General's body. This gibberish was useless. Max had to use this time to learn more about the General. It was the perfect opportunity, or as perfect an opportunity as he would ever find.

The very next night Max lay in wait for the General's night ramblings. Usually they began at 11:30 PM and this evening was no different. The General was right on schedule. It began as usual, with bloodcurdling screams. Max mentally took note. He needed to check for any repetitive names, subjects or symbols. The General then began his dialogue—and dialogue it was—though it would take a series of thirteen such evenings to decipher the basic characters, sequence of events, and culpability. Yes, the General had his own ghosts and horrors, as Max systematically discovered. How he would use this information to his advantage was still not clear—but somehow it could be the link to freedom.

Each evening the General's pattern became increasingly coherent and Max was able to piece together a scenario. The General was waging a battle with past demons, camped in a solid fortress bunkered in his subconscious. Max had to find the key to this puzzle, and fast. He did not know how much longer he could maintain his present levels of productivity. One slip up, one minor error and the three brothers would be quite dead. Of course, that also depended on how badly the General needed timepieces whose 'salvation had come.'

Max found that in the insanity of the times; he had a new appreciation for the melodramatic. After all, this was a time when clocks, watches and priceless fobs achieved priority over human life—unless of course—that human life bore the correct pedigree—namely blond, blue eyed Aryan stock, possessing an extremely obedient nature to the existing government—in other words—the ultimate oxymoron—namely—a good Nazi. What a deafening, blinding, mind numbing contradiction of terms. His mind raced back and forth from piano lessons to the present situation.

Piano lessons; how far away from reality could a simple thing like that be? How his life had changed, from a mild semblance of normalcy in a hostile country, to this murderous insanity known as the Third Reich. Why hadn't the adults seen it coming? Why didn't we secretly arm ourselves like those crazy Americans? Max had seen two John Wayne movies when he was younger, and wished 'the Duke', (as he was called in Hollywood); was Jewish. The Duke went down with a fight. He never worried about 'appeasement'—he got the bad guys. No,' the duke' didn't do appeasement; he saw it for what it was—unconditional, cowardly surrender. Let's face it; the Nazis were probably the clearest, most obvious case of villain or pure evil on this Earth.

Max used to think that ladies who went to certain German Nazi doctors to get rid of their unborn babies—were monsters; but upon further reflection decided otherwise. He realized that some situations weren't so simple and that the world would have been better off, if some people had never been born. Adolf Hitler was in that second category. Think how different the world would be if the Fuhrer had never been born. This Third Reich might not even exist. All these thoughts raced through Max's mind faster than a Nazi empties his machine-gun clip into the Jewish ghetto.

He seemed comfortable with this hypothesis; that is until a rogue thought seeped into this nice, neat, little mental compartment. The thought was simple enough; could the Nazi regime, this affront to humanity, have formed without Hitler? The answer which found residence in his conscious mind—was a bone chilling—yes. The German people were very comfortable abdicating any responsibility or personal morality. Any people so selectively blind and deaf to the atrocities being committed in the name of patriotism—would not have the need for an Adolf Hitler to sound the battle cry—any hateful lunatic would suffice. Perhaps Hitler was merely the excuse. Max did not fully realize his own political sophistication. At his age he was more politically astute than half the world leaders. The Germans, as well as other Anti-Semitic Europeans were willing and able to pretend that torture was merely 'enhanced' interrogation, imprisonment was 'protection' by detainment, mass murder or genocide was 'ethnic cleansing', and stealing property was 'appropriating' payments 'legitimately' due the Third Reich for these 'services'. They believed what was emotionally easy and expedient.

And they kept their kitchens clean. No stains or soil ever crept onto obsessively scrubbed floors; and mercilessly polished furniture. The cleanliness police were everywhere—but the death camps. Dirt preceded the grave. This was the graduate study Max received. Yes, how his life had changed—selections were always fatal.

THE ADVENTURE BEGAN. The Generals voiced screeched tightly like an old rusty hinge. "Please, please—don't, don't!"

Max wondered what was so terrifying that it generated such fear in this heartless man. Whatever it was; Max prayed it would haunt the General forever. That would be a small justice.

In the General's subconscious, the nightmares always began with darkness; pitch black inkiness. The darkness stretched across a vast horizon; a few torn seams of light peeking through a taut canvas. He was walking through the darkness, pushing through air which had the consistency of filmy bubble gum stretched to the limit. It clung to his skin refusing to be summarily disposed. The General systematically pushed this adhesive slime away, but it rebounded onto his skin with an even greater urgency. He used a scrubbing action, employing his uniform coat as a rag, but with no success. In fact, the harder he 'scrubbed', the more furiously the slime clung to him. It seemed to have a life of its own, and bonded to the General with a vengeance. This 'slime' burned upon impact; searing his dream flesh like branded cattle being prepared for the kill. There was no stopping it. Relentlessly it continued to burn, eating away at his flesh, leaving fear as the sole remnant, which was cannibalizing his soul.

Finally the burning stopped. The air had cleared, and there was a more distinct light at the outer perimeters of this place. This 'horizon' resembled a manila envelope; the light tracing the edges so as to distinguish the shape. The General walked toward the light. It was impossible to estimate distance in the place. In fact distance, like time itself, had no relevance here. The only constant was the blinding light. The closer he walked to the horizons edge the more intense the light became, to the point of total blindness; except for the corner of his eye. What the General saw now was perplexing, beyond belief. From this 'envelope' horizon that swamped his senses, grew a floor, ceiling, and walls—all manila colored like the envelope edges.

Then the hooks came. All assorted sizes with odd curvatures. They were suspended from the manila ceiling by a series of levers and pulleys. Everything was still as a tomb. Each hook had a dingy lampshade hanging from it. And the smell. It was foul, choking off his wind, making him gasp. Sounds came independently from his throat, much like the last death rattle he heard so often from the prisoners. Usually the General enjoyed such sound effects, but this time the resounding echoes were more like painful harpies ripping flesh from a carcass. Suddenly the hooks began to move. They jerked spasmodically in all directions, like an epileptic in the final throes of seizure. He crouched from these hooks, but as soon as he did they moved his direction. While attempting to evade these hooks; he imagined the impossible—that they were tracking him—like prey. Realizing he had no other course, he stood still and studied them. While the earlier lines appeared to follow him, he noted that some lines independently moved in tandem. So harmonious were these coordinated movements; it was clear that these hooks seemed to possess an intelligence all their own. The General barely kept out of harm's way, when suddenly one hook—larger than the others, reeled straight into him—slamming the back of his skull. It knocked him out on direct impact.

When he came to; the sight in front of him was certifiably insane. The lamp shades had sprouted arms and legs. Some had faceless bloated bodies and distended abdomens. Others had blood and maggot filled sockets, where eyes had once been. The tandem movements all ceased when they saw the General. There seemed to be a collective stare.

The hooks began to move once again. Suddenly a large, solitary rusty hook with a blood encrusted jagged edge swooped down like a hawk. It stopped an inch short of piercing one of his eyes. He stared furiously at this immobile hook. It was at this time—the General felt two empty uniforms lift him like a small child's teddy bear, and carry him for approximately 666 meters, as indicated by signs along the path. These signs were written in blood.

The uniforms walked by themselves—with no bodies to inhabit them; yet they had strength and an invisibly solid form. The suits looked familiar to him, but not quite identifiable. Then the true horror set in; the cold black realization, they were the uniforms of Jewish prisoners. They were carrying him to a still much larger hook; one that had been polished smooth. This was a virgin hook, no blood or skin, just a clean mirror surface. And it was waiting. It was patient. It knew him.

His image reflected in the mirrored sides, and he was stupefied by what he saw; the immense ugliness of the vision. He released a silent scream. His face was no longer his own; but a Frankenstein like composite of dead human skins in various stages of decay or tanning, like some sort of leathery animal hide. Not only that, but adhered to the side of his head was a miniature woman sewing new skins to his neck. The number 666 was there again; tattooed on his half rotted forehead.

He just stared in total disbelief. She was quite mad and singing a rather joyful ditty. He could make out some of the words, something to the effect: "There once was a Jew, who lived in a shoe—covered with skin of leather;

So whether ready or not,

Here I come,

Making lampshades—out of your bum!"

The light went on—she was making a lampshade out of skin from his face, and creating this monstrosity from the remainder. How could this be?

And then he remembered Goff's pleas—and so many others—Jews, gypsies, homosexuals, cripples, Catholics, intellectuals and political prisoners. Of course there were assorted others, who could keep track? Theirs were the silent screams he refused to hear. It was only the dark silence. Yet here he was being punished as a criminal; how was silence a crime? Then the crazy woman sewing human skins together into a grotesque crazy quilt halted her work to lead a chorus of equally grotesque voices.

"Silence! We can hear your thoughts—such noisy questioning thoughts!"

Her voice was low, guttural, sounding like a multitude—not the vision of a small benign looking society matron. She had on a properly starched lace collar. Still, the ugly voice continued; "Just be still, and do your job. Be still, say, hear, see nothing—while I stitch your ears shut and poke out your eyes. You will be the perfect Reich citizen."

Visibly shaken, the General replied; "Madame must I be blind, deaf and dumb to achieve this dubious goal? I am a General. I know the ways of the Third Reich." His voice was shrill like a piece of sharp smooth glass screaming down an elementary school chalkboard.

The matron replied; "Yes, indeed the job must be completed. Now don't fret so—it is the way of history—the truth, as those in power, twist and pervert. It is the only way. Now just stop fidgeting—I need to complete this by the, excuse the term, 'deadline'." Her voice was still full of mirth as she delivered this punch line; much like a silly schoolgirl who can barely contain her own laughter. In fact, she could not restrain her giggles, as she released girlish squeals of delight. She exclaimed; "I just love my work!" The matron continued sewing until she received an unexpected message from another empty uniform, and grew an irked expression, as if some unknown 'they'—had robbed her of this fun. The General could still hear and see out of one side of his face.

The matron ceased sewing and said; "My orders have changed. You are to be too impaired to say or do anything before your pronouncement—whatever that means. I have been ordered to sew up only one ear, one eye, and one side of your mouth equidistant to the midpoint of your nose."

The General tried to mutter a reply, as he felt the stitches begin to close and tighten around his mouth. The job was nearing completion; uniforms were once again approaching. The matron signaled to them—to cart the General away. Again he faced prisoners; but this time—as one.

The hook secured a firm grasp on his uniform coat and carried the General like a limp ragdoll to a docking area. Around the dock like structure were two receiving lines of the type one would encounter at a formal gala, or an 'official' state function, completely staffed with full dress uniforms.

In fact, that's what he saw out of his remaining functional eye; the one receiving line composed of every type of uniform imaginable—Jewish prisoners with yellow stars, homosexuals with inverted pink triangles, gypsies, Slavs, Catholics with small deformed inverted crosses nailed into their foreheads, cripples holding limbs that had been amputated, and multitudes beyond them.

The other receiving line was populated with a very different type of uniform; these were the familiar, comfortable uniforms of Nazi soldiers. SS men, Gestapo, Luftewaffe—these were his people. The reception was not what he expected; his 'own' had turned on him; like he was of the mud races. He looked down at his jacket and discovered a yellow star pinned to the lapel. In a furious panic the General attempted to rip off the vile symbol with the open end of his distorted mouth; much like a desperate animal chewing off a leg, to escape the trap. It was to no avail. He could not be branded a Jew, this was the ultimate indignity. He had to convince these people on the receiving line that this was all some vicious mistake—surely someone would recognize him. No one responded.

Again, this was not the order of things; this 'B' rated movie version of Dante's Inferno. Where were the parades, reviews, the flag waving, and that sense of belonging to something larger than one's self? But he was wrong; a parade was before him—celebrating his fall from grace. Fellow officers were now lining the extended route further down the road. Very familiar faces were at the end of the line; occupying the space next to an open, raging crematorium. He was heading directly towards them on a collision course. They were all there—the Fuhrer, Goering, Goebbels, in full regalia and all smiling. This must be some sort of hazing, it couldn't be real. As he passed by the infamous three, supported by the jackbooted spirits; he could feel his now mutated flesh crawl. How could they smile through his execution? He was not some scum, not a member of the mud races; he was one of them.

The parade halted directly in front of the crematorium door. His feet were still on the ground—barely—as the two uniformed ghouls tightened their grip—holding him motionless. The General stared straight at the death chamber unable to process this horror, and as he did, his mind retreated to a strange anecdote; namely the times he ordered cleaning crews to scrape residue from inside the crematorium smokestack. Usually the crews called upon to perform such work developed mental problems or became alcoholics afterwards.

He then recalled one particular crew that committed suicide after they realized what the residue actually was. Even the General himself was revolted by the sight of 18 inch thick, wall sized slabs of an unknown, solidifying, gelatinous substance. They had to bring in a chemist to identify what was clogging the crematoriums smokestacks so badly, that it had to be shut down for regularly scheduled scrapings. The chemist was made to 'disappear';(presumably executed), after he gave his official report. The substance clogging the smokestacks—was human fat.

What was indeed amazing to the General, is that even with adult Jews starved down to 37 or 40 pounds; some fat tissue remained. The General once estimated numerically, that several hundred thousand bodies had to have been processed, to create this solidified wall of human fat. Just the numbers involved in such an undertaking, were staggering.

The fatty residue issue was the procedural disgrace of the death camps. It impaired efficiency on a consistent basis. If the scrapings weren't done on a regular basis; the stacks effluent would revert and explode onto the ground troops.

This would be very difficult to explain to the locals, (not that the Reich needed to explain anything), but keeping things neat and tidy avoided complications. Besides, there was the propaganda ministry and their job to consider.

They had to make the Final Solution appear not only patriotic—but profitable—and clean.

Images of eighteen inch slabs of human fat kept flooding his mind; forming walls, ceiling and floors. They began to move in on him closing the space, choking off air. The slabs were melding with his mind, body, so much so that he was drowning in the human fat of murdered slaves. Why he was able to recall that particular episode seemed quite absurd and yet, it fit, given this time, this place, this reality—or was it an alternate reality—subordinate only to the laws of a new physics created by that insane Jew—Albert Einstein.

They said Einstein was retarded but the General knew better, Einstein was brilliant but crazy. It was the only conclusion a reasonable person could deduce. Yes this was a new dimension in reality and when he willed it to change—the whole nightmare will end. He will be back in his command, completing the transfer of special materials, from the watches, clocks and assorted timepieces this little heathen—this Max child, repaired like some surgeon bringing a soul back to his body.

His mind traveled back to reality and the subject of smokestacks, for now he was facing one. The two guards reinforced their grip; bone like claws digging into the General's half rotted flesh. Perspiration beaded up on his distorted upper lip. He searched the reception line for any sort of ally, as the truth of the situation became all too real. He wondered if they could see, smell his fear. It was feral and basic. He clung to his fear, as it was the only constant in this reality. At this time of utter despair a small guard came forth while the others served as witnesses. The General could hardly believe what he saw; this small guard had courage but no cunning, for he was obviously committing suicide just by coming forth. The shock registered on the General's now distorted remnant of a face.

What the General saw next was even more astounding; this small, child size guard motioned to the two uniformed ghouls, and as he did, the General was released from their grip. The General felt like issuing a knowing grin, but was prevented by his altered facial features. The petit sauvage had a child size body, but an incredibly old weathered face, rich in deep crevices and wrinkles. He marched straight up to the General and stared him down. The General actually lowered his gaze. The petite guard smiled.

An amazingly youthful voice emanated from the guard's body. "You have exactly 60 minutes to complete the job, on the 61st minute—you die."

The General looked up in raw fear—he recognized the voice.

It continued; "Relish your 60 minutes, while you can."

A blur of random thoughts raced through his mind; had some act he committed in the past created this alternate reality? The General felt his head explode with these impressions, pushing out logic and reason.

A plain chair was brought out for the prisoner and he was directed to this contrived piece of civility. He sat down. It was, upon first inspection, a plain wooden chair; but as the minutes passed it began to undergo a metamorphosis. Within minutes; this same chair was larger and definitely richly upholstered. The wooden sides were finely polished and glistened with life, while the cushions displayed fine embroidery and intricate detailing. How could this furniture become so elaborate with no apparent explanation? Then again did any of this seem to fit in with an explanation of any type? The General heard an incessant ticking out of his one good ear. It was an even rhythmic beat.

The ticking became louder and louder, to a point that he thought he could hear nothing else. Somehow the provision of the upholstered chair added to the aggravation of the constant ticking. It paired insult to injury for as the seconds passed, the chair became more comfortable—the ticking more pronounced. He looked around to determine the source of the ticking, only then realizing it was his timeline. This little guard had a perverted sense of humor thought the General. He muttered to himself, "much as I do."

The clock continued to the final seconds, then—time was up. The young guard was back, staring him down face to face. The young guard spoke; "You don't have any idea who I am."

The General resented the question. He then realized that the stitching loosened and he could speak once again, so he kept the conversation going. "You possess an enjoyment of the perverse and ironic. It adds to the flavor of the suffering, don't you think?"

The little guard turned towards the prisoner and responded; "Yes, I do find a sense of pleasure in this activity, but there is a basic difference between you and me." The boy continued; "I am right, and you are wrong."

The General took the bait; "Oh, in what way?"

The boy continued; "I am right, and you are wrong."

Explosive laughter came from both men, from their very bowels. It shook the room down to the rafters. The General began to come to his senses at least enough to realize the insanity of the moment.

The clock was winding down towards the 61st minute. "Your time is about up;" the toy soldier mused.

The chair began to grow hard and stiff. It sprouted small wheels. The guards began to roll the General closer to his fate. All he could now see (out of the one good eye), was the raging inferno, coursing through the crematorium passageway. The fire became too much to witness, so he turned away.

The little guard turned his back and began to explain. "I have waited such a long time for this type of justice. I want to savor the taste revenge brings."

At that moment, the ticking ceased. The General's body was impaled through the chair on that large virgin hook, and flung, chair and all—into the waiting crematorium.

V

PROPAGANDA
AND PEARLS

THE FILM PROJECTOR was still plugged in, long after the reel had broken away flailing about wildly. Max had wandered into the room as the General sat straight up in bed, eyes large as saucers. He walked over to the still raging projector, flipped the off switch, and pulled the plug. It was dead.

The General had been watching the latest documentary accounting of the model German citizen's life. It was a Leni Riefenstahl piece. Max had heard old Mr. Goldman speak of Madame Riefenstahl—and not kindly. Mr. Goldman had a contact at a newspaper and was leaked information through a discussion group of local artists, intellectuals, and as Mr. Goldman put it—"people of conscience."

Max thought, that's how he knew, or at least suspected. Most of the time the group discussed international newspaper clippings; but sometimes films would be the topic. And where films were concerned; Leni Riefenstahl topped the list.

Her propaganda was supposed to sanitize state authorized robbery, rape and murder. The face of hatred wore pearls.

Max thought some more. So there were warnings, signals, but the Judenrat wouldn't listen. Their solution was uniform over time—appeasement. Don't make waves or the Germans will get angry. The Germans want to enforce a curfew on Jews, just ride the storm out—it too will pass.

The General's stunned face suddenly looked as if he had seen a ghost. Not knowing what else to do, Max froze. Perhaps the General was still dreaming even though his eyes were wide open. He hadn't said anything up to this point. There was no reaction from the General—he just kept staring straight ahead. Max knew that he couldn't remain where he was, so he made a bold move.

Without a second thought, Max kept a fixed gaze on the General's face, walked straight to the overstuffed bed, placed his hands on this Goliath's rigid shoulders and pushed them back on the pillow. Placing a single finger on each eye; he mechanically closed the sockets and walked out. That night Max prayed.

Max wasn't summoned to repair any watches or timepieces the next day. His meals were sent to the room where he, John and Henry waited. They didn't dare speak; it could mean any of their murders. This was the hallmark of the Nazis; murdering babies and children—and all sanctioned by the chain of command. To survive you were told to get with the program. Silence was both a haven and a sin. It all depended on context. Max, John and Henry waited for two more days and on the third day, at sunset, they were escorted to the General's room.

The boys were led to three chairs. The General motioned for the guards to leave. He paced the length of the room. His words were slow, deliberate and aimed at Max.

"I have unusual dreams." The General surveyed the children's facial expressions. No terror there, just confusion. The General continued; "Do any of you interpret dreams? I have heard that Jews possess this ability. I am curious about the accuracy of such claims."

Max saw his opening. The General doubted his own sanity. Max answered the query. "Yes my General, I am able to interpret dream signs."

Without looking at Max the General pointedly interviewed him on the spot. "Oh, and did you also learn this skill from your father?"

"No my General." Max knew the General's mysticism was newly found, and like most neophytes he was bound to be blinded by superstitious fear. So, Max played to that fear and let the General's imagination fill in the blanks.

"How did you discover this hidden talent? Surely a simple Jew boy with no education cannot possibly be so gifted." The General's voice trailed off and became little more than an unintelligible mutter. He appeared to be in a trance, not sure of his own location in time and space. The dream was beginning to invade his waking hours. This was his greatest fear. Could this boy help and even if he could, why would he? The answer was simple, to keep his brothers alive and safe. He could always have them executed after they outlived their usefulness.

The General's mind returned to the present. "Explain dream interpretation."

John and Henry watched this sideshow of Max's, and now felt their hearts sink. They both knew Max to be a bit of a con artist, but not so talented that he could convince a General of such nonsense. John and Henry were soon to discover how wrong they were. Max was just beginning to hit his stride, while both brothers held their breath.

Max began to speak in Latin, when mid-thought he switched to German, then to Hebrew, Yiddish and finally ended his performance using an ancient Gallic tongue he had read about in one of Mr. Goldman's illegal books. At any other time speaking in a language other than German, would have served as cause for a difficult prison term, but that worry was irrelevant now.

The General was enthralled, never had he seen such a strong child. He began to question Max in Latin about his dream sequence. Max answered in Latin for the first half and nonsense syllables for the remainder of the message.

The General was confused as he distinctly heard real words intermingled with some tongue he could not understand. The unintelligible jargon had the sound, feel of real language; yet meant nothing to the General's mind. The General halted Max; "It's clear my thought process is impaired from the sleep deprivation. We can continue this discussion later."

Max leaned forward and asked; "Are you fatigued my General? Perhaps you have been working too hard on the program."

"How did you know about the program?" The General's eyes became small slits, more resembling a venomous cobra ready for the strike—than human.

Max responded with rapid deployment. "We could not help but overhear the instructions you gave to the Colonel while we were waiting."

"Who gave you clearance to listen to anything?"

"You did, my General."

"And for what purpose?"

"To serve as witnesses in the event any of your officers were to turn traitor against you."

"Oh really, and why would I place Jewish children in such a position? Why would I trust you, especially against any of my officers?"

"Because our very lives rely on you—and your success. None of them recognize the importance of these timepieces to the High Command." (Fishing expedition).

"That is a much more conciliatory tone than your previously arrogant answers. Why have you changed your mind?"

"Again, the answer is simple. You have kept us together and alive. And for this, we earn our keep by repairing timepieces."

"Very well. You are a clever boy. I will retain your services both as a watchmaker and an interpreter of dreams. Pray that you are as lucky as you are skillful." (Fish takes bait).

"I will, my General. I will." Max sat motionless by his brothers as the General surveyed all three of them. The silence was once again there, heavy on the air. He wondered if the General would detect the ruse. Surely a man who rose to the rank of General in any army couldn't be so gullible as to believe in dream interpretation by a 13 year old boy. Maybe the General wasn't gullible; maybe he was that emotionally disturbed.

Max wondered which image was the key to this evil man's perverted psyche. There had to be a weak spot and he would find it. It was their only chance. The silence was then broken. It was the General. "I will expect a full interpretation of one of my select dreams as a test of your competency." He walked out of the room and locked the door behind him.

Max was surrounded by his brothers. Both John and Henry looked shocked. Henry began; "Since when do you know how to interpret dreams? Let me guess, you can read my mind too!"

Max expected this but had to respond; "Would you prefer that he find us suddenly expendable?"

John looked at Max and said; "And we're not that now?"

Max shot back at John; No we're not, at least not yet. As long as the General believes he needs us, we'll be kept alive."

John snorted back; "Yea, and the minute he doesn't need us, it's off to the crematoriums. After all we're too small to be useful as workers."

That last remark left all three brothers cold. Henry interrupted the stark silence; "So we have to keep the General strung along, believing you can read his dreams. I get it. What information do we need to maintain the deception?"

Max was amazed by his baby brother's level of street sense. Henry had never before shown such gall. Max actually liked his little brother at that moment. You always love your brothers, because they're your brothers, but you don't always like them. That was something special. Max was beginning to like his brothers, especially in the midst of all this chaos. Max motioned to them and they huddled like undersized American football players. "I'm not sure what the General is going to come up with, but whatever I interpret, has to be something that terrifies him even more. At the same time, the interpretation has to be just incomplete enough to convince the General that he has to have more information on a regular basis."

THE THREE BROTHERS repaired timepieces by day, and plotted psychological warfare by night. They had to be cautious to avoid detection. Any mistakes or miscalculation would result in torture and then summary execution. They summoned memories of old archaic superstitions, stories of the occult, and warnings of strange creatures they had heard from great-grandma Esther. They paired up specters of the most terrifying demons from Jewish mythology with old German Teutonic superstitions. This was their weapon of necessity.

John look at Henry and Max, and whispered; "What if he figures it out? He's not exactly stupid."

Henry cut his brother off short; "Then we're dead men."

John added; "Men, men, you're not even showing a single whisker. How can you call yourself a man?"

Henry answered the question with the utter resignation of an aged cynic; "Can you honestly say that we're still children?"

Silence engulfed the proceeding, much like a snake swallowing its prey whole.

Max continued; "I think we're ready." He looked at John and Henry and amended his statement; "God willing—we're ready."

The three brothers knelt and prayed. This was the childhood of a Jew during the days of the Third Reich.

T HAT EVENING THE General sent for Max. He arrived to find the General huddled over the open fireplace, staring wildly at the flames. The General remained there long enough for Max to become uncomfortable waiting. Finally acknowledging Max's presence; the General signaled for him to approach. It was a dignified motion Max thought, and he followed through. The General finally spoke, "I have had another disturbing dream and it has the same symbols and sequence of events. I must have an interpretation now."

Max studied the General's face. It looked gaunt and worn. He found some satisfaction in this turn of events. Max replied; "My General, perhaps your staff scientists should witness this information, and not a mere boy such as myself."

"You were not so humble the other evening, when you made claims to these skills. Have you been toying with me boy?"

"No sir, I merely need to remind the General, that your dreams may contain material which is of a sensitive nature, possibly issues of National Security. Such information may be in your subconscious mind, and forming through your dreams."

"Why would a Jew be so concerned? You of all people should desire the weakening and downfall of the Reich." The General looked straight through Max, as if he weren't there at all.

Max saw a possible trap, and he had to keep the lines of communication open. He had to concoct his answer rapidly and give a response that would be generic enough to be believed.

The General grew impatient, raised an eyebrow, and said; "Come now boy, you rarely seem to be at a loss for words. Surely you can give me a straight answer." The General looked down at his Italian loafers, (that had been seized in a raid earlier that year), and muttered to himself; "You are probably the only person I know—who would give me a straight answer." Max saw the General shake his head, as if in disbelief.

Max looked up at the General and replied; "My General, I am at a loss for words."

The General was stunned. Never did he expect such an answer from this child, who had such obvious skill at manipulation. The General had long recognized that Max had manipulated his way into protective custody, but he also realized that he needed this talented gremlin. He looked into the fire again, and asked; "Why are you suddenly at such a loss for words now?"

Max knew the way to go with this conversation. He said in a very soft voice; "If I tell the truth, I may jeopardize the protection my brothers and I have enjoyed with you, my General. If I lie, you may see through the deception. Either way, my brothers and I risk what security we have."

The General looked energized by this comment and said; "Boy, you may be sure that such security as it is dubbed, is quite tenuous and dependent upon my moods. It will be most definitely lost if you tease in such a fashion. Now speak!"

Max realized the time to spring the trap was either now or never. So he began in a soft, deliberate voice; "Your dreams, are they of a repetitive nature?"

The General felt his blood turn to ice water on that inquiry. "Yes." The answer was small and unsteady, like a clumsy infant's first steps.

Max continued. "Do any of these dreams ever differ on any detail, or are they identical to the previous ones?"

The General coldly asked; "Is that information even pertinent?"

Max answered; "Yes my General."

"How so Jew boy?"

"It establishes a firm pattern if identical, in which the entire body of the message is equally important."

"And if the dream varies in some minor details?"

"Does the main theme remain constant?"

"Yes."

"Then the changes in details, even when the theme remains constant, would indicate a special significance in either those details, or their place in the overall sequence. It also means that the theme is highly important."

The General winced on this proclamation. The pain on his face was clearly visible. Max made a mental note of this reaction. The General continued; "What if the dreams had one constant theme with a variety of events, different places, people, actions and reactions, but obviously the same moral?"

Max looked puzzled; "Moral?"

The General stammered his response; "Moral, theme—same idea." Exasperation controlling his voice box.

Max calmed himself and asked further; "What theme would that be?"

The General's voice grew cold, robotic and steely. "Victimization."

"HE SAID—WHAT?!" JOHN'S voice was high and shrill, matching his total disbelief.

"How can he, of all people, even speak the term? How many people has he murdered, raped and butchered?! And he cries about victimization?"

Max grabbed his older brother by the scruff of his neck and desperately screamed a whisper in John's face. "Look, we need this vile man."

John broke loose from his brother's surprisingly strong hold and countered; "Why, to keep us as collaborators for these bastards?"

With those words, Max lurched at John's throat, ready to rip it out. Henry intervened, with his nose intercepting John's fist. Max and John halted like two ancient dinosaurs frozen in ice. They had never before turned on each other.

Henry then shrieked at his brothers; "I need my nose."

Both brothers stopped immediately at the announcement of such an obvious statement. It took his brothers a good ten minutes just to realize the absurdity of their situation.

Henry spoke quietly; "It doesn't matter if the General's feelings are insane or insulting. We know he's evil. We know that we hate him; but John—were buying time."

John turned away from his brothers long enough to feel the bile building inside his mouth and his soul. "Yeah, watchmaker's buying time. Did you hear that—buying time—in the death camps."

John just stared at Henry, unable to argue against the truth of the statement. Several minutes, or was it hours, passed before anything was decided.

Max broke the silence. "Henry, you're exactly right. We're buying time in the middle of the death camps. We're doing that, because we have no other choice right now."

John looked up at Max. "We do have other choices."

"What choices are those?"

"We can fight."

"Have you lost your mind? Fight—with what—our fingernails?" The voice was Henry's and his patience was gone. Henry looked old and tired; like he was tired of living itself. He continued; "And how far will we get, that is before we're shot by the guards in the yard, or the tower?"

John glared at his baby brother and said; "It's better than just waiting to be executed like dogs!"

"So it's smarter to dive into the crematorium?"

John's voice was equally timeworn as he explained further; "No, but it would end the pain."

All three brothers became silent. They could hear the casket door creaking shut; slowly entombing them.

"WAKE UP JEW bastard! Move, move!" John's head was reeling as an enlistee hit him with a riot stick. Henry and Max helped him up. Sirens were shrieking through the camp, nothing could escape the excruciating noise. The boys were pushed through the door and faced the chaos of the outer compound. It was clear to Max that no one had the smallest clue as to what was 'supposed' to be happening. It was morning, and being obedient, no submissive, was the order of the day. Henry and Max helped their brother to his feet as they made it to the outer yard.

A loudspeaker boomed down at the half dead populace. "You will strip down completely, and form lines to the showers."

Max felt the panic in waves. He searched the quadrangle for his General. This fate was not correct. They had a deal. They could fix watches and other expensive timepieces. His fear became unbearable, and he was looking for somewhere to run. It didn't matter where, anywhere would do, anywhere far away. They had to escape. Max understood now, this was the time John meant, the time to go down fighting. Max looked wildly at his brothers; he was about to give the signals designed to start a small riot. In just the amount of time it takes for a heart to skip a beat; he had made his decision.

Max then felt the ground escape from under his feet. Before he realized what was happening; all three brothers were being dragged towards the alley behind the crematorium. Max and his brothers had been lined up opposite three like-aged Nazi Youth Corps volunteers. Max was confused; then he saw the General's familiar form and knew a plot was in the works.

The other three boys looked fearful, even more so than Max John and Henry. Perhaps it had to do with higher expectations; somehow possibly dying in a mud soaked alleyway didn't fit the recruitment poster. The General cocked an eyebrow, and a border guard gave the order for the three brothers to strip and exchange clothes with the enemy. The three Nazi Youth Corps members followed their orders, though with trepidation. The next few minutes seemed to stretch for an eternity—mere seconds pounding away at entire lifetimes. The only signal that triggered the execution style murders was the General calmly turning his back. The three boys dropped like flies. The guard ordered the bodies to be thrown into the crematorium directly; much like the disposing of a used candy wrapper.

Max, Henry and John found themselves ushered into the General's private car, speeding off to an unknown destination. The General had all the windows to the car sealed tight. He found the fumes from the active crematoriums distasteful, particularly during a mass fumigation.

They drove for approximately an hour before a single word was spoken. The boys could see the clouds of smoke rise from the camp in the rearview mirror. In fact for a while, all they could see was smoke. It blanketed the countryside. Finally, the General leaned back into the leather upholstery, and began to speak; "We are headed to the woods. I have additional quarters there. We'll remain at those new quarters until I receive counterintelligence orders."

Max was confused. Was the General a double agent for the Allies, or was he just a mercenary poised in the high command? Max supposed he would find out soon, for they had arrived at their final destination. As the car pulled up to an old stone drive, a dark castle rose on the horizon.

Looking up at the castle growing closer in the foreground, Henry envisioned himself advancing in a receiving line, shaking hands with various luminaries, until he reached the end of line—to wit—he would say, "Dr. Frankenstein, I presume?" He could feel a smile emerge, though he knew to suppress any normal reaction in these dangerous times. Random thoughts raced through Henry's wandering mind. Why couldn't he live in a normal time? What was normal? Wouldn't even Dr. Frankenstein be shocked by these pig butchers called Nazis? And frankly, wouldn't a comparison to Dracula be more fitting—as Dracula drained the blood of innocents to feed his evil appetites—so did the Nazis follow suit.

Max saw the faraway look on Henry's face, and he knew exactly where his younger brother was hiding. Max knew that inside each person was a place no one could disturb, or touch. It was a place where there are no bullies, no evil, and no Nazis. It was the ultimate safe haven. And it's true; no one can touch you in that safe haven. There you can find your humanity. There you can find God.

Breaking the silence, the General gave a signal to his regular guard. The two additional guards attached to this temporary envoy, followed the old veterans into a wooded area some 50 meters from the car. Two shots were heard in the distance, followed by the sole return of older, battle ready hands. The General wanted no additional witnesses to this exodus. Max, John and Henry tumbled out of the staff car and stood at attention, like young draftees. They knew that their survival depended on this ruse. For the time being, they were Nazi Youth Corps buck privates.

The German Sergeant routinely stationed at this post, ignored the perfunctory executions; such dealings with unnecessary witnesses had become accepted practice. Instead he decided to look over these suspiciously childish enlistees. Glaring at these boys, he barked the command to turn 'about face'. The boys remained in place. The Sergeant repeated the order, and still the boys remained in place. The sergeant looking confused and angry, released the safety latch from his service pistol, cocked the trigger and rammed it against the back of Max's skull. He squeezed the trigger.

"Halt!" The order came from the General himself. The Sergeant was stunned beyond his senses. Why would the General spare a youth corps private, a scrawny inductee at that? The General motioned for the Sergeant to approach. He stood at attention. The General spoke; "These three recruits are to be stationed in rooms adjacent to my personal quarters. See to the details."

The Sergeant now fully understood the situation, or so he thought. These three recruits as he put it, really just boys, were the General's personal playthings. Funny, he knew the General to be sadistic, but to sexually molest young German boys, this was a new low. He had heard of a Colonel Goff who regularly raped young boys, but they were Jews, so it was forgivable perhaps even a service to the world. But these were German boys, they were not meant to be so used, even if they were incompetent dolts! They deserved to die more honorably than a whore! He could feel his revulsion towards the General grow like a festering wound that's been left unattended. He could not stand by silently. He spoke up, unaware of the very words he was uttering. Time, in the Sergeant's reality, had stopped dead.

This was the first time in his life he had ever questioned the actions of superiors, even subconsciously. Yet here he was about to address the General. The Sergeant was not the type of person to break with tradition. He had always followed orders, and taken pride in his ability to get the job done. He was the epitome of effectiveness and efficiency. He got with the program, but this time it was different. It was no longer a matter of just doing your job; these were good German boys, once again perhaps inept soldiers, but Germans. If nothing else, they deserved to die like soldiers.

A cold steely voice broke the silence; "Sergeant you are to escort these three to my personal quarters—immediately!"

Still stony dead silence, as the Sergeant stared straight ahead.

"Can you not hear my orders?" The General's voice was shrill, cracking with the sound of fear.

This detail was not lost on the sergeant. "Yes, my General." Then the unthinkable continued to evolve as the Sergeant suggested; "Perhaps these young soldiers would be more useful to the unit in the enlisted men's quarters."

"Are you questioning my judgment Sergeant?" The General raised a brow but also felt the taste of sweat draining off his upper lip into his mouth. The General stood there, praying internally to a higher power, that this rather bright non-com didn't see through the ruse. His heart beating in his throat, racing at a maniacal pace; it took all his nerve to control the urge to scream, but silence was maintained. Silence was the key.

"No my General, I was merely presenting an option."

"An option which was duly considered at an earlier date and deemed unworkable."

"Yes General." The Sergeant snapped to attention.

"Oh Sergeant," the General's voice waited.

"Yes my General?"

"The last soldier to make suggestions that were not solicited was sacrificed to the crematorium." The boys were escorted to the General's private quarters without a second's hesitation.

VI

SECRET
HEADQUARTERS

THE SERGEANT MONITORED the General's movements for several weeks to come. Every morning the General inspected the small barrage of troops as they performed their duties. This was followed by an immediate retreat to his personal quarters. The Sergeant knew something unnatural was going on, but had to be cautious. One error would cost him his life and that of his entire family. Was it even worth the gamble? Could this be a test to see who was a loyal Nazi, and who was a mere impostor, a sleeper, hiding in the shadows, waiting for the moment the shooting stops? The Sergeant's days were filled with a new type of uncertainty, always looking around the corner, double checking each minute detail. It was easier when the enemy was clearly identified.

Finally, one seemingly ordinary day which normally carried no import, the secret was exposed to the light of day. It happened during a dinner break; a communique had been delivered to the General's office by special envoy. Upon opening the envelope and reading its contents, the General motioned for his private guard to usher the boys to a different locale within the compound. The Sergeant watched this choreography for the following week. Every day that week a new private communique would arrive and the General would disappear for exactly one hour. When he returned his entire demeanor had changed. His voice was more relaxed, his stance still very military but not quite so defensive. It was during this time that he let his guard down. The Sergeant began a dangerous game at this juncture. He hired informants, (with nothing left to lose), namely certain prisoner trustees to spy on the General.

Actually it couldn't be truly considered a hiring; sometimes the reward was maintaining their position as prisoner trustee and at other times (usually with the bolder trustees), cigarettes or small bits of chocolate would serve as currency. What they discovered was suspiciously benign, (at least by the Reich's standards). The General was receiving a variety of timepieces that these three boys were able to repair. In fact these boys repaired the timepieces within a span of exactly 60 minutes, (at least that's what his hirelings reported).

His prize informant Mika Schloss was summoned to a dark corner of the compound late at night, for an explanation beyond this drivel about repairing clocks and wristwatches. The Sergeant began, red faced but cautiously inquisitive. He knew that showing too much concern would give this Jew weasel the edge. Though he could have this weasel, this Mika eliminated easily; he had no idea how many others this lowlife also spied for. Not many insiders even knew—how many weasels like Mika turned traitor against their own; it had become an actual network with suspected players at the highest levels of Jewish society.

Among Nazis, the paranoia generated from living in an age of constant surveillance, had grown so deep that there was even talk of insurrection, talk that the Fuhrer had become totally insane. Everyone had to be cautious. Times were changing like twin tornadoes blowing in opposing directions. Those caught in the middle were trapped in the vortex. Temporary safety until one force dominated all (which one ultimately will), became the password of the day. Then selections.

So the conversation began with Mika granting the Sergeant some not too serious groveling; "You called, my benefactor? How can I, your miserable servant, be of some aid to you?"

"Miserable weasel, what kind of crazy nonsense have you brought me?!"

"What are you saying my gracious employer?"

"The cryptic messages about these three German boys repairing time-pieces for the General"…

Mika saw the opening of opportunity. He could smell the Sergeant's fear, so he risked interrupting him mid thought. "What is so cryptic about repairing timepieces?"

"But German boys, hidden away like…"

Mika risked his intact throat again, and interrupted; "Who ever said those boys were Germans?" Mika's face revealed an oily grin; the type all Dathans develop with time. He mentally noted the bone white panic on the Sergeant's normally well-disciplined features.

"What are you saying?"

"I am saying those boys are not Germans." Mika let the force of this revelation wash over the Sergeant's boringly handsome, monoculture, Aryan features. He enjoyed playing both ends against the middle.

That sole moment of satisfaction was broken by the Sergeant's revolver savagely pressed up against his non-Aryan penis. "Before you become a castra-to, I suggest you inform me just who those boys are!"

With an obviously strained voice Mika released the information; "They are Jews."

Shock forced the Sergeant to withdraw his weapon. Several minutes passed in seemingly slow motion, before the obvious question was given life.

"What?!" The question fired volley like from the Sergeant's mouth. "You had better explain the garbage that just came from your ugly Jew mouth." The Sergeant was sensually caressing the barrel of his gun as he uttered this generic warning.

Mika knew that the game had turned sour. Through his temporary panic, he explained; "The three boys are Jewish watchmakers employed by the General."

The Sergeant continued his masturbatory massage of the gun and said; "Why would a man like the General save three Jews from the gas chambers or crematoriums merely to repair clocks and watches?" He cocked the trigger and took square aim on Mika's organ. "You had better conjure up a more creative response than that tripe—my hand is becoming tired."

Mika blurted out; "These boys are quite ingenious. They have repaired his-toric timepieces the finest watchmakers in Europe have been unable to revive."

"What like Lazarus rising from the dead? We are talking about clocks, not the, the…"

Mika rose and interrupted;…" The living dead?"

The Sergeant sneered, slapped Mika to the ground and said; "You talk too much Weasel."

That was his nickname and that's what he was, a cowardly but clever weasel, just high enough on the food chain to be useful, but low enough to be nothing more than a bottom feeder, only he fed on his own, mused the Sergeant. If they were not baby eating Jews, they would almost be worthy of pity.

The Sergeant looked away and continued; "Let's say, for argument's sake, that your information is correct. Why hasn't the General employed good Aryan watchmakers? Why has he risked such dangerous talk?"

Weasel looked up, his cowering arm shielding his face; "Simply because the best watchmakers tried and failed." Weasel hunched over in preparation for the Sergeant's next blow. Nothing happened. Weasel looked up and saw the Sergeant staring into space, muttering to himself; "The best watchmakers in all of Europe," over and over again. He was dumbfounded. Finally the Sergeant looked down at Weasel once again and inquired; "Exactly where does the General house these boys?"

Weasel looked down at the ground fearing any further confrontation of the kind direct eye contact might induce, and replied. "They have been issued a room within the General's suite."

"There is nothing new about that information. That is where they sleep. I want to know where they work!"

Weasel never looked up from the floor, but he could feel the fear build to an even higher climax. (Fear had become an animated living force). In a shrill voice, a voice that could shatter glass, Weasel explained. "They have been shuttled to different rooms in the mansion. I do not know why."

"And"… The Sergeant's voice was hoarse and sultry from anticipation.

"At other times they are blindfolded and driven to secret locations, presumably to repair other antiques." Weasel's body shook like a dry, dead leaf at the time of the fall. "That is the extent of my knowledge. I know nothing else!" His was the dangerous voice of cowardice, willing to commit any atrocity—in return for dubious salvation.

"What would be the purpose of such shuttling as you call it? Why not keep them here in one room?"

Weasel watched the sergeant pace the floor, muttering, much like a true believer mumbling some nondescript prayer.

The Sergeant knew something more dangerous was evolving far beyond some profiteering on the General's part. He could smell the deception as it penetrated the air. As a rule deception was normal operating procedure; that is as long as the deception victimized the undesirables in a group. But this deception, at such possibly high levels, was a very treacherous game. He reconsidered the prior knowledge he had of the General.

For the most part the General's reputation was clear-cut, like a perfect diamond, ruthless and goal driven, undeterred by any conscience. No attachments to speak of, other than his carefully engineered self-promotion. So returning to the question; why risk so much on the dubious talents of these three boys? The facts did not add up, yet here he was in the middle of a potentially explosive situation. He needed more information, and that information had to be somewhere. Generals of the Third Reich—or elsewhere, do not suddenly become sentimental. What was the real plot? Who were the players? The Sergeant could feel the pressure mount like a volcano minutes before a major eruption. The question of explosion was not 'if', but 'when' and how far the aftershock.

The Sergeant looked up and sneered at the cowering body of Weasel, curled on the ground waiting, expecting searing red retribution. "Weasel I have another task for you." As he motioned for Weasel to approach, he watched the sunset sink into distant clouds of smoke, probably crematorium smoke. The Sergeant realized at that interval; death has its own timeline.

TIME PASSED SLOWLY at the house. One job followed by another made time itself seem stagnant, weighing down on a soul like quicksand pulling in a giant wild beast. Eventually all life would be siphoned off, leaving only a shell of a carcass. The boys constantly wondered when they would outlive their usefulness. Which job was the last job? A month later they would receive the answer.

Weasel had been exceedingly busy, attempting to fulfill the mandate received from the Sergeant. Fearing the future he pushed onward trying to maintain the status quo; but change was in the air, coming from a secret motorcar envoy. They arrived by cover of night, fully uniformed in Nazi regalia. Weasel was privy to such information as unofficial secretary to the General's personal assistant—and as such, he witnessed all the comings and goings in the compound. This mysterious elusive 'they' took the form of Herr Wiener—an American born scientist with early Nazi party sympathies. Weasel didn't know it yet but his livelihood as a snitch was about to change, and this stranger, this Herr Weiner was the cause.

Herr Wiener was accompanied by an entourage of five uniformed strangers. The talk inside the office was in hushed tones and cautious strains.

"When can the items be delivered to the pickup destination?" The man was tired and drawn, and it registered in his voice.

"We must do this in small increments or the items will become too unstable to handle." It was the General's voice this time and Weasel could tell by his tone that these items demanded the utmost care. He wondered what these items could be, to command such attention.

The unknown man pressed his point; "So when can we expect delivery? We are ready to proceed with the next phase, and have received intelligence reports that the enemy is much closer to parity than was previously thought." You could all but hear the sweat form on this stranger's brow. "We must close the gap, and have first strike capability."

"We will have the first strike, but we need some additional time."

"Time isn't a luxury that can be spared." Herr Weiner was speaking through gritted teeth. "Our latest communique indicated that the Allies are closing the gap."

"But the Fuhrer has assured us that the Reich has all but devastated the infidels." The panic in the General's voice betrayed him.

"The Fuhrer may not be in charge for much longer." Herr Weiner motioned the General closer; "The Ides of March are not the only powers that the Reich must guard against. The Fuhrer has lost contact with reality. He believes that soothsayers and other such humbugs can more accurately advise him—than his military experts."

Weasel was actually peeping through a keyhole as a result of this last proclamation. Through this small opening, he further witnessed this unbelievable drama unfold between the General and this visitor. The General was mopping his brow with a silk kerchief; "But the communiques we received were so brilliantly organized and conceived. Surely the Fuhrer is in command of all his faculties." The General turned his back on his high ranking visitor. He was visibly shaken, so much so that his entire pallor had become a deathly bone white. The General continued; "I will not speak anymore of such things, what you say—is treason."

Herr Weiner look at the quivering mass before him, whom Weasel knew as the General, and coldly said; "No; what I speak is the sane voice of reason. In the very near future, the wise path involves cooperating with those in power, or those on the threshold of gaining ultimate power."

The General looked up and their eyes locked. Herr Weiner further added; "And there are many more who prefer the saner rationalist, to the moon crazed ideologues. You see General, ideologues may inspire, or should I say incite throngs of sheep, but their vision is limited to the idea. They have no method to implement or create a delivery system. No General, it takes cold headed realists, pragmatists, to make the plans, the ideas, come to life."

A dramatic pause punctuated the air. "The war is not going well; we're losing ground just by the drain of maintaining the death camps. We waste manpower and fuel running the crematoriums. This preoccupation with the Final Solution is counterproductive; slave camps are much more efficient. When they die, you just dump the bodies in mass graves as we had before. There's no need to waste valuable fuel on giant ovens—baking humans."

The General looked worn during this entire revelation. He was like a man without a country. "What do you mean the war is not going well?" Panic continued to ravage his face. "Our troops, weaponry and overall readiness are far superior to any of the Allied forces."

"That is not everything." The stranger was serious. "There are times when military equipment, readiness and brute strength are not enough."

"What?" The General gasped for air. He could barely believe his ears, an officer of the Third Reich admitting imminent defeat. How could this be? What was this Herr Weiner's true agenda? It certainly couldn't be this defeatist rhetoric he was presently forced to hear.

Herr Weiner noted the suspicion growing on the General's face. This was the time, to either make or break the rise of Germany as the sole world power. Would this corrupt, simpering General have the foresight to join the pragmatists, or was he also an insane, moronic ideologue? This was the moment of truth and Herr Weiner had no time to waste. "General, I do not have the patience to argue the merits of the case like a first year law student. You must comprehend the urgency of the situation; without first strike capability, we could lose the war."

Herr Weiner looked up at the General's puffy face; "We are fighting the clock and every second counts. This race is to the death, whoever loses dies. It couldn't be simpler than that." Herr Weiner stared straight into the General's eyes; "We are all in this together. There is no room for squeamishness or indecision. Honestly, I don't see how you can be so naive. Times are changing and those who are left behind; will be left very dead." He watched the General's reaction to this new information. He needed the General's cooperation, (at least in the short run) otherwise he would have to kill him now. There was no room for leaks; the game being played was too dangerous and Herr Weiner was far too implicated.

But then so was the General. That was the confusing part; the General should have been more direct in his reaction. It was difficult to read him and his allegiances. The party had to drop Adolf Hitler like a bad nightmare. Word had leaked out that Hitler was half of out of his mind from syphilis. As it turns out the stories passed from gossip to gossip were true. But only the top echelon levels of government were privy to such information. Herr Weiner sized up the situation rapidly and it did not bode well for the General. He couldn't kill the General right there and then, since he didn't know the location of the uranium—or the decoy packaging. He still needed the General; and he needed him alive and lucid for this vital piece of intelligence. Yet he realized that once this information was harvested, the General would be a messy afterthought, much like a dangling thread hanging from an imperfect garment; it had to be excised, cut off, eliminated.

Not only the General, but the three boys engaged in repairing the decoy time pieces, had to be eliminated as well. A pity though, to waste workers with actual skills, but without intending to be trite—this was war and—war was hell.

He had to plan his next verbal strategy. The room was deadly silent. Walking over to a large cherry wood desk he leafed through some papers resting on the surface blotter. As he accidently pushed over a brandy snifter that had been poised on the desk since his arrival—both men watched the dark red liquid course down the blotter, being duly absorbed to some degree by the paper—studying how a few precious drops escaped the fate shared by the remainder. Both men stood transfixed watching this seemingly useless reaction, unable to turn away.

Herr Weiner waited and watched for a few more minutes. Finally he broke the silence. "General, whether you view my opinions as dangerous, is not the issue, we must…"

"We must do what; turn traitor to the Fuhrer?" All the General's senses were heightened by this new awareness. "How do you plan on getting away with this impeachment? Will the Reich suddenly rule by committee? Or is this some sort of test to determine which officers are loyal and which are questionable? Surely Herr Weiner, you must have more specific information which would clarify this most confusing situation. You cannot seriously expect me to conform to the plan you are suggesting without some sort of confirmation from higher levels."

"You're requesting confirmation of what? High treason as you say—or a pragmatic German response to rapidly changing situations?" Herr Weiner and the General's eyes locked once again in that second.

The General broke the temporary silence. "I demand clarification!" His eyes flashed as he challenged this dangerous alien stranger. Herr Weiner was nothing more than a solitary uniform; that had managed to sprout arms and legs like a rotten potato sprouts roots. He was certainly not a party man.

The General paced the small room, tickling the belly of Max's latest patient. Mentally he had to admit that the boy was like a physician who healed diseased timepieces. His finger traced along the edges of this finely detailed Swiss cuckoo. He continued to caress the clock as he challenged Herr Weiner further. "I reiterate, upon what authority do you base this revelation concerning the war?" Looking down he appeared to be speaking to the clock. "Surely you must appreciate my position. I am a loyal Reich officer who will not undermine the cause. I must have some kind of official authorization or code word for this change in plans." The General took a deep breath and said; "If you are ordered as you claim, the code word will be simple to produce."

Herr Weiner was ready for this challenge. The General had taken the bait. There was no code word, but rather an elaborate ritual that involved smoking cigarettes with specially treated wrapping papers. When held to the light, a faint impression could be detected which appeared as a brand name impregnated on the paper. The brand name is A.H. Fuhrer. He was ready to respond, yes time was running out for the General and his three protégés.

Herr Weiner had finished wrapping a cigarette for his personal use, when he presented this contrived signal. "Herr General, have one—I insist. The tobacco is a rather smooth blend and the wrapping papers are my own special order. I apologize that the tobacco is not your usual private imported blend, but we must all make sacrifices during such trying times."

He observed the General's face become totally drained of all color and expression as he handed over the wrapping papers. The General cautiously approached the light and inspected the 'brand' name. It was as it should be, A.H. Fuhrer. This was the highest clearance code for his sector. Only specified individuals knew of this code and the method of transmission, namely the cigarette wrapping papers. But why would this particular emissary have such high clearance, if he is speaking virtual treason against the Fuhrer?

Or was it treason? Could the Fuhrer be testing various individuals in the field? He found himself in a terrifying position, and had to consider all possibilities. What would logic dictate? Earlier that month a communique had been sent concerning the transfer of command structures from centralized control, to more diversified teams based on academic or military education and experience. It did make some obscure sense on one level, and yet, why would the high command make even the most top secret directives appear as a treasonous act?

The wrapping papers could be a counterfeit even under tightly controlled intelligence precautions. The General was deep in thought over this quandary when Herr Weiner interrupted; "Is there a problem with my wrapping papers—are they unsatisfactory?" The grin on his face was all too telling. Both men knew how this interlude had to end. There was no cavalry arriving in the nick of time, sent to save the day. Destinies were already entwined; the drama merely had to play itself out.

"No Herr Weiner, the wrapping papers are quite excellent—though." His voice trailed off as Herr Weiner inquired further—"though what?"

"Well, the insignia imprinted in the paper is rather unusual." His voice betrayed the panic he was failing to fight back. How could this man possess the genuine papers approved by the high command for clandestine operative identification, and yet be speaking of overthrowing the Fuhrer?

Could this insanity be true? Is it possible that the very masterminds of the war, of the Final Solution, were disposing of the Fuhrer and forging a new alliance, in order to save the Reich? The General felt his heart beat in exact time with every second the ornate, Swiss cuckoo struck. He had heard stories of the Fuhrer's erratic behavior of late. And it was also true that the war was turning against the axis powers. Rumors from respected sources abounded, that defeat at the hands of the Americans in particular, was imminent, unless Germany developed and deployed the atomic bomb first. This was absolutely critical. Perhaps the Fuhrer was going mad. If that was the case should not sensible heads carry on with the burden of state?

Herr Weiner read the General's face and counted the minutes it would take to win him over. It would not be too much longer now. He recognized the General as the quintessential company man, ironically a valued commodity, even in America. Yes in America the General would have been Mr. Upper Middle Management, carrying a briefcase, attending the 'correct' church on Sundays, and belonging to a sufficiently segregated country club. He would have been Mr. Republican Conservative, rabidly voting against Roosevelt's 'New Deal', while discreetly hiring Pinkerton uniformed thugs tasked with breaking up union meetings—all the while disavowing any information concerning worker deaths. Further adding to the hypocrisy of it all; he would have spent his Sundays decrying how society had deteriorated to chaos.

He would have spearheaded creation of legislative programs which strengthened police authority and brought 'law and order' back to society, while bankrolling sympathetic racist groups like the KKK—effectively subsidizing lynch mobs and necessary police silence.

Family values would have been his political lightning rod, featured prominently in public appearances where he lavishly praised the flag, motherhood and apple pie. Such would be his day job. Night would find Herr General scouring the clubs and cabarets looking for any number of perverted pleasures. Yes, he thought, the General was the ultimate company man, drunk with hypocrisy, and thus the ultimate patsy.

He would weaken. It was only a matter of time. The problem was to speed up the timeline. Herr Weiner did not have the privilege of time. He had to obtain the General's cooperation now, not later. He had less than two days to convince the General to cooperate, or find the uranium himself (the latter was certain to arouse suspicion among any double agents). The alternative was to admit defeat, kill the General and then commit suicide. There was no other way out. He was gambling on the General's overall level of pragmatism and cowardice, hoping that this was a man who knew when to switch loyalties to the more rational group—one with an actual chance of surviving.

His gamble was about to pay off. As Herr Weiner stood contemplating the General's temperament and position in an alternate society; the General himself was considering many possibilities.

The General found it simpler to concentrate if he stared solely at the wrapping papers and nothing else. One thing was for sure; if he stood with the Fuhrer and the Fuhrer proved insane—he would lose everything. If he stood with Herr Weiner & Co.; he would either risk being accused of high treason or be lauded as a good party man, a team player. A flood of thoughts went through his mind, cascading fears, spilling doubts, until he came to the only decision he could. It was like watching a movie of his life play back in a matter of minutes. His decision had been made.

Even if Herr Weiner was a traitor, his plan made sense, and in this realm success was the only criterion. The General realized at this juncture that his life would change forever. There was no tactical retreat; no turning back.

He continued to stare at the wrapping papers as he responded to Herr Weiner's proposal. The General was musing to himself seconds prior, that his fate was sealed by the same benign looking wrapping papers that would be absorbed by the flame of a single lit match.

The General chuckled under his breath and said to his adversary; "The uranium will be ready for your project in a timely fashion." The General took an individual wrapping paper, a pinch of tobacco from his silk lined pouch and meticulously rolled a cigarette for himself. He sucked hungrily on the slim stick releasing curls of smoke which formed small cloud like formations surrounding the top of his head, almost like an angel's halo.

Herr Weiner observed this and thought to himself that this man would soon be sleeping with spirits, but not on the side of the angels. No the General was heading the other direction, that is if you put faith in such spiritual matters.

The General continued; "It can be ready in 12 hours. You understand we had to place it in several different containers just to allay suspicions."

Herr Weiner raised an eyebrow and said; "I am glad to see that you are a sensible man Herr General. Some of 'us' were worried, but I had a feeling that you would come around to the right way of thinking."

The General interrupted Herr Weiner at that exact point in time."Some of us? You mean to say that this movement has a broader base of support than was suggested earlier?"

"Why yes Herr General. The movement as you call it has grown in recent months exponentially."

"Not among the general population?"

"Well no. The brain dead masses still blindly follow the propagandist line. They believe the Fuhrer will deliver them from their own inadequacies."

"But, among command ranks"?

"Exactly the reverse. With expanded news of the war, real news"...

The General interrupted Herr Weiner again. "Real news as opposed to what?" This was the General's move; he had fed Herr Weiner just enough rope and now it was Herr Weiner's turn to finally give some proof of his previous claims. It was his final paranoid move on a real life chessboard, in a game where he was definitely outclassed.

"As opposed to skillful propaganda continually painting a picture engineered to softly lull the populace into a false sense of security. They actually believe that we're winning the war."

"That is the second time you have stated the opinion that we're losing the war. How many sources have reported such reversals? Surely this assessment cannot be based solely on a few claims?" The General knew what he had to do, but he needed more specifics. After all, this stranger, this potential arbiter of change, had single-handedly convinced him to follow this dangerous path. He needed some additional background, if for no other reason than to quell his nerves.

The General had been won over, but was still amazed at how this man gained such power over him merely by feeding some targeted knowledge of certain key details, while withholding the remaining information. So the General pushed onward; "What propaganda lies are you specifically citing?" The General took another puff off the cigarette, easily inhaling and expelling the passive but ever present smoke.

Herr Weiner responded; "Leni Riefenstahl's works for one—have been a major influence on the average Reich citizen."

"In what way?" The General was absorbing the cigarette's life at a more rapid, frantic pace.

Herr Weiner continued; "Frau Riefenstahl has done, what the party alone could not. She sanitized the Nazi movement. Party membership has become as common and respectable as living behind a white picket fence, or scrubbing the sidewalk. No one person has to face any sense of responsibility for 'political' excesses. They were just doing their jobs, while being good, loyal, Reich citizens. Declaring oneself to be a good Reich citizen, a good Nazi, became a rite of passage."

"And this propagated lies about the war?" The General's interruption was unexpected, but welcome.

"Certainly. This made the success of the Fuhrer's Big Lie theory possible, by making this entire lifestyle appear normal. It was normal to retake what we had lost at Versailles. It was normal to have a curfew placed on the Reich's citizens, just as a curfew had been placed on the Jews prior. The party was acting on the people's behalf, for their own good."

Herr Weiner went on; "Initially in the early stages; the official party line was to sanction any and all violent acts against non-Aryans. This became a problem with a few church lady busybody types, apparently the reality being directed in plain view—was distasteful." Herr Weiner took another drag off the remainder of his cigarette, crushed the butt into an ashtray and went on with his explanation.

"You see, these good German citizens sought to divorce themselves from any sense of responsibility. They wanted us to murder Jews, homosexuals, cripples and the like; steal their property and discredit their accomplishments. They wanted to erase the history of any mud races. Now personally, I don't have any problem with these actions except—when the mass exterminations place a drain on our armed forces. Then it becomes a problem. However, the political forces at large led a feeding frenzy which used all these minority groups as scapegoats, while simultaneously demanding a pristine sanitary explanation."

"You see, we weren't really murdering Jews; we were placing them in protective custody. Unexplained disappearances were the by-product of hysterical women of low intelligence. We didn't steal their property, we appropriated taxes from those very same Jews we were protecting, and making them pay for the cost of that protection. Yes, in spite of the drain these Jews placed on our mighty and virtuous German nation; we summoned enough decency to protect these greedy leeches. What a virtuous considerate people we are!" Cynicism spilled from each word like cascading maple syrup drowning a stack of dead, burnt flapjacks.

Herr Weiner selected another wrapping paper and prepared two more cigarettes, one for himself, and one for the General. He wrapped the cigarettes with lightning speed and offered one to the General. "You see, Frau Riefenstahl provided the politically correct whitewash. She concentrated on the positive aspects of Aryan life, the traditional family and the good, clean, orderly way of things. In Frau Riefenstahl's world, there are no gas chambers, no crematoriums, no children raped and no disgrace. There is only the clean, pure sanctity of the good Aryan people, all neat, tidy, and swept under the rug. Everyone is just doing their job. The public is saved the 'discomfort' of viewing the ugliness, on the other side of the ghetto wall. Later the same public is spared the messy details of the 'detention' camps. These 'good Aryans' actually deceived themselves into believing that Auschwitz, Bergen-Belson, and the others—are mere 'detention' camps, complete with calisthenics, decent food and honest work."

Herr Weiner took another long, hungry drag off his cigarette as he continued his cynical commentary. "For those in our midst with a delicate stomach Frau Riefenstahl provided a more palatable alternate reality. In short, the propagandist tells lies in order to sanitize atrocities. The propaganda stories are to the beholder as pure and clean as the driven snow. John and Jane Aryan can go to bed every night with an artificially cleansed conscience. Subsequently propagandists like Frau Riefenstahl knew their duty, and did their job—namely to popularize the war and sanctify the Final Solution."

The General had been listening intently, watching Herr Weiner's face as he described the events. The General then asked the obvious; "So the war was popularized by Frau Riefenstahl's movies—what bearing does this have on the accuracy of any news we receive on the war?"

"When news is sent via official channels, it is heavily censored. Put bluntly, it is not news. Since there is no free independent press; most people have no way to find out what is happening to their loved ones on the front, or to the troops working in what is euphemistically called—the labor camps. The public has no way to objectively verify any claims made by our propagandists. Frau Riefenstahl produces films which are nothing more than intellectual pablum and we know it. We serve it up like my Tante Clara serves strudel—unhealthy, but sweet and warm. As a result of this shallow presentation, and the collective denial of the general population; no one seems dissatisfied."

The General reasserted his previous claim; "How does that affect the news we receive as officers of the Third Reich? Surely you're not saying that the intelligence reports we have received are nothing but more propaganda?"

Herr Weiner closed his eyes on that response, as if doing so would make the blow softer.

The General continued his ill-fated dialogue. "But, that is insane! What you say is little more than suicide."

"You sound shocked, Herr General. I honestly can't understand why. Are you now only first discovering that real news—is not a luxury which we receive?"

"What is the point of unreliable news? How can our troops succeed?"

"Don't you understand? They are not to succeed. Certain troops are pre-ordained cannon fodder—nothing more than a decoy meant to draw enemy fire away from their real target."

"The real target? What are you saying?" The thought produced such terror that the General felt his heart jump into his throat. So, this was the moment he would become expendable. He knew this time would come if the war started to go sour. Nothing could prepare him for the answer he received. Herr Weiner delivered the response in slow, calm, deliberate tones. The General, shocked and confused, nevertheless agreed to the terms.

VII

RAINING URANIUM

THE URANIUM HAD been stored in small secret compartments of the various antique clocks, (particularly the larger pieces), that Max and his brothers had repaired. The secret compartments had a protective casing made of lead, but the timepieces still required multiple repairs within a few weeks. Max had wondered about the constant recalibrating of the larger timepieces.

The General had earlier threatened the boys with sudden death, if a watch was so much as two seconds off; yet on these larger pieces weekly repairs were not only forgiven, they were eagerly anticipated. It worried his older brother John who was convinced they were unwittingly part of a secret experiment. John came to this conclusion after he noticed a peculiar effect on his one, (and only), possession. John had smuggled two old photographs, one of his family, and the other of his girlfriend from home. He had been hiding these photos in a variety of makeshift places. Over the past several weeks the photos reversed to a film negative. "Maxie, I'm telling you, something in these timepieces is radioactive."

Ignoring John, Max kept working. John would get more reaction from a stone wall. Finally Henry couldn't stand the monologue any longer, so he interrupted John. "How do you know about radioactivity?" As the youngest brother, Henry's opinion was given as much credibility as the full worth of a dirty diaper.

"Shut up!"

"Why should I? It seems to me that we're all in this together." Henry couldn't recall the last time he stood up to his older brother. It felt good, like smashing a cream pie in a bully's face, laughing at him, and actually getting away with it.

"You don't think it's even possible that this stuff is radioactive and very dangerous?" John glared at Henry with cold black eyes.

"I don't think the subject is important one way or another. Here you are worried about a health risk, when our whole lives are a constant health risk. Does it matter whether we're killed off by the guards, the crematorium, or radioactivity?"

"Look Henry, I know something will kill all of us, unless we are unbelievably lucky, and we all know how that story plays, but it's important to know what kind of materials the Nazis are using, so we can find a way to sabotage them."

"So which one of us gets to play 'hero', John?" Henry practically sang John's name. It was one of the very few times Henry had ever shown any temper. John stared at Henry in total disbelief, while Max bit his lip to force back the 'shmegatz' or 'smart ass' grin that was growing on his face. Here was Henry, the baby of the family, (a bit spoiled and sheltered by mama), the ultimate pragmatist, trying to pick a fight with his oldest brother—just for the hell of it.

And all this was taking place while they were arguing about what John thought could be hidden radioactive materials—possibly uranium—being smuggled in through these antique clocks. At that moment, Max realized that they may possibly have near access to the raw materials needed for a prototype nuclear bomb—the ultimate doomsday weapon. Max considered this absurdity and began laughing. John and Henry started to swing at each other, when both stopped as if frozen in midair and stared at Max. They suspended their punches, but not their disbelief.

The laughter was cynical, crass and raw, like an overripe melon rotting in the last hours of the summer sun. The laughter soon became nearly riotous as Max lost himself in the insanity, the absurdity of the moment. Max felt this laughter emerge from the very depths of his soul, from every ounce of the hatred and anger directed at his evil, petty oppressors. It was venom rich and creamy as mother's milk.

John and Henry looked at each other and reexamined each one's respective fists. Somehow Max had drained the passion from their brawl and reduced it to an infinitesimal wart. Their stares were sustained and drew Max's attention.

It was at that moment that Henry and John truly felt the ludicrous horror of the times. The criminal insanity of an entire era had rooted itself in this one absurd laugh. This went on for an undetermined period of time. Max received sustenance from this laughter, and then stopped as suddenly as he began, looked at his brothers, and proclaimed; "Pick your poison gentlemen. We'll all die soon anyway. Shit, we may as well go for broke and blow up the whole damn compound. Should be interesting."

The brothers stood there and watched this diatribe. Max continued; "Who knows, maybe we'll blow up Germany, and Poland. Wouldn't that be entertaining! Then we can nuke Russia, just for fun—and this time we'll kill all the Pogroms!"

Each brother at that moment became lost in the temptation of that scenario. Then, as suddenly as it stopped; the laughter resumed, contagious as the plague. All three boys were laughing and pointing fingers at these timepieces. Once again, the laughter stopped as furiously as it had begun. They all knew—the laughter had died in that split second. None of the brothers knew how, or where to respond. The Golem was within their reach—if they can find the smuggled nuclear materials in time. Max realized time was the enemy.

THE GENERAL AND Herr Weiner unlocked the door and walked in the room. The boys stood three in a row, mimicking the line facing a firing squad. They knew. Judgment day had come. Herr Weiner totally ignored the boys, seemingly walking through them with the General in tow, progressing to the present work. It was a handsome mantel clock with ornate gold and porcelain paintings of edelweiss or evergreen trees, set in the Alps.

The General and Herr Weiner spoke in low clustered tones for a few minutes, nodded in black agreement and exited the room without another word. Max, John and Henry burned with curiosity. Each brother glared at the others, desperately trying to read faces for some meaning, some clue as to their precarious future. No such information was forthcoming. Again, silence was the password of the day. Only waiting remained.

Nobody slept much that night. The General felt like the recipient of a dozen chain letters who had just run out of postage stamps. He knew this plan was about as foul and vile as the skinless corpses haunting his dreams. The General and Herr Weiner were finishing details on tomorrow's activities while the boys were sent to their room. A few hours had passed when the boys were unceremoniously thrown out of their bunks by the same sergeant who was suspicious of their presence since their arrival.

"Rauss! Herr General has use of you boys."

The boys picked themselves up off the floor and stood waiting. Max was thinking—this was the end. No more last minute reprieves surfacing in his mind, rescuing him and his three brothers. No American cavalry always 'making it on time'. No happy endings here. This was real. Escape was irrelevant and impossible.

To have survived this long—only to be murdered in something less than a split second was beyond anticlimactic. This was scaling the glass mountain and falling off into a chasm, mere inches from the peak. Max truly felt trapped for the very first time, not just physically—but spiritually. He always knew he was in a trap, but that's a completely different story, with potentially different outcomes, (and far more consequential)—than 'feeling' trapped. One situation was a state of mutable physical reality which affected your outlook, if you allowed that to happen. Feeling trapped is the outlook itself, independent of the situation.

Max supposed that Hitler himself felt trapped his entire life, and that his phobic hatred of the Jews only testified to that feeling of being hopelessly trapped. He only hoped that someday Hitler's suspected feelings of being mercilessly surrounded by enemies, trapped like a terrified animal in a cage, would become reality for that paranoid monster. Yes, someday Hitler, and the rest of them should face this kind of terror, and be made to atone for their crimes against humanity.

Max was filled with energy, the type of energy supplied by blind rage. He willfully ignored the pounding on his back. For the past five minutes, the sergeant had been beating Max with his Billy club. What the sergeant failed to understand, was that prior to his stint as 'watchmaker' to the General; beatings were so commonplace that he could barely feel anything. Max looked up at the sergeant as if astounded anyone would bother with him. He knew this was to be their final 'job'. Why worry about total compliance? Who could obtain total compliance or obedience from a dead man? Yet this self-absorbed little bully persevered. He was much like the pimp who beats his whores to death, before attending church—all while sitting in the front row.

Max looked up, glaring daggers at the sergeant, and silently stood by his brothers. All three boys were lined up once again and led to an unmarked truck outside. The General and Herr Weiner left camp in a private staff car minutes before the boys.

The General watched the scenery race past the car window. A patch of woods here, a burned out village there; the picture seen from the window more closely resembled a detached road map—than reality. It seemed like they were perpetually traveling in circles. A gnawing suspicion grew in his belly regarding his mystery colleague. Herr Weiner was far too unmilitary to have ever been commissioned, yet he had the authority to override a General's commands.

The small convoy pulled up to a singular drive and expeditiously expelled the contents like a chimney belches smoke. Herr Weiner motioned for the General to approach. The General silently complied.

The boys were led to a small room in the main house. The lock was sealed from the outside. It was waiting time again.

FINAL URANIUM DEPOSITS were to be delivered to this unnamed destination on Friday of that week. A constant flow of traffic coursed through the small driveway of the makeshift campus. The General was more tight-lipped than usual, barely speaking to anyone; that is except Herr Wiener, and of course the tormentors in his recurrent dreams.

The boys heard the screaming every night. So did Herr Weiner. Talk was circulating in the compound that the General had gone quite mad. That, in and of itself, was considered trivial; many in the high command had previously been asylum residents. Usually their 'lieutenants' provided cover for any difficulties or incompetence. What was unforgiveable was the appearance of cowardice. What kind of a warrior cries like a baby each and every night?

Herr Weiner was apprised daily of each previous evening's discourse and ramblings. He met every other day with certain key informants to discuss possible acts of sedition on the General's part.

One could never be too careful. After all, the uranium smuggling had to be maintained at present levels. It was too close to the target date. Gossip in the ranks was beginning to fly. Herr Weiner had just finished a conversation with some unknown courier, and was preparing to implement instructions, when the General walked in through the doorway. He cradled the receiver as he hung up, and motioned for the General to approach. His thoughts were racing. Did the General suspect anything? Would it be necessary to dispose of any witnesses this soon before the project comes is completed? The slip of paper resting between two duplicitous fingers was skillfully spirited away into the darkness of his coat pocket.

The General pretended not to see this covert action. He began the dialogue. "The final shipment is ready. We can now break down this delightful operation and go home." Newfound calm was clearly visible on the General's face. He mopped his brow with a plain cloth.

Herr Weiner replied tersely; "That is not the final shipment."

The gasp released from the General was loud and clear; "How can you say that? We don't dare risk any further engagements; it's becoming too dangerous."

Herr Weiner coldly looked through the General, not at him. He continued; "Is that your final word?"

The General could feel his blood turn to ice as he prepared himself.

"Yes."

The reply hung barely suspended in midair, but slowly lost altitude, like a balloon running low on helium.

Herr Weiner spoke next. "Then permit me to reassert the purpose of our mission. We are under a mandate to deliver the exact amount of uranium required to build a small, but fully functional nuclear bomb. This weapon will bring about the turning point of the war."

"So by my estimates, we should presently have the needed uranium while still maintaining a surplus." The General's voice mercilessly cracked with fear, like exposed frostbitten skin.

Herr Weiner nodded his head to the contrary. "Your estimates are incorrect. It seems that the earlier figures were overly optimistic. We do not have sufficient uranium for the prototype device, much less any surplus. Additionally, the Allies are dangerously close to a completely functional atomic bomb; we have no time to spare." Herr Weiner's intense stare burned holes in the General's psyche.

"How could this happen? The Third Reich seconded by lowly barbarians and mud races? Surely you exaggerate the severity of the situation."

"No General. I am not exaggerating. Such a trait is beyond my limited ability."

"You have limitations, Herr Weiner? Say it's not true!"

Herr Weiner flashed the General a cold, dry look and said; "I actually expected something better from you, than mere sophomoric humor. You disappoint me General."

"I apologize for any disappointment; it's just that I am not accustomed to such admissions."

Herr Weiner interrupted the General's feeble attempts at sarcasm and reasserted his orders. "The shipment must be readied for transport within 24 hours."

"To where?" The General was a man consumed by his fear.

"I will advise you of the necessary logistics on a 'need to know' basis. That is all for now." He turned his back on the General and proceeded to work on some blueprints draping over the edge of his desk, forming a shroud.

"You will advise me of the necessary logistics on a 'need to know' basis! No, that is not sufficient Herr Weiner. You will advise me right now."

"Why should I? You forget too soon where the power lies. I am your superior. You will comply and get with the program. No further explanation is necessary."

"So you have said from the very beginning, yet none of your claims have been proven to date." The General pinched the bridge of his nose between his soft thumb and index finger as if nursing a migraine. "Could it be that your alleged power base is rather limited?"

"You dare to question my mandate or my credentials?!"

"Yes—I dare." The reply was terse and dry like a martini overdosed with vermouth. No shaking or stirring required; the ingredients spoke for themselves. The General continued, "Other than those unusual wrapping papers and some official looking communiques; I have yet to see any true credentials."

"What do you need in the way of credentials?" The inquiry had the tone of a predictable expectation, clear, bored, and possessing a firm tone. The words fairly ringing from Herr Wiener's mouth.

The General was visibly shocked by this consolation. Fighting back the panic the words fell from his mouth. "Some sort of official orders from the High Command."

"You know I can't do that." The General saw the truth register on Herr Weiner's normally disciplined face. "There are security considerations."

"You just asked me what I needed to see for verification and I told you. Why do you ask if you have no intention of fulfilling the request?"

"I will supply you with information within limited parameters. That should suffice your needs, and mine."

"Why do you have such a need? Surely a top official such as you has everything he requires Herr Weiner. I can't imagine you wanting for anything."

"Does it matter whether or not I'm politically omnipotent? Settle for the compromise General. You won't obtain a better deal in this time or place."

"Settle, for what?" He looked Herr Weiner straight in the eye with un-blinking hardness. "And just what am I settling for; half of the truth or half of a lie? Do you even really know, or are you also a mere pawn?"

"Does it matter?" The statement was worn and old, like a concentration camp prisoner being sent to the showers. "We both want the same thing, name-ly to win. To that end, uncomfortable measures must be taken. As military men we accept this premise, it is in the truest sense—a 'fait accompli'."

"Or as the Americans say; the ends justify the means." The air fell flat with that painfully true statement. That was the crux of the issue, at least in the General's eyes.

Herr Weiner grinned; "Perhaps another place, another time..."

The conversation abandoned the level of conjecture, as earnest plans were made for two additional shipments of this invisible killing machine, this uranium.

IN THE FOLLOWING weeks it was literally raining uranium at the compound. There was a flood of work to be done, in a small ration of time. John noted the changes in the daily details of life, or what passed for life in this purgatory. Meals were a bit more generous if not more hurried. The Fuhrer's picture became a reverse negative. Ironically he was depicted as a black man, one of the cursed mud races. Actually with the reverse negative he more resembled a black man with a very bad glandular condition, or so John thought. John let his mind wander further. It's not that he meant any disrespect or disparagement to any black people; truth be known, he never knew any. But, he was sure they must be of a noble bent if the Nazis hated them so. Someday if he ever escaped this prison, he was going to meet people from all over. Yes that would be interesting. And if the rabbi didn't like it, well he can enjoy his 'kinipshin' fit. Yes, it was a good dream, maybe even enough reason to keep fighting for life.

What would the face of fascism look like, if Hitler were a black man or even a Jew? What if all these Aryans woke up tomorrow as either black, homosexual, gypsy, crippled, or worst of all—a Jew? Would these 'Aryans', and their 'white, Christian' supporters, then question the perversion known as, white, Christian privilege—that is, after they became the victims of racism or anti-Semitism themselves? Would they then see the schism between 'rule of law' and 'rule of privilege'? Or another thought, wouldn't it be entertaining if the tables were turned? John thought deeply, could he return the cruelty the Nazis had so generously doled out? Could he sign the death warrants for millions, or even for one? Could he slam the crematorium door shut on something as evil and insane as Adolph Hitler or his Aryan cheerleaders?

John's teenaged psyche then left these more mature, philosophical thoughts and revisited his basic needs, namely revenge and safety. He contemplated these more instinctive needs for approximately five minutes and arrived at his answer, clear as a blue spring sky, and clean as a church lady in her 'Easter best'. Sure he could. With joy and satisfaction would he reap his appetizing revenge. To Hell with Hitler! To Hell with the Nazis! To Hell with Germany! Revenge was a dish best serve cold, on an empty stomach—and with relish.

The sound of fantasy was broken by a taunting voice. "Enjoy your privileges of employment while you can. Not all prisoners are treated to such generous accommodations." The voice was cold and detached from a body or person. The boys weren't sure, but it sounded like the voice was smiling.

IT WAS A new day. Max, John and Henry woke up to the sound of moving furniture. Noises were particularly nerve wracking as the boys had barely slept three hours since completing the last timepiece. It was an unusual sight; furniture being removed at such a frantic pace, it seemed to disappear in the blink of an eye. All of the General's possessions were going; the elegant cherry wood desk, a Tiffany style lamp, paintings which were sure to be the original works, carpeting, in short everything. Henry wondered if they were going to take up the wooden floor beams. His unspoken question was soon answered as soldiers began tearing up individual floorboards from each of the four corners of the room.

Ushering the soldiers out; the General pulled his trophies from the building's bowels and drew them next to his bosom. He appeared to be 'nursing' a series of boxes. Slowly, tenderly, he opened the combination locks to each box and cradled every individual glass enclosed radioactive mass in his hands. John gasped when he saw the uranium; this furnace of stone.

"Did you see that? Did you?!" John's compulsive tugging on Max's arm nearly broke it.

"Yes, I see it. Now that we've established that fact—what do you propose doing? Work a deal?" I suppose we could just march up to the General and negotiate our fair share of the profits! I'm sure he won't mind. He might even see the reasonable nature of our request. Yes, let's do that. John, you can be our negotiator. Of course, you don't have the requisite suit—or uniform. Wait, what am I saying, you do have a uniform—one with a yellow star in prison stripes that is." Max's sarcasm was sharp and bitter much like the herbs Jews have eaten for centuries on Passover. These bitter herbs were said to symbolize the bitterness of slavery in Egypt, before the Exodus led by Moses. Where was their Moses now?

John replied; "You know better. But Max, it's uranium for God's sake! They're making a bomb! We have to stop them!"

"How, John? Maybe, we could storm the tower..."

"We don't have a tower here."

Max continued, "Fine, we'll storm the Bastille and rush the guards. We'll knock them down, take their weapons and seize the uranium. There, we settled that!"

Henry glared at his two older brothers incomprehensibly. "Does it even matter? Does any of this truly matter? We're little more than the walking dead."

The exclamation hit hard like a runner sliding into home plate on the local baseball diamond anywhere, USA. The boys felt the silence entomb them. They wore fear like a blessed and ordained funeral shroud.

The seconds spent themselves like old, worn lovers, near death and too much in denial, to admit that the end was near. Everything and nothing sped through their minds. How would a decision be made? Sadly all three knew. There was no way out. They could only comfort each other as they faced death head on.

Max began; "Look, we may have to make a run for it." He watched his brother's faces and found them curiously cooperative. That's when it was confirmed—this was the end. But that didn't mean giving the damn Nazis the emotional satisfaction of seeing, smelling their fear.

Max continued; "It will probably happen when we deliver the last clock. By then, they'll have enough uranium." Lowering his head, he made a final point, a final choice. "We may not make it, but I think we should steal their uranium and hide it somewhere, long enough so the Americans might make a bomb first. I think we owe that much to our people. I need your help, so it's up to the two of you."

Henry and John looked at each other, walked over to their brother and shared a giant bear-hug. The decision was unanimous. The boys waited and watched the activities for the next week. Movement came within eight days. All signs of life had been removed some time ago. Soldiers were wandering around the compound listlessly, literally twiddling their thumbs.

Enough supplies remained so everybody ate and slept on some sort of bedding. More jobs were completed in those eight days then in the previous month. Max, John and Henry completed their last job, including removing the uranium hidden within the internal mechanism of each timepiece. The boys stole the uranium from the last several jobs they finished, (in addition to the General's treasure trove). They surgically replaced the uranium rods with any cylindrical object they could find; pipe cleaners or wire from hangers. One time, they coated simple twine in melted wax from a nearby candle, so as to make the twine stiffen like a glass rod.

The boys collected a significant number of uranium rods in a short span of time. It was staggering to think of the destructive potential this benign looking metal had. To add further insult to injury; they buried their hidden treasure underneath the General's bed.

Max was able to sneak in during the General's frequent delirium spells and make his dubious 'deposits'. They couldn't take the chance of being caught with this notorious haul, so setting up the General as a treasonous smuggler just added some spice to the crime. Max liked this notion; that of the General 'at the fall.' There was something almost poetic about this unlikely twist of fate.

This gathering was accomplished, once again, in a mere eight days and eight nights. The boys took turns posting sentry, attempting to eavesdrop on the General's conversations, both during his waking hours as well as his restless sleeping hours. Apparently the General was receiving the slender grass like uranium reeds individually on the third of every four shipments; with the exception of the last eight days.

Since the project was nearing completion, the amount of uranium sent through the 'underground railroad' had increased tenfold, so the operation could be shut down quickly. There was to be no trace of evidence left behind. It was to be left clean and sanitary, like the digestive tract of a patient who was swept barren from a high colonic. That was the comparison used in the official orders that Max read in the memorandum. Thank God for these night terrors that afflicted the General, as they afforded Max opportunity and access to such critical intelligence.

Yet, ironically the General was a gift from the angels—the one thing which kept the boys from the gas chambers at least for the time being. What a thought! Max's mind tasted the irony, not like a fine wine, but more of a wine gone bad and become lowly vinegar, unsuitable for even the most rudimentary culinary uses. That's what the Third Reich was—rotted vinegar in the wine cellar of life. Max mused to himself, it's a good thing he's a better watchmaker or spy than philosopher. Max stared out into space, when suddenly, like a page out of a spy novel, a sonic boom hit. The room seemed to tremble with a life of its own. John and Henry scrambled from their cots, rubbing trace remnants of sleep from their haggard eyes, hunting madly for the remaining uranium rods. The time had come. John frantically searched the room, unable to calm his fears; they had grown like clinging vines anchored in his brain, choking off his windpipe. He ran around the room in circles much like a hamster on that tirelessly cruel wheel—going nowhere fast.

He barked at his brother; "Now what do we do Max?! Well, I'm waiting! Don't tell me the greatest watchmaker of all time finds himself without a plan?" John's voice spilled out with anger.

Max shot a halfhearted glance John's direction. He just didn't have time for anger and; there was too much work. Silently he collected the uranium rods from their hiding places. Max mused to himself; much like the Jews in Egypt gleaning straw for bricks. Only these reeds were uranium, and they would never build a pyramid. Yes, Moses had the burning bush; but the Hirsch brothers had uranium. Unknown to Max; uranium also burned while appearing to be unconsumed. The radioactivity generated by the uranium 'burned' human tissue, eventually causing cancer in a matter of decades; while the half-life of the isotope would take millions of years to be completely consumed. The boys were ready to begin their Exodus.

Collecting all the uranium sent Max scurrying for approximately twenty minutes. Once accessed, he placed the slim, weed-like reeds in several odd containers of haste—multiple old hatboxes. Max actually stole a moment and glanced at these hatboxes. They were rather ordinary looking, some spherical, while others were cubical but all assembled in two pieces, one being the receptacle and the other the lid. Such common objects hiding this deadly treasure in plain sight; no one would miss these boxes for a moment. Max wondered where he could hide this unusually gift wrapped arsenal. There was no time to bury it, and he seriously doubted they would be allowed this trivial luggage. He couldn't risk the Nazis reclaiming this threat. Turning to his brothers he asked; "Now, what do I do with this 'sartorial nuclear arsenal,' gentlemen?"

Henry and John glared at Max their eyes becoming saucers of wild creamy fear. They fairly shrieked in unison; "You don't know?!"

Max answered in typical smart ass teen aged fashion; "No, but I'm open to suggestions."

"I'm open to suggestions! I'm open to suggestions! What does that mean?!" John's reed thin face turned purple, like American Welch's grape jelly. Max stood there, refusing to react to John's tantrum, studying his brother's transformed purple jelly face. He remembered once seeing a photograph of some American friends of his mother, eating sandwiches made with this Welch's grape jelly. The Welch's grape jelly jar was prominent in the photograph. And to think, John's face reminded him of a strangely pleasant picture. Life is crazy sometimes, and just when you think things might start to make sense—they don't—things just get crazier.

The memory seemed to last an eternity, for time had dropped dead at that point. He envisioned the photo again, his mind like a movie camera, performing a 'close-up'. So close was the jelly jar; he could practically see the pores of the paper label. Letters were so intensely dissected, recognition of their original form was impossible. It was no longer anything recognizable; it was pure form. His camera eyes zoomed back to a more reasonable level so that the picture made sense.

He read the label once again. It was 'Welch's Pure Grape Jelly'. Max liked the picture. 'Impure' Jews were eating 'pure' grape (Aryan) jelly. Only one other thought came to mind; "Mazeltov".

A second later, the clock running again, Max felt reality slap them in the face with relish. John was shrieking in his ear and Henry was staring incomprehensibly at the latest predicament. Unable to control himself any longer, Max slapped John square in the face. White hot finger marks, like radioactive contrast dye, marked John's cheek. John held his jaw while Max spoke.

"We don't have time for this crap. A decision has to be made now." Max waited for some response from either Henry or John. Nothing. The silence permeated everything.

"Well?" Panic was beginning to register in his voice, red bleeding panic.

Finally, after what seemed an eternity, Henry spoke to the issue. "Why don't we just stick it in our jock straps? John could hide it; he'd have plenty of room."

"You wish baby brother—you wish." John's eyes were gleaming green with submerged anger.

"I know." Henry's grin was practically maniacal, while returning John's stare.

"You have no ideas?!" It was Max again. He continued. "Let me remind you, we don't have any time to spare. We have to make a decision now."

Going on, he reiterated a theme they knew all too well. "What we decide today could have serious consequences for our people. Remember, we're not smuggling comic books; we're stealing uranium scheduled to make an atomic bomb that could kill thousands."

Dropping his head low; then looking heavenward, he stated his final case. "This bomb is the Golem." All three boys stood still, frozen like an ice block waiting for the spring thaw. They knew far too well the reference Max made. The mythical beast recalled from ancient times, named to destroy any and all enemies of Israel. The Golem left nothing in its path. Max's voice was low and older than his 13 years. "It's a gamble. If we take the uranium with us, we risk the Nazis getting hold of it again. If we hide it, they might find it, or we might deceive them just long enough to buy time for the Americans."

"You make the decision." It was John. Henry nodded in agreement. It shocked Max how his brothers trusted him so implicitly.

"What if I'm wrong?" Max was coldly serious.

"Then you're wrong." Henry responded in sober grey tones, evenly modulated, which complemented the silence. He continued; "You've done more than most so called heroes, but then again most heroes never had to live in a death camp either." Henry shook his small head, looked down at the plain floor and added; "Hell, most heroes are adults at least, they don't have to face this when they're 11 years old."

John and Max stood silently while Henry had his say. They knew he was right and much older than his years. Truth be known, if a person looked as old as they felt, Henry would be a shriveled, wrinkled centenarian.

The decision was made. Max was going to hide the uranium in the most benign place he could think of—the closet. All of these old hatboxes, (approximately 12 of them), would be neatly stacked in the General's closet. The logic was simple. Who would think to look for uranium in these old hat boxes? And there's nothing unusual about some hatboxes placed in stacks on a top closet shelf. It's the most natural thing in the world next to putting mothballs in with your woolens. The boys laughed. The joke was simple. The' boy next door' was putting away his things, only this time his things included an entire uranium arsenal. How precious. Just in the nick of time.

Seconds later the door split in two, resting on the plain, splintered, wooden floor. Two guards ushered the General into the quarters, his face ashen with worry and wear. Without looking at the boys, a fully gloved commissioned finger pointed their direction, while jackbooted guards escorted them out of the room and into the General's private car. They had ridden in this hearse of a car several times before, yet this time had a sense of finality more fresh and crisp than ever.

They rode for approximately an hour, before the car came to a sudden halt. All the passengers popped out of the car like overdone, burnt bread, fresh from the toaster. Two guards, the boys, and the General were standing out in the snow, somewhere in the dead icy mountains. All parties involved stood at attention, waiting for the fall. Time once again had become comatose, having no sense of itself in the grand scheme of things. Waiting was the watchword of the era and the boys were expert in this field. At least if they were waiting, they were still alive to speak of such things.

Max felt the sweetness of the bitter cold air maraud his face, gnawing, swiping, clawing, at his consciousness. This was better than the concentration camps if nothing else. The boys stole glances at each other cautiously; they didn't know any other way to relate. Tension was a fact of life, there was no escape. The air was thick with tension; you could practically slice it like American 'Wonder' bread.

Everyone felt it; the General, the guards, Max, Henry and John. Their waiting was soon remedied as the executioner of the day arrived—in the person of Herr Weiner.

"What is the meaning of all this? Have you lost your mind Herr Weiner, or are you merely a criminal? Certainly you have an explanation for this outrage!"

"It is quite simple General; you have outlived your usefulness. It is now time to die, or as the poet said, 'for whom does the bell toll, it tolls for thee.'

"I have outlived my usefulness! What do you mean by that? I am a loyal Reich officer and you would discard me like yesterday's foul smelling rubbish?!" His fear ate at his gut, in the same proportions as his shock. "By what power do you authorize this outrageous travesty?" Voice foul with anger. Smell of death thickly sliced with equally proportioned servings for all.

Herr Weiner knew he had his prey in sight. "I will answer your tiresome inquiry only out of courtesy for your years of service, but the question is rather elementary."

"What do you mean?" Red hot indignant voice. Plague of locusts for Pharaoh. "I have followed orders to the letter."

"Have you General?" Cat toying with mouse not yet dead.

"Is that the issue? You're questioning my loyalty? But, I have been an unquestioning loyal Reich officer; how can anyone doubt my record?"

"Many voices have proclaimed loyalty, while practicing treason."

"I don't understand. The mission has been unbelievably successful..."

Herr Weiner's face flashed white hot rage at this pronouncement. Time for play was over. Without any further words, Herr Weiner motioned for the guards to restrain the General and carry out the sentence.

Max saw the opening. Lunging forward, rocket like, he pushed past the armed guards not by the might of his body, but the force of his free will. Max was a warrior possessed by a mission; Herr Weiner had to be convinced the uranium was buried elsewhere even if it meant the brother's lives.

He began; "I'll not tell them, I'll not!"

Curious about this particular outburst, Herr Weiner motioned to the guards to spare the General, at least for the moment, while he investigates this strange child's soon to be fatal, outburst.

"You'll not tell who—what, boy?!" Voice raised; curiosity killing the cat.

"Nothing sir." Venomous tone seeping through falsely guarded expression.

"Nothing? Nothing? I think not boy! You had better speak and quickly, or I will kill your brothers before I finish off the General."

"Why should I tell you anything if you are determined to kill us anyway? The order of the executions is irrelevant; we will all be just as dead."

Herr Weiner had never witnessed such an impudent and strong willed child. This was not only a challenge, but a curiosity, unfortunately it was the type of challenge he could ill afford at this time. "Boy, I'll kill you and your brothers any time I please." One of the few times Herr Weiner felt a loss of control, sensing the anger which losing control generates. He did not relish this sensation; it made him feel weak, much as a newborn baby's grasp. This had to be a ploy, it was too transparent and yet why would this child risk his worthless life? Then again, the General was their ticket out of the concentration camp, and when he dies—they die. Simple as that. Yet, it might be entertaining to hear the boy out, before he's killed. He'll pretend to grant clemency, anything; then go back on his word. Yes, that's the plan.

"Very well boy, you have a point. Now what do you propose I do about this?"

"I don't know what you mean sir." Sticky veneer of hatred, like filmy bubble gum slime only a child could understand. Max played this to the hilt.

"Fine, if that's the game you're playing, shoot him and his brothers now."

Guns took square aim. "Wait! I'll tell you what I know. Please don't shoot!"

"Well, speak. What is the great mystery? Did you hide a secret weapon somewhere for the General, or are you upset that you missed snack time?" Searing hot uncertainty. Knowing he was being manipulated; puppet on a tight string.

"It's the uranium." Max saw the raw power this one word had on all these grown men. Thrill of the hunt. At that moment Max realized his next move. Herr Weiner and the rest of his entourage had to fully believe that the uranium was gone.

Even with the uranium safely hidden; these Nazi bastards must be convinced it's gone for good. It was payback time for the General. He continued; "The General shipped the uranium to his contacts at the Allied underground forces."

(Foaming mouth—like a rabid dog in the final throes). "That's a lie! He's crazy!" General held tightly, vice like grip pushing him into the car, seating him in the back.

"Continue boy." Herr Weiner genuinely interested.

"We had several contacts through your main office."

"What do you mean? There are traitors in my own office?! I want names!" Desperation dripped from his jowls.

"I never had access to any real names, just code words. Our job, my brothers and I, was to repair the timepieces, extract the uranium reeds, and hand them to the General in some ordinary container so as not to arouse suspicion."

"What happened then?"

"The General took the uranium and hid the glass reeds, container and all, under his bed at night. He liked to know exactly where his 'nest egg' was."

"That's a lie, by a desperate thieving Jew boy! Surely you won't take the word of a Jew over that of a loyal Aryan officer!"

"I'll take whatever word pleases me, too much is at stake! But tell me boy, why should I believe you now?"

"What do I have left to lose?"

"Your life, for one."

"I knew that was already done for; it was just a matter of time."

"Then why confess now? What does it profit you?"

"Revenge." Steely hardness. Cold raw hatred.

"Revenge you say?" This nervy Jew boy had entertainment value.

"Yes, I can't get all you Nazis, but I can retaliate against one."

"The General." Herr Weiner's voice that of the realistic pragmatist.

"Yes." Never had one word said so much for Max. The question in his mind—was Herr Weiner buying this lie? Answer soon to come.

"It appears we have a situation here which was not planned for. Boy, I need some sort of proof for your accusations."

Max was ready for this. During one of the General's midnight terrors, he took John's photograph, (the one that turned into a reverse negative), and placed it in the General's billfold. It was near the end of the war, (not even the Nazis had much opportunity or need for money), and consequently rarely checked their bill folds. Not only that, there was an extra surprise, this picture was of a Jewish family; Max's family (and John's girlfriend), with yellow stars blazing. The solution to his ploy was at hand. Masada in Europe. "The photograph in his billfold is very telling."

"How so boy?"

"It will clarify to you, my need for revenge. This desire for personal revenge is even more manifest that my hatred for you Nazi dogs."

"You're very bold for one who will die soon."

"It is because I will die soon, that I am comfortable being bold. What more do I have to lose?"

"True." Herr Weiner directed the guards to stand the General spread eagled against the car. "Take his billfold."

Flesh crawling with fear. The General protested. "I'll not allow this! This is absurd! I have no photographs, or any need for them."

"Here it is Herr Weiner." Naked hand producing unusual photo.

"That is impossible! I will see to it that you are dealt with severely, Herr Weiner!" General's voice—a mad barking dog, rabid with fear.

"Restrain him. In fact, gag him so I'll not have to listen to such pathetic drivel." A large grease rag formerly used to clean a rifle, was balled up, and in an unceremonious motion—rammed into the General's mouth. The gag nearly suffocated him at that point.

"Is this your family?" Herr Weiner handed the reverse negative to Max, and as he did, the boy nodded his head in agreement. "Why is this picture like a negative?"

"It's from the uranium."

"Hidden under his bed at night?"

"Yes. The uranium turned all the photos into negatives. I don't know why." Big lie. Max knew why, radioactivity, like John said. It burns without consuming itself. Burning bush. Moses. Uranium. "The uranium's strange like that."

"True. That establishes where the uranium was stored, but what is the General to you, that you hate him so much? Surely you know, he's the one who has kept you alive all this time?" Genuine confusion.

"He's more revolting than the rest of you Nazi pigs; he's, he's"...Dramatic pause, more believable story that way.

"He's what?!" Curiosity killed feline.

"He's our father." Dropped the bomb.

Fear choked off every sense the General could perceive. The ball of oil soaked cloth gagging his throat, freezing his voice, grew to Golem size proportions. The situation was out of control. What was going on with this crazy Jew boy? Had he finally lost his little mind? He could feel ponds of sweat flood the inside crevices of his mouth, a tickle teasing his throat, a scream that will never surface.

"Your father, you say? I see. So this revenge is more, personal." The situation was beginning to make some sense. The Jew boy wanted one last hurrah, to skewer the bastard that sired his worthless hide. Why not let the boy have his last wish? "Very well, it seems that your words have granted you a last wish. What do you want?"

To Max, the words were comical—to the point of insanity. What did he want? An absurd question. He wanted to be free from this horror that was his life. He wanted to kill the monsters that murdered his mother and slaughtered his people. He wanted to rip Herr Weiner's face off and feed the flesh to the dogs. God forgive him; but he wanted to throw these demons into their own ovens, their cursed Wagnerian music blasting from the loudspeakers. He really wanted a miracle.

Screaming voices filled his mind as he faced the oncoming winter air. The screaming became louder to the point that it made no sense, just babble, useless babble. Babble. Suffocating him. Cold, biting winter blast.

Herr Weiner continued; "What do you want boy?! Last chance!"

Max came back to his senses, realized what he had to finish.

"I want to whisper something in my—it revolts me to say it—my father's ear. Something he never knew."

Intrigued, Herr Weiner pursued the question. "Will this knowledge increase his suffering?" Salivating dog enjoying moldy bone.

"Definitely, but only if shared seconds before his execution, and not for public consumption. He may shout like a madman. I suggest you alone enjoy the floorshow. The less anyone else knows, the more isolated he will be during his last moments on Earth. And, he is more terrified of isolation, than anything else."

"How did you come by this information?"

"He has night terrors. I'm sure you have heard the gossip around camp."

"Yes, I have." At this moment Herr Weiner realized that a great deal of thought had gone into this last attack. He almost admired the boy for the cold blooded hatred this plan engendered. "Very well, you may have your last request, but before that, I wish to reveal to the General, the reason for his execution." Herr Weiner's revenge for a failed plan during these waning days. With that, Herr Weiner looked the General straight in the eyes, with an unblinking stare. "You are to be sentenced to death, for crimes against the Third Reich."

The General took all this in, silently; the oil soaked rag gagging his throat, rendering him mute. Proud chin, defiant eyes, tear escaping down pockmarked cheek. If only he could understand what had happened, but this time he was the helpless one. Seconds pounded away, wearing years, maybe even decades off his now shortened life. He wondered about this God of the Jews, how such faith could be inspired in the doomed; the hope of the hopeless. Glancing Max's direction he saw newfound defiance in this mere boy.

Herr Weiner went on. "It wouldn't have been so rough on you—had you completed the uranium deliveries; but you made other choices. You will possibly derive some satisfaction knowing that we never found the necessary uranium to complete the bomb prototype. You realize any knowledge of your illustrious career no longer exists. Any evidence of your commission, past education, family background or military accomplishments has been destroyed in Berlin. You are now a 'non person'."

Turned back on General 'non person'. Cold, stiff wind invading the mountains. There was one last torturous insult to add, and then of course, the boy's absurd last request. Facing the General once again; "The high command thought it only fitting that you suffer the same indignity as Colonel Goff."

He watched the General's swelling face, gag tearing into the flesh of his jaw line. The General's eyes, two tired, swollen sockets with small raisin centers, flashed pure horror and disgust. Yes, he had the General living his last moments in his night terror, by bringing that same night terror—to reality. How deliciously ironic! "You see, the high command needs to set an example against any other would be traitors."

Turned back, dramatic pause, clawing ground with black boot, like angry bull about to close in on the kill. "The war is going badly for the Reich. Discipline is breaking down in the ranks as we lose experienced older soldiers, and are forced to use more teenaged boys." Turned again and faced General. "Soldiers are running from the front lines. These Americans in particular, are insane. Just when we are certain they're trapped; they come at us from nowhere. They have no discipline, no sense of military strategy; they are totally unfit for any organized assault, yet they have decimated our forces. We're at a turning point in the war."

Looking out at the growing winter sky, Herr Weiner noted the pink and golden glow as it grew to fill the entire panorama, like a giant ceiling mural. "You are to be executed in a most unusual way; one that was devised to maximize the length of your suffering."

He motioned for a guard, armed with tattoo needle fully inked. "We have arranged for the execution to take place in orderly, sequential steps, with full explanation as it is implemented. Very efficient procedure. I'm sure you can appreciate that aspect."

Tattoo needle prepared, the guard approached, the plot thickened. "First you will have a giant Star of David tattooed on your face." He watched the General's eyes grow red, weary with horror. "Of course your serial number will also be included. After the execution, your nude mummified body will be displayed in museums as a Jewish reprobate." General's eyes closed in blinding pain. "You do realize that the body will have to be preserved for as long as possible. For that purpose, we have prepared a mixture of formaldehyde and some other ingredients which will petrify the remains." Dramatic pause.

"You will notice that there are two needles, one is for the tattooing procedure; the other contains the formaldehyde mixture, or as the funerary professionals referred to as—the forever stuff." Herr Weiner motioned to the guard to begin the tattooing as he spoke.

Two massive gloved hands blocked the remainder of the General's view. Large hands suspended in sky. Puppet clown appendages, digits for hire; no job too dastardly. Just doing their job.

"It may satisfy your intellectual curiosity to know that the formaldehyde will be injected in small increments, allowing for scientific observations regarding the time necessary to complete the entire embalming process. We will be noting how much time is required for certain appendages to die."

The General's eyes registered pure raw animal fear. He knew what was to come, just not the exact moment. All was pending. Pending patent. Pending execution. Pending formaldehyde. Somehow the knowing increased the horror.

"Of course, you will have to be conscious during the procedure, reporting how it feels to be...mummified live."

Death by inches.

"One other thing; remember to circumcise him before the formaldehyde solution is administered."

Blinding pain. Silent scream. Clumsy butchered circumcision, but one last detail for the sake of accountability.

The tattooing was nearly complete. An hour had passed, and an IV solution, (probably stolen from a MASH unit), was wheeled to the General's side. Smelling salts unceremoniously rammed up his nose violently brought him back to consciousness. It was all too real. Watching the IV bag sway in the increasingly violent wind; the General realized his night terrors were prophetically coming to pass.

Another jack booted guard wearing disposable sanitary rubber gloves inserted three different syringes into the IV solution. End of his life visited by sterile gloved hands, measuring increments of death much like an engineer measures the dimensions of a structure. Beads of sweat slid down his forehead, coursing into his eyes, instantly burning on contact. A mirror was placed in front of his face, so he could view the new creation. Describing this picture as ghastly, would have been the understatement of the century.

Presented with the flourish reserved for beauty contestants during the final selections, Herr Weiner displayed the look 'for all ages', as he so dubbed. Exclaiming with hot dripping sarcasm, Herr Weiner added; "Certainly you cannot argue with the craftsmanship that went into this job." Flashing greasy smile. He continued; "You will note that a special touch was added as per your young friend's suggestion, (nod of recognition towards Max); that of the smaller Jewish stars situated at the upper quadrants of your forehead. Apparently when the large full facial star was planned, we had not considered the possible abstraction of this symbol when applied to the contours of your face. For a brief moment we had toyed with the idea of breaking every bone in your face, but your little friend reminded me that if we had followed this plan—you would not be able to give feedback regarding the partial mummification process of this experiment."

Turned back, issued cold order, steely sarcastic voice. "You are truly fortunate to have such a son."

Gloved hands signaled orders like a traffic cop giving directions. "Bring the boy here. I want you to appreciate this irony while you are still able to understand." Sends sideward glance the General's direction, before issuing next order; "Strip the rest of the body. Oh, I'm sorry—I forgot—you're still alive, and here I referred to you as 'the body'. Oh well, just a temporary error." Voice traveled from charmingly amused and lilting, (very much a high tea/country club tone); to a place of cold amusement. Moving furniture, moving Generals, moving bodies—same difference.

"Bring the boy here."

Max wondered what Herr Weiner was up to now. Feeling that his body was in far too close a proximity to the notorious IV drip set to systematically petrify the General; he wondered what the next little surprise might hold in store.

"Hurry, you are moving too slowly." Impatient voice invading the air. The guard finished stripping the General and waited for the next order. "Now dress the little Jew boy in the General's uniform. I find the irony of a Jew bastard child playing dress up in his Nazi father's uniform quite entertaining. Hurry, I want the General to relish this mild amusement."

Wind whipping his flesh, searing both visible and invisible scars; the General tortured himself with the unspoken, gagged question—why? Why was this happening to him? He had followed orders to the bitter end. He was just doing his job. (Unwittingly the ultimate company man/the ultimate company patsy).

Herr Weiner's voice interrupting fragmented thoughts. "You will now see General, or should I say number 131313666, visions of a better, new and improved Reich soldier. Introducing your future mirror image (albeit in a distorted world) the future that you will never live to witness. But then isn't this world we live in, that you are about to depart, a series of distorted images, a circus sideshow if you will?" Cheshire cat grinning.

"You will describe the new sensations in minute detail. We don't wish to miss a single second of information." Dramatic pause. "Consider that you are contributing a valuable resource or wellspring, if you will, of scientific information."

Silence filled the frozen dead air. Herr Weiner continued his taunt; "Don't be shy—we at the Third Reich value your input. You're a valuable team member. Get with the program!"

Still more dead silence. Herr Weiner becoming impatient. "Now General, what is the problem? As the Americans say; cat's got your tongue?" Each word crisply clipped.

Formaldehyde mixture administered. Delivery system located in plain sight of the General; a man viewing the last moments of his life frozen in time, drop by drop. He was becoming a human statue. His thoughts wandered into madness. It's not death, but a long sleep. He would go quietly into the darkness, he had no choice. Just as conformity to orders had frozen the direction of his decisions in life; the formaldehyde would freeze his body in death. Whatsoever ye shall sow, so shall ye reap. Amen.

IV solution beginning to take effect. Legs frozen, dead to world. Still hearing Herr Weiner's, deadpan voice. Only Herr Weiner's voice was growing, becoming more animated, as his body was dying inch by inch.

Herr Weiner seized opportunity. Rubbed salt in soon to be mummified wound. "I forgot you can't talk with the gag locked in your throat. Pity. We will have lost that data." Looked to the wind. "There's a storm rising over the horizon. I do so love rainbows, all the hope and such." Dead sigh. "I suppose that's one rainbow you'll never see, what with the mummification and all."

Another dead sigh stabbing the silence. "Guard, I require a clean cloth; my hands are soiled from inspecting the procedure." Winked at General. "I don't wish to soil my clothes." Washing hands of situation. "By now the mummification process should be advancing rapidly. I imagine you should be feeling the effects upon your lower extremities. You see, we fed the IV drip through the veins in your legs, so you could better appreciate the sensations, as they approach your face and head. I suppose the boy can whisper his little message to you." Satisfied grin. "Make it good little man."

Max faced the General, the vision of a toy soldier, an oversized uniform wearing him, bending over the partially paralyzed frame while he whispered his news.

The General's eyes grew big and Herr Weiner noted this change, could smell the honey sweetness of betrayal—only not so sweet on the receiving end. Motioning to the guard he issued the order; "Remove the gag; I want to hear his last gasps."

Max froze with fear, wondering if the General would be physically able to reveal his secret. The entire plan could be destroyed, and all because he had to rub salt in the wound.

Seconds passed, and then they saw the spectacle. Here was a man, being mummified live, after being informed that every detail of his existence had been destroyed—and he was laughing! A large, uproarious belly laugh came from this unknown message.

Opening his swollen mouth, the General unwittingly issued his own epitaph; "The hatboxes," more laughing, "hat hat hatboxes." More words laughing; "Beware the hats, beware the hats we wear in a lifetime...,hats, ha ha hats."

Rushing to the General's side, Herr Weiner demanded; "What hats? Is this some secret code? Reveal your source—I demand it!" Flushed purple cheeks and pulsing veins in forehead. Panic obviously registered in face.

Frantically shaking the General's now lifeless body, Herr Weiner continued grilling his subject; "What hats? Give me the code! I must have that code!" Minutes passed, or perhaps hours; time had every meaning and no meaning in this godless place. Sensed futility of questioning. Slamming the body on the makeshift slab, he directed the guards to dismantle the IV setup.

The General's body stiffened seconds later, a lopsided, maniacal grin frozen in time. Disappointed, Herr Weiner turned his attention to the next problem at hand, the boys.

No witnesses could be left behind; this was Herr Weiner's way. After reading literally hundreds of official communiques speaking to the issue regarding public recordings of such strategic events, (the Third Reich desired its successes broadly publicized, reaching the largest audience numbers); he still felt this course of action ill advised. There were some things which were better left unsaid. He didn't have any problem disposing of witnesses; he just failed to see the need to advertise such activities. The decision regarding disposal of these miserable juveniles had been rendered. They obviously had to die, but method was still the problem.

Herr Weiner issued the final order. "Cart up the body, and prepare it for shipment to Berlin." Voice raw with conviction. Noting the pink hue in the sky and dropping temperatures, he knew a violent winter storm was merely a matter of an hour or so. Inspiration arrived on the edge of the storm. He barked the order. "Bring the boys here." Finger pointing at a small clearing facing the winter winds.

Evil smile plastered on mealy face. "You will now see how the Reich completes what it begins." Sudden gust of wind blew Herr Weiner's hat to the frozen ground. Stooping to pick it up, he felt the raw iciness surrounding all of them.

Max and his brothers remained silent. Herr Weiner continued his diatribe. "My original orders were to kill you as soon as possible, leaving no trace of this operation. I see no reason to postpone that order." Raw wind striking, beating all the players. "The question remains regarding methodology. You see, we must conserve ammunition at this time, due to the drain you Jews have been on our economy. I see no point wasting a single bullet on your worthless hides."

Cold wind blowing clean, cheery death, welcoming boys to icy sleep. Henry shuddered uncontrollably. Noticing the blue color of the boy's lips, the answer came to Herr Weiner like divine inspiration. "So you don't care for the cold, boy? You are a frail little thing, aren't you?"

Voice of feigning interest. The boys remained silent while the wind screamed like a banshee. Still toying, Herr Weiner made his decision. "It seems as though Mother Nature is helping my cause. Perhaps you are curious as to the method I've chosen for your execution?"

Max responded flatly; "Not particularly."

Amazed, Herr Weiner attempted to bait Max again; "You are not the slightest bit interested in your own demise? I would have thought that by now you would be absolutely frantic."

"Why should we be?"

"Because you are about to be put to death."

"We knew that all along."

"Yes, but knowing and experiencing it directly, are two different things."

"Not if you're a Jew." Max was coldly indifferent to the slap, viewing it as the act of a desperate coward. Besides, his face was far too frozen in the growing wind to feel anything other than the bitter cold. "Striking me won't change what I feel." Pause. "What I know."

"And what is that little man, or should I say...little dead man?"

"I know that you never acquired the materials needed to make your bomb."

Max was relishing this bit of power over an enemy, no matter how short lived. It was definitely worth it. Yes, in these last few moments—'hitting back—made him feel better'. And frankly, he was becoming a teenager now, (he finally had a few whiskers), and disrespect for authority figures was part of the package. Continuing, he added something abysmally irritating; "We might be dead soon, but you will be demoted." Grinning, he offered, "Who knows, maybe you will become an expert at something truly earth shattering—like cleaning latrines, and then write a bestselling book."

That statement hit Herr Weiner, slamming his consciousness like a wild rabbit punch. He couldn't believe the gall of this, this child. What's more, he couldn't believe how this conversation was undermining his confidence and getting to him. This strange child hit a raw nerve, much like tearing off one's own toenails and sticking pins straight into the red, raw flesh. He shuddered. The wind was picking up. Daydream time. He actually entertained for a brief moment, a vision of himself cleaning toilets and scouring the sink, like a worn out house frau. Just as rapidly, he changed the picture, back to the freezing wilderness. "Enough of this nonsense! Guards, line them up—over there." Pointing to a small clearing.

"Strip them." The order was cold and direct. Rough, menacing, robot like hands ripped the tired, worn clothing from each boy, revealing thin, pubescent, prematurely aged bodies. The effects of the surrounding cold took effect instantly, as all three brothers stood there shivering, like electricity was shooting through them, triggering severe convulsions.

Repulsed by the entire idea of showing fear or pain in front of these cowardly monsters; John steadied himself. He didn't want his shivering from the cold to look like he was trembling from fear. He would never give these bastards the satisfaction.

Herr Weiner noticed this change in the older brother's demeanor, seeing him obviously steel himself against the cold. This single act of bold acceptance and courage infuriated him to his core. Even as these little thieves faced imminent death; they dared to display this arrogance towards their clear superiors!

It wouldn't matter, for he would teach this Jew parasite about respect, before he died. Turning his back away from the boys, Herr Weiner toyed with the 'mouse' one last time. "So the cold does not appear to trouble you—eh boy? It soon will as you three freeze to death. Oh, and don't even think of trying to run off, for as you see, the guards are in possession of some very potent land mines, which are being planted all around you."

"Guards, turn them around so they can't see where the mines are being placed." Smug grin followed by the additional comment. "Shoot all three, if even one attempts to glance your way."

"Oh, and when you're done—turn them, no—twirl them round in circles until they are so dizzy they can hardly stand." A childhood game or favorite pastime—now an instrument of torture.

Grinning wider; "We wouldn't want you to think that this is shoddy workmanship."

Still no satisfaction from the oldest boy. Next tactic. "So, are you enjoying the crisp weather?! What, still not enough, eh, Jew kike!"

Max and Henry both shot strong looks towards John, taking in his spectacle, for here was their older brother standing stolid and still, in spite of growing, mind numbing cold.

John gave his brothers a pleading look in response. Understanding their older brother's last act of defiance; they too 'froze' their bodies into a still growing aggressive form of physical submission. In essence, though their bodies submitted; their minds and souls proclaimed open defiance. "Though you may torture my body, you will never conquer my free soul." Hebrew proverb.

Infuriated further, Herr Weiner turned his back and marched away from the spectacle forming before him. Turning back again, he issued the command; "Empty your canteens into those buckets."

"All of them Herr Weiner?" Questioning voice from a lowly, confused Sergeant.

"Yes, all of them!" Dramatic pause, then menacing query; "Are you in the habit of questioning your superiors?"

"No, Herr Weiner! I only meant that..." Voice shrinking to miniature empty shell.

"I expect my orders to be carried out, immediately and without question." Studying the boy's frozen and defiant stance, he offered a menu of the forthcoming activities. "I hope you three are cozy and comfortable." Three buckets are produced, and the Sergeant begins to empty the canteens into the containers. When the job was completed, Herr Weiner had the Sergeant stand down.

"Apparently the cold does not seem to affect you boys too terribly."

"No not too terribly." John's voice trembled with the increasing cold temperatures, as he returned an angry glare.

Well, we must remedy this situation. We wouldn't want you boys to miss any part of this experience—at least before you die."

Signaling the guard, he issued the command; "Douse them."

As the water hit each boy, the effects of the growing cold multiplied to a painful level no human being could understand, unless of course, there were in the same situation, same conditions. (Walk a mile in my shoes).

Watching them for a period of exactly five minutes, (checking his Swiss watch which was exact to the second), he had their bodies pointed directly in the path of the unforgiveable North wind.

Noting any visible changes. Hoping to see something, anything, invoke additional terror in these three outrageous little trolls. In rapid fashion, each child was becoming an interesting shade of blue. Every hair on their bodies was standing at attention like hypnotized minions of soldiers, unable to do anything but obey the insanity of the moment.

T H E   S I L E N T   C U L L I N G

Within a period of forty-five minutes, the boys were clearly an opaque blue with no remainder of normal coloring. Each boy faced his brothers with a knowing look, like some sort of secret communion was taking place.

This shared intimacy in the face of death enraged Herr Weiner further. He had them turned outward so that they were prevented from looking at each other.

Watching the boys shaking violently like otherwise inanimate objects, (such as houses or cars in the midst of an earthquake); gave Herr Weiner no delight. These boys were not shaking out of fear or terror, but merely from an automatic physical response to extreme cold. In another few moments, (for the boys had no way to monitor or measure the time remaining allotted them); they performed what had to be assumed, a last ritual of rigid defiance—they chanted the Kaddish, or prayer for the dead. None of the boys could see their brothers, and yet they were together in spirit. The chanting grew from a cracked whisper (on Henry's part), to a somewhat larger voice.

Herr Weiner could feel the veins bulge out from his temples, painful pressure emerging from his head, a parasitic growth, eating away at his mental faculties. Finally, his last shred of sanity died; a cancerous organ destined to painful atrophy. Screaming at the top of his lungs he tried to rid himself of the constant chanting, but the boys paid him no mind.

He continued to shriek the order; "Cease! Cease and desist!" Painful throbbing in each temple kept pounding, much as jungle drums spreading news of the last battle. "I said—stop it! Stop it, I say!"

Running in circles from boy to boy, he resembled a lunatic on the loose. (More resembling a dog chasing his own tail). "I can have you all killed! You'll die the most painful death, along with your entire family and friends!"

With that offering, the boys stopped for a brief moment. John turned from his stationed position, weakly walked up to Herr Weiner, and spit in his face. At that point the stunned Nazi could do nothing but stand and listen, as John calmly and coldly replied; "They already ARE all dead." John then quietly walked back to assume his station.

Herr Weiner, amazed at this last act of defiance, responded; "And of course you assume the position like the cowardly dogs we Germans know you Jews to be."

No response from John.

Continuing the harassment; "Why do you stand there Jew boy? Is it because you know the Germans are a good people and you deserve this type of undignified death?! Or could it be that you're too stupid to run?!"

Still no response. The chanting resumed. Herr Weiner tried to shriek over it, but his own voice was not strong enough. Motioning for the guards to join him in song, this group of grown men, many probably average people under ordinary circumstances, (normally decent to their family and neighbors), joined together and sang, to drown out the last prayer of these three young boys, sentenced to death—for daring to live.

Unsatisfied that the group of grown men had drowned out the voices of three dying boys; they sang a Nazi war song meant to further rub salt in old festering wounds. At that Herr Weiner signaled for the guards to shrilly shout this war song in each boy's ear. Six guards were stationed in this profane situation, bellowing Nazi war songs and beer songs, at the top of their lungs. The boys continued to lovingly chant the Kaddish, refusing to give any recognition to the screaming uniformed banshees.

Totally exasperated and emotionally drained, Herr Weiner gave the signal to stop all action, and come to attention. Dutifully, the guards responded. After all, they were not to blame for this pitiful situation; (or so they thought); they were just doing their jobs. Always the good company man.

The boys, though half frozen after two hours of this activity, were nearly hoarse, yet still chanting, of their own free will.

Herr Weiner stood there, totally shocked by this single stubborn act of defiance; no this single act of pride. Here these boys were stripped of their clothing, their naked bodies at the total mercy of the winter storms, robbed of any heritage, possessions, or future, and they were proud. He just stood and stared. Struck mute, a dumb animal, lost and separated from his pack, he just walked away to lick his wounds. (Wash hands of it).

Relief shook from the boys as the convoy of hate drove off. Each brother looked at the others with a newfound respect. They were facing death together with strength and love.

Max could see the storm clouds forming over the horizon, much resembling giant scoops of mashed potatoes, spilling over the blank vastness of the sky, while Henry's mind made note of the small icicles forming on John's eyelashes and brow. It was becoming harder for John to keep his eyes open, for the water dousing had hit him directly in the face. John was becoming a bit giddy.

Henry recognized John's giddiness as the first mental sign of hypothermia setting in, and reasoned that with the storm coming their way, the end was very near. Motioning to his brothers, John suggested that they huddle in an effort to stay warm. Henry nearly laughed at the idea, but bit his tongue and humored him. They would have found somewhere to hide, but then remembered the land mines planted around them like daisies. They dared not go any farther. They just stood together and waited.

They didn't have very long to wait. It began as an ice storm. Bullets of ice sprayed the landscape. Within minutes, perhaps lifetimes, the boys were buried in a tomb of ice.

SLOW COLD NUMBNESS, this was the order of the day. Sights, no visions of whiteness enveloped the small iceberg. They were ancient scarabs trapped in amber. A curiosity piece. The other side of the looking glass. Fossils for the museum. Figurines trapped inside a glass ball with artificial snow. Frosty the snowman, who will never grow up—or old. Everything was slow, frozen and silent.

Each brother saw parts of their short lives flash before them. John envisioned the girl of his dreams, warm smile lighting up the sky; while Henry saw vast multitudes of great books amidst an enormous library engorged with even more food. Max saw his bicycle, and his father droning on about the intricacies of watchmaking. These visions played over and over, melding the past, present and future, much like mixing ingredients to make a cake. Life, death, whatever…was one long sleep.

VIII

TRAPPED IN AMBER

S PRING ARRIVED THREE months later. Trees were beginning to bud and birds were building nests. It was warm, short sleeve weather. The small iceberg in the middle of nowhere was shrinking after a long hard winter. A small puddle formed under its base. Once cloudy ice became clear and shiny as newly blown glass.

Max saw a butterfly land on the far edge of the iceberg. It fluttered down to a perfect landing. Facing his brothers all suspended in the ice; he saw their frozen naked bodies. Was this heaven or hell? It was too confusing to say. Do the dead think such thoughts?

Then feeling something totally unsettling, his hand began to move ever so slightly, through the iceberg. A slight tremor, but definite movement. Becoming aware of the sleepy cold surrounding him. Never quite believing in heaven or hell, he merely suspended judgment, watching in total awe.

Max saw perfect crystalline formations, much like beveled window panes interlaced in a complex web, turn several colors when the sunshine tickled its glass skin. He then realized that—he was waiting. The clock was ticking. Boredom, fear and anticipation were growing, gnawing at his gut. At that point, John's eyes opened. This terrified Max, not knowing how to take in the new information.

Henry had closed his eyes earlier in this ordeal. They remained closed. Thinking he saw John's hand move closer towards him; Max watched helplessly as one brother attempted to approach the other, all the time trapped in this tomb of ice. Henry's body was still motionless. John and Max stared in total disbelief at each other. Neither boy fully comprehended what was before their eyes. It was impossible. Mirror visions of each other; they waited and hoped.

MAX BROKE THROUGH first. One finger, (a thumb to be specific), found its way to the surface. Warmth, he felt warmth! In about an hour or so, (time had no meaning in this situation, this nightmare); his entire right hand embraced the warmth, the light. It was happening to Henry, too. The top of his head was exposed, and the light danced on his thinning, sandy blond hair. Henry's eyes opened and he became aware of the vision before him, his brother's frozen bodies trapped like prehistoric fossils in amber.

Henry was dazed, reacting like a spectator to a strange dream. Slowly, he tried to move, but the thaw had not progressed to that level. Time was on their side, only the boys didn't know that yet.

All in all, an entire day and night passed before their casket of ice melted away like a strange nightmare. Silently the three boys stood there, staring at each other, unable to believe the sight before them. Not yet convinced of their newfound mortality, each boy stood and stared again at the other two. They stood for hours as living statues, stunned, confused and frightened.

Pain, white blind pain stabbing at John's gut. Henry felt it too, wondering how a dead man could feel pain. It made no sense, but nothing about this war made sense. Max grabbed his bloated stomach, bent over in the same kind of pain and then realized the great secret—he was hungry.

Max knew he had to get his brothers talking and thinking, or they'd all die in spite of this miracle. Not sure how to approach, Max tried humor to get his brothers going. Looking over at his brothers, Max spoke in a hoarse, breathless voice; "I see we're all hungry. What shall we eat first? An entire chicken, or several cakes and pies?" Beginning to laugh from the absurdity, he grabbed his midsection again. "Seems like I'm not quite ready for heavy meals. Guess I'll have to start with oatmeal and toast."

John glared up at Max, shocked at this revelation. "Hungry! Hungry! We're dead! Dead men don't get hungry!"

"Well, obviously John, we're not dead—if we're hungry! And I don't know about you, but I'm really hungry!"

John continued to berate Max, hoarsely shrieking at him; "We are dead!" Max waved off the statement in typical teen fashion. Grabbing his brother's shoulders, John shook him as he breathlessly shrieked; "We are dead! We froze to death in the middle of the mountains! No one can survive that Max!"

Icy look shot towards John; "You don't know that for sure."

"Right, I guess we just dreamed all this, the death camps, the watch-making, morning selections, Mom dying...." Sentence cut off as Max pushed John down on the ground. Max shook violently, not out of cold, but from the intense rage of grief. John revised and added, "Mom is..." Voice cut off, choked from emotion. "Mom is...with the angels." John, Henry and Max all stood silently for an unknown period of time.

Henry interrupted the silence, and added; "We still haven't settled whether were alive or dead. Let's face it—Maxie is hungry and frankly so am I. How do you explain that John?"

Stuttering from the shock of it all, John offered the following; "We're hallucinating, that's all." Feeling the air, trying to establish substance.

"But John, how can we hallucinate if we're dead? You have to be alive to have delusions." Again Henry's voice was mature, wise and always logical—beyond his few years.

John added; "I'm not sure, I just know, we can't be alive after all that. It's impossible."

"John, what if I could supply some proof as to our mortality." Henry was always too smart, always using big words, even now.

"Like what?" John really felt like saying 'Duh'.

"Some sort of evidence, some bodily function." Henry noticed that this line of reasoning just didn't register with John, so he simplified the explanation. "John, dead people don't eat or drink, and don't have to whiz."

"Yeah."

Looking incredulously at his brother, Henry suggested; "Well let's find something to drink, and then try to whiz."

John was still not sold. "We still could be in some spirit state."

Henry tried again. "Look at us."

"Look at what?"

"John, your hair hasn't grown. The haircut you got before we closed shop is still freshly trimmed."

"What does that have to do with anything?" Max was now the one intrigued.

"When a person dies, the only part of them that continues to grow is their hair." Blank looks on his brother's faces. Henry continues exasperated; "After someone dies, their hair and nails keep growing."

Silence for a few more minutes—then the dawning for Max. "And our hair is freshly trimmed, and our nails are short."

Henry nodded, with a look of utter exasperation on his face, as if they finally got it.

"Exactly."

Max added; "In fact, John had short whiskers before the camp shut down, and his whiskers haven't grown at all."

Henry shook his head in agreement; "That's right. By now, John would actually have a beard."

Max poked Henry gently and whispered; "Took him long enough."

John's face began to soften, but he was still unconvinced.

Henry chimed in his final 'two cents'. "All right, now that we've established that Max is hungry, and John is convinced we're all dead, I suggest we do something about these hallucinatory hunger pangs, and find some clothes for our 'deceased' bodies." Shaky voice, with a quality much like a raspy whistling tea kettle. "Besides, if we are still alive, and found stark naked, we're either going to be arrested or at least, die from exposure."

Staring at his two brothers, voice raised; "I'm ready to go NOW." Henry had never been so forceful. Max and John silently took their younger brother arm in arm, and walked away.

"Wait!" It was Max sounding the alarm. "What about the landmines? How will we know which path is safe?"

Henry answered again; "We won't—we'll just go forward." Like angels dancing on the head of a pin; the boys choreographed this dance with death—praying with each step.

THE BOYS WALKED for hours in the mountains, naked as the day they entered this world. After hiking through miles of rugged, rocky terrain, their feet had become mounds of raw, broken flesh, more closely resembling dirty hamburger meat, than human appendages. Henry had become so weak that John and Max had to carry him on their shoulders. Though the path before them seemed endless, it was better to go down fighting than die in the concentration camps. Unable to walk any further all three boys collapsed in the middle of the glen. They remained through the night.

Rain beat down on the small huddle as they woke the next morning. All debates regarding their mortal or possibly ghostly state were suspended until they found some sort of cover or shelter. In spite of their pain and fear, they ran through the glen and down some local hills not really caring what they might find. They kept running and running, feeling drenched, cold and alive—very alive.

Though the run left them winded, (in truth the 'run' wasn't much more than a hobbled limp); the exertion made them feel more alive than dead. The quest for shelter seemed unending. Then at the bottom of a valley, they saw the impossible—an old farmhouse, barn included. It was an unexpected oasis in the middle of this European purgatory. Under cover of heavy rain, they dragged their broken bodies into the barn. Each boy, totally beyond exhaustion, looked at the other two, and began to laugh—hysterically. Fingers pointing like accusatory judges, but thankfully, no judges were anywhere to be found—so they laughed. They laughed themselves to sleep. There was nothing else to do.

Henry woke hours, perhaps days later. (Time was irrelevant here). His eyes scanned the area of the old red barn, taking mental inventory, when he noticed an odd looking old clock. Henry rubbed his eyes. The clock had a pentagram on it, and even more oddly—it was still running! Shaking Max violently, he shrieked in his whisper; "Maxie, get up, get up!" No response.

Desperate to know if this was real or a hallucination, Henry plowed his bony elbow into Max's equally bony abdomen. Max woke in a sputter and a muffled scream, as Henry slapped his hand over his brother's mouth.

Henry continued; "Quiet brother. We don't know where we are, or who might live on the property." Max's body relaxed its stiffened pose while Henry apologized. "Sorry about poking you, but I had to know if you were still alive." He released his hand from Max's face.

Max sarcastically added; "Well now you know!" Exasperated look. Lasted about five seconds followed by an anemic bear hug for his little brother. "Thank God you're alive!" Looking around for John. He's still huddled on the floor of the barn. Nothing's stirring.

"What do we do?" The question firmly established on Max's lips.

Henry responded in a very matter of fact tone; "Why don't we kick him?"

Max looked at Henry, amazed at his gall. It was good—Max liked gall.

"All right, but who should do the honors?" Max considered the lunacy of the situation where two brothers decide which one will kick (or otherwise abuse), the third brother—to see if he's still alive.

Henry volunteered. "I'll do the honors." Almost grinning, he added; "It's the least I can do." Taking square aim, Henry prepared his swing, (for the kick), when Max stopped him in mid-air and sent both of them falling on their— uh—'dignities.'

"What's that for Max?" Voice of red hot anger. Max swore he could see sparks flying from Henry's eyes.

"I'm sorry Henry, but if you kick him with your bare foot—well you might injure yourself and that won't help either of us—if John's dead." Voice lowered on last word spoken.

"So what do you suggest Mr. Genius?"

"I don't know." Max was stuck like a mosquito trapped on flypaper.

Grinning like the Cheshire cat, Henry suggested; "Let's poke, or hit him with a big stick."

Max then shot a quizzical look at Henry; "What if we hurt him?"

No response from Henry.

Again. "Henry, we might hurt him, you know." Wild look at his brother. Empty look from Henry, volleyed back to Max. "Henry?"

"What?!" Henry looked at Max as if no one who survived all this could be that dense.

The argument could have continued for a week, had the boys been in a 'normal' situation, and if John had remained unconscious. But, as luck would have it, John woke to see his brothers (with backs turned), arguing over his assumed demise—and over who gets the 'honors' of kicking, striking him etc., in an effort to establish his ongoing mortality.

Voice from the grave; "Kick him." Heads turned towards familiar voice. "But don't hit him with that stick—you'll damage his manly features."

"What?!" Violent gasps came from both Max and Henry. Standing more still than during their deep freeze. Looking directly at Henry—John gave his youngest brother some advice. "Never turn your back."

Gulping from shame, Henry accepted. "I'll remember that."

Eye to eye, John replied; "See to it. Someday it may very well save your scrawny life."

Watching his two brothers standing there with 'egg on their faces' was definitely fun, but it also made John realize the danger of the moment, and the need for him to take charge.

Seeing a way to break the tension, John pointed out the obvious; "I don't know about you two, but happy as I am to see you guys—I'm seeing way too much of you."

Laughter broke through the silence as the brothers hugged, horse-played with each other, and completed other such brotherly duties. The next activity of choice was to find some clothing. Some thirty yards from the barn was a small, anemic grey farmhouse. The boys decided to go under cover of night. Even if there were no clothes in the house, they could make some crude garments out of torn upholstery from a sofa, or even old draperies. Anything would do at this point in time.

The boys waited in anticipation for a couple of hours. Though they had dreamed of freedom for years since this Nazi nightmare began, the next few hours proved more trying—after all—they were so close. The time had arrived. John planned a course through the yard, much like a relay runner plans to tackle an obstacle course in high school, only this was peppered with possible landmines and Nazi snipers, instead of plastic cones and homemade chalk lines. (Chalk lines for relay races; chalk lines for dead bodies—all dependent on context).

The order was decided; John would go first, followed by Henry and backed up by Max. They were about to make their run when Henry stopped dead in his tracks chiding John; "Wait a second, Mr. Brain surgeon."

"What's the problem?" John offered this as less of a question, and more of a promising threat.

Henry answered in his usual banal tone. "Have you even considered what happens if we get caught?"

John snapped back at this. "I suppose we'll be left stranded on a mountain until we die from exposure, or perhaps merely killed on the spot. But, I'll take those odds against freezing naked in this stinking barn."

Henry was stumped on that one. "Fine, I agree with you on that part, but what if we run out in the cold, only to find the farm house locked tighter than a drum—then what?"

Astonished at baby brother's naivete, John stared at Henry and answered simply. "Then we break some windows—whatever—so we can get inside. Any more stupid questions, or would you like to pause so we can take our tea time?!"

Without any further discussion or arguments; they headed out into the cold night.

Standing in front of the farmhouse door, the boys found themselves arguing once again. (Boys will be boys).

"Go ahead, open it already." John's voice—cold and impatient—boomed into the night, his hot breath heaving on the back of Max's neck.

Flashing back, Max glared at John; "And if you keep talking so loud, we'll all be caught."

"Gotcha." John decided not to rattle his brothers any further.

Max leaned down towards the presumably locked door—only to find it gently give way. The three naked boys walked through the doorway, taking each step as gingerly as they could. They were three condemned men trying to escape the executioner's axe—by walking on eggshells.

The house was pitched black, with the exception of moonlight invading from the open door. All was once again still and silent, that is until Henry's big toe connected with a large wooden leg belonging to an even heavier, overstuffed chair. His howling could have awakened the dead, and probably did. All three brothers spun around in place, desperately searching the darkness for any strangers, any Nazi predators. No one was in sight.

Max couldn't resist jibing his little brother a bit further, even in this life threatening time. "Good going Henry! Could you scream a little louder—I don't think Hitler heard you in Berlin!"

John chimed in; "Too bad we don't have a microphone, his voice really carries well. In another time Henry could have been a radio star."

"Yes, and then he could support his two brothers in a style to which they could very well become accustomed."

"Just think Maxie, while we spend his fortune; all the girls would have been swooning at his feet, of all people!"

"I know what you mean John, but somehow I think we could have survived such a fate. Who knows, maybe we could get his leftovers!"

"Speak for yourself, Maxie, I can do quite well for myself in that department. I definitely don't need baby brother's sloppy seconds."

"The entire issue will be academic if both of you don't shut your mouths!" The corners of Henry's mouth were tightly drawn down. He could feel the veins in his temples pulse with anger. "I really don't understand your fascination with my future sex life, especially considering the fact that I have not been physically endowed with those needs yet. Besides don't you two have more important things to think about?"

"Like what Henry—our future fortunes?! Besides we are fascinated by the thought of your very first wet dream." John had always been Henry's loving tormentor. As he said, everybody had to have a hobby.

"How about finding some clothes and shoes—and let's not forget some winter coats so we don't..." Henry was soon interrupted.

"So we don't freeze to death; is that it Henry? Maybe the Nazis left us some fashionable fur coats."

If it hadn't been so dark in the house, John would have seen Henry's face turn an angry blazing red. Henry continued; "And what if I'm right? Would you rather go without a coat than admit I'm right?"

"Let's get some light on the subject so we can find something to wear and not freeze our privates off." John's perspective had begun to change as he became more aware of the new surroundings and the promise of some warmth.

"Here are some candles and matches." Henry was in the kitchen, thumbing through an odd assortment of drawers, pantry shelves and window ledges.

"How did you find these?" John was genuinely sincere this time.

"By looking." Henry had just struck the match and saw the dumb, blank look on John's face. So there was some pleasure to be found, even in these circumstances.

John feebly returned the volley; "Oh yeah, that makes sense."

The boys spent the remainder of the dark hours scavenging the house for food, clothing, shoes, and any money or identification documents. These items were as necessary as air for breathing.

Max signaled his brothers using a catcall type whistle, that apparently only Henry recognized. John was clueless asking; "What in the devil is that? Are we infested with some kind of animals?"

In an exasperated voice, Henry answered; "No—that's Max's signal to come."

"To what?"

Henry couldn't believe the thickness of his oldest brother. "All's clear. We can approach!" It didn't seem to be sinking in. "It's ok to come out."

Hands on naked hips John relayed back; "Well why didn't you just say so in the first place Mr. Brilliant?!"

"I didn't think it would be necessary to paint you a picture!"

"No Henry, painting me a picture was not necessary, though spoon feeding me might have been entertaining. You know how us oldsters drool and dribble so."

Max interrupted, "Enough of this jibing at each other."

John played the puzzled sibling in this rivalry; "What jibing Maxie? It's just a little harmless horseplay."

Shooting John a harsh look Max responded; "Especially you John. Henry is trying his best and you're"…

Interruption from the peanut gallery in Henry's voice; "…just trying?"

John saw this could escalate further or turn into a good laugh (which they all desperately needed), and chose laughing.

The search for supplies continued on into the dawn.

Morning came. The three bodies huddled in the corner, so intertwined it was difficult to determine where this human knot ended, and where it began. Henry could feel something long, hard and sharp poke him in his all too evident ribs. Panic struck Henry as his imagination raced. Could it be a knife or a Billy club, or even an electric cattle prod? He had seen such electric prods used on the old in the camps. They were regarded as 'useless eaters' by the Nazis. The procedure was simple; a Nazi guard brutally rammed the cattle prod up the ass of someone's eighty year old grandmother, and electrocuted her, in a matter of minutes. The howls of pain lasted only a few seconds, as the victims couldn't gather enough breath to scream. It was execution by sodomized rape.

Readying himself to face his executioner, Henry turned around with the grief and sobriety of a hundred year old man. What he saw would have enraged him earlier, but now provided necessary comic relief. John's bony elbow had been prodding him in the ribs.

"Get off of me!" Henry fairly squealed the command. His voice hadn't totally changed yet, and cracked from time to time, like a little girl.

"What?" Rolling over on his little brother, John looked around in another unsuccessful attempt to locate the complaint.

"Get off of me you stupid Neanderthal!" Still no lucid response from John. This time, with a more urgent intensity, Henry aimed squarely—and bit John in the ass; THAT got his attention.

Jumping straight up a few feet, John reeled around, ready to choke the jackass who so insulted his 'dignity', only to find his baby brother grinning gleefully at this 'juicy' conquest. "What is your problem, you little jerk!" Rubbing his better half, (or as Henry saw things, his brains), John strained to control his temper and remember who the real enemy was. "I know you're hungry Henry, but wouldn't looking through the pantry be a better idea?"

"Don't flatter yourself John, believe me—you're not that tasty."

"You little jerk..I'll..." Verbal sparring partner hijacked away, in a move engineered by Max.

"You'll do nothing, except help find clothes, food and some way to escape to Switzerland." Max was seething with determination.

"Oh yeah, sure—how could I forget?" Banging a far too thin hand on pasty forehead, mocking forgetfulness. (How could anyone forget anything, anywhere near this maelstrom of insanity?) John enjoyed baiting his brothers from time to time. And with times, being what they are—'time was of the essence'. There was no time to waste. A stitch in time saves nine. Scratching his head, he wondered nine what? Nine lives, like some wayward misbegotten cat?

Look incredulously at Max, John kept talking. "I suppose it's my turn to call for the limo. You did that the last time."

Max had just about enough of John's smart ass attitude. "You may think your sarcasm is clever, but we just don't need it."

"My what—my sarcasm! At least I'm not living in Never Never land!" No response from Max, so John kept jibing baby brother. "What am I saying? I forgot, weren't we supposed to have some brilliant plan, something about taking a little jaunt to Switzerland?!" Hands flying in mid rage. "That's right, three little Jew boys are going to waltz into the local mercantile, demand clothes, and let's not forget—some money—and why not borrow the Mayor's car while we're at it?!"

"That's not what I meant." Attempted voice of reason.

"Oh really! Exactly what did you mean?"

"I'm not sure."

"You're not sure—about what—your non-existent plan? Hands on hip bones far too prominent.

"At least I'm working on some sort of plan, instead of acting like a jackass!"

"Well forgive me your highness, or is it hind-ass? We can't all be so perfect! Tell us mere mortals, what is it like 'walking on water'? Do you consult often with his divine grace?" Smirk on face with a mind of its own.

Grabbing John's bony arm, Max faced him down, eye to eye, nose to nose, and schooled his older brother. "Listen you jerk, when you can come up with something better—then share it with us. Until then, I don't need two sets of enemies!"

The silence that followed was definitive. Apology offered and accepted. "Fine, what do you need done?" Tone of resignation.

The boys kept rummaging for food and other necessities. A Saturday Evening Post photographer snapping pictures of the fall harvest in the dust yellow corn fields of Iowa —couldn't have created a vision more human, than these children rummaging through this alien kitchen—for anything to eat. Except in Iowa, the kids would have had Norman Rockwell faces, round and sun burned, glowing with energy the corn exudes. No olive skinned ethnic faces full of torment and dignity, would ever grace the cover of America's little piece of heaven—the Saturday Evening Post. No, only good old fashioned 'family values', 'wholesome entertainment', with no foreign commentary, would be allowed inside the covers of America's makeshift cultural bible. Calendar portraits with bare bottoms presented to the country doctor for childhood inoculations. (Bare bottoms presented to pedophiles—raped by 'pillars' of Nazi society.)

Americans were presented innocent photos of freckle faced boys going skinny dipping at the local water hole, followed by a sweet ride into town to get an occasional ice cream soda, or a phosphate. And the smells, pumpkin pie, fresh from the oven. (Human corpses fresh from the oven.)

Our boys faced starvation and pestilence growing tall in the killing fields, as opposed to chocolate cake destined for the local church's bake sale. Our boys viewed crumbs that a bird would turn away—as a feast. Anything to continue—anything. Any scrap would suffice—a rotted melon rind, or a rodent infested piece of raw potato.

Max found a heel of bread—half green with mold. Leaping on it, all three hungrily devoured this remnant. Even a self-respecting roach or mouse would have turned it down. Resembling piranhas, they decimated the mass unlucky enough to fall before them. This 'feast' lasted for an estimated duration of mere moments; (it was unclear as to the exact amount of time spent on this activity, as none of them had a timepiece handy—or so Max thought.)

In a matter of moments, Max noted a broken clock on the wall—still as death. Beginning the repair job was simple enough as he appropriated some tools from the pantry, and dug in for the duration. (Old habits die hard). None of them were ready for the opportunity ahead.

IX

NUNS AND BAD GIRLS

MARY HAUSEN WAS part of the local color and scenery. Tall, sinewy and every inch the poster child for blond Aryan womanhood; she could have been Eva Braun's daughter. The boys had never seen hair that incredibly blond; it bordered on a luminescent white. And there she stood, in the doorway, like Helen of Troy, studying these three boys—these three very naked boys. Feeling the raw white fear of the moment, all parties froze into flesh and blood statues. Time had frozen as well. Every second counted. The silence broke as Mary spoke in fluent German. The boys were astounded to say the least.

Max didn't know what else to do, so he responded to this blond goddess, using the German he managed to remember from protested lessons that seemed so long ago. He decided to play the 'crazy' card. With the most pitiful, lost expression he could muster, he managed to produce a few tears and ask; "Mother? Are you our mother? Please tell us, we are so lost. The bad men hurt us and left us out to freeze."

He knew their only chance for survival was 'snowing' this woman. She had to be convinced that the boys were slightly insane, 'touched' in the head, as the old timers would say. The question was did she take the bait? John and Henry watched silently as their brother tried to work his magic once again.

Max was totally unprepared for her answer. "Yes children. I am your mother."

The statement hit like a tidal wave. Max, John and Henry felt the nausea which terror brings. Henry always thought terror would feel somehow different than it had in the past, more dramatic or—heroic, but it just nauseated him. Henry wondered if Nazis ever got this nauseated. He hoped so; it would be poetic justice. The thought of his torturers, these would be conquerors, 'worshipping the porcelain god,' constituted his only available entertainment. Now his daydream abruptly halted; Henry was back to reality—and back to Mary.

The boys only heard certain words as she kept guiding them into her lair; a black widow taunting them into her web. They were amazed at how composed this woman was with her lying. She was either a pathological liar—or just plain crazy—meshuggah.

Mary continued her sweet monologue aimed at these boys. "Boys, come hug your mother." Voice of a calm con artist in the midst of her own element. "You poor things! Is that bad man still nearby? Should I call the authorities? The Reich will deal with him severely." All three boys felt their blood freeze once again, just as it had during the ice storms. "What is wrong my children? Why do you look so frightened? You are all as pale as a sheet."

Max had to come up with an answer right there and then—or they were dead. John and Henry were waiting. Nothing happened.

Mary continued; "Perhaps I should send you three to hospital, since you are too much in shock to speak any further." Sarcastic tone. Calling their bluff. (Time to show their cards.)

Henry finally spoke. (Time to lay cards down on the table.) "Obviously you don't believe my brother." Wall of truth slamming in their faces.

"Is he even your brother?" So the boy took the bait, interesting. Waiting for the moment of truth. Calm look, belying the tension of a high-wire artist—working without a net for the first time.

"Yes, all three of us are brothers, but you already suspected as much. And while it is true that we were left to die of exposure in below zero weather by evil cowards; it is not true that you are our mother." Voice of defiant pride, stiff-neck Jew—thank God. "Our mother would be shorter, poorer and kinder. Our mother would also be very dead." Silent pause punctuating the cold. "Our mother IS very dead." There, it was said. Out on the table, nowhere to be denied. No Judas Kiss this time around. This was the end of their story. It was the only way things could be; at least, that was the only solution the boys could understand. Exit world.

Walking back into the room, Mary pulled out a plain splintered wooden crate. Expecting to see a gun, the boys prepared themselves for execution. No elaborate crematorium or pseudo experimentation on their immature bodies, just a plain bullet to the head. This was the plan for their brief adolescence. There would be no awkward boy-girl 'mixers'. They would never experience teen-aged angst over their first broken heart. No wallflowers sitting on the sidelines at the school dance. The only dance they would see was the dance of death.

Opening the crate with care, Mary reached in, aimed squarely at the boys, and cast aside—three pairs of trousers. "Here, put these on. You're probably freezing to death. Besides, all three of you are much too thin—it's truly quite ghastly."

Each boy looked at the other two in total amazement. Were they to be executed fully clothed? No Nazi had ever been that decent. A noisy silence filled the void.

Mary couldn't wait any longer. Reaching for the smallest of the bunch namely Henry, she pulled a shirt over his halfway bald head. Wriggling like a worm on the end of a fish hook, Henry only managed to entangle himself further, shirt collar twisting, noose-like against the skin and bone forming his emaciated neck. Finally released from her grip he screamed; "Go ahead, kill us! Stop toying!" Mouth foaming and wild eyed, he kept screaming; "There's nothing more any of you can do to torture us further! We have nothing left to lose, so be done with it already!"

Aiming an all too tired look at Henry, this blond Aryan creature issued the order; "Finish getting dressed, then sit down in the living room, be quiet, and be respectful!" Look of exasperation. "Do it—and don't give me any mouthing back!"

Too shocked to argue any further, the three boys did as this strange woman commanded. It felt strange to wear clothes again, not to mention the fact that the clothes were warm. John's trousers were too short, and Henry's were falling off his skeletal frame. He held them on, by gripping the waistline with one bony hand. Max's shirt sleeves hung down to his knees and he more resembled an apparition with emaciated phantom limbs hidden in the fabric, than a young boy. They inspected each other while moving to the living room. Seated on the couch, they were a living, breathing caricature of sickly children.

Mary entered the room, gave the boys a heavy fish eye and placed some fruit, cheese and bread on a large plate. She watched the boys hold back their drool, realizing they probably thought the food was poisoned. "Since you boys obviously think the food is tainted, I'll have to prove to you otherwise." Cutting off a slice of apple and breaking a piece of bread, she calmly and silently began to eat.

The boys waited approximately ten seconds and attacked the plate like troops invading their shores. Max spoke between gulps; "So, why are you feeding us? Is this our last supper?"

Mary looked straight at Max and answered; "You speak like you're the walking dead."

Max, returning the gaze, added; "That's because we are."

Isn't that statement a bit strong?" Mary testing the waters.

"For what—the times? Do you mean to tell me that it's normal for children to be hunted, tortured, butchered and finally murdered?" Taking a breath to say more. Max on a roll. "I suppose it doesn't matter, considering we're just Jews." Bitter taste of hatred, bile spilling into his mouth. (Sweet taste of oven fresh apple pie in the Iowa world of Norman Rockwell).

Mary noted his spirit and challenged; "And of course, your chances for survival are instantly improved by insulting me. Aren't you even curious why I haven't turned you in to the authorities yet?"

Max's answer startled Mary down to her soul. It was an indifferent response, cold and battle weary like an ancient warrior, just a simple—"Not particularly."

"What do you mean, not particularly?" The gall of this child nearly took her wind away, yet she couldn't help but admire his courage.

"Look, you're going to do with us what you want." Looking at his brothers for acknowledgement, if not permission to continue. They nodded their approval in perfectly silent, three part harmony. Max added; "It's not like we have a choice in any of this insanity, and frankly, if our curious behavior tortures you in the slightest—then that's all the better."

Mary's next statement landed flat, which told her so much more than a million interrogations. "You hate us, don't you."

All action stopped dead. John and Henry nodded again at Max, as he issued the response for their triad. "What do you think?!"

"I don't know. That's why I'm asking." Unblinking, she repeated her statement. "You hate us. Well don't you?" No response. She was determined to get her answer. Again. "Don't you?!" Still, nothing but noisy silence. Decision to taunt. "What's wrong with you? Are you as cowardly as the Reich has said all along?"

This got a rise out of Henry. He knew by the looks on his brothers' faces, that his rebuff met their full approval. All three were more than ready to die for each other. Regained composure, (the type that acceptance of a final fate gifts the bearer); they became Henry's staff, armor and shield. With quiet dignity, he informed this 'blond' woman; "We have no fear of you or your people. Do with us, what you will—it makes no difference."

"Have you lost your minds, you little halfwits? Do you actually believe that some heavenly reward is waiting for you in the next life?" Mary was dumbfounded. These boys had courage and something more—raw faith.

Henry continued. "No matter what you do to us—we will not knuckle under."

"Why is that? Are your bodies, bullet proof? Or, let me guess, some fairy godmother will land on my roof and rescue you three magpies. Is that the story? Is that the only way you'll accept help? Or will you trust someone else?"

"That depends." John's voice interrupted with teen aged sarcasm. (Motioned to Henry to calm himself).

Mary took the bait. "On what?"

Smiling broadly, John delivered the punch line. It was now or never, and he dearly wanted his say, (like any normal teen aged boy)—before he dies. "On her having an IQ equal to her bra size." Grinning from ear to ear, he added; "You know, about a 38 or so."

And that was how the wise crack landed, flat on Mary's …dignity. She was astounded. After all the horrors these boys had endured—they had enough spirit left to make noises like normal, 'pain in the ass' teenagers. She was about to respond, when John interrupted her promptly. "One other thing."

"Yes?" Mary almost afraid to ask.

"She has to be a bimbo."

"A what?"

"A bimbo—you know—a BAD girl—the kind you NEVER bring home to mother."

"And how would you identify such a girl?" Mary knew she shouldn't ask, but found herself trapped in this obnoxious boy's game. It had to play out.

"By her looks of course! THEY have a certain look, you know."

"Oh, and what would that be?" Mary already regretted asking. Too late. Trap sprung.

"Blond, big tits and easy." He sang the 'easy' part. Smile of victory. Battle cry sounded.

"Now where would we find a girl like that? Why—I know—you! You're that girl! Only one last problem—how much do you charge, you see, we're a little short." Big grin once again. "Of money, that is. We can handle the rest, if you know what I mean." Cheesy grin. "Oh, wait. One more problem—that little execution thing. Oh, well—life's a bitch—but then, you'd know about THAT—wouldn't you?!"

Henry and Max stood there applauding big brother's little tantrum. Henry, who usually had something smart to say, was so flabbergasted that all he could manage was a heartfelt, "Yeah—so there."

Mary knew right then that she had the right boys. Obviously hating the Nazis, risking imminent death and still persisting in these immature barbs and insults. Yes, they would be perfect.

Walking out of the room, packing her belongings, was the one thing none of the boys anticipated, but there she was, placing a few sweaters, a skirt, scarf and a solitary book into an old, worn, leather suitcase. There were no jewels, or expensively cut clothes. Odd for a Nazi operative. Usually they had the best of everything (namely anything they could steal).

Following her into the bedroom the boys found their attention centering on one small item, carefully bedded in an old book. It was a small gold crucifix. (Miniscule piece of jewelry. Miniscule religious symbol). There was no way of knowing for sure if this bimbo was a true Christian, or a religious hypocrite.

(Max remembered stories of a commandant's wife who said the Lord's Prayer, as she sewed the skins of Jews into lampshades. She was known as the Bitch of Buchenwald). Max pondered the odd thoughts that flash through the mind as he—and his brothers, once again, faced imminent death. He figured their time was at an end. (Time was a cruel mistress). Patiently, the boys waited—every moment a blessing and a curse.

Then they saw the final piece of evidence, the one tell-tale sign—the final sacrament, a carefully folded black habit and some worn rosary beads. The boys were stunned to the point that the silence was actually painful.

Mary continued packing her few things. She was wondering how long it would be before at least one of them would take the hint. Apparently none of them were taking the bait, so she finally put on the small veil, collar and crucifix before confronting them. "You may as well know the truth, while you're standing there gawking—I am Sr. Gabriel and I'm part of the underground movement."

The boys were still standing there, staring at this curiosity. She was either a master spy with a brilliant cover story, or she really was a nun. The only problem right then, was which theory they could afford to believe.

Henry broke the silence. "You're a nun." The statement was more of a disgusted and confused exclamation than anything else. (Flat tone, like ruined cake remnants after the oven door slammed shut). (Dead cake remnants left in oven; dead Jews left in oven). Leaning against John and Max, he added; "If that's what all the nuns look like—then I'm joining THEIR religion."

John countered; "How do we know if this isn't some sort of Nazi trick? Why should we trust you?" Serious tone. No jokes in sight.

"I don't know." Mary was solid and straight. "Perhaps you shouldn't trust me. After all, I could always turn the three of you in—for an extra ration of petro, or sugar." Hoping they'd take the bait.

"You're not supposed to say that. You're supposed to talk us into trusting you." John's voice ripe with anxiety. "What kind of Nazi spy are you? Don't you know how to do this right?"

Mary saw Henry's eyes roll back in his head with exasperation. So the little one was the brains. It was an interesting trio; the oldest one had the guts, the middle one was the leader—shrewd and streetwise, and the baby was the intellect. And in spite of their youth, (screaming hormones and all); they could function as a team. They would be very useful to the underground movement.

Adding to their promising talents; they did not resemble the Jewish stereotype pictured in the Nazi propaganda books. These boys looked like little Aryan brats, with dirty blond hair and fine, chiseled features. Of course, they'd have to be fattened up a bit—their level of emaciation would otherwise be a dead giveaway, but that's easily remedied. Yes, Mary thought—they would do nicely. Her smile was not wasted on Max. She was right—he was the strategist, and he knew a decision had to be made rapidly.

Max interrupted the stalemate. "All right, let's say that we believe you. What do you want from us?" Nothing left to lose.

"Follow me." Flat statement. Out on the table.

"Follow you where?" Bait taken. Hook, line and sinker.

THEY SOON FOUND out. They followed Mary to an old barn; that in Max's mind was situated between the middle of nowhere, and the last dead man's mile.

John began the banter. "All right, great esteemed leader; what do we do now?" In fine form that morning. Actually, it was barely morning, when they reached this weary old barn. John continued on with his teen-aged, hormonally driven rant. "What was I thinking?! I know what our mission is—we will march on in, bite the bullet, stare down the enemy, and—milk those cows!" Pretending to listen to a far off sound; "But, quick—I detect…excrement… fetch me the royal hip waders!"

For once Henry agreed with older brother, and chimed in; "I see that we're on the secret mission of the barren cows, otherwise known as Bossy's lament!" Not as good a cut down as big brother, but you had to give the little brainiac credit for trying.

Patiently waiting, Mary endured the adolescent hijinks. Finally she couldn't stand any more nonsense and said; "Are we quite ready yet?"

Max looked at his brothers and decided; "Sounds like a nun to me."

"I don't know if that's a back handed complement, or an insult." Frowning further she added; "And I don't know if I want to find out."

Henry chimed back; "Believe me, you don't.

Looking back at the worn faces of the boys, Mary gave one last bit of advice; "You'd better try to get some rest while you can. We have a long journey ahead and there's no turning back."

"WELL, IT'S TIME." The statement slamming the air; making it suddenly hard to breathe. Mary looked seriously at the sad trio and wondered if they were truly ready. Then again, is anybody in this life, or any life, ever ready for life's perverted twists and turns? Mary thought some more and came up with the answer, (at least from her perspective)—and that was a resounding—no. We're never actually ready for many things, but perhaps that's not even important. After all, the Lord works in mysterious ways, and maybe that's why His works are mysterious. (Kitchen table philosophy). There are things in life that we are kept from knowing. Nodding at the boys; they followed her to a back stable.

Henry, once again was becoming impatient. "Let me guess, this is mission headquarters, the only problem being—you have to walk in between the horse turds."

Mary responded as if she was only half listening; "If you'll just be patient a few more seconds, I'll be able to get us on the next leg of our journey."

"If you'll just be patient, blah, blah, blah," Henry added, showing his bratty side. This was instantly stopped by Max's bony elbow slamming Henry in his ribs. "Hey, what's your problem, big brother? Are your hormones also raging for Sister big titty?" Another elbow slam. "Alright, I'll shut up, for now."

"Thank you baby brother." Looking back at Mary, Max popped the question. "So where do we go from here—to get to the 'next leg' of our journey?"

"So are you ready to trust me?"

"No."

"Then why are you going along?"

Max heaved a long sigh and stated the obvious; "As I see it—we have nowhere else to go."

THERE IT WAS; a dusty, makeshift latch door, that opened outward from the bowels of the hay carpeted floor. It was time.

More like rats, or gophers, than people—they crawled through a space which John thought must have been smaller than a virgin's privates. John knew that he had to calm his thoughts and concentrate, but he just couldn't help himself. All he could think about were the kind of bad girls his mother would have thrown out of the house, (that is if they had a house). He thought about Mary, this whore-goddess—(this nun); oh, that can't be—how could that be?! He decided at that moment. In his mind, Mary was the whore-goddess, (at least until further notice).

Yes, there she was—just begging for it, crying and moaning for him. She began 'working' him. (More crawling in a new tunnel, barely room to move— much less breathe). (Nun—Sr. Gabriel). (Too much information). His fantasy had grown along with his member. Smoke filled his breathing space, teasing, caressing every inch of his experience, of his being. The tunnel no longer constrained; he was in a distant world, one where he was among the privileged class.

There Mary was—half naked, writhing in front of him, proposing a lap dance. He was seated in a smoke filled cabaret, in the heart of Paris. Barely nodding approval; he accepted Mary's warm body swallowing him, straddling his lap, moving in perfect rhythm. (More digging, clawing), groping for his member, (Mary pummeling dirt impasse—clawing at remaining collapsed tunnel). He could smell her raw desire, her feral essence, like newly planted soil.

She was ripe—all he had to do was reach for her, just a few inches; (tunneling stopped, her body squeezing through a small opening, his body squeezing through the same small opening). Definitely not the type of 'entering' he had in mind. Henry and Max followed. No privacy here. The quest continued and John's teen-aged lust was put in long term storage.

THEY TRAVELLED FOR approximately a day and a half, crawling at a pace that would bore a snail. Alternating between anemic tunnels, small forested areas and sad church graveyards, they persevered. Mary shared no information with them during this leg of their journey. She wondered if the boys would bolt, or even try to attack her, but as it was, they kept following. Finally they arrived at an open clearing. Mary then announced; "We'll have to travel silently from this point."

Henry, already taxed beyond his years demanded; "And how much longer will that be?"

With the deadpan expression of an experienced Mississippi poker player, Mary answered; "Approximately two more kilometers, before we reach our final destination."

"And that is?" Henry losing patience more rapidly than his childhood, wanted a straight answer.

"It's not only better that you don't know, it's safer." Mary's only response as she resumed hiking.

"Safer for who?" Henry's voice struck the silence like long scraggly fingernails screeching down an overused chalkboard.

Mary recognized the fear in the boy and responded with her typical calm. Turning from this unlikely exodus, she blandly said; "Safer for my colleagues." Reading even more mistrust in their faces, she added; "Until you prove yourselves to my colleagues, certain precautions must be taken."

Henry spoke up again; "And we shouldn't be wary of your colleagues? Why is that? As I recall, we were the ones being tortured and held captive, while you lived quite comfortably. Why should we ever trust you or your colleagues, as you call them? Just give me one good reason—why." His face was red as a ripe tomato, waiting for the fall.

Mary knew that time was a luxury, that they didn't have. She had one last strategy to get them moving once again. With desperation that she couldn't let show; Mary walked away.

Henry took the bait. As he watched Mary walk out of their lives, her form becoming ever more distant with each second lost—he panicked like the child he really was. "Why don't you answer my question?" More distance as each second slowly died. "You don't have a legitimate answer, do you?" The air filled with a dead silence as she kept hiking.

The boys followed her for another hour, wondering again if this was their last mile. As they neared the underground headquarters, their answer was forthcoming.

"WE HAVE TO stop here for a while." Mary began collecting several items from her pack. Henry watched her with a type of suspended fascination. Why was this woman so unusual? She didn't seem like a Nazi, and yet, how could they trust anyone? Henry continued to study this curious woman as she kept digging for some nondescript yet specific item.

Finally Mary gave the boys instructions. "Turn around."

The boys just stood there, watching, studying their subject.

Again, in a strict voice, she ordered them; "Turn around."

No answer.

Finally in a larger voice, much more authoritarian—she barked out; "NOW."

This time the boys did as they were told, much to their own surprise. They spent each moment waiting in a manner similar to how Ebenezer Scrooge spent his fortune before his epiphany—begrudgedly pinching off each second like it was some sort of scrap material, to be saved for an unknown later use. Their time was spent, and they knew it.

Mary continued her transformation. Within a span of minutes, Mary went from sex goddess for hormonal teens—to Sr. Gabriel. To say that the boys were astounded was the epitome of understatement. It seemed as if time had been precariously suspended like the deadly blade of the 'welcoming' guillotine tentatively swinging in the wind.

Mary, (actually Sr. Gabriel), finished adjusting the final details of her habit and surveyed this motley crew. They didn't look like freedom fighters, but then—neither did David when he faced off against Goliath. Knowing she had to end this awkward silence and get moving; she gave additional instructions to her little band. "Now as you see, I'm either an extremely clever spy, or very simply—a nun. Right now I don't care which theory you happen to believe; we have to finish our journey before the Nazis catch up with us."

Signaling each other, the boys dutifully followed Sr. Gabriel. Surprised by their sudden cooperation, but afraid to look a gift horse in the mouth; Sr. Gabriel led them to the new 'promised land'—of the resistance.

I T WAS AN entire month before the boys met their 'real' boss. Mary was a courier, a clever undercover spy, at least that's what Max thought. Then again, what did a typical undercover spy look like? After all, if they looked like—what most people thought a spy should look like—then wouldn't that defeat the purpose? Realizing the question was unanswerable and irrelevant;—he pushed such thoughts aside, much like piles of unwanted trash. Besides, as Henry pointed out, (like so many times before); this was no time for such unproductive speculation. Max rolled his eyes, (like so many exasperated teens), amazed yet weary of all the games, weary of all the big words his baby brother knew. Imagine what Henry could have become if Jews had been admitted to the same schools as the children of Nazis. Henry, in another life, could have been a brilliant scientist or diplomat—instead of being branded as a treasonous insurgent by the Nazis, merely for the 'crime' of breathing;—and all before he even entered puberty!

As he finished this supposition, Max came to a dark and (unfortunately credible realization)—that anyone—even Henry—could become just as corrupt and cowardly as their tormentors, merely by consenting to collaboration with their silence—simply as someone—'just doing their job.'

X

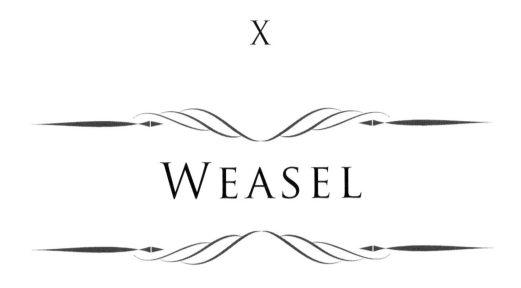

WEASEL

HIS NAME WAS a secret to all but a privileged few. So tight was the security around him that several small myths surrounded this new Moses, elevating him to the level of a mystique, a legend in his own time. In truth, he was no Moses or even a simple resistance fighter, but a double agent looking to hedge his bet. He was the Weasel.

The boys remembered hearing a few stories in the camps, both from inmates like themselves, and from their Nazi jailers. Weasel's escapades had grown beyond the boundaries of the concentration camp walls, directly to the hearts and hopes of the hopeless. Weasel had become a hero—who (unknown to his desperate admirers)—worked for both sides. He had supplied the Sergeant with enough information to send these boys to their deaths—but somehow they survived.

Unknown to the boys—they had become a problem for Weasel. Three boys surviving the camps and a death freeze in the wilderness—all while issuing their own peculiar brand of revenge (best served cold), against a General of the Nazi regime—is the stuff of legend. This was impressive, and yet, Weasel was acutely aware of these dangerous and deadly times. The very fact that these three boys survived this entire litany of dangers, also begs the question—could they be plants—spies in deep cover? Worse yet—(and far more likely)—could they identify him as a double agent?

In better times, an adult could take in a child and grant protection—the decent thing to do, but these weren't even times that try men's souls—they were times that callously raped—the naked, charred remnant—of men's souls.

Weasel had to see if these boys could identify him as a spy. There was no room for error. So, here Weasel sat, waiting to see whether he would be their new, but deceptive ally—or their immediate executioner. Days like this one made him feel much like Solomon of old—rendering a calculated and cold blooded decision—to take this 'baby' and cut it in half. Such a move was viewed as a strategic decision engineered to force the truth. Solomon knew that the genuine parent would relinquish any rights, would self-sacrifice in order to save their child, regardless of any blood connection. It was the ultimate test of loyalty. He had a feeling that these boys could be useful instruments, (though with a very limited shelf life)—in a time when valuable tools were a rare commodity. It was a win-win; if the boys couldn't identify him as a double agent—then he would easily sacrifice them on a suicide mission. Since he never uncovered the real reason for the watchmaking jobs they completed for the General—he lost out on some very lucrative information. Either way, he lost business, so this one-way mission he had in mind would serve his need for revenge.

Proving their worth to the resistance was merely a ruse; they had to prove their worth to Weasel in the short-term, without alerting his Nazi sponsors. Weasel loved increasing his power base—at the expense of all involved. He knew that you had to make deals with the devil—in order to survive—even thrive.

Weasel began; "So you three wish to work for our 'friends'."

Always impatient with any subtleties, John shot back; "Friends? No, we don't wish to work for your friends—or anyone else's friends—we're her to fight for the resistance!" Walking away from this small enclave, John heard Weasel's final words before they became resistance fighters; "So nebish, how far are you willing to go?"

This got John's attention, like discovering your fly was open for the whole world to see. Max and Henry formed a skeletal wall on either side of their brother. Shooting from the hip, (like American cowboy hero John Wayne), John answered; "How far are you willing to go?" Deadly silence, treasonous silence from the other side.

"How far am I willing to go? I am one of the most wanted criminals in the Third Reich!" Walking around in a circle, Weasel stared John straight in the eyes and said; "I can't believe you have the nerve to even say that." He shook his head in a deceptively benign fashion before suddenly slapping John in the face. The slap was so hard resistance fighters at the next campfire heard the blow echo in the wind. "You'd better be ready to prove yourself—or all three of you are dead men."

John stared back, and with the calm of a Mississippi gambler replied; "We have heard these promises before."

Henry then nudged John, and added; "By all accounts, we should have been dead three times over. Either we are very solvent ghosts or led by providence. The question to be asked is why should we trust you, or your dubious organization? You claim to be one of the most wanted criminals in the Reich, yet I don't see any reconnaissance teams assigned to hunt you down. How is that?"

Smiling from ear to ear, Weasel attempted to tease more information out of these three boys. "You'll have to take me at face value."

Finally Max said in a low voice that was more of a controlled growl; "How can you claim to have a monopoly on suffering? You, who are supposed to be some kind of a leader, brag about being a wanted criminal? You've placed horror and cruelty on some kind of a measuring stick, expecting a superior grade like a school boy competing for a spot on the honor roll. We're all wanted criminals, everyone from the oldest grandparents to newborn babies."

Sneering, Weasel said; "What do you know of suffering?"

"We know suffering as intimately as any Jew on the planet." It was Henry speaking this time, while returning an angry stare so intense, that Weasel had to drop his eyes, and walk away.

Weasel was impressed. Turning his back, he issued the cold command. "Send them on the next mission. Mary, you will accompany them."

Nodding, Mary accepted the order, (Sr. Gabriel accepting the habit). "I trust that you will want the usual precautions."

"No." The response was cold and calculated like a firing squad. Weasel was dead serious.

"What?!" Astonishment in her voice, (showing her poker hand). Gathering her composure, (gathering her habit, folding it gently as she left the order); she realized the danger of this test, and accepted her lot. Thinking swiftly, passing thoughts, perhaps the boys were right; her role in this underground was a bit too 'cushy.' It was a long way from the convent, from the shelter of cloistered walls, walls that ignored screams of conscience. In the beginning the walls were a source of comfort. They gave a flush of warmth like an old broken-in quilt from childhood, which protected all from unseen monsters. Monsters in the closet, monsters under the bed, monsters with evil hearts 'possessing' old favorite toys like teddy bear, (monsters 'possessing' old favorite friends, 'possessing' old neighbors, monsters in her own heart). The walls would protect her from all. The walls would protect her from her own heart. So she thought, but that was not to be. Soon the walls became too closed in. They no longer protected, but suffocated. Walls closing in, surrounding, choking off her soul. In due time, she realized that the walls could not protect or insulate her—from her own thoughts, her own conscience. She had to face her own demons. She had to...

"Mary, you are to help them prepare." The voice was Weasel's and the tone was anything but pleased. For the first time since her initiation into the resistance, she noticed how Weasel looked far older than his twenty years.

She wondered why this sudden change in procedure. It was very unorthodox. Raising her voice, she questioned the wisdom of this change in plans. "I do not think it prudent to omit our safety mechanisms. Perhaps we should rethink the..."

She was immediately silenced by Weasel's hand signal, and two machine guns jabbed in her side. Looking around her in a state of shock usually reserved for dire emergencies; Mary spoke again; "I don't understand." Voice cracking with fear and confusion. "What did I do? What reason could you possibly have for this?" Hope lost. No chance of rescue this time.

Weasel walked away for what seemed forever. When he came back his mood was calm, but dead serious. He directed his talk to the entire group.

"We have strangers in our midst. I know that some of you are questioning my sudden change in procedures. I can assure you that there are very compelling reasons for my recent decisions." Looking back at the boys and the blonde whore/goddess/nun, they knew as Sr. Gabriel, he pointed a finger and continued his diatribe. "We are expecting a very important shipment of munitions coming through our outer sector that will be transported over a certain bridge." Dramatic pause intended to heighten the effect. "I need to see if these boys are trustworthy as well as crafty."

"And me? What additional information do you need concerning my involvement in this organization?" Exasperation in her voice, leaking out in sweaty desperation. "Haven't I proven myself by now?!"

"What do you think?"

"What do I think? What kind of question is that?" Few seconds of anger. Remembering guns poking at sides. Not caring any more. "I think you're a pompous little ass! That's what I think!" All voices halted. No one knew what to make of this outburst, even in these crazy times.

Weasel grinned. "Is there a problem with me Mary? What's wrong? Did you forget about your vows?" He knew about Mary's past, and on occasion took advantage of her fears. He knew all too well, that information was power. And certain information that fell into his hands, gave him power over Mary—and it felt good. "I'm sorry, but I can't hear you. What did you say?" Grinning satanically. "Can't find the words to express your emotions now? I'm so disappointed. Don't worry—you will find the right words—soon." Tone of threat in the air. (Spring in the air). Her days were numbered. He found a certain perverse pleasure in that. Issuing next order; "You will accompany these boys through a secret road, where you will encounter a small motor caravan. Once you meet the group, you will receive instructions telling you how to proceed from that point." Forefinger waving dismissal. "That is all you need to know at this juncture."

"That is all we need to know at this juncture?! That and we're dismissed like yesterday's rubbish?" Mary's face was on fire.

No response.

Again, she fired at Weasel. "So, I must somehow get these undisciplined boys through enemy territory once again, meet an unknown motor caravan, and wait for instructions—and all without any support or planning? Have you lost your mind?!"

"No. I expect that you will follow orders, like a professional." Nasty side-long sneer. "That is, if you can handle it."

"You cheap little fraud!" Mary/Sr. Gabriel sputtering fire. "I made you! You were nothing but a street urchin, a small time terrorist about to be captured..." Stopped dead in tracks. Had said too much. Fear of the dead in eyes. (We each have our own demons).

Looking back at the entourage, she gave the order; "We'd better get some sleep now. We have a long, dangerous journey ahead of us."

THE TREK BEGAN late. Weasel had purposely delayed issuing supplies to his little band of brigands. He enjoyed seeing Mary squirm. More importantly though, he knew it made her a more effective operative. She needed to hunger for the victory. Little did she know that even the victory would not suffice the hunger—this time.

They hiked for approximately three days and three nights, before spotting a small group of cars and one antiquated farm wagon. Crouching under some bushes, they waited for some sign of recognition, of safety. They waited for an unknown period of time. No signal was forthcoming. Silence dominated the scene. Finally Mary broke the stalemate. Walking straight into the clearing, where a small, unknown band had stopped a moment to rest, she was an arresting figure. Never had the boys or these unknown travelers seen such bold action. Not quite knowing what to do; the boys froze in place, (much like deer freeze in the path of headlights), (out of sight, out of mind);—as Mary met the unknown party. (We have met the enemy—and it is us).

The new operatives were rather ordinary looking, (four men of various ages; one seeming more 'worn' than the others). He had the look of a person who carries an evil and perverted burden, but one that was of his own doing. Henry was especially fascinated by that one fellow traveler. Something about his face; he had seen this man somewhere before…

Max worried about this meeting. Mary had been talking for some time. Would she double cross them? Only time will tell. He knew that longer negotiations often spelled out unexpected outcomes—good or bad—and he wasn't in the mood for any more surprises.

An hour had passed since Mary disappeared into one of the vehicles. When she reappeared, a nod was given for the boys to join her. Walking like souls who had no other choice, they followed her path into this makeshift 'oasis.'

It turned out that the 'cargo' to be transported was a device—and it's creator. This wasn't any small job at all. The boys were there to serve as decoys, while the cargo made its way to the underground safe house, and finally to Switzerland.

CONRAD ZUSE WAS a Nazi scientist of some renown, who was defecting. He had been the Reich darling in scientific circles for his completed work on a calculating machine which he named the Z4. In theory, the high command had visions of Z4 forming the 'brain' of a smart bomb, which could kill thousands with a single warhead. Subsequently, Zuse was a valuable property.

The war had been going badly for the Axis powers lately. Berlin itself had been bombed. Zuse was ordered to dismantle the Z4, and transport it by wagon to an underground factory in western Germany.

It was rumored that once Zuse arrived at the factory, and saw the concentration camp nearby—the conditions—the evil being done there—he secretly packed up his Z4, and escaped towards the Bavarian Alps. Zuse suspected what the boys couldn't know, that the war in Europe was nearing an end, and Germany was losing. Zuse wanted to make sure that when he was captured, it would be by the English or the Americans. The underground was quickly contacted and Zuse was on his way. Unfortunately, the Nazis discovered the Z4 missing and launched a desperate search. Much like a Chinese finger lock trap; the underground risked all to assist this one time Nazi scientist. Even the most trusted members of the underground did not know of Zuse, and his doomsday device. That's where Weasel came into the picture.

Weasel had a scientific background himself, being a type of 'wunderkind', who had escaped from German society. He knew all too well the significance of the Z4 and the implications for the future balance of power worldwide. His mission was to create enough confusion by providing a false target, so Zuse could escape successfully. The German command couldn't risk issuing a general alert for Zuse, without leaking the information that a computerized bomb was very near completion. Several components of this project were being completed separately, in multiple locations. If any single component were destroyed; the chance of the others surviving intact still remained. This type of scattering to the four winds was part of the genius which epitomized the Reich. Ironically this same genius allowed Zuse the opportunity he needed to escape.

Zuse sat quietly in the wagon, uncomfortably cradled between well-padded boxes of glass tubes. This was the Z4, his creation, his baby, his doomsday device, (that is if the Nazis kept possession), but that was never to be—not after what he saw—what he smelled. The stench of evil abided in the well-kept uniforms of the Reich. Never again could he close his eyes—or his conscience to the evil around him.

For years, Zuse was one of many professionals 'just doing his job,' never wondering how the finished product would affect others. It simply wasn't relevant. He was a scientist; he would leave such moral dilemmas to the philosophers or theologians. Zuse was a microcosm within himself, emotionally an unborn embryo seeking to remain in the dark, silent womb of academia. This was where he was most comfortable, until that day.

It was a day so like any other, that it might have remained totally indistinguishable in his memory—until that unmistakable odor. An odor so strong, it slammed into his pores and choked off his anemic soul. At that point, incidents and people became entwined in a seemingly endless collage of sights, sounds and smells—(those inhuman smells); climaxing to the apex of insanity. In short, it was the day his wagon train arrived at Auschwitz.

Up till that moment, Zuse either believed the Nazi propaganda machine, or at least, convinced himself that it was the truth. Zuse needed to believe the Nazis, for that was the only way his Z4 could be born. Yet, this barrage of foul, ungodly smells, rank with filth, screamed at his orderly sensibilities. All around him there was suffering, torture and death.

To the right of his small convoy were mass graves, containing living corpses. As his wagon passed by this dubious landmark, his eyes locked with one of the many victims, lying in an open grave, a living skeleton that blinked lifeless eyes and whispered 'why?' Barely a whisper, yet spoken with the intensity of millions. He wanted to fly far away from this hell on earth, but the wagon steadily crept through the camp.

This was the beginning for Zuse. His eyes were open for the first time in his cloistered life. All that remained was a plan, and the actual escape. Escape from this hellish place, escape from long delayed guilt, and escape from his own sin of silence. That was the point when he decided to contact the underground. Determined to keep Z4 from the Nazis, he made his move. Hopefully if captured, it would be by the British or the Americans.

The actual details of the escape to Switzerland are unimportant, and frankly, it is doubtful if the world will ever know the entire story. Suffice it to say, that Zuse was well on his way to the 'promised land' of allied forces protection. The plan called for multiple decoys and diversions. So intricate was this plan that Weasel only had privy to small portions of the strategy. No one person had knowledge of the full scope or planned implementation.

Weasel had been contacted about this coup some seven months earlier. He was told that new operatives were required. New faces, unknowns—to serve as decoys. Status of the operation; critical. No other information was provided.

Decoys! How in the hell was he going to find decoys? What was he supposed to do; run up to the first yid who can 'pass' for a goyim, and say; "Excuse me, how would you like to serve as cannon fodder, so we at the underground movement can play hero, and have one more successful operation?!" Somehow the whole thing lost meaning in translation. But, being a 'dedicated operative'(who also saw the Z4 as a valuable asset that he could acquire, copy and sell to the highest bidder), he 'followed' orders, and delegated the responsibility to Mary. She was always better at such tasks; she had a way with people that he so plainly lacked.

Now seeing these three boys, who were so much like him—(a lifetime ago), he wondered where the line between good and evil crossed over, or how such lines of distinction blurred and melded into each other. He knew, nevertheless, that Mary would succeed, ragtag group and all, even though some day—decades from now—all of this will start again, somewhere—anywhere. It was the way of the world. So it was written, so it shall be done. His mind was full of wonderment.

After being fitted with 'proper', civilized clothes, (and some decent grooming), the boys looked very much like little Aryan brats. Dishwater blond hair and hazel eyes, they looked nothing like the grotesque, exaggerated features of the Shakespearian 'Jew' character—Shylock. Ironic, Weasel thought, these boys looked more German than actual Germans. Well, life deals many odd blows. You never know when suddenly, (like a flash of lightning in the summer sky), everything you call reality, changes. Yes, lightning, life—very similar. Thoughts interrupted by a banal, sour toned voice; "We're ready."

It was Mary. Resigned to the task at hand, she was a modern day Joan of Arc. It was a bitter pill to swallow, this suicide mission. She always hoped that the end would come after a prolonged series of heroic struggles—but not like this. Babysitting was to be her legacy. Deep down inside, she knew—it was her time. No one would ever see her again after this assignment.

Weasel handed Mary a small piece of paper, with a few lines of script. He told her to memorize the information and destroy the instructions. The message was simple and to the point. Mary read silently. "There's the name of a bridge on your orders. Even I don't know the destination; it's that important. You are to destroy that bridge, then create a diversion by getting captured."

XI

SUICIDE MISSION

"So what's the suicide mission?" Henry glared at this blond, shiksa goddess. He didn't expect a straight answer, but making her a bit more paranoid than she was, served as a small comfort. At least they would go down fighting.

"There's no suicide mission, merely a routine sabotage job." Lie Mary lie.

"If it's so routine, then why the deviation from your 'normally accepted procedures'?"

"There is no deviation. We're just being flexible. If every job were characterized by a signature style, we'd become very predictable, and very dead." Jesus, having problems explaining a con to an eleven year old. The kid's just too damn brainy. What a waste.

"Oh, so this snafu is a strategic change." Rook takes Queen—check. Henry loved chess.

Stifled breath; "Yes, that's right." Mary's in trouble. Moving King back a space.

Ready to pounce, but like a cat playing with its food before devouring. "That's a relief. For a moment I thought we were merely a diversion to be used, and subsequently sacrificed." Checkmate—game's over.

Mary stood there in absolute shock. How could a child out maneuver an experienced operative?

Seemingly reading her mind, Max interrupted; "Henry was a chess master, self-taught, in fact. He read your actions and your moves, and he figured all of this was a strategy meant to deceive us. He's gifted that way."

"Enough!" Weasel was becoming bored with these little adolescent games. Had to face facts, he blew it. No secret there. Looking straight at Mary, he decided to reveal all, knowing full well that if these boys made one false move, he'd finish the job that the Nazis botched. "You wanted to know why we cancelled our usual security measures," pointing nervous finger at Mary; "and you, (changing aim, finger shot directly at boys), you wanted the truth. Well I'll tell you the truth. At least, as much as I know." Playing with unlit match, trigger finger itchy. "We have to get Zuse and his machine out of Germany and to the Swiss Alps." Still playing with matches. (Children shouldn't play with matches, or so mother always said). "The Nazis have been monitoring all the border exits. Apparently Zuse's machine, his Z4, is one hot property."

"And you can't get it out of Germany without some diversion." Dead silence. Silent as a cemetery. Henry continued. "We're your diversion, correct?"

"Yes." Weasel tired of the endless games of subterfuge. It felt good to tell the truth; but not the entire truth.

Sensing there was more unfinished business, Henry pushed the envelope further. "More precisely, our capture, systematic torture, and subsequent executions are the actual diversion." Stone dead silence. All eyes were riveted on Weasel. (Time was the silent killer). No response. Again Henry prodded; "During the torture phase we are expected to cause enough of a delay for this Zuse—to make his escape. There's no rescue plan for us—we were written off as 'acceptable collateral damage'."

Weasel stood there—stunned by Henry's raw courage. No one in this group ever had the sheer nerve to question his motives. He couldn't move.

Henry stared Weasel straight in the eyes and demanded an answer. "We're the human sacrifice—AREN'T WE? Answer me!" Looking past his brothers and directly at Mary, he finished the equation. "And did you realize that you'd die too, or were you counting on some perverted sort of loyalty from Weasel?"

Mary's eyes grew as big as saucers. Once again, the finality of it all penetrated her mind like a long slow rain. She was going to die, along with these three boys. No one would ever remember her, or any of her good works. She hadn't been known long enough to even be a memory. One morning, everyone else in this indifferent and cold world would wake up, not knowing that she had ever been part of it. No mysterious lover in her future, no fantasy, no leaving the order. This was wrong. Her legacy was supposed to be different. She was going to …to…

"Did you count on dying for the cause?" There it was, gauntlet thrown down, for all to see. She had never really faced this possibility before.

"Enough! I've heard quite enough of your childish tantrum." She knew a losing battle when it faced her.

"Right. Can't stand losing to a 'child', can you Sr. Gabriel."

"Time to leave." Weasel's order was firm and direct.

Before realizing how fast things were moving, a pair of armed guards dressed as farmers escorted the entourage to their sad destinies. They traveled down an old, tired road that seemed to head nowhere fast. In less than three days they were a scant hundred yards from their target. A new envoy of large men in their twenties continued along the path with Zuse and his amazing machine. That was the last the boys ever saw of Zuse. In later years, Max heard stories about him from time to time. Nothing elaborate, just a detail here, a memory there. Conrad Zuse, his entourage and the Z4, disappeared in the cold mist.

"THERE'S THE BRIDGE. It's about fifty yards from this point." Mary could feel her voice tremble as she shared the information. "Our mission will be completed quite soon."

"Tell us when we get our party." Sarcastic tone which Henry had now mastered. Henry continued to grill Mary. "So after the job—then what? You parade us in front of the enemy, or do you do the job yourself?"

"You're crazy." Looking down on the scrawny boy with the giant intellect, Mary raved; "Don't you think I want to survive this as well?" Up in the boy's face, squeezing his shoulders so tightly it bruised; "Do you honestly believe I enjoy any of this?" Realizing that she's hurting the boy, Mary backs away. "None of us have any other alternative. Like it or not, when you joined the underground—you accepted certain debts—and risks. There's no backing out now. It's too late to change your mind—or your side."

"We know that Mary." Max was now standing directly next to Henry. He motioned to John, and soon the three were standing there like conjoined triplets. "Henry just wanted to be a teenager, even for a short while—that is, before he died. Do you blame him?"

Startled by the obscene naked force of this statement, Mary looked at these pathetic boys, cradled her own face in her hands, and cried. This wasn't the way things were supposed to be. She was one of the heroes. Heroes were supposed to win, and the villains punished. But that wasn't the real world. In this reality, the villains would probably win. The deck was stacked in their favor from the very start. No Moses to rescue them, because, very simply, there was no promised land. It didn't matter anyway. If there was one thing she learned during all this—was that—life was cheap. Looking at the trio, Mary answered the question; "No, I don't blame him at all, but that doesn't matter."

"Why is that?" Max asked more out of contempt, than actual interest.

"Because we'll all die during this assignment, no matter what any of us want—or hope." Lowering her head, (but not in prayer), she continued; "There is no hope."

"I thought you were some kind of nun or something." Max hoping to get some sort of protest or reaction from Sister Mary Hopeless.

Henry looked at her contemptuously as he asked; "You really have lost your faith?!" As he stood there, looking up at the beautiful sky, he turned his small back into the wind. "I thought your faith came before anything else, or is that only when things are going well? I suppose we'll never know." Silence filled the air. Henry couldn't stand it any longer, this woman's hypocrisy was topped only by her fear, and he had to believe that someone—somewhere, possessed the faith of a small child. Something had to be bigger than all this. "So, we just martyr ourselves, without slashing back at the bastards?! We just lie down and die, and say 'thank-you' for the privilege?!" Facing the cold wind he kept on with his little tirade; "Well—the hell with that! You hear me, the hell with that!" Pushing his nose up in her face so close, she can feel his brave soul along with his hot breath; "And the hell with you lady!"

The shame that Mary felt served as a cold reminder of her duty. She had to get these three working together—with her, so she decided to outrage them. "So you just walk away like a little coward?! I thought you little Jew boys had some guts, but you're just as spineless as the old men of the Judenrat—who sell your people into slavery and death!"

Anger hit all three boys like a fire consuming fuel. Max looked at his brothers and responded with a full frontal attack. "We're not the ones who murder grandmothers and babies. We're not the ones having sex with corpses, or raping small children. We're not the ones desecrating synagogues and cemeteries. We're the good guys. As for you, well, we're not sure if you're even human."

It had been a long time since someone made Mary feel anything decent or honest—too long. It took these children to remind her of her Christian duty. Looking down at her feet firmly planted in mud, she said; "I'm sorry. That was totally out of line. I've allowed the coarseness and vulgarity of the times to drag me down. I have disgraced my vows."

"You're really a nun?!" John was absolutely paranoid about his obscene day dreams. He never believed the nun story, but now he knew—he had lusted over a nun.

"Yes, I'm really a nun. What did you think; that this was all a very elaborate charade?" The light of sudden comprehension dawned on Mary. "You thought just that! Mary hated her role in all this, reached into her purse and handed a small gun to Max. "Since you don't believe or trust me, you may as well kill me." Seconds passed, and still no execution. Mary looked over the small band and waited. She then added; "Since you have no stomach for this, I would suggest we move on with our assignment." That was the last protest of the mission that Max could ever recall.

They all settled down for a few hours of sleep—waiting for godot. No one truly slept, but it felt good to pretend. That's all they had, make-believe. There was no beginning, no middle, just the end. Somehow, a nap was so civilized, so normal. It gave a façade of daily life, to impending death.

Mary thought back to an earlier, simpler time when she carelessly enjoyed an espresso and biscotti, while seated at a small, terrace café facing a side alley. Handsome gigolos and intense intellectuals filled the space, adding just the right amount of ambiance. Her hair was fresh from shampoo, and she felt the sun tickle the back of her neck, like a lover's soft kiss. These boys were being shooed to their piano or violin lessons, while the oldest was at his apprenticeship. Life was civilized. The only sneaking around she had to do in this scenario, was snitch an extra biscotti and some chocolate sauce.

Max's dream was more basic. His mother was still alive, Henry was in school teaching the teachers, and John had more invitations to parties than there were hours in the day. He was just an ordinary boy, doing ordinary things. Eating ice cream, reading comic books, teasing his brothers and watching his mother prepare for the Sabbath. Running out of the apartment with his mother chasing and chastising him simultaneously, shrieking her complaints about his being an ungrateful son, not practicing his violin. "When will he ever throw away those horrible comics? He'll make me old before my time—that boy!" Throwing her hands up to the heavens, as if they could really hear her complaints. How will she ever survive such a son?! Yes, it was a good dream.

John dreamt of the perfect girl, slender and sweet with soft brown curls framing her face. He would take her to the school dance, and they would hold hands gently as they walked down the street on a calm spring evening. Life would be lovely.

Henry found his dream in a university library surrounded by the world's greatest books and the world's greatest philosophers. He was discussing abstract questions with the likes of Leonardo da Vinci, Benjamin Franklin, Buddha and Jesus, till late into the night, (long after Mama said light's out); and never feeling freer. (Later he would explain to Mama that his curiosity about Jesus was strictly philosophical). In addition to his fantasy intellectual 'salon';

Henry's dream included a banquet table filled with nothing but desserts of all kinds; cakes, pies, cookies, candy, and other assorted sweets. In short, Henry was in heaven. He wished it could go on forever, but duty waited. Since Henry woke up first, he had the thankless job of rousing the others.

Shaking each member of their motley band, Henry also began to organize the few supplies they had. "Well, let's go." Looking back at the others, he chided; "What are you waiting for, we have a bridge to demolish." Accepting their fates, the small band followed.

As they made their way to the bridge; Henry realized that their little team didn't have to sacrifice themselves to complete the job. If the entire battalion were destroyed in this explosion, then this little band could walk away from the entire escapade—live. No suicide mission after all. They just had to destroy the entire battalion.

Looking around the area, Henry spotted multiple large metal cans laying by the side of the dirt road. They were unmarked so Henry opened each container and realized what he had. It was kerosene! Highly flammable, and very available—kerosene! Henry knew—this kerosene was 'mannah' from heaven,(strategically speaking), gift wrapped in rusty, dented cans.

Instructing Mary and his brothers; they soaked the bridge in the fuel, creating an incendiary boost to the charges. Henry realized—that this kerosene was the miracle they needed. To make the explosion even more flammable, they littered the bridge and the surrounding ground on both sides with sticks and dried leaves to serve as additional fuel. The team backed away and hid in the forest. The charges had been set, just a matter of minutes now.

They set the charges at key points on the bridge, and waited. They didn't have to wait long. Battle weary troops were bearing down on the bridge. More resembling an army of ants than blond Aryans; an entire battalion began the march across this nondescript chasm. Little did they know—everything was ready for their deaths. Mary had it down to the second—ninety seconds to be exact—before all hell blows. On the 91st second…

They never felt what hit them. What a beautiful sight! The explosion sent bits of Aryan garbage flying through the air. It actually made Henry smile. Mary, John and Max were in shock. Henry never smiled. Yet, here he was, sporting a broad grin which would make any connoisseur of the infamous Cheshire cat—proud. Henry turned, faced his 'gang' and proudly announced;

"Mission accomplished." (As a side note, Max would discover later in life that 'Weasel' was a double agent working for the Nazis. The suicide element of the mission was unnecessary; but Weasel needed an excuse to murder the boys, and protect his cover.)

With Henry's pronouncement, the ragtag triumphant four, joyfully walked away. No fanfare or patriotic drum beating; just a pleasant walk down the last mile.

XII

HENRY

T HEY WALKED DOWN the country road arm in arm, laughing, enjoying the sunshine, practically dancing, much like the characters from the Wizard of Oz. Unfortunately for them, there was no wonderful wizard, no emerald city, and their 'yellow brick road' led to nowhere. But it was freedom, at least for now. Nothing else compared.

They never noticed the old woman staggering down the road. You could call it walking, but her gait more resembled a perverted toddler bent on destroying the first thing it found. She had a tattered, worn look about her, much like an old, soiled dishrag, ripe for the garbage heap. Seemingly having no rhyme or reason, she barreled directly towards them.

John was playfully slapping Henry on the back both living for the moment, being kids. They hadn't been kids for a very long time. Max was pleased with the results of their project, but still felt the need to be cautious. Mary was in a fog of self-induced shock. Never in her wildest dreams did she think they'd succeed, and without a casualty. Such things did not happen to ordinary people. But then, were any of this group, ordinary? This random thought caused a smile to erupt on her face. Not the kind of thing she usually let show, but these were troubled times, calling for some joy, anywhere you could find it. Normally during such a lull, something disastrous would happen; something to do with an unwritten law of nature. The thought dredged against her memory like a rusty rake striking pavement.

Nobody saw the butcher's knife. Coming from nowhere, it struck a major artery, sending blood flying, liquid streamers celebrating; announcing death. They all knew the wound was fatal, just a matter of minutes. "Funny," (gasping for breath), "I would have loved to score on a shiksa," (barely able to whisper), "it's up to you big brother." Tears running down Mary's face. Henry was dead. The old woman skipped down the road. She toyed with the bloody mess, like a child plays with finger paints.

They all looked at Henry's lifeless body, stunned by the act. John openly wept, cradling Henry in his arms. Max stood silently for a few moments and then began to recite the mourner's Kaddish.

John looked up shrieking; "What good does a prayer do for him now?"

Max continued his prayer, indifferent to his one remaining brother.

John rested Henry's body on the ground gently, grabbed Max by the collar, spinning him so hard, he nearly fell. Again he demanded, "What good will prayer do for him now?" Beads of sweat swimming on his brow, "What kind of God stands by and does nothing, when little children are murdered? In fact, where was God for Henry, or for any of us?!"

Max turned his back on John and kept reciting the prayer. John pushed him down with murderous force. "I said; where was God for Henry, or for Mama, or for any of our people? Why has God forsaken us? Can you answer that, you little hypocrite?!"

Max picked himself up, turned his back once again, and returned to his prayers. Mary was totally speechless as she watched this scene. John kept hammering away, determined to pound on someone for this impossible pain he felt. "Why is it little brother," (voice of bile filled sarcasm), "that when Mama was alive, you had to be beaten with a broomstick to get you to Hebrew School, yet now, all of a sudden, you're super Jew?!" Still no interruption in Max's irritating prayers. John knew, just a little more banging away would do the trick... "You never believed in God anyway, I don't understand the sudden pretend piety."

That did it. Max twirled back and punched John right in the stomach. The force of the blow knocked the wind out of John. He had no idea that Max had such strength. Regaining his own force, John stood, caught his breath, and hurtled back at Max. The dirt flew, while the two boys lunged, punched and gouged at each other. This had built up inside of them for a long time.

Ignoring those two, Mary dug into her bag, located the required tool and took off down the road. Her cause was simple; she was after the old woman. Blind raw hatred fueled her body. She saw nothing but the enemy. Poised to kill, Mary stood within physical reach of the of old hag, aimed and shot. A split second between aiming and actually firing; their eyes met. The old woman knew what was coming, but grinned insidiously at the nun. Mary saw for the first time, that this crazed old woman—enjoyed the senseless viciousness of her crime.

The bullet grazed the old woman in the leg, sending her reeling to the ground. Mary's anger had not subsided, but had grown like a cancer, bringing her closer, forcing her to aim squarely at the old grey head. Looking heaven-ward as if waiting for a thumbs-down sign from God; Mary stalled too long. As she kneeled down to consummate the deed—(eye to eye),—so close that she could smell the hag's foul breath; the old woman slashed at the nun. Warm blood drenched her face and throat in a matter of seconds. At that point, something stopped Mary from finishing off the old witch. Throwing the gun as far as her strength allowed, she spat on the old woman, turned her back and walked away.

The old woman laughed wickedly and said; "Too weak to kill me?! You Jews have no backbone! Unbelieving devils!"

Mary kept walking. Desperately searching for a cloth, anything to stop the bleeding on her face. She found a rag and created a makeshift tourniquet. Searching further in her bag, she took out her veil and habit, rapidly changing into them. The transformation was complete. Now she turned her attention to the old woman. It was time to teach this old reprobate a lesson about life.

Walking back to this evil old crone, Mary offered another tourniquet and some additional first aid. The old woman was happy to see an official from a Christian church, (even though she wasn't Catholic herself). She thanked the nun. "You should have seen the evil Jew girl who did this to me! She had blond hair like one of us, but she must have colored her own hair to 'pass' for a real human being. I honestly thought she would… " The old woman stopped dead in the middle of her speech. Mary calmly removed the habit's veil revealing her blond hair, and the new gash in her face. Stammering, the old woman said; "How can this be? You are a nun, yet you are a fellow traveler, a collaborator with Jewish trash?!" The old woman's face was as red as an overripe tomato. Continuing, the old woman pushed further; "What are you?!"

The answer was simple for Mary. "Something you're not—human." At that juncture, Mary walked away, leaving the old woman lying in the dirt.

THE BURIAL WAS simple. Everything seemed to move in slow motion in a surrealistic montage of sounds and images. Pain and loss became sentient and palpable, a living, breathing monster that feeds on anything human. Nothing made sense to Max. After all they had been through; Henry was dead.

The one with the most potential was forever gone. Max and John settled their fight, and began digging a grave for their baby brother with shovels Mary found at a nearby farm. Each pitch of the shovel buried any residual hope, right along with Henry. Max pretended that he was digging a grave for the Nazis, and it made the task much easier, that is until they had to lie Henry's body down, for the final time. Suddenly these freedom fighters cried like babies on their mother's lap. Theirs were tears for humanity lost. Mary cradled the two children in her lap, crying alongside them. She hadn't truly felt like a nun, until that moment.

By the time the burial was completed; it was pitch black outside. There was no point in trying to go any further. That first night, they slept beside the new grave. It had occurred to each one come morning that they were leaving without Henry. Thinking to himself, John muttered under his breath, "Life stinks." Not a lullaby, not a liturgy.

AS THE SUN rose, the ground shook violently, like the earth was having a giant seizure. The dirt road belched up smoke and dust, barely withstanding the pressure. Max and John stumbled on top of each other, waking up from a nightmare. (Waking up to a nightmare.) Not yet able to pry the gooey sleep from the corners of their eyes, the boys found bayonets and jackboots kicking and prodding them from this inertia.

Mary could barely believe her eyes. After all the close calls, all the risks, now they're captured as they wake up from a nap! (The gods must indeed by crazy!) Before any of them could make sense of the situation; they were being shoved towards an entire convoy of military trucks, jeeps and active troops. Each one of them could feel the point of a bayonet piercing their backs.

The boys were separated from Mary, and stuffed into an old truck filled with cow manure and half dead bodies. The boys would have choked from the stench, except they were used to the smells of war. Before anyone could utter a cry or protest, the boys were ushered off to their fate.

Mary screamed; "Where are you taking them?! Why are you doing this?! Why?! We are good citizens of the Reich!" Still playing the role. Had to survive. Life may stink, but it's the only option we know of for sure. Trying to tear away from her captors; Mary was sent reeling. The force of the blow was so hard it broke her jaw. She saw the young face of her attacker a split second before he rammed a rifle butt against her face, before the lights went out.

XIII

CRUCIFIXION

WHAT FOLLOWED WOULD make a night terror irrelevant. Mary woke to severe stabbing pain so unbearable, she was unable to yell. Only a silent scream emerged from her worn body. Her neck was tied to a stiff wooden vertical mast by the throat with coarse rope while her legs dangled. As she watched, two Nazi soldiers attached a horizontal cross piece to the main mast. She could not believe what they were doing. These devils were crucifying her. With eyes as big as saucers, she watched as one soldier nailed her wrist to the wooden bar. The pain was too much. She passed out after the first two blows of the hammer.

When she awoke, the soldier had nearly finished the job. Planting the crucifix into fertile soil; he then removed the rope which was supporting her neck and torso. The extra weight of her body against the nails tearing into her flesh, made breathing that much more difficult. Mary recalled having read in a history book that in biblical times, crucifixion victims died from suffocation, not blood loss. She fought to keep her head and torso erect. Her breathing became more labored and shallow, and she prayed for death. Looking up with one last effort, she saw her tormentor—a pimply faced teen—'playing' soldier. Without a second thought, she uttered; "Why?" It took most of her remaining breath. The young soldier briefly stared at her, like he would any common inanimate object, not saying a word in reply, and walked away.

With her last breath, Mary began praying. Humbled and awed, for the first time in this vocation—she understood her mission. She finished her epitaph with "Father, forgive... " Nothing more. She was dead.

The last two soldiers looked up at Mary, casually turned their backs and compared notes. One was grinning with delight. "So, do you think that she was saved?" The one soldier playfully poked the other quieter comrade.

"I don't know. She might have really been a nun. What if we made a mistake?" Looking frightened; spooked. Thoughts of ghosts and old childhood night terrors seeped into an immature, superstitious subconscious, absorbing any remnant of free will—much like a gentle spring rain soaks into an Iowa cornfield of fertile soil—slow, steady and deep.

His comrade patted him on the shoulder. "Look, you didn't give the order; you were just doing your job. Me, I wouldn't have a problem with this whole thing, but I have more wartime experience." Stroking his immature whiskers, he went on; "It won't even faze you—once you get used to it."

Hearing their Sergeant's orders, they prepared to leave. "One more thing, I forgot that you're new at this." Picking up a rather large camera, he pointed, aimed and fired. "We always have to collect a snapshot of any execution. The brass just loves this stuff."

XIV

AUSCHWITZ

AUSCHWITZ. THE NAME alone was a nightmare. Max resigned himself to this being the end. They had come so far, and yet—it was to end here. There was no escape or rescue from Auschwitz—only death.

He thought of those he had lost along the way. Mama first, then Henry and finally Mary; only he and John remained. They had survived 'selections' this morning, but it was night now and John was looking awfully weak. Max had already decided that if John were taken for 'selections', he would sabotage his own chances for survival. John would not die alone surrounded by strangers. They would stick together to the bitter end.

Thinking back to the events of this morning, he found himself wanting to kill that little shit of a soldier. What kind of perverse satisfaction did he get from murdering a skeleton of an old man? It would have been poetic justice if he got a dose of 'his own medicine.' Max knew an easy way to a fast kill. Weasel taught him. One of the few decent things he did. It would have been simple enough, just push that one bone at the base of the nose up into his wormy brain. One quick way to a kill, and it would have been worth it, even if he had died in the process.

They were all going to die in this hellhole anyway. Yea, Max figured if John were selected, he'd go for their throats. He was damned if they were expected to lie down and die. He looked forward to killing one or two of those bastards before they finished him off.

Tomorrow would be the day. Max was ready. He would stay by his brother's side no matter what. Come to think of it, selections had begun earlier this morning. As he and John lined up in their spots, Max noticed that John looked even weaker than before.

They had been at Auschwitz six weeks today. John was noticeably sicker the last two days. He caught a chill which turned into pneumonia. Fact is—John didn't have much more time in this world, without some sort of miracle—and miracles were in short order at Auschwitz. In truth, they were nonexistent. There was no hope. There was no peace. There was no mercy. There was only Auschwitz.

Max watched that morning, noting how John could barely stand. It was time to stage an 'incident.' They grew up together, fought together—and now would die together. Max had already decided, no ovens or gas chambers—just a bullet. It was a braver, cleaner death, and he'd try to take a few Nazis with him. (Every small action matters—every little bit counts.)

But, that plan never had a chance. They would not die in this barracks. Within minutes of making his momentous decision, reality once again slapped him in the face. The camp was a flurry of activity. Sirens wailed while prisoners were rounded up like cattle. Before they knew what was happening; Max and John found themselves in the middle of a stampede. Nazis were running for cover, some using prisoners as human shields. An old, white haired officer grabbed John to use as a shield, but he was so weak; he more resembled a limp rag doll that had lost most of its stuffing. He could barely stand; much less shield this coward, yet the officer carried John like a toddler would an old worn blanket trailing to one side.

Suddenly a window exploded, landing a small missile on the opposite side of the barracks. Fire, smoke and ash poured into the air. The sound of approaching tanks and bombers shook the building clear to the foundation.

Max spotted the opening and lunged at the officer, falling on soldier and puppet. He couldn't get the gun away; the officer was too strong. All three bodies rolled on the ground in this clumsy choreography. Wrestling between the gun and John's limp body; Max could feel the barrel of the gun intimately embraced between them. Desperate to free his brother and having no other form of self-defense; Max bit the officer's face, and held on for dear life. His blood tasted thick and bitter as it dribbled down both faces. It distracted the old officer and in the next few seconds, a shot rang out. Max stiffened. The nameless officer arched his back, his lifeless body slammed against the ground.

It took Max a good twenty minutes before he was able to roll the body off of John. He wasn't sure if John was alive or dead. Trying to feel a pulse, Max screamed at his brother's body, which looked like a puppet whose strings had been cut—permanently. "C'mon John!" Shaking him—desperate for any evidence of life; "Wake up you jerk! Wake up!" Slapping the body, sweat beading on Max. "You can't die! I'm not ready to let you go!" Still not working. No pulse. Thinking fast. "What do I have to do—breathe for you?!" Nothing else made sense, so Max did just that. Locking mouths with his brother, he breathed into John's lifeless body. Nothing. Hysterically, he pounded on John's chest; "You've got to live! I need you!" He tried again, still nothing. Once more (and the closest thing to a miracle in this hell—happened); John began to cough weakly. It was barely a cough, but enough to register life.

Another explosion, this time even closer. Max tried to help John up to his feet, but he was too weak. With no other alternative, Max grabbed his brother under the arms and dragged him outside, as far away from the sounds of artillery fire as he could. Though he barely weighed 60 pounds; Max's arms nearly broke under the strain of the dead weight.

The scene outside was pure insanity, (even for Auschwitz). Chaos ruled the day. This wasn't the battle scene of an American John Wayne movie—but consistent with Auschwitz—it was pure butchery. Still dragging his brother's body; Max spotted a parked jeep just five feet away. Perfect cover from the shelling and bullets. At least they would be safe there for a short while, or so he thought. All they had to do was remain low, and they could stay alive. Max thought to himself—that's what all this amounts to, staying alive a bit longer. He didn't have much longer to wait, as a bullet barely missed his head. They had to move.

Just as Max turned to scout a new hiding place; a rifle was once again pointed at his heart. Staring into the face of his captor, he noticed that the uniform wasn't German. It didn't matter, as this alien soldier shoved him along to a central collection area. Max resisted as he pointed to his brother lying there, more dead than alive. It did no good, for the rude soldier forcibly lifted Max and carted him away. Squirming just enough, again biting this soldier's arm, Max broke away, running back to John. They would have to kill Max in order to separate him from his brother. The British soldier ran after the boy, gun aimed square down the middle of his small emaciated back. He never made that shot, as another rifle beaded down on the British soldier. It was an American Lieutenant at the other end of that second rifle. The Brit was angry, asking; "What's your problem mate? Just taking in a little target practice. Where's your sense of sport?"

The American angrily flashed back; "My sense of sport left when I saw grown men firing on children! Maybe I should do my target practice on you—eh Mate?" Growling red hot contempt. Ready to spring on the bottom feeder before him, and tear him up.

Brit feeling a brawl building; "What's that supposed to mean, Yank?" Brit sensed the hatred, raw and dank. He could smell it, ripe, explosive and base.

"It means that once we finish this mission rounding up these refugees, you and I have some unfinished business. Maybe I could teach you some manners, eh Mate?" Ready to rip his face clear off.

"We have a date. We'll finish this later in a manly way. In the meantime, what do we do with these walking skeletons?" Waiting to toss them in the garbage heap.

"Our job," replied the American Lieutenant. Glaring at the Brit, daring him to argue.

"So give us orders, Mate, I mean Lieutenant, Sir." Brit's tone filled with bigotry induced judgment and bitter resentment.

The Lieutenant was disgusted with this seedy Brit, but they had a job to finish and he was going to see it through. He owed these refugees at least that much. Issuing the order, he bellowed; "Round up as many of these refugees as you can, and send them over to the far corner of the camp where our medics can assist."

Interrupted by the Brit once again; "But what about these crips? I ain't about to wait for them to stand and walk over there! What do we do then, Mr. American Lieutenant?!" Eyes glowering with hatred.

Shoving his rifle up the Brit's chin, practically impaling him; "Then you carry these people and children to safety," growling his answer… "or I can't guarantee your safety. You might have an unfortunate, but gruesome accident. Do we understand each other?" Reluctantly releasing the vise-like grip.

Growling back the Brit replied; "Perfectly Yank." Muttering under his breath; "Just don't turn your back in a dark alley any time soon." Still catching his breath.

American reply also under his breath; "Or yours."

I T TOOK ANOTHER five days to round up the refugees, scouring through smoke and stench so thick you could cut it with a knife. Bodies lay everywhere, most emaciated beyond recognition. They more resembled skin covered sacks of bones, than human beings.

Max and John were lying in a pile of half dead remains, along with other victims barely breathing. Max heard two American soldiers talking. "What are we supposed to do with these corpses? Look at this mess! Why didn't someone do something about these places?"

His friend turned, indifferently lit a cigarette and answered; "Look, all we're here to do is dig the graves." Ignoring the suffering all around them; they began digging.

LATER THAT EVENING the British allied forces began singing drinking odes, which, as they became more inebriated, rapidly turned into bad renditions of various 'patriotic' songs. Eventually, they sang O' Brittania and God Save the Queen. The French bellowed 'La Marseillaise', followed by the Americans screaming an extremely off-pitch round of the Star Spangled Banner. It was a gaudy, rainbow cacophony of song, pride, uniforms and drunkenness.

Finally, the Jews in their weakened state started to sing the HaTikvah. Softly, barely a whisper, they clung to each other—desperately trying to stand, young and old paying homage to their faith. The Allied troops couldn't believe what they were witnessing. Outraged soldiers howled with bigotry; how dare these pathetic creatures interrupt the singing of patriotic songs?! Have they no respect?! So enraged were these combined armed forces by this impertinent interruption that they started shoving and beating the Jews with their rifles, forcing those who had managed to stand, back down to the ground. The weakened prisoners were violently struck by some of the same soldiers sent there to rescue them.

Suddenly, a solitary shot pierced the air. Everyone froze. The American Lieutenant who had rescued Max, fired his pistol into the air and bellowed at the combined forces. "Have you no decency? What's wrong with you?" Looking around at these military minions. "Can't you see—these PEOPLE are singing THEIR national anthem?!" With that, the Lieutenant motioned to his men to help the old and weak stand, as he sang the HaTikvah alongside his people, in a voice filled with rare humanity.

For a few moments the Lieutenant's voice was the only one heard, then something miraculous happened; the prisoners began once again to sing their song of hope, their beloved HaTikvah, while the louder voices from other lands softened their coarse banter. A new harmony had been created that day, that some of those soldiers would take home. It was at that moment the Lieutenant had learned the true meaning of heroism.

XV

DENOUNCING TRUMP

M AX SURVEYED THE spacious lawn filled with a sea of virginal white folding chairs, all leading to a ribbon festooned podium clearly identified by the presidential seal. Various aides from the West Wing public relations office explained the order of the program and when he was expected to read the prepared speech crafted by the same public relations staff. The White House Rose Garden was filled to capacity. National and international dignitaries were there to honor Max, both as a Holocaust survivor and for his longstanding work in the civil rights struggle. Friends and foes alike were in the audience waiting to hear his words of enlightenment, while grabbing some face time with the news media. He never felt more lost.

John was spending his days in a nursing home mired in the final stages of Alzheimer's. He didn't remember his wife, children, grandchildren or Max. Thankfully, he didn't have any memories of the camps either. Max stood there waiting for his introduction by the head of the Anti-Defamation League, yet his thoughts were of another time, another place. His mind wandered to Mama nagging at him to study his piano, or of wrestling with John over a dog-eared

Superman comic book sent from an American cousin. Most of all he thought of Henry. He remembered Henry's intellect, but more importantly—his courage.

Now here he was, expected to give a gracious acceptance speech to an audience of affluent Jews and their token Christian friends comfortably ensconced in the White House Rose Garden. Both US Senators from his home state of Missouri were in attendance, and Max wondered how the Republican Senator could smugly sit there after helping to elect a monster like Trump. International, national and local press huddled in the 'free speech' pit, far away from the Senators. No doubt, the Republicans wanted to make a show of this award; a ceremonial statement denying any Nazi sympathies on the part of the GOP. No, Max thought, they wanted to demonstrate a peaceful transition of power, in order to silence critics and legitimize or 'normalize' the simple minded thug they were sending to the Oval Office—Donald Trump.

Trump had just been elected President on a platform of propaganda and hate. The parallels between Trump's election and that of Hitler were far too close to ignore. Neo Nazi groups had become outspokenly bold in the US both during and after the election, resulting in an explosion of hate crimes. This award he was receiving today offered rare opportunity to speak out with the press in attendance. He knew the speech that he was supposed to give—and he knew the speech that he had to give.

As he waited, he thought of his life's journey and of his family. He worried about his grandchildren and the world they were inheriting. They were both grown, working in the business world and waiting in the audience. His son, Nathan, had given him his only grand-daughter—Julia. She was a strong, smart civil rights attorney. She had also recently come out to him as a lesbian, and introduced her wife to him. Max worried about the ugliness Trump had unleashed, and was fearful for her safety. She was very vocal against the various alt-right groups, and had already received multiple death threats. (Max realized that alt-right was just another word for Nazi.) He couldn't have been prouder of her.

Then there was his grandson, Henry. Named after his uncle, this Henry was nothing like his namesake. His grandson actually worked on Trump's campaign. Max had not spoken to him since this revelation. Henry had also worked for the new governor, Eric Greitens, the first Jewish governor of Missouri, a state not known for its religious tolerance.

Since Greitens was a Jew, Henry rationalized that Grand-dad would forgive him, his other political 'sins'. Henry was wrong. Max regarded the new governor-elect of Missouri as just another opportunistic politician. It looked like he was trying to be the 'Trumpian'republican version—of a Jewish JFK. Max could not comprehend how any Jew could run on a political ticket headed by what can only be called—a neo Nazi.

As Missouri's first Jewish governor, Greitens was a curiosity. He conveniently invoked the name of the late Rabbi Heschel in a magazine interview aimed at liberal Jewish groups in Missouri. This is the same Rabbi Heschel that marched with Dr. Martin Luther King Jr. in Selma. Too bad the new Jewish governor didn't invoke the actual lessons of Rabbi Heschel, and stand firm in fellowship with racial and religious minorities—against this Nazi Trump.

In his inaugural speech Greitens mentioned two famous black icons in Missouri history—Dred Scott and Langston Hughes. In a fit of political correctness, Greitens cynically condemned the Dred Scott decision, which declared blacks to be a mere 3/5th of a person. He then applauded poet Langston Hughes' demand for the same equal rights as whites. His entire inauguration was little more than an amateurish theatrical production of overflowing hypocrisy, fully accessorized with a 'sincere' smile plastered on his face. Greitens managed to accomplish this politically manufactured event while maintaining an eerie silence regarding Trump's Nazism.

No, this new Jewish governor only seemed to speak about Judaism when it benefitted him politically. He was a walking, talking public relations invention, who couldn't separate the daily minutia of keeping the Shabbos from the larger lessons of Rabbi Heschel or Hillel the Elder.

Instead he pandered to the religious bigots of Missouri by giving empty speeches praising the importance of family and 'virtue' as defined in white, Christian churches, while remaining silent to Trump's dangerous incitement of hate crimes against those deemed not white, straight, or ironically, 'Christian' enough. He spoke of religious liberty, knowing full well that religious 'liberty' in Missouri, translated into 'White Christian Male Privilege', and the subsequent power that grants open license to discriminate with legal impunity.

Greitens also recently claimed that he and his wife were fairly observant of Orthodox Jewish practices like keeping kosher, (again conveniently similar to Ivanka Trump's specious and shallow claims); but what good is keeping a kosher kitchen if you remain silent to the ugly voices of fascism?

The ceremony was the first time Max had seen his grandson Henry, since their argument about Trump back in September. Though Max loved his grandson; he was ashamed of him. He wanted to forgive Henry, but he had to teach him a lesson. Those who ignore the strident voices of Nazism must face the shame of their silence. Yes, Max knew the speech he must give, and the time was now.

As he waited for his introduction, Max found himself drifting in and out of a fugue state. Past, present and future were all part of a symphonically blended mess, bouncing back and forth with no rhyme or reason. The death camps melded into Trump on the campaign trail, sycophants chiming his infallibility, Hitler's rants on the rally circuit, and Mama's dead, lifeless eyes—begging the question—why? Before he could mentally register these images—his name had been called.

Max took the podium and began. As he crumpled the canned speech given to him by White House staffers into an angry shredded ball contemptuously thrown down to the ground; he began to speak. "First, let me say how honored I am to receive this recognition from the ADL. I was asked to speak on the blessings of this country and my life here, but I find that I cannot, no—I will not give that politically safe speech. Instead, I am going to speak about the America that I am now ashamed—to call my country.

I am going to speak out against the new president elect, Donald Trump—a clueless billionaire who has gleefully incited violence against racial and religious minorities using coded language all too familiar to the bigot; namely 'dog-whistle politics'.

I am going to further denounce this new president elect, who is now filling his administration with white supremacists and neo Nazis such as Steve Bannon, Senator Jeff Sessions and Sebastian Gorka. This same president elect who cannot tolerate any criticism without throwing a tantrum only worthy of a three year old toddler—has repeatedly slandered persons of color, religious minorities, gay people and women. Donald Trump has encouraged xenophobia against anyone deemed 'not white, straight, or Christian enough.' He has done all this while enjoying virtual impunity from the press and the justice system. Like a spoiled prince; he demands total obedience from the rest of us 'useless eaters.' Trump does not intend to be President—he expects to be Emperor. His supporters don't want equity, rather they demand revenge for imagined crimes against white Christian males—crimes that never happened.

I am going to speak about a resurgence of neo Nazism and the impotent response from our government officials, far too much like the cowards of Vichy. And I am going to speak about my own two grandchildren—one who I view with pride and joy—and one that I am ashamed—to call family.

I was called here to speak about how the human spirit overcomes hardship. The organizers wanted me to recount the terror of my childhood—as a prisoner of Auschwitz. I was to then praise my adopted nation for the gift of my comfortable life in the suburbs. That will not happen. As I stand here, my granddaughter Julia is fighting for the civil rights of blacks, Hispanics, Gays, women and religious minorities including Jews and Moslems. She is not only facing professional censure, but actual death threats coming from Donald Trump's rabid followers. I couldn't be more proud of her.

Meanwhile, my grandson, Henry has become a card carrying member of the brain dead Trump brigade. I couldn't be more ashamed of him. How any Jew could cooperate with a GOP determined to win elections at any cost, including fanning the flames of resurgent Nazism—is beneath contempt.

Max looked up from the podium and caught his grandson leaving. "Henry, you need to hear this."

Henry stopped dead in his tracks, turned around and glared at his grandfather. Max continued. "If you think that you are man enough to support a fascist pig like Trump—then you are man enough to face me—and you are man enough to face your people—the very same people who were murdered by bigots just like Trump."

Henry looked at his grandfather with empty eyes, turned his back and walked out. Max knew that he had to finish what he started.

"To those of you, who like my grandson, think that this critique is too harsh and would rather turn a blind eye, or to those who mistakenly claim that Trump hasn't slaughtered millions like Hitler—I say that your arguments are flimsy, cowardly and both intellectually and morally bankrupt. None of these atrocities, these crimes against humanity, start at full strength. They build up gradually."

Max was shuffling note cards on the podium as he continued. "In my hastily scribbled notes there is a quote from the late Supreme Court Justice William O. Douglas—describing how fascism begins. To quote Justice Douglas;

… "As nightfall does not come all at once, neither does oppression. In both instances, there is a twilight when everything remains seemingly unchanged. And it is in such twilight that we all must be most aware of change in the air—however slight—lest we become unwitting victims of the darkness."

Removing his glasses, Max looked his republican Senator—Roy Blunt—straight in the eye. Max knew that Blunt was a member of the national GOP leadership team. He was outing Blunt as a Trump collaborator to the world.

"Justice Douglas inadvertently captured quite poetically the Nazi build up to power during the age of the Third Reich. Hitler, like many dictators before him, consolidated power gradually by using the 'rule of law.' Unfortunately far too many people confuse the contrived technical 'rule of law' with actual justice. They are not the same. There was a time in this land when slavery was upheld as the 'rule of law' in spite of its base immorality.

The Supreme Court at the time ruled in the Dred Scott case that a black man had no rights under the law. Under the 'rule of law'; a black man was deemed to be a mere 3/5ths of a person; receiving less legal protection—than a worn out plow horse.

Though technically legal at the time—this decision represented a grave miscarriage of justice."

Max removed his glasses and aimed his commentary directly at his republican senator. "I'm sure that Missouri's new Republican Attorney General, Josh Hawley would have then argued that the slave holder's rights to religious 'liberty' would have been jeopardized by any other decision, as many alleged Christians, then claimed their white privilege to be a judgment from God, punishing blacks—and naming whites as their masters. After all isn't the conservative movement a demand for consistent maintenance of the original status quo—namely 'white, Christian, male privilege'?" Max was smirking at his republican senator. He then continued.

"True justice demands equity, truth and compassion. Historically when dictators seek the overthrow of a democracy—they first reduce 'rule of law' to petty squabbling over mere technicalities or the 'letter of the law', conveniently ignoring any true sense of justice.

Nowadays, these technicians refer to themselves as 'original constructionists', 'strict constructionists' or 'originalists.' These legal theologians are often attorneys who work to subvert democratic rule through a perverted reading of the Constitution. Utilizing tortuous false logic; they read the Constitution and the Bill of Rights as static documents never straying from the exact concrete details of the first writing. There is no room for any interpretation except the literal and original wording. If a human right has become accepted by the majority; these original constructionists vehemently argue that no such right exists under the constitution, unless it was explicitly stated in the original draft.

Under such a limited reading; no one would have voting rights except white men who own property. The right to self-govern is then usurped to the false assumption that human rights remain the sole reserve of a preselected privileged class. Subsequently, the concept of human rights is now reduced to that of privilege—the same privilege which can be given and—just as easily taken away. This is the long term strategy of the tyrant; their end-game being the total destruction of democratic rule.

Like selfish children rigging a game for their own delight; 'rule of law' is now firmly maintained to benefit one class of people—by destroying another. The Nazis did just that." Max is now glaring at his republican senator. He has no need to look down at his notes—his mission is clear.

Max went on. "They acquired and consolidated power legally, by building on the work of Hitler's predecessor, Reich Chancellor Heinrich Bruning. Bruning wasn't a National Socialist or Nazi, but a centrist, who incrementally chipped away at German democracy. He took power away from the Parliament while further restricting civil liberties. Hitler then used the newly weakened laws to legitimize all his actions.

In fact, Hitler boasted that… "We will overthrow Parliament in a legal way through legal means. Democracy will be overthrown with the tools of democracy."

Looking back into the history of that era; Hitler didn't have to work that hard to gain power. Most of the work had been done for him by cowardly members of the Reichstag, or their version of Congress. Lawmakers then believed that if they made Hitler the Reich Chancellor; they would be able to control him. They were wrong. Like many con artists, Hitler and his inner circle engineered a 'false flag' terrorist threat—namely—the burning of the

Reichstag building. Nazi provocateurs torched the Reichstag and blamed the Communists and Jews. No proof was required.

This provided the flimsy excuse needed to strip away civil liberties in the name of national security. These fascists then gleefully eradicated free speech, free assembly and of course, a free press." Max is now aiming his speech directly at both senators—the democrat and the republican. The media focused the cameras in on their uncomfortable facial expressions. He proudly continued.

"In addition to these abuses, the police were given the power to hold people in custody indefinitely—without a court order. The Nazi high command codified these new powers and gave this miscarriage of justice a very benign name—"clause 2". To top it all off, Hitler then demanded a Constitutional amendment that would allow him to further eradicate other parliamentary powers.

He demanded the legal right to tap phones and open mail without a warrant. His demands were granted with a law called the Enabling Act.

If any of this sounds familiar, well it should, because George W. Bush made the same demands after 911. Barack Obama then took these practices further with the NDAA 2013 and codified them into law.

Now a president has the legal power to designate any person as an 'enemy combatant,' thus stripping them of their human rights. No formal evidence is required by any civilian court. The decision of the president is unquestioned and final with no oversight, much like a monarch.

From that point a president can legally kidnap, torture and eventually murder any person they desire with absolutely no restrictions. Of course like most dictatorial regimes, the vocabulary used to describe these extra-judicial procedures is a whitewashed jumble of public relations jargon. Kidnapping becomes known as 'extraordinary rendition,' and—'enhanced interrogation techniques' are the replacement phrase for torture. At least the phrase for murder uses the word 'killing'—as in 'targeted killings.' All this is done by targeting dissenters and labeling them as 'enemy combatants.' Such a label removes any legal status as a human being. 'Enemy combatants' have the legal status of slaves, which protects any politically ambitious tyrant from legitimate challenges. What had been clearly acknowledged as crimes against humanity in the Bill of Rights and the International Declaration of Human Rights—has now been 'legally' justified as prudent statesmanship—and all with the blessings of Congress."

At this point, the republican senator leaned over to an aid, and walked out of the program. Max smiled as he realized that he gleaned in part—a pound of collaborator flesh. He placed his horn rimmed glasses back on his face and continued.

"We have been stripped of our due process rights with the single stroke of a pen as President Obama signed the NDAA in 2013. What had been recognized historically, as legitimate rule of law regarding our due process rights, since the time of Charlemagne has now been thrown out, as politicians demanded 'legal cover' for crimes against us all.

Designated 'enemy combatants' face the ultimate oxymoron—namely military justice. They have no right to an attorney. They are denied the right to view any evidence being used against them. They are even denied the right to know the charges they face. The accused have no due process rights during this fraudulent military court procedure.

Even before any conviction in this kangaroo court under military hunta; the president retains the right to legally sanction torture, and execution—before, during and after this farce of a trial.

The sickening part is that this entire litany of injustice is all once again—considered 'rule of law,' just as it was during Hitler's regime.

So, you see that 'rule of law' does not necessarily translate into actual 'justice.' Unfortunately the American people have traded their right to overthrow such injustices, for the dubious privilege of witnessing the televised version of a lynch mob, featuring the full frontal corruption of militarized police tear gassing people—who had the audacity to be born the wrong color. They prefer politically correct fairy tales that elevate the many irrational fears and hatreds of the bigot—to a pseudo art form.

Once again, during this slow buildup towards oppression, many of us use television as a form of emotional anesthesia. We look for escape rather than face our problems. It is far easier to worry about some celebrity we will never know, than face our own moral shortcomings—and we are talking about morality.

As such, we live in a world of trivialities and empty unearned celebrity. Idolatry has replaced humanity.

Trump and his followers worship materialism, false praise, greed and hatred. An emotionally immature people have embraced the scapegoat, rather than accept responsibility for their failings. Into this shallow world enters

Trump, a pied piper poised to entice and entrap the minds of the bigoted class, in order to fulfill his own narcissistic needs.

In the period of 10 days since Donald Trump's election, the Southern Poverty Law Center has reported over 900 hate crimes. Innocent people have been beaten, humiliated and even lit on fire. Police have taken reports but somehow those same police—and bystanders—saw nothing in many cases.

Trump has half-heartedly told followers to stop—but they already heard his dog-whistle, his signal to violence thinly camouflaged in coded language; a semantic Trojan Horse—to civility. Trump incited the violence with great ease and a level of plausible deniability sufficient for the intellectual wasteland known as reality television.

If Donald Trump had not been running for president; someone else could have just as easily lit that incendiary fuse. We cannot continue to ignore the deep history of bigotry in the US which has led to the election of a fascist.

Beginning with violent kidnapping and slavery, we have continued the ancient hatreds of the old world. Racism has been the scourge of this nation, like anti-Semitism was to Europe. From the evil of slavery came the conjoined births of Jim Crow and 'dog-whistle' politics.

The preferred class; namely white, Christian men were self-appointed as the political masters of the universe. No blacks, Jews, Moslems or women—need apply. This systemic bigotry worked well—for white, Christian men. For the rest of us—it was Hell, though you wouldn't know it by the representation in movies and television.

As racial, gender and religious minorities—we were invisible, except for an occasional token character granted for comedic relief—or serving as a villain. We were inconsequential—as story generators—and as humans. This was the shallow world of the sanitized 1950's sitcom, where racial and religious minorities did not exist, and the most serious problem was whether Mary Sue had a date to the prom.

There was no memorial for the Emmett Tills of the world. The denial went deeper, so that even after the Holocaust—slavery, rape, torture and genocide, did not exist in the American psyche. This is the 'great America' that Trump hearkens to—an apartheid state for white Christian supplicants fully accessorized with perfectly manicured lawns—and equally 'manicured' historic amnesia. Bigotry is scrubbed clean and closeted. All is well with the white Christian majority.

Trump's America has no racial or religious minorities, at least not in plain sight. Women are subservient yet gracious to their pre-ordained masters', with this gender slavery enthusiastically endorsed by conservative religions—Orthodox Judaism included. Gays, lesbians and the transgendered do not exist. It is Mayberry in Trump-Ville and all is well in this apartheid state.

So you see, I was to speak about my great respect for this country, but I cannot. My anger is not merely limited to the obvious neo Nazis on the 'alt-right', but includes the 'nice' people who didn't approve of Trump's vulgar language, yet voted for him regardless. These are the kind of people who don't like to talk about politics. They are moral cowards.

Writer Naomi Shulman recently explained this phenomenon quite concisely. Her own mother was born in Munich in 1934 and survived the Holocaust, in spite of the alleged nice people in her neighborhood, who remained blind and silent during Hitler's rise to power.

Shulman wrote that… "When things got ugly, the people my mother lived alongside chose not to focus on "politics," instead busying themselves with happier things. They were lovely, kind people who turned their heads as their neighbors were dragged away." To put it bluntly, Naomi Shulman said that… "nice people made the best Nazis." In fact, if I were to create a slogan for the 2016 presidential election it would be… "nice people make the best Nazis."

The late Elie Wiesel, a fellow Holocaust survivor and Nobel Peace Prize Laureate spoke to the true issue buried deep in the bowels of xenophobia—namely indifference. When the rage of the xenophobe subsides; indifference settles in—and it is that very indifference which is the real cruelty, when any abomination or atrocity is possible because the object of the bigot's hatred—becomes just that—an inconsequential object. This is the state of moral atrophy.

Wiesel put it quite succinctly when he simply stated that… "Indifference, to me, is the epitome of evil."

He explained further in his 1986 Nobel Peace Prize acceptance speech… 'I swore never to be silent whenever and wherever human beings endure suffering and humiliation. We must always take sides. Neutrality helps the oppressor, never the victim. Silence encourages the tormentor, never the tormented."

Now we have a president elect who has consorted with known racist and neo Nazi groups, while the opposition party, namely the Democrats, sit idly by trying to normalize this situation. Various public figures that posed for decades as defenders of equal rights have visited Trump in his gaudy golden tower, kissing his ring, like a mafia don of yesteryear. The 'for profit' news media carefully ignore stories linking Trump to Nazi groups. We are told to give this monster a chance, as he continually slanders communities of color, religious minorities, a free and robust press and, to use his term—nasty women.

Yet, there are a few rays of courage and one of them is New York Times Op-Ed Columnist Charles Blow, who refuses to paint Trump as the new normal. Calling out the president elect as an "unstable, unqualified, undignified demagogue"; Blow challenges each of us to reject despair and defeat.

To quote Charles Blow… "the only thing that can protect America from the man who will sit at its pinnacle of power is the urgent insistence of the public that radical alteration of our customs and concepts of accountability are not on the table, that authority in a democracy is imbued by the ballot, but it is also accountable to its people."

Blow also reminds us that our civic responsibility includes rejecting any president that… "surrounds himself with a rogue's gallery of white supremacy sympathizers, anti-Muslim extremists, devout conspiracy theorists, anti-science doctrinaires and climate-change deniers."

Blow continues to denounce this incompetent billionaire dictator and issues an invitation for us to join in the call to action. To quote Blow; "I happen to believe that history will judge kindly those who continued to shout from the rooftops, through their own weariness and against the corrosive drift of conformity: This is not normal!"

Once again, we are confronted with a choice between silence and standing as witnesses for our neighbors. It was Dr. Martin Luther King Jr. who spoke about … "the silence of our friends," and how such silence constitutes not only betrayal, but also confers license to evil. Granted that it takes courage to stand up to lynch mobs, but what is the alternative? The silence of cowards and bigots allowed atrocities like the murder of 14 year old Emmett Till. Far too many in white society know nothing of the atrocities committed against this innocent child. Emmett Till was a 14 year old black child who was accused by a white woman of pushing sexual advances. The result of this evil woman's lies produced a lynch mob that not only murdered this child, but immolated his corpse beyond recognition. None of the perpetrators felt any remorse. This is the result of lies that go unchallenged. This is the result of silence.

Thankfully not everyone has been a silent coward. There have been heroes as well. Sophie Magdalena Scholl was one such hero. As a founder of the White Rose Society, Sophie practiced non-violent resistance against the Nazis during their reign of terror. After witnessing German citizens execute naked Jews by firing squad, and watching their bodies fall in a dirt pit on the Eastern Front; she helped form the White Rose. She also paid for her courage and her conscience—with her life.

The election of Trump has emboldened racist and neo Nazi groups, who now feel safe to openly threaten and violently attack blacks, Hispanics, Asians, Moslems—and Jews. A new leader named Richard Spencer has risen through neo-Nazi ranks in 2016. Spencer has given the American Nazi movement a politically correct makeover, including a new name—the 'alt-right'. Rather than sport the favored skinhead look, Spencer more resembles a young urban professional working on K Street, but don't be fooled by the business suit and model looks; for underneath the façade is the amoral mind of a Nazi.

Spencer is from a small town in Montana called Whitefish. His mother still lives there. Once Richard Spencer's notoriety became public in the national sphere; his mother contacted realtor Tanya Gersh asking for help selling a commercial building she owns in Whitefish. Sherry Spencer was worried that the building would be targeted by protesters because of her son's open support of the alt-right, especially after his very inflammatory keynote speech to a white nationalist conference in DC, days after Trump's election. The speech was on video and it included Spencer and others using the old Nazi salute. Ms. Gersh agreed to help Ms. Spencer. Ms. Gersh happens to be Jewish.

Shortly after this decision, Sherry Spencer experienced an epiphany, and changed her mind, which prompted a call for an armed march against Jews in Whitefish. Inspired by Spencer, (and the boost white nationalists received from Trump), another alt-right leader named Andrew Anglin launched a troll storm by publishing an article only worthy of a Nazi regime, attacking Ms. Gersh. With Anglin's help; the 'alt-right' proudly announced that they were going to openly—hunt Jews. His article incited hundreds of threatening emails, letters, social media messages and phone calls. Here are some prime example of these threats—and these are direct quotes:

… "Thanks for demonstrating why your race needs to be collectively ovened."

… "You have no idea what you are doing, six million are only the beginning."

… "We are going to keep track of you for the rest of your life."

… "You will be driven to the brink of suicide & We will be there to take pleasure in your pain & eventual end."

"Even Ms. Gersh's 12 year old son received a threatening tweet featuring the image of an open oven and the message: "psst kid, there's a free Xbox One—inside this oven." Like my brothers and I—her child was mortally threatened. So, who is Andrew Anglin?

Anglin runs The Daily Stormer, a racist, anti-Semitic, openly Nazi website. He has organized this armed march of some 200+ Nazis with military weapons present, as they prepare to invade the streets of Whitefish. Anglin virtually confesses to conspiracy and premeditation, as he brags that his attorney certified that the march will be legal due to Montana's liberal 'open-carry' laws. Anglin goes further with publicity on his site.

The 'March on Whitefish' poster features the image of those infamous front gates—to Auschwitz.

Anglin's post includes the names, phone numbers and addresses of various Jewish residents in Whitefish. The poster includes photos of Tanya Gersh and her family wearing the same yellow stars worn by concentration camp slaves. One of the photos is of a child—Tanya Gersh's son.

The local CBS affiliate merely reported that the Whitefish, Montana Police Department is 'aware' of the white supremacist group and its call for an 'armed march.' The police did not see fit to denounce the armed march or to issue any sort of warning against these neo Nazis.

Now to be fair—the Montana Governor, Attorney General and both US Senators did give a joint statement condemning… "attacks on our religious freedom manifesting in a group of anti-Semites." Unfortunately, these same public officials failed to see the greater danger of—blood in the streets. They also fail to see the danger of liberal 'open-carry' laws. The only reason to march en masse flaunting assault weapons in an 'open-carry' state—is to intimidate, threaten and murder. This could easily turn into a bloodbath, but it is nice that the police are 'aware' of this armed march.

How is it that 'Grannies for Peace' are violently arrested for peaceful protest, wheelchairs, walkers and all—but the neo Nazis can plan an armed march—with no legal challenges? In spite of 'liberal' open-carry laws; how is this not considered assault & battery, or conspiracy to commit assault & battery? The selective enforcement of our laws by legal agencies is alarmingly similar to the same selective enforcement of the civilian police under the Third Reich.

Just recently the online 'hacktivist' group, 'Anonymous' released a data trove of documentation proving growing police membership in white supremacist and neo Nazi groups. Names were released. Still there have been no investigations or prosecutions. A heavily redacted version of an FBI internal intelligence assessment dating back to 2006, raised the same questions. The FBI was alarmed at how many white supremacist groups showed interest in ... "infiltrating law enforcement communities or recruiting law enforcement personnel." The FBI further stated that this potential infiltration could ... "lead to investigative breaches." The memo also mentioned concern over officers using the term 'ghost skins'; a term used solely by white supremacist and Nazi groups to describe ... "those who avoid overt displays of their beliefs to blend into society and covertly advance white supremacist causes." This is a direct quote. One case specifically mentioned, dealt with a skinhead group encouraging 'ghost skins' to become police officers, or become employed in law enforcement—so they could warn white supremacists of any pending investigations.

There is more. The U.S. District Court found that members of a sheriff's department in LA, created a neo-Nazi gang that routinely terrorized black and Latino residents. In Chicago, a police detective named Jon Burge, was fired and prosecuted in 2008, for the torture of 120 black men during his career. Burge referred to the electric shock device that he used during interrogations as his 'nigger box.' Burge was rumored to be an active KKK member. In Cleveland, racist and Nazi graffiti was scrawled through police locker rooms. In Texas, two police officers were dismissed when they were 'outed' as Klansmen. One of the officers admitted to disseminating applications for the KKK in order to boost Klan membership. He gave applications to fellow officers that he thought shared his... "white, Christian, heterosexual values."

How can these police officers honestly 'protect and defend' ALL of us—when they harbor such bigotries—and from groups pledging to destroy the 'outsider'?

At what point do we—as people of conscience say—enough?!

I realize that I am rambling somewhat, but issues of conscience take precedence over stylish rhetoric." Max leaned over the podium as if in pain. He saw the concern in his grand-daughter Julia's face—so much like Mama's. As his eyes welled up with bittersweet emotion—he noticed a single tear trace a path down Julia's cheek and jawline, like a lone sage bearing witness to an audience of closed minds and cold hearts. In a show of strength, Max straightened his back and steeled his heart. He was going to finish—not even stomach cancer would stop him.

"We are living in a time of great selfishness, bigotry and fear. Trump voters continue to make the slanderous claim that this is a time of 'white genocide'. Their bigotry is loud, profane and honest. They actively incite new genocides against everyone who is not a 'White, Christian Male.' These neo Nazis openly present themselves as our mortal enemy; there is no guesswork.

Other self-avowed religious conservatives are swearing that we live in a 'post-racial' society, and that while the Lord hates the sin—he loves the sinner. These same religious people—some actual clergy; preach love and forgiveness—while they support a systemic racism and institutional discrimination which like a cancer, has been killing us. Their hypocrisy is legion."

Max thought to himself—they have their cancer—and he has his. By far—theirs is worse. Soldiering on…

"Though both groups are different in outward appearance; they have the same goal—to restore white Christian supremacy as the sole authority in this country. They also have another similarity—their enthusiastic willingness to embrace the 'big lie'.

This battle is about morality." Max grabs his left arm as he feels a sharp pain, enough to make him crouch down a bit. He soldiers on.

"As Sophie Scholl faced the executioner at the tender age of 21, she heroically spoke to us all when she said…"

"How can we expect righteousness to prevail when there is hardly anyone willing to give himself up individually to a righteous cause? Such a fine sunny day, and I have to go, but what does my death matter, if through us thousands of people are awakened and stirred to action?" "

Max added; "We must stir people to action against these evil cowards, even if we sacrifice our futures, including this fine sunny day… "The room begins to spin for a second, as he remembers the oncologist's warning—that the chemo drugs 'may' damage major organs like his heart.

The spinning reminds him of the starvation he faced back in the camps. At times the spinning became a hallucinogen—that is if you let go of reality—that is, if you could. He grabbed the lectern—and then collapsed. Inside his mind—the spinning is a grand, beautiful mess—and he is screaming from the rooftops—THIS IS NOT NORMAL.

A week later, Henry gave the eulogy at two funerals—one for his grandfather and the other for his sister, Julia.

Grandpa Max died suddenly from a massive heart attack, during his speech—in the White House Rose Garden. His doctor attributed the heart attack to complications from the chemo drugs he had been secretly taking, though the treatment was not going well. Max was on borrowed time. He had less than two months to live. Henry had no inkling that his grandfather was dying.

Julia knew, in fact she went with Grandpa Max to many of his appointments—including the fateful day when his doctor told him to get his affairs 'in order.' And now—both of them were dead. Henry was heartbroken. The last time he saw his grandfather alive—he turned his back on him.

In spite of their fights over Trump, Max had forgiven him. In a sealed letter sent via a courier service, Grandpa Max explained his final actions. After both funerals Henry sat down in his grandfather's worn recliner, just smelling him, and began to read.

"Dear Henry,

Know that I will always love you. I realize that our relationship has been extremely strained by this election. Please understand that my public disapproval of your choices was done with love. I was fighting for your very soul.

I do blame myself in part. In an attempt to shield you, your father and Julia; I refused to talk about my life in the concentration camps. I didn't mean to deceive—I just believed that no child should ever have to face such inhuman terrors. I finally told Julia my story as she pressed me with that non-stop ferocity of hers."

Henry chuckled at that. Julia was a force of nature. He had to stop—it was too much. He had never cried so hard. His entire body was shaking convulsively. After drying his eyes, he resumed his reading.

"There is too much to explain in this note, to do justice to the entire horrific experience, so with your sister's help—I have written my story. Julia has instructions on how and where to publish the final work. I hope that you take the time to read my story and grow to understand the plain fact, that those who refuse to learn the mistakes of history—are doomed to repeat them.

I never want any children to suffer like your uncles and I did. It doesn't matter where these children come from—they are children and they are entitled to loving families and happy childhoods. Your uncles and I were robbed of that. All children, whether they be refugees from Syria, Iran, or any other war zone—have a right to the same happiness as American children of privilege.

Your sister has made all the preparations for the book publishing and subsequent tour. She will be promoting my book to multiple human rights organizations and I pray that you join her and fulfill my last wish.

I love you Henry. I will always love you.

Grumpy Max"

Henry sat there in shock. There it was in his messy handwriting, the nickname they loved so much—Grumpy Max. And he would never hug or argue with him again. He just sat there and wept until he ran out of tears.

HENRY FOUND OUT about Julia's death minutes after he had finished making arrangements for Grandpa Max's funeral. He would always remember the phone call from the police station, so cold blooded and sanitized. No condolences and no explanation, just the bored, banal tone of the desk sergeant, asking where to send 'the body.' He just stood there, on the other end of the phone, numb and in shock as he felt his heart break. He could hear the sergeant repeatedly demanding, where to send 'the body.'

Julia was working as a legal observer or LO, at a protest staged directly in front of the 'Old Courthouse' downtown, (the same, infamous courthouse where the Dred Scott decision was rendered)—that is before it went to the Supreme Court.

The police claimed that some individuals in a 'known black anarchist block'—began the violence. Actually, the police report specifically stated that a masked anarchist threw a brick at police which triggered retaliation. Police responded by using 'surgical taser strikes' at those they claimed were 'known' combatants.

According to witnesses that came forth on Julia's behalf; the police repeatedly tasered anyone within close striking distance, including four children and a pregnant woman. People began to run as police 'kettled' the crowd.

Julia was at the back of the protest. She came forward in an attempt to reason with the police. When that failed, she used her own body to shield that same pregnant woman. At the time of her death, doctors estimated that Julia had endured the equivalent of 200,000 volts as the result of 4 taser shocks. Julia was 28 years old and died from a full cardiac arrest. The autopsy report cited 'excitement' as the cause of death.

Police did call an ambulance some 20 minutes later, though they made no attempt to administer CPR. In fact, witnesses reported that police threatened violent repercussions against anyone daring to attempt CPR. Police further barricaded the street so the ambulance could not gain access. Paramedics were forced to park several blocks from the wounded. They had to run into the crowd, to locate casualties requiring medical triage. By the time they found Julia—she was already dead.

Paramedics filed a formal criminal complaint against the officers at the scene. Predictably, internal affairs responded swiftly and saw no evidence of wrong doing. Later that year, Henry heard of another data dump by the radical activist group, Anonymous. The data came from the same classified FBI report his grandfather spoke of, which revealed police recruitment and involvement in multiple white supremacist and neo-Nazi groups.

Henry later found out that Julia was well known to the police—and reviled. What Julia never told Grandpa Max or Henry—was that she had been receiving death threats for months over her work fighting the immigration ban Trump was proposing. Some of the threats had a cartoon of Pepe the frog—wearing a police uniform. (Henry found out later that Pepe the frog—was an anti-Semitic symbol used by virulent neo-Nazi groups.) Her car had been vandalized on multiple occasions, usually slashing her tires. During one routine maintenance visit to the car dealership, the mechanic showed her where the brake line had been severed slightly so she would slowly but eventually—lose her brakes.   -

After her death, a colleague revealed that Julia's eight week old puppy—had been poisoned by a doggy treat, soaked in anti-freeze. Again—there was a cartoon of Pepe wearing a police uniform—next to the tiny body.

XVI

NICE PEOPLE MAKE
THE BEST NAZIS

T HREE MONTHS AFTER the funerals, and a week after Holocaust Remembrance Day; Chesed Shel Emeth cemetery in St. Louis, was desecrated by vandals. Over 200 gravestones were damaged. The story made international news. True to Grandpa Max's admonishments; the police and the FBI argued that it wasn't a hate crime. Henry noted the timing, days after Trump refused to mention the suffering of Jews during the Final Solution.

People in the interfaith religious and ethical community came together one day in an act of friendship to help clean up the cemetery. Henry found out later that the local branch of the Moslem group CAIR, made an online appeal and raised approximately $90,000 dollars to repair or replace headstones, in 24 hours. Local Syrian refugees came to help. It was a beautiful expression of tolerance and love.

This warmth and goodwill was shattered when Governor Greitens, Vice-President Pence and Trump staged a fraudulent goodwill visit to make political points. As an attempt to manage this story, Vice-President Pence was sent to the cemetery for a photo op with the first Jewish governor of Missouri, during what should have been, a day of interfaith worship and assistance at the cemetery. Apparently, Trump called Greitens some 12 hours earlier and this visit was the result. Both men pretended to rake and pick up stones, but they were really there to make speeches and receive adulation from the crowd.

Henry arrived as the Vice-President was speaking. He noted how families who actually had loved ones buried there—were forced to wait until Greitens and Pence finished posing for the cameras and making shallow speeches, before they could enter the cemetery. As a final insult, they had to go through security, because of Pence. It was like being violated all over again. Henry realized that this day of friendship and interfaith fellowship, had been cheapened by Trump, Pence and Greitens all working to promote their own careers.

Henry noted that other Jewish cemeteries in the US had been vandalized that week, in the same manner as Chesed Shel Emeth.

A YEAR LATER; Henry renewed his passport and traveled to Syria, searching for truth. On his first day in Aleppo, (after dodging bullets and mortar fire)—he found himself a guest in a local family's apartment. They were among the lucky ones. They still had a place to live. And here he was, sitting down to a Shabbos dinner—with the enemy. These were the enemy combatants, the terrorists—and they looked like family.

The mother showed Henry a photo of her late son, Mohammed. Henry was about the same age. The resemblance between the two young men was haunting. The mother then explained in broken English that Mohammed died from a missile launch as he was coming home from the pharmacy. He was bringing his mother her insulin.

Henry became uncomfortably aware of his own responsibility in this tragedy. The barrage of vicious lies he had once so willingly believed—because those lies fit a comfortable narrative—the very same lies that elevated an evil, incompetent man—to the presidency.

Henry could hear the screams of children throughout the night. Homemade bombs aka IED's and Apache missiles exploded with an insanely predictable rhythm. You could almost hum Sousa's "Stars & Stripes Forever" to the beat; and envision the local 4th parade, resplendent in the red, white and blue of our flag—except the red here—was the blood of children.

S EVERAL MONTHS LATER, Henry wrote an overdue letter of resignation to Missouri Republican Governor Eric Greitens. In his letter, he denounced the hatred and bigotry that dominates the GOP. As a fellow Jew, Henry chastised the Governor on his silence regarding the rise of the alt-Right.

Henry was on tour with his grandfather's book, aptly titled—The Silent Culling. In honor of his Grandpa Max and his dear sister Julia—he ended each reading with a special dedication, which featured a short film. The film was staged at the Lincoln Memorial. Standing at the feet of the 'great emancipator', Henry explained that the film was in response to one of his Grandfather's final requests. His Grandpa Max called out slavery, Jim Crow and racism itself—as the—American Holocaust. This film served as further testimony to the shameful and shared legacy America has with the Third Reich. The end of the film featured various human rights activists reading the names of Holocaust victims alongside victims of racism in America.

They read the names of Holocaust victims alongside the names of slaves from our racist past. They read the names of Holocaust victims alongside the names of those lynched during Jim Crow, and they read the names of Holocaust victims alongside our most recent losses—-Trevon Martin, Sophie Magdelena Scholl, Medgar Evers—and finally—-Walter Scott and Anne Frank.

Henry ended each talk with questions from the audience, in a round table type discussion. A local Fox affiliate asked; "How can you accuse President Trump of being a Nazi, considering his daughter, Ivanka—is Jewish. She is raising her children in the Jewish faith, and even keeps kosher. She is such a well-mannered and nice person. Surely President Trump has done something right in your eyes, if he raised such a wonderful daughter."

Henry shook his head and explained; "My grandfather told a story of a Jewish writer named Naomi Shulman. Shulman's own mother, born in Munich in 1934, survived the Holocaust. Naomi Shulman wrote about her mother's recollections, regarding these 'nice' people who were their neighbors and alleged friends, and how these same 'nice' people granted license to these atrocities—with their silence. To quote Naomi Shulman; … "When things got ugly, the people my mother lived alongside, chose not to focus on 'politics,' instead busying themselves with happier things. They were lovely, kind people who turned their heads as their neighbors were dragged away."

Henry added; "To put it bluntly,... "nice people make the best Nazis."

Made in the USA
Middletown, DE
13 August 2018